Mock Cob Village

Book 1

Mock Cob Village

Jackie Sonnenberg

4 Horsemen
Publications, Inc.

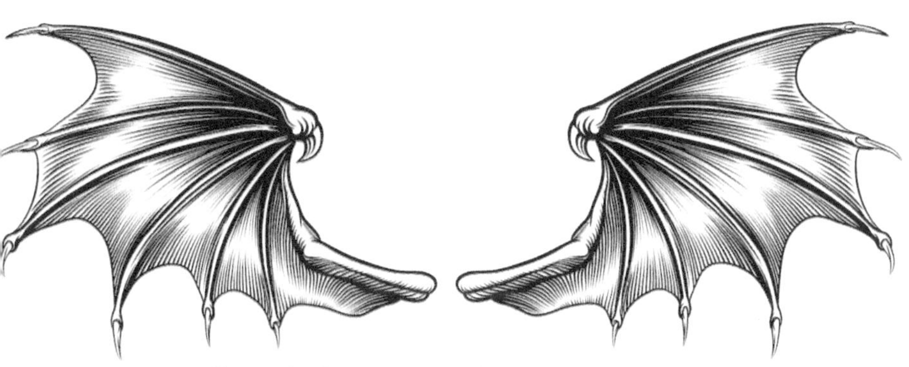

Table of Contents

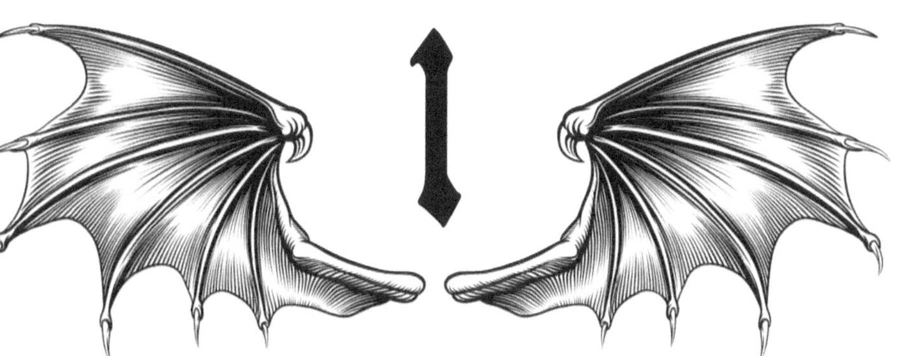

She liked blowing candles out because when the smoke tendrils floated away they looked like ghosts. And like ghosts, they were only seen for a moment or two before disappearing into the darkness.

Just like what she was good at.

Poe was certain they settled to sleep now, as all was quiet on the homestead, and that meant it was time for her to act. She took her cloak—the one she made of different patches of fur from different animals, dead and discarded. It was a new creation now, a new life of leftovers that made her her own creature of the night when she wore it, camouflaged and unbothered. She put it around her shoulders, leaving the antlered hood down her back until the last minute so she could get out. The boards on her window were all in place, or they all appeared to be in place. All she did was get the nails out of the window frame but keep them in the wood, and she could remove them anytime she wanted without anyone knowing, and toss those wood planks to the floor when she wanted them to know. Like now.

Her current caretakers—her employers at the orchard—learned about her strange little quirks early on after they brought her from the last place, a small inn with too many rooms to clean. They found Poe out climbing on the roof. She put her climbing skills to use on those apple trees, testing her agility at reaching every single branch all the way up to the top. But sometimes Poe would refuse to come down, and they would punish her for being idle by being locked in her room. They all learned how to home that wild child and tried to tame her. Especially once they heard her wandering about at night ... both inside and outside. The little footsteps, the doors opening and closing, and the playful scamper in the dead of night answered to only one. They knew that she did not sleep at night. Not until after the sky bled blue and pink in the dawning sun did she ever go to sleep. There was just something so exciting about the nighttime. It was when the rest of the world finally quieted down, when all the hustle and bustle of the day was complete. Nighttime was her time. When everyone else was asleep, the night was hers. They all learned this, and all tried to make her outgrow it.

But at age fourteen, the wild child, although no longer considered a child, was still wild.

So, with her pack bundle of everything she owned, everything being very little, Poe fastened the last clasp at her neck and opened the window.

She felt the cool breeze that brushed her face and the symphonic chirp of crickets coming from every direction as she scaled the roof. She crawled across at ease, coming to her favorite tree and walking across the branch thick as a plank. This tree had a nook that could cradle her in place comfortably, putting her in a nurturing hold that put her at rest better than anything else. It was here she often faced the night sky, letting her mind get lost, looking to it for answers. Sometimes, it was the only thing that could give her answers. One of her caretakers told her growing up that she was convinced fae dropped Poe on the doorstep. Even as a baby, she had a full head of jet black hair, like a little piece of nighttime itself, and golden-green eyes for seeing in it perfectly. It was like the universe made her that way on purpose.

Poe descended from the tree and landed in the grass with light crunches. She watched a toad covered with brown and green warts dart away into the bushes. Sidestepping a plump mushroom overlapping over the walking path, she remembered all too well the last time she stepped on one and got red flakes all the way up her shin. She had a rash for weeks that looked like her leg erupted in purple boils, so as light as her steps were in general, she practiced extra lightness around that shrubbery. The wind whistled through the trees, but mainly it had a good time whistling through the servants' home. It blew around the sign near the front path, *North Thistle Apple Orchard and Farm,* so much so that it caused the chains to creak. The home itself looked like an odd assortment of wooden boxes stacked on top of one another, the wind always finding its way through every uneven angle and making an instrument out of it on particularly breezy days. Right then it blew a small flutter of leaves against the door that crashed against the papers in the mailbox, the forgotten mail from the day prior. The farm owners sometimes forgot to check it. When there was anything, Poe got to it first.

It was after a long day's work, and she had stopped short at something sticking out near the bushes. It was the angle it was in that made it easier to see from this point of view, but also easy to see how easily it could be missed. She had walked right over and bent down, pulling the end to see it was rolled up tightly and covered in cobwebs. Her eyes followed the trail of webs to see them attached to a much wider one stretched out against the window, and saw what lived there. Its body was the size and shape of a lightbulb, speckled with yellow against its black form and long spindle legs. The front two legs were holding on to the end of the cobweb attached to the rolled-up parchments like it was protesting her taking it. Well, spiders could not read, so she gently pulled it away until the webs broke. The spider rubbed its front claws together, making itself comfortable again in its web as Poe came away with the prize. She wiped excess webbing off as she pulled on the string holding the parchments together and unrolled them, seeing an issue of *The Thistle Bugle* that was a week old and jumping ahead immediately to the postings at the back.

They were all mostly the same, as they always were, and another quick scan told her that she might not find anything this time either.

But it was when she turned a page and saw an ad that only took up a square among the columns. There was something about it that grabbed her gaze and kept it there.

The language was the same, but its vernacular seemed different, out of order like it just wanted the right words to hit first. The font used was different than the rest of the ads. It seemed thicker ... fatter, something that whoever had it printed paid for extra ink to make sure it stood out.

Chapter 1

Wanted: Only the brave to apply

An apprentice I seek

With a keen eye and knack for stealth

If danger you do not mind

Then you can come

Mock Cob Village

Poe held her burlap bag with the farm logo stitched across it and hung it across the mailbox. The smallest one, the one with the tea stain on the front—there was no mistaking that one was hers and her message was clear. She left the farm and walked down the street to the train station, pulling her hood over her head.

The town of Thistle had no carriages running in the dead of night. There was one parked along the side of the street with its door left open, a breeze blowing it all the way open and then back in the gentle snore of rusted metal. Poe, herself, settled into a steady pace until she reached the train station. There, small groups waiting to board stood together with various baggage.

Poe got in line between what was a large group of serious travelers, those with many bags per person and hats that have seen every kind of weather. She dug into one of the pouches around her waist for coins while others settled in line behind her. She looked up when the line started moving forward, still digging around for the right amount. When her turn came, the little man at the ticket window said "Next," while counting his own.

"Right, hang on," Poe said, placing some coins on the counter.

"How many?" the man asked, leafing through papered tickets and not looking up.

"One."

"And where to?"

"Blue line, destination Shorthills."

The man slid a ticket across the counter to her and chose that moment to look up, and he formed an expression Poe was not expecting to see. His eyes bulged out more than they could, transfixed and frozen.

"Oh, my..."

He suddenly slid the maroon-colored ticket back under the window.

"I do apologize, I didn't realize you..."

He scrambled through the tickets in the box before producing what he thought was the right one and slid this one to Poe.

"Okay, there you go. Thank you! And my apologies again!"

He scooped the coins without counting them and gave Poe a frazzled smile.

"Enjoy your trip and the many accommodations we have on board!"

Poe walked away with her own confused amusement and viewed the ticket. All that was different was that it had green lettering instead of maroon. She went to board the train to find where her seating was, not noticing other travelers staring at her and moving out of her way. The train car compartments were all open and ready to receive travelers, and many of them piled into the compartments closer to the front of the train. Poe looked at the numbering and placement on her ticket; her assigned section was toward the back and less busy. She went to this section and climbed aboard.

Her eyebrows shot up a bit in shock at the thought that this had to be a mistake. Everything looked almost brand new from the chestnut walls and doors to the gold knobs and borders. Poe walked down the aisle to her compartment seat and slid the door open. Her little gasp that she made did no justice to the explosive reaction she had on the inside.

The cushioned seats were made of pure velvet, color coordinated with black, raspberry, and cream blankets and pillows lining up against the wall. There was a sophisticated table in front of it that was either polished frequently or could never rust, and when she leaned into it, she could see her reflection: the girl in the homemade cape of a hodgepodge of furs ... her two bright green eyes sticking out from under the hood. The hood sat on top of her head comfortably. Though made too big, she loved her little addition to it—curved antlers, found from the skull of a jackalope in the woods. She fastened them on, deciding she liked the profile very much. Around her neck, she wore a layered necklace made of animal bones, the remains of a shrew she dissected from an owl pellet once. She stepped inside and let the door slide shut on its own, plopping down on those seats in a euphoric release. The cushions sank and hugged her in a soft embrace, molding themselves to fit her and making them exclusively hers. The table held its own dinner set of three plates of different sizes in one another and sibling sets of utensils. Next to it was a silver chalice with a small note:

*"Enjoy our finest herb teas on the house! And don't forget
to view our selection of meals in the dining car."*

Poe picked up that chalice and leaped to her feet, not believing nor understanding how she came to this. Had she had so little pleasure in life that it only seemed like a luxury? She left her compartment holding the chalice in front of her like a holy relic and made her way down the aisle. Another compartment door slid open a few doors down and those occupants trickled out. Poe's mouth opened to give them a cheerful co-existing greeting. When they came out, she stopped walking and stood there, her mouth still open.

The tunics they wore were long enough to be capes and gowns, some even dragging a bit on the ground as they walked, but it was their hair that was even longer. Some were tied into intricate braids, whereas others hung from their heads and covered some of their faces like curtains. It was the trinkets they wore around their necks and wrists that did it, many having gems and rocks that were too colorful to be found in common lands ... and different kinds of bones. It was difficult to tell just what kind of bones they were, or where they came from, but Poe was too distracted by their long nails to think about the bones. They were real, and they were their own. All of them had very long nails curled under at the ends making them look like claws, grown and shaped that way on purpose, for a purpose. Many of them were black all the way up to the finger joints, so there was no telling where the finger ended and the claw began.

Still standing there, with the chalice clutched in one hand, she pulled the rim of the hood down to almost the tip of her nose. The occupants in front of her walked down the aisle with their own chalices. Thousands of tiny bubbles exploded in her stomach. Her first impulse was to shut herself in her compartment for the whole trip, lest someone found out, but the amazement of it all won over and she told herself to stay calm, stay cool, and try to figure out where she was. And whose company she shared. She patted the hood on her head and continued down the aisle to this particular dining car. This one held more occupants with more long and elaborate clothing and accessories made from things in nature, though she did not stare at any of them long enough to see what they were, but they were all women. She kept her face casual and moved quietly, sidestepping to the wall to make sure she was always next to or behind someone. They were all too busily engaged in their own conversations, sitting together with their heads close and telling stories with wide gestures. Once in a while, someone would look up, see her, and return her look with a knowing smile. This made something prickle on the back of Poe's neck, and although she could not read what it meant, it was not altogether unpleasant. Many of them appeared to be trading with various things in mason jars, corked and wound tightly with leather cords. They held everything from bright magenta liquids to tiny bundles of sticks to red-brown spices she could smell from where she was standing. She saw where the stations were that held the big barrels with faucets. She walked over to them in sync with the people in front of her, instantly mesmerized by the melodious and strange-sounding language they spoke. The barrels had little labeled signs indicating which one was jasmine, oolong, or peach, though under their labels was something written in entirely different characters that were not even letters, possibly just a translation. Poe filled her cup and took a sip, smiling instantly at what was the same as taking a bite out of a peach. She kept it right at her chin as she made her way back to her compartment undisturbed, head down, stealing a sip every once in a while.

And so her trips to and fro were undisturbed, though she only did one more to get herself a meal of a rice bowl with beef and vegetables that she enjoyed very much, this time with jasmine tea. While she ate, she watched the passing landscapes separated only by the pane of glass. The rolling hills of green on the plains varied in size, with small forests speckled all throughout. Farther in the distance, she could make out the purple-black mountains disappearing in fog and clouds. The open fields next to her had a horde of wild horses that all of a sudden decided they wanted to race, picking up trots and turning into full-force galloping right next to her car. The way they threw their heads back and let the wind tease their manes looked almost human, like they were enjoying themselves. They kept up with the train at impressive agility and speed. She watched them disappear into a forest, and once that forest passed, it seemed to pass through the daylight as well. A shadow fell over her window as the sunlight dimmed down, all the way down, almost all the way down to nothing, almost skipping the afternoon to evening.

Poe diverted her attention to the lantern above the window that was blinking, on and off, on and off, before it went out completely. She crossed her brow, watching the forest continue to stretch. She took the last gulp from her chalice and set it down, standing up to leave her compartment. The water closet was down a little past the dining car and it gave her an excuse to wander, and work her bored legs. It wasn't until on her way back that someone noticed her, really noticed her, giving her more than just an interested smile. Or, she noticed her for the first time. The woman sat alone at a booth; her legs stretched out to take up the entire seat. What made Poe stop to acknowledge her was that she had already been acknowledging Poe, possibly from the moment she came into the dining car the first time. She was looking right at her and smiling, but in a way that made her entire face smile, including and especially her eyes. Poe became entranced by these now, ice-blue and piercing right through her mind. They stood out as the only real trace of color about her black-and-white image, as her hair and skin were both so pale they could have been white. She wore a black lace black shawl over a gown with leggings and boots and held her hands together as though in prayer, or anticipation. Poe thought that it was hard to tell if she was young, or old, or somewhere in between.

"You," she said in a voice that was deep and scratchy. "You're interesting."

Poe couldn't move her feet. "I am?"

The woman didn't blink. "Yes. You call to me. I think I know some things about you."

"Like...what?"

The woman put her legs down and stepped out of the booth.

"That, and more. And I can show you things about yourself you don't know."

"What do you mean?"

"Would you like to find out?"

It should have sounded threatening, but oddly, it felt inviting. Poe believed every word she said, and she very much wanted to know what the woman meant. Especially by the way she was looking at her like she had known Poe her whole life. She nodded.

The woman smiled. "I am quite good with looking inside people. Come."

And the woman took off for the opposite row of compartments. When Poe trailed behind her, she could make out just how long her hair was in the back, swaying down at her bottom like the tail of a horse. She led Poe to her compartment and slid the door open, allowing her to go in first. Poe had expected this room to be the exact mirror of her own, but she felt like she stepped out of the train completely. Even in the dimmed lighting, it looked like a suite inside a grand hotel, because there was no way the train compartment could be that large. Red mesh curtains decorated the walls, where some of them appeared to have openings to go elsewhere. In the middle was a rounded table decorated with a thick, black tablecloth and cushioned stools to match. Poe barely took a breath but she could smell something spicy, something that tickled her nose and made her want to cry, but it also very much made her want to taste it.

Poe stood there while the woman slid the door shut and came inside, not even realizing until she walked around to the back side of the table and sat down.

"Come in, and have a seat," the woman invited.

Poe sat down on the stool opposite the woman. The amber lighting in the room made everything a bit dimmer except for this woman's face. For now, sitting across from her, Poe could see that her eyes shone enough to cast their own light down her nose and across her cheekbones, illuminating a gentle and otherworldly glow. She was smiling pleasantly, arms folded across the table.

"You are an unusual girl, and you have talent and appreciation for the unusual."

"Thank you," was all Poe could say.

"So perhaps this was the correct train for you to travel in, after all."

Poe froze, but the woman smiled at her knowingly. She said nothing as the woman pulled her arms away and began shuffling a deck of cards. Poe did not even see where the cards came from, but now the woman was weaving them in and out of one another. The woman now placed the deck in the middle of the table and drew one card, placing it face-up on the table. Poe watched her as she took the time to study this card, putting a nail to her chin in an unreadable expression. She drew another one and placed it next to the first, her eyebrow rising like it was a compliment.

"An odd one out, I knew. Someone with creative talent, I knew."

She drew another card, looking immediately into Poe's eyes. Poe tried to get a good look at the card, but it did not make sense to her either way.

"You have another gift, a gift you will get to explore and practice. It is something that you have already begun to master and it will help you get out of difficult and dangerous situations."

Another card.

This one the woman blinked at, and from what Poe saw on the card, it looked like a mass of black fog.

"Your truest self is foggy and is something of a mystery. Coming to find yourself is a journey that you will take in the years to come."

Another card.

This fifth one the woman stared at the longest, folding her hands on the table. Poe could see that she was digging her nails into her flesh, veins popping up by her knuckles. The card appeared to be a very long face, mouth wide open. The woman licked her lips and raised her eyes to Poe again, making her voice low and calm.

"You will have connections and encounters with beings from the other side. That is something that is— as already has—come naturally to you."

Poe sat back.

"How did you know?"

The woman smiled.

"So you have already?"

"A little," Poe admitted. "I could always ... sense something since I was little, and I saw things a few times, but nothing ever really happened, and I never really knew what it was."

"There are things that linger between this plane and ... others, and you will have brushes with them. There will be a time when the veil between planes is the thinnest... and then you will have more encounters."

Poe moved slightly enough to make the stool squeak, and she didn't want the woman to think the noise came from her. Before Poe could think of anything to say, the woman got up from her seat and disappeared behind one of the red curtains. She came back holding something that looked like a little icicle broken off the top of a frozen cave.

"Take this. It's a quartz crystal, good for protection. When the time is right, it will be useful to you."

Poe took the crystal, clear as ice, or a mirror. She wondered if looking into it at the right time would reflect something behind her. She looked back and forth between it and the woman, regarding the crystal as a most personal gift and her heart filled.

"Thank you," Poe said. "Thank you so much."

The woman was all smiles. "I knew you appreciated the unusual. And I know that while you may be afraid, you are also brave. Good luck on your travel, and your tasks to come."

Poe thanked her again, feeling like it was already doing its job. On her way back to her compartment, she held it close, watching for any signs, wondering just what she would be encountering in Mock Cob Village.

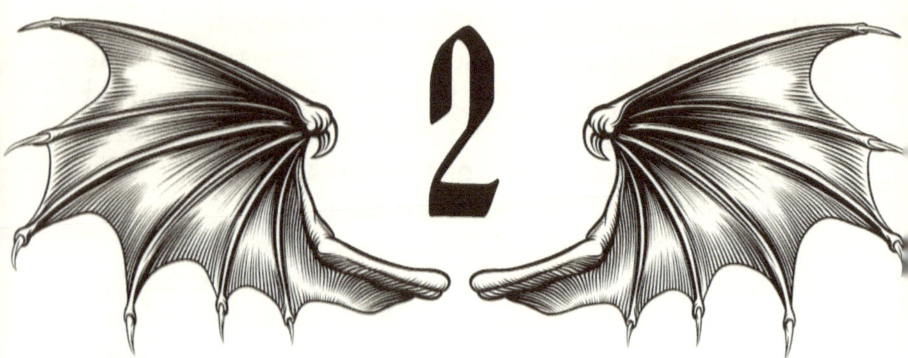

oe's body became alert when the train stopped, waking her out of her daydream. The orange and pink washed the evening sky all the way down to the horizon line, where she could see, not knowing how far the colors ran behind all the buildings she could see now out the window.

"Blue line, Shorthills," she heard the conductor call out, as she thought her stop would be soon. She got up, pocketing some taffy candy she meant to save for later, and slid out of the compartment door with her pack.

She walked down the hall and out the train door exit, noticing not many getting off at the train depot. The map inside the depot was large and stretched out, showing the blue line she took and the corresponding points to indicate neighboring areas and towns. She reached into her bag to pull out her own map, comparing the two; hers was more wrinkled and thus more difficult to read. Mock Cob Village was a short distance away, nestled in what looked like a nook below the mountains. She approached the horse carriages absent of any riders and pulled out some coins.

"Mock Cob Village, please," she told the driver.

The man sat up and looked at her as though she had asked for a decapitated head. He made a show of trying not to stare, instead giving a short nod and picking up the reins.

"Yes, I...I will take you as far as I can go. As far as the carriage can go. Are you...you are you prepared for your journey?"

When Poe paused, the man quickly came up with his own response.

"Oh, no, forgive me. You seem like you are. You have a lovely lantern. It can get quite dark. Not that it would matter. It is all right. Yes, come aboard."

This time she had a ride of the open countryside. She had her hood down and let the evening wind blow through her hair, leaning out the side of the carriage to catch the lukewarm lamp of sun before it retired for the night. The carriage rolled up and down streets with gentle rises and declines; the wind giving her the rush of flying like she was keeping up with the hawk that dipped from the sky. She rode through one town where all the buildings were the same deep brown color and smelled of freshly baked bread, though it was gone the minute they passed into a more wooded area. Poe looked around at all the trees, and the further in, the more they looked like they were sinking. Here the path steeped just enough for her seat to squeak as her weight adjusted, as did her curiosity. The trees spread out, some becoming scarce and some morphing into shrubs and bushes. Here, the horse grunted as its steps became more cautious and more hesitant. The man with the leather reins wrapped them very tightly around his fists. There was a point where most of the trees were behind them, and when Poe turned around she saw for herself the big slope, higher than she thought it was, trees sticking out like they were growing sideways. Poe looked through the trees and realized that it was not the canopy of leaves that was shielding the light. The sky itself seemed to surrender it, needing to bloom darker down there.

She turned around when the carriage came to a halt, the wheels sliding a little in the mud. The man stood there and pet the horse on its neck.

"This is the farthest I can go," he said.

Poe frowned. "Why?"

"It gets steeper from here, but there is a path you can take that is easy to follow and safe on foot."

Poe climbed out of the carriage, stepping on grass so dry it crunched and so long it nearly covered her boots. The man pointed the path out to her while soothing the horse again and adjusting the reins. He unraveled the reins and stepped in front of the horse to help it turn around, getting the carriage to travel back around in a sort of half-circle. He seemed to want to move faster only when Poe pulled on her hood and brought out her lantern.

"Best get going. It's almost curfew."

Before Poe could ask what that meant, the man and his horse were off.

Poe looked down to the path, her eyes following it going as far as they could before it disappeared into another decline she could not see. It was small and not all that steep, and she knew that the carriage would have had no problem going farther. The driver just would not. Poe made her way now, immediately putting her arms out to her sides to balance, though her belief she could fall was in her head. It was not all that difficult to walk normally. The imbalance was gone and her boots found traction in the dirt. She walked all the way down where the hill started to break off into little steps, stepping down, and for a minute almost believing that the temperature also dropped. A cool breeze blew around her nose, challenging her, asking her if she was sure she wanted to proceed. She came to another section of woods and stopped when she reached the edge, the clearing to the valley below, and that was when she saw it.

It curved into a deep basin, hidden almost by the layers of fog floating above, but there was no mistaking the arrangements of triangular roofs and squares of light speckled everywhere one could see. Now, with the dusk settling on the land, and given how deep it nestled into the valley, it made it look like it was the first to welcome darkness before anything else. With the sky's pink and orange colors long gone, the deep blue around the town made it look like it sat at the bottom of the ocean's deep. Poe sauntered down this path in a gentle slide as a chorus of crickets greeted her from the grasses. The path she walked merged with the land and though still easy to follow, seemed to blend too much: something that lost its straight and well-kept form and instead became directionless, giving her free range to go as she pleased, or having her go wherever she ended up. When Poe got up close and personal with the town outskirts, she could see just how layered they were just like the rest of the surroundings. It seemed that the basin scooped deep down in the valley wasn't too steep, and still had some more layers to go. The houses were all stacked in layers, on some hills and even nestled along the edges of hills. The entire town was a series of tiers, with places and things to see high as well as low. From where Poe was standing she could make out a little bridge over a river, the moon's reflection making it look like a silver snake.

Poe found the entrance to the village, right where someone staked the sign in the dirt rather lopsidedly. The letters looked like they might have been dark blue once, now faded to an almost gray. Poe lifted her lantern, holding it at arm's reach with her own glow. The letters on the sign could use some repainting, all the way down to the *"circa 808."* Her glow stopped at lettering that was not part of the sign, but rather sketched in free-handedly by locals: *"They come from below, and beyond."*

"Those finding yourselves alone in the dark…you are not."

"Beware those who walk at night."

Poe jumped, nearly dropping her lantern at the sound that thundered across the sky. It sounded like a repeating chime, only lower, almost like a gong.

Don, don, don, don.

She turned so the lantern lit up as much as it could of the mouth of the town and what was inside it. She could hear a few doors closing, windows shutting, and a voice yelling at someone else to get inside, quickly.

Ahead of her, the path curved and disappeared behind a building with most of its lights still on, even the yellow paper lanterns hanging from each corner. Poe held her lantern near her bag to search for the paper she'd kept with her. Although memorized by now, its message rang something closer with her setting foot on the scene, especially after reading the cryptic warnings added to the sign and kept there. She smoothed the paper out and held it to her light.

Wanted: Only the brave to apply

An apprentice I seek

With a keen eye and knack for stealth

If danger you do not mind

Then you can come

Mock Cob Village

She looked at the sign again, then back at the ad. She walked past the sign holding the ad with her thumb near where the address was, moving quickly with the realization that she needed to find it before it got too dark.

She walked past a house with a blooming garden with the start of vegetables poking through the dirt, hearing something scuttle through the grass. A gust of wind blew across the back of her neck, making her break out in goosebumps all the way down her arms and legs. She pulled her hood up over her head, though she still felt the next one. Poe looked to the houses, and buildings, able to still make out the numbers and street names she walked by in the still-evening dusk. The farther in she walked, the more the chill traveled down her spine, something trying to tell her something about her surroundings that she could not shake. The evening was in the area between warm and cool to be called cozy; where normally it would be just the right setting to want to be out taking a peaceful stroll, and although she had it all to herself, she somehow knew that she was not alone.

The chimes sounded again.

Don, don, don, don.

She came to a yard with two swings tied to a tree with a long, stretching arm behind one of the houses. Strange enough, the wind was only making one of them move, and even stranger it blew that swing straight in line, just as if a person was riding on it, gentle and steady. The swing seemed to stop altogether as she passed, just as she walked up the side of the house and watched it fall in line with the other, and the wind not blowing through it again. She walked down the sidewalk with her boots picking up subtle crunches of stones she stepped on, the scuttle or two of a small creature hurrying out of her way with the twitch of a tail.

When she walked past that house, the sound of slamming shutters made her jump. She turned, hearing a creak coming from somewhere else. And then something that sounded like a whisper. She turned around from her right, in the direction the voice was coming from. It was barely higher than a whisper but too low to make out what was said; it was close enough to her ear for the speaker to be right behind her. And yet, there was no one on the path. Even lifting the lantern to the sidewalk revealed nothing. She scanned the area, sure of herself, and then turned back around to continue walking. Here on the path, the cow tails were fairly long, and sometimes when the wind blew through them they could sound like voices. The path deterred to some wood steps made into the grass as it went down into another small slope. She followed these, and the houses around her seemed to merge in closer, blocking out any open space, and forming an outline of crooked triangular shapes. Here, she could see these shapes were not just houses, but they had odd structures all about them. She could make out a large wood frame of something that used to be whole, but now had pieces broken off and strewn about the lawn. Poe steadied her lantern at it, noting the roughness of the broken, splintered off at the ends. Whatever this was had been torn apart, and it had done so recently. The house next to this one had shutters and boards across every window, and when she passed the sidewalk, she could see an outline of something chalk white sprinkled on the lawn. Poe bent down, seeing clumps of crystals sprinkled thickly, all around outlining the entire house.

She lifted her lantern to the newly formed shadows. In the instant she did so, something fell away and something disappeared down an alley, knocking over a garbage can. Poe jumped, moving her lantern down that alley but seeing nothing but the garbage can rolling toward the wall. She sidestepped, backtracking so that she was not near this alley, focusing on the street sign a few feet ahead. She lifted her light to the names there, reading the one matching the one on the ad:

46 Matchstick Lane

Matchstick Lane pointed to the right, leading down an irregular-shaped street. Poe turned the corner to a patch of blue outside, lifting her light this way and that to read the numbers on the buildings, and any signage for businesses. From what she gave cursory glances, one looked like it was a post office and another was a barber shop.

A figure in a store window caught Poe's attention, making her stop right in front of it so that she was almost chest-to-chest with it. The figure might have been female but was not all the way in the window, though it was facing her and not moving. She thought she was looking at a mannequin wearing a fashionable jacket. She stepped all the way up to the window to see the jacket better, when all of a sudden those mannequin's arms shot up and closed the curtains. Poe sauntered back, making her lantern shake, standing before the curtains, looking at nothing but her startled expression. She backed up, trying to make sense of it. The person was tall enough for their head to be concealed, but somehow they saw her, and for some reason, they did not want her to see them.

She quickly made her way back down that street, one hand over her heart and telling herself that it was just past their closing time, and they just forgot to shut the curtains to indicate they were closed to customers for the evening. Poe walked on, turning first into a sprint then a light jog, scanning the would-be business places on either side of her to see all curtains closed, all windows secured with shutters. Some even padlocked. Some even had flat sheets of wood across them, like they were all preparing for some kind of storm. Poe stopped short at the one thing that appeared up ahead, the one thing she did not see anywhere else at all: a light. A single light was on in the first-floor window, bright enough to be known, yet dim enough to not stand out. Poe's heart elevated when she realized the light was meant for her to find. #46 Matchstick Lane was there, up on a little elevated hill.

Poe raced up the little steps around the bend, knocking over a stack of bowls that crashed and rolled to the ground. She picked them up as they rolled away to place in the grass, cringing at the noises they made that were loud enough to knock over the street signs. After steadying her lantern light, she stayed crouched to the ground in anticipation of the house's owner opening the door to see what the commotion was. She heard no sound, no activity from within, so she stood up and carried on. When she walked up to this house, she turned to what was in the front yard, not just the disturbing shapes beneath the tree, but also the disturbing smell. There was something on the lawn she could not quite make out, some pile of leaves and something in the middle. Poe steadied her light as her nose twitched. Whatever it was, it was no longer alive. And it was in pieces. She crept up the lawn, careful in her steps to not make too many leaves crunch, viewing it from where she stood. The meat was all in chunks, skinned all the way off so that it was nothing but pure red, almost like something positioned them together to look like the animal was still solid.

The next step Poe took made her drop her lantern and yelp as the leaves shot up around her, the hidden netting closing her up in a bundle and lifting her all the way up to the tree.

The moments that followed blurred together in a series of panicked fidgeting, pushing, and pulling. She stuck her arms out through the netting as far as they would go, reaching as high as she could go to the coil of rope at the top, not able to feel high enough for any knots she could fumble it. Her breathing came out in quickened heaps and she forced herself to quiet them, straining her ears should she get the company she did not want.

She pushed at the netting to give herself some room, opening her pack bag and rummaging through it. Her fingers found them, the small silver pair of scissors, the kind for a quick sew. They would have to do. She opened them and began to snip away at the netting.

Poe swallowed when she heard the faint creak of wood somewhere. Something opening, and then creaking again to shut. There was the crunching of leaves coming around the side of the house, and a new lantern light glowing from around the corner.

Poe turned down and to her right just as the massive figure appeared from the darkness with something long and pointed directly at her, something with a sharp end. She moved aggressively in the netting only to realize that the antlers in her hood were stuck, sticking right out and giving her a false silhouette that was no doubt against her. She pulled on them, keeping her eyes on the figure approaching, staying still and quiet. The figure kept the spear pointed at her, and, not losing aim, reached around the tree to unravel the rope. Poe felt the bundle loosen and descend from the air enough, but only just enough. The figure kept it at that level and then approached Poe in her frayed and knotted prison, the lantern now raised enough for her to see her captor.

This man looked made of mostly hair and beard, both so long and shaggy they grew into one another, a color between black and gray that suggested his age was unknown. She could smell a musky sweat coming off of his pores that suggested both adrenaline and non-stop labor. His eyes were almost the same color as his hair and could have been soft, though at the moment they were crazed. He was portly due to fat, but also due to muscle, and Poe thought it was something that should not be overlooked. The spear he was holding had a design etched of symbols and lines she wanted to look at but could not distract herself. The spear end was inches away from her body and the lantern light was right by her face, forcing her to shield her eyes.

"What in the—"

Poe moved enough, just enough, so that she could wrap her fingers around the netting.

"You're—you're human!"

The man rushed back to the tree and undid the rope all the way, lowering the net bundle all the way down until Poe could feel the ground again. She remained in the bundle, looking up at the man as he made no rush to undo the bundle, positioning the spear at her just as before.

"You are *human*, yes?"

"Yes!" Poe cried.

The man held the lantern at the bundle, his eyes and jaw stretched to ovals.

"You're ... you're just a kid."

The man tossed his spear and approached the bundle, untying it and allowing Poe to tumble out and away from it. He waited while she stood up, fumbling with the bag around her back and lowering her antlered hood, showing him she was exactly what she said she was.

"What in the hell are you doing out after Shut-In?!"

He paused, still peering at her. "You aren't from around here.

"No," Poe said. "I came to answer your ad."

The man's shoulders fell like those were the last words he was expecting. He quickly looked all around him, to the right, left, and behind him.

"Come, get inside! Quickly!"

He waved his hands at her to speed her pace and follow him to the back of the house, around a bend of bushes to a side door with a crack in the windowpane. The man shut the door behind them and locked it, even taking a minute to double-check out the window that nothing else was there.

She came to a living room area with a pulsing fire in the fireplace. There were two big sofa chairs near it with three or four old shirts draped over the arms, some caked with dried mud, and a few caked with dried blood. There were two pairs of boots thrown astray by the wall with missing shoelaces and one with a missing bottom. Poe stepped in, seeing the labyrinth of boxes piled up on one another, some empty packages with foam packing peanuts littered all over the floor and loose papers neglected inside. And the books. Poe spotted them all over the table near the couch, even at random places on the floor opened to various places with underlines and notes. She could smell something so sweet it was sour: rancid meat combined with old dairy, and it all came from the dishes with partially leftover turkey leg bones and bits of bread, and something else that had crusted over time that lined the bottom of a bowl.

The man turned to Poe as she pawed through her hair.

"Where did you come from?"

"Thistle. It's a town in Engle City."

"Thistle. I did place an ad there. Funny, I thought to myself that no one would answer it from that far, but why not take a chance ... and here you are."

Poe stood there, some leftover leaves still stuck to her cloak and in her hair.

"You are the first, and only one, to answer it."

"I found it in the paper," Poe answered. "I found it intriguing. I had to come and see."

"You alone?"

"I am, yes."

"Does your family know where you are?"

"I'm an orphan."

"An orphan, gee. What's your name?"

"Poe."

"Poe."

"That's right."

"I'm Rex. Rex Arken. You made me almost wet my pants out there. You looked like a new kind of demon beast with that on your head," Rex said with a disgruntled tone, fists on his hips. "I thought I caught a new one."

"Caught a new one?" Poe repeated.

Rex smiled now.

"So, you think you're the one for this kind of work? The only way to find out is to put you to the test."

Rex turned to the hall closet and went to work searching for things, knocking over other things clinging and clanging to the floor. He emerged with another spear similar to his but a tad smaller and presented it to her.

"All right, come on then. No better time than to continue right where I left off. You're going to need this."

Poe and Rex went out into the night, the cool blues now morphed into the deepest black. The light from Poe's lantern lit up a small circle of the lawn where she dropped it in the dark. He picked her lantern up and handed it to her, adding another guiding beam of light to the night. Rex kept his voice low, saying things to her that were quickened and quiet. He held a finger to his lips, gesturing to the outside as a whole, and instructed her to stay close.

"Up this way," he whispered. "We are going to check on all of them."

Rex walked forth, his stride careful yet authoritative. They steadied their lanterns at their sides so they could see where they were walking, every once in a while scanning what was ahead. Poe could feel the jumping of her heart that came when she first approached Rex's house in a combination of anticipated fear—a thrill of something mysterious that kept her guessing. They walked along a path in the street curving behind some houses, Rex aiming his light toward particular points on the ground and up in the trees.

"Sometimes they linger," he whispered. "Sometimes they stick around one place, especially if they're hunting."

He guided farther down the path to a small cluster of trees, where, even in the dark, Poe could see a familiar bundle of netting hanging from a branch. She froze, lifting her lantern only enough whereas Rex raised his all the way. The next breeze that picked up sent the bundle swinging and they could see the massive hole on the side of it ... the torn, frayed ends hanging out by the sides. Rex approached the side of the tree where the rope was and lowered it down. Poe watched that familiar trap come down, the holey netting bouncing up and down like a mouth eating or laughing.

Poe joined Rex at the scene as he turned the netting this way and that, inspecting the rope ends and brushing them with his fingers.

"Torn right through," he commented. "Either torn by claws or bitten by teeth. It's hard to tell. Most likely by claws. There's no trace of saliva here... could not have been bitten. No traces of fur or anything."

Poe looked at everything he did, keeping up.

"Some have fur. Some do not. I saw one furrier and bigger than a bear. But I did not catch that one."

Poe helped him bring the netting down and tie it into a bundle for carrying.

"Come, there's another one a little ways ahead."

They passed through the tree cluster and back around to some small hills and a bridge. They crossed the bridge, their footsteps creaking and groaning under them. Rex tensed, stopping and putting an arm out in front of Poe.

"Look," he whispered.

Poe thought she saw a shadow dance across the grass, and when she went to move her lantern, he pushed it down.

"Steady, we don't want to scare it off."

He gestured for her to follow, and they crept off the bridge toward whatever Rex saw. Poe stared at nothing but darkness. But Rex had found something to focus on. He reached into his bag and pulled out a mason jar. He half turned his head so that he was speaking to Poe out of the corner of his mouth.

"Come up here," he said. "Quietly. I want you to raise your light this way just a little, only a little, and keep it there until I say to move it. You'll see it. Don't make any noise."

Poe tip-toed forward, keeping steady, lifting her lantern, and then stopping at the part of the darkness that moved and opened into a big hole.

It looked like a little scribble on paper that floated off the page, but it was nothing but smoke. It could have tiny arms and legs... but it mostly just had a big open mouth. It opened that mouth wider, revealing tiny sharp teeth, emitting a hissing noise that sounded like steam.

"Easy," Rex coached. "Walk toward it with the light. Bring it over to me."

Poe steadied her lantern on this thing, this tiny thing that seemed to be all mouth now, nothing but a mouth wanting to bite. It scuttled backward with Poe's advance, hissing at her and trying to tear at the light with its jaws. Poe saw Rex come up behind it with the open jar ready, and then, in one quick swoop, he gathered it in the jar and sealed the lid. He and Poe leaned in, Poe's own mouth open in awe and disbelief.

"What is it?" she asked.

"It's a little snapping shadow. They love to hide in very dark places on the ground and attack things when they're moving. Pesky things. When they bite, it feels more like sunburn. They can't tear at flesh, but they still can leave marks that can't be explained otherwise."

Rex held the jar out to Poe, allowing her to take it to view for herself.

"Hang on to it. Watch its movements and how fluid it is. They're fast, but slow at times."

And so Poe tucked the creature of shadows under her arm, watching what looked like smoke swirling around in the jar. Every few minutes the smoke would open up an angry, spike-lined mouth and snap at nothing, anything, fury at its capture. Poe would watch it and watch where Rex was taking them, one after the other.

"You see, I am a cryptid and spirit hunter. I have been hired by the town mayor to study the things that come out around here. It's greater than anything I had ever done before. So I needed an assistant."

Rex shined his lantern on the remains of a squirrel in the road turned into carnage from something other than roadkill. All that remained was its tail and back legs, the top half torn away.

"Cryptid and spirit?" Poe asked.

"Oh yeah, all kinds of things. This place, this town, is in an area that is very susceptible to the strange and the otherworldly. It is located right on the edge between realms, so it gets a lot of ... visitors. There is one time of year when the veil between worlds is thinnest, and they all come out full force. It's called The Night of Passing, and it is like a full invasion."

Rex pointed out the houses they passed.

"But every night, right after dusk, everybody boards up their homes and goes into hiding. It's called the nightly Shut-In. No one is safe being out after dark. This town learned it the hard way years ago, and it has been this way ever since."

Rex stopped her before a patch of earth that had something only he could see. He leaned in, frowning.

"Nothing fell in there this time. Let's move on."

As Poe passed, she glimpsed the jagged spikes lining the bottom.

"Whoa."

"I cover all that during the day," Rex continued. "There's one more trap."

The ground underneath them slanted, moving them in a downward path into a valley. Rex took to using his spear as a walking stick as the ground turned bumpy and uneven, and Poe followed suit. With her lantern around her right arm holding the spear-stick, she turned her attention to the thing she had in a jar in her left. It looked like she only had a jar of smoke that every once in a while opened up to show teeth. What was Rex to do with it? She wished she had a camera on her to take a photo. See? She wanted to show the world. She wasn't the only one who saw things.

Rex stopped walking abruptly and held a hand out to Poe.

"Shhh."

Poe looked ahead, where a pond had mostly dried out enough to become a murky marsh. There were stumps and logs scattered throughout, but nothing else. Rex kept his lantern steady, though he was shaking a little.

"There," he said in a hush. "Gently. Do you see it?"

He guided her lantern to his level carefully, to where the bunch of logs sat, to reveal one of them was not a log. It could have passed for one, even in the daylight, with its wrinkled leathery skin, though she did not know any trees that were that red in color. Its back was turned to them with its head drooped down to its chest, and it appeared to be sleeping.

"That's a flyer all right," Rex said. "Almost sure of it. Do you see its wings?"

Poe raised her light just a little higher enough to see the two shapes that made up the bulk of its body staked right in the ground like anchors. There were spikes at the top, and there was no doubt the bottom had spikes as well.

"Geez," Poe breathed. "What is that? Where did it come from?"

"It's a Nether flyer," Rex said. "From below and beyond."

Rex reached into the bag around his waist. "I need to get my camera."

His behavior changed from steady and careful to elevated and jumpy as he rummaged through his bag, no longer caring so much about noise or speed. He pulled his arm back out holding said camera, but bringing with it other items that clanged together and scattered to the ground. Poe felt something sharp poke her stomach as those wings shuddered and the leathery log stretched. The thing now sat upright and revealed its head. She held her breath at the spikes curling out at the top, visible now once it turned its head—and self—around completely. It had the body of a vulture, though it had short, skinny arms coming out of its chest like a reptile. Its face would have been human if it weren't for the yellow eyes and the protruding beak. That beak opened and screeched before it leaped into the air.

Rex pushed Poe down and held his spear.

"Get down!" he yelled, aiming his spear at the flyer a good five feet above them. It flew over the marsh within seconds with open talons for Rex. He swung and missed, ultimately ducking while the flyer dived and caught something in its talons before taking off.

Rex sat up with his spear raised.

"It's got the camera!" Poe said.

Rex jumped up, holding his spear, cursing.

"It's attracted to shiny objects."

The flyer landed back at its previous spot, now holding the camera in its skinny front claws. Rex continued to curse while Poe kept her light on it.

"I've got other pictures on there I haven't developed yet! Ones of the big beasts, you know, ones from the other night and maybe even some ghosts from last week, and if that demon hell spawn ruins them I—"

Rex paced in place, his feet debating on whether or not to cross to the marsh and how.

"If I try to cross it, I'll scare it away."

"I think I can get it," Poe offered. "I am very quiet."

She put down the shadow demon jar, her lantern, and her spear and dug through her messenger bag. She opened her palm to show a bracelet made of pieces of aluminum and then turned toward the marsh. The flyer was keeping busy inspecting the camera, scratching it here and there, trying to figure out what to do with it. It did not stir when Poe walked down the grass and did not move or become alert when she stepped on the first log sticking out of the marsh. Behind her, Rex hissed through his teeth, lowering himself to the grass and holding his spear close, very close.

"Careful, kid," he muttered so low it was possible she did not hear him, but she did.

Poe stepped along the log and leaped lightly to the next, crouching to make herself as small as possible. She did not disturb the marsh just as she did not disturb the flyer, every once in a while jerking its head out where they were, but making no reactions to anything. Rex held his spear tightly while Poe crossed, squeezing it extra hard whenever she lumped to a new log. When she made it to the last remaining log before where the flyer sat, she raised herself up just a little, just enough. She took her steps in a slow stride, not making a sound, holding the aluminum bracelet in one hand. She was now close enough to see the wrinkles on that thing's skin and small strands of hair that stuck out, too close to human. It continued to play with the camera, shaking and poking it. In her peripheral vision, she saw Rex walk to the edge of the marsh with one toe pointed to the water, ready to bypass the logs should he need to cross in a hurry. Her breathing was easy and rhythmic, and she kept the pace as she moved. The last step she took landed on the very last log, the one barely sticking out of the water, so much so that the water seeped around her shoes, and she had to allow it to happen. The Nether flyer, the red demon creature straight out of Hell, was so close she could smell it. She lifted a fist to her nose, immediately thinking of smoke, gunpowder, and anything that was burning, for the thing smelled like it had come from the bowels of a fire pit. Poe held back a choke as she balanced on the log, shifting her weight to offset the water making its way around her leather boots. She could still see Rex out of the corner of his eye, one foot on an already sinking log, but she could not tell him not to move. He was not what she needed to focus on.

Poe tossed the aluminum bracelet a few feet in front of the creature and ducked, stepping to another log a little further away. It took the bait, flexing its wings in response before emitting a little screech. It diverted its attention while Poe made her way to the little island, walking one foot in front of the other and barely making a sound.

Poe spotted the camera straight away, and with each inch she took, Rex inhaled and gritted his teeth. She crouched down. The creature busied itself with her distraction, even attempting to take a few bites out of it. It did nothing when Poe scooped the camera under her arm and crawled away. It did nothing when she allowed a small breath of relief. But when she stepped onto a small pile of leaves, it created a crunch that was enough for the thing to lift its head, horns silhouetted and looking like a fork ready for a meal. It turned its head, beak opened into a snarl, where a thick line of drool fell to the grass. The thing growled a sound lower and deeper than any dog she had ever heard. Poe froze in place, although she had to keep her balance, sidestepping just enough and keeping her head low. The creature snarled again and lifted its head higher to survey the whole area. Poe kept steady and, on the other side, Rex crouched low and hid his lantern. She braved a moment to make her way onto the log, taking a leap that had a little too much force, causing her to slip. The creature caught this movement, eyes boring directly on the wavering log in the murk. Poe tensed her whole body as she made herself as small as possible, acting like she was shrinking her head inside her body. Her antlers on her hood had their own silhouette, and although a different shape, were indeed a bigger size. The creature then made a noise that was an octave higher and spread its wings. Poe ducked where her nose almost touched the water as she watched the thing take off. The wings expanded, curved and sharp enough to look like an umbrella in the sky. In a split second, Poe held up the camera and captured a shot. She took a few, watching the winged demon disappear somewhere in the darkest parts of the night sky.

Rex stood up all the way and was waiting for Poe right at the edge as she made her way back. She held out her camera to him as he stood there staring at her.

"Well, you're hired."

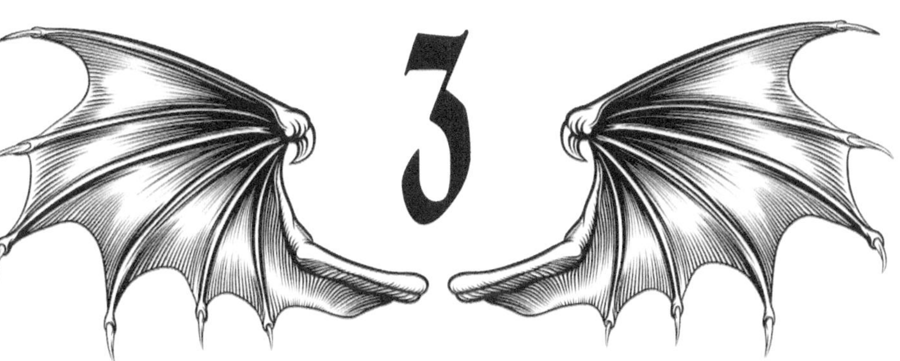

3

As quiet and reserved as Rex was before, he had turned the complete opposite. At the end of the night on their walk back to his house, he was the equivalent of a child talking with high energy and high speed.

"Just incredible what you did back there," Rex repeated. "That was parts sheer dumb luck and skill. I came close several times myself to things, but not as slick as you. Especially this one time, I nearly got out chased by a ghoul. They're stupid enough, but not that stupid."

"Ghoul?"

"Oh, and then some. There are many, and I know there are more, and that is what I am trying to get a hold of."

"Where do they come from, exactly?"

Poe leaped over a puddle in the road slick with mud. Rex would have stepped right in it the way he did when he did not look where he was walking.

"The Nether realm. The other realm. The beyond. Whatever you want to call it, there are plenty of names for it. They come out, they terrorize, they feed... and they leave at the break of dawn. Their time on this plane is so short, but there is plenty of time for them to do their damage."

They rounded the corner down the street, where the horizon revealed a deep blue rising out of the black.

"It's about dawn," Rex said. He turned to Poe as they walked. "Remember that snapping shadow we caught? Take it out."

Poe rummaged through her bag until she found the forgotten jar. The little black mass still floated around, bouncing around its glass walls.

"Open it."

Poe untwisted the lid and the black mass poured out, diffusing itself thin enough so its gaping mouth became a yawning O. It swirled a few inches above Poe and Rex's heads and stayed there, its gaping mouth opening and closing on nothing. As the dawn blued, clearer and clearer to a soft dim, it seemed to dim as well. Poe never took her eyes off of it as it started to vanish in the lightest tendrils of smoke until there was nothing left ... until it yawned its last yawn and showed her its tiny pointed teeth one last time. Poe held the jar and the lid and said nothing. Rex chuckled.

"Dawn of a new day," he said. "Once it hits daybreak, wherever these little beasts are hiding, it's enough to disappear them back to the shadows where they belong."

He rubbed his eyes and produced a yawn himself.

"Well, I'd say it's about time for some shut-eye. You— you must be tired."

Poe did not need to rub her eyes or yawn, and only considered it when Rex mentioned it.

"I am a little," she said. "To be honest, I don't sleep very much."

Rex just shook his head.

"I don't know where you come from, but I hope that once the sun comes up, you don't disappear, too."

"I won't."

They got back to the house just as those sky blues mixed with pinks and oranges, and Poe realized just how tired she became with the increase of Rex's conversation. She was tired from trying to keep up with it, interested as she was.

"I'll show you," he said again. "I will show you everything in my study and my books and all my notes and my sketchy drawings, just not tonight."

They climbed the stairs and Rex opened the door to a room he insisted was nothing much, but when the door opened all the way, Poe raised her eyes in surprise. It was an actual room, made up for someone to live in, as opposed for someone to simply sleep in only after they finished working. The bed was made up of colorful sheets and patchwork blankets that she immediately felt a connection to with a dresser next to it. Fun, curling designs carved into their woodwork adorned both the dresser and the bedframe. There was even a comfy ledge underneath the window with blankets and a few books decorating the back. On the far wall was a painting of a bowl of candy.

"I like it," Poe said.

Rex grinned. "It was like this when I moved in. I guess the previous owners used it as a guest bedroom. But, since you're my employee, that doesn't apply now. It's ... it's yours, if you want it."

Poe felt the bloom of warmth in the pit of her stomach, viewing what was nicer than any living quarters she ever had.

"I would love it."

"You get some rest, now."

"Thank you!"

Rex lingered by the open door.

"No, thank *you*. Just the fact that you got here in one piece."

Poe dropped her bag to the floor and hung her cloak on a peg on the wall. She started to unlace her boots.

"Right, well, see you in the morning. Or, day. Or, whichever. Sleep as much as you want and we'll figure out whatever we need to tomorrow. Or later today. And, welcome."

Poe grinned.

"'Night."

Rex shut the door, and she listened to his footsteps go down, then make their way back to the kitchen. She started walking the room, taking in every nook and cranny, but immediately she knew her favorite part would be the little ledge and the window. The books lined there were old classics, those she would not mind reading, and could picture herself doing at that very spot. She looked out the window, trying to imagine just how the afternoon sun would light up the room during the day and just when the perfect reading time would be. She moved the curtains slightly to see out the window. The moon was still visible in the pinkish-blue dawn, and yet, it was still the only thing that was out to see the entire town. Perhaps the sun would be the only thing to come out. Poe thought about what Rex said about the entire town going into full lockdown by nightfall, hiding behind bolted and boarded windows and doors. Everyone in the town wanted to appear like they were not there at all, and they knew just how to do it.

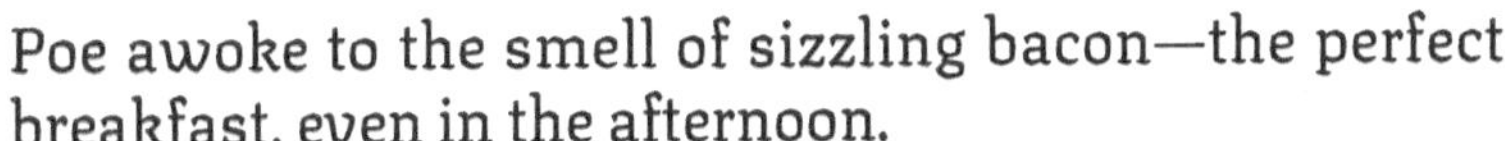

Poe awoke to the smell of sizzling bacon—the perfect breakfast, even in the afternoon.

It stayed in her nose while she dressed and washed up in the bathroom, rubbing her eyes and combing through the ends of her hair. As tired as she should have been, she was not, instead she mentally rewound the previous night's events and made her way downstairs.

Rex stood over the kitchen sink wearing a dirty, very stained apron. The stains ranged from reds to browns, smeared together and splattered, and could have been anything. Anything at all. He turned his head at the sound of Poe coming down the steps and, unlike her, he did not get the sleep out of his hair.

"Would you like some coffee? I just made a pot, and there's some toast and bacon here, too. Come on and help yourself. I don't know if you're a big eater, but I sure am, especially after a hunt."

Poe followed him into the kitchen, a quaint complement to the living room. It had equal parts trash and dishes in both sinks, and a few dented, empty cans lined the counters. And yet, it felt just as cozy with the rounded table and chairs with matching cushion seats. There were three, but Poe could see the scuff marks on the hardwood floor meant that only one was ever used.

Rex busied himself with the cabinets, pulling out a mug with a chip he took care to wipe off.

"Sorry, uh, can't say I spent a whole lot of time maintaining the place, but ... food's on the table!"

Poe went over to the table and chose one of the lesser-used chairs. There were two plates on the table with piles of bacon so crispy they hardened to curls and slices of toast with golden-brown centers. They were the only plates there. Poe waited for direction from Rex. He poured more coffee into his cup and brought Poe hers, sitting down on the chair to her right.

Her cup steamed, the trail of cream swirling in the middle. It smelled strong, though she could not place it. She blew on it and took a sip, pleased at the hazelnut aftertaste. Rex reached over and started buttering a slice of toast, and she followed his cue.

"Where did you come from again?"

"Thistle, I already told you."

"So, Thistle. You saw my ad, and you decided to come all the way over here to answer it."

Poe nodded, cradling her cup. "Yep, it got my attention. I just had to see it for myself."

"And now you have. No one responded. Even locals. Honestly, it's a small town, so I thought why not try to get a few new faces in here? That is, if anyone even answered. But you haven't seen everything yet ... I have much to show you."

"You do?" Poe asked.

Rex's eyes answered for him, taking on a sharper and more serious edge, the same look Poe first saw when he found her in his trap.

"This town..." he said softly, like he was afraid someone would hear. "This town gets invasions from other creatures for a reason. That's because it's by a border to another world."

Poe regarded him with one eyebrow lifted yet ate her breakfast.

"We got paranormal things. Things that go bump in the night, things that visit from the other side. You ever have … encounters? Thinking you see something and then it's gone?"

Poe blinked. "I have."

"We got 'em. We got … everything. This town has a lot of history. The early settlers came here and built the town and knew it, believing it to be something special, and they worshipped it. And now we're here. And now you're here, and the encounters we already had didn't seem to bother you at all."

That last thing Rex said hung between them as they ate, the two of them sharing a meal almost synchronized, picking up one another's patterns in an amicable fashion. They ate until it was all gone, two more plates filled with black and brown crumbs, and they even took their last sips of coffee at the same time, placing the mugs down in dual completion of the meal.

"All right," Rex said with a heightened voice. "Leave the dishes for now and come with me."

Poe followed him to another door she had not noticed before, one against the wall and nearly hidden in the wood. Rex reached up and grabbed the cord above him, turning on a dim light that only showed the stairs in a spotlight triangle. The stairs squeaked under them as they descended, and although Rex was talking a mile a minute, Poe could not help but be distracted by the pungent smell that hit her. She crinkled her nose and stifled a gag as it brought tears to her eyes. It was something she never smelled before, but it smelled strongly of a chemical.

"…just like the one you saw," Rex continued. "You'll see all my photos too, and then, once I get that film developed, I can show you more that I got in person."

Their triangle of light ended, and Rex knew where to reach to click on another light. It revealed a section of the basement that looked like a lab of pure chaos. Small squares pasted over sections of the walls that made it almost seem like wallpaper. Some that had various stages of age and decay, along with décor. They were mostly full of scribbled designs that in no way complemented one another. When Poe walked further into the room, she saw the scribbled designs for what they really were: wall-to-wall sketches. Some were sloppy and quick, while others had more details, focusing on one particular face, set of teeth, or claws.

Rex was already at a table near the center of the room that was so full he knocked over a few rolls of paper and some metal things that crashed to the floor. He continued to look for whatever he was looking for when Poe saw what was behind him, and the source of that nauseating smell: The glass vials, beakers, and mason jars were all in rows on the shelves, all holding different things, some of which looked like they could still be moving.

Or ... just floating in the gray-green liquid that held them in there.

Poe approached the shelves, seeing some of her reflection and the form of her face change shape as the jar shape did. One had a single eyeball with part of the severed optic nerve still attached, ends frayed like red yarn. The eye itself looked like it was more red in color, a bloody pink, and instead of a round pupil, it had an angry vertical slit. The jar next to it was larger and needed to be, for the nails at the end of each digit were bent up against the glass. It could have been human if it weren't for the claws, and the tufts of fur that was hard to tell what color it was. The liquid in the jar made it look green, but perhaps it had been green to begin with.

"Found them!"

Poe turned to Rex, who stood at the table holding up a pack of photographs. "You'll want to see these." The photos were mostly taken in the dark with the help of a lantern light to capture what was in them. Poe took two or three at a time.

"Woah," she breathed. "These are all creatures? Just like the ones we saw?"

She looked longest at the one that was the clearest, the one where the subject was looking right at the camera and right at her. Its eyes were small pinpricks, but bright enough to almost cast a glow, but invisible almost to the giant hole that was its mouth. Its skin was so wrinkled and so dark she could not tell what color it was, as it was pinkish-gray, a drab color of dirty wash-cloth wrung out. It even almost looked like one, drapery heavy and dripping wet.

"This one," Rex said, pointing to the picture she held. "One of the howlers. It sounds like a higher pitch wolf call, or like a child yelling, and it alerts others of where to find prey. So if it sees you and lets a howl out, that means company's coming, and you'd better run and hide."

Rex gave Poe more pictures to hold. She felt the jump in her stomach at the next one but otherwise did not react.

"Look here. This is actual evidence. There had to be multiple ones at once, otherwise it wouldn't have been such a clean job."

"Clean?" Poe repeated. There was not anything clean about this picture, aside from the bones themselves, which were completely polished off of all blood and meat. The grass held most of the spills, and the remaining ribcage and skull rested in its own pool of dried gore. Some of the other pictures were similar from different angles.

"I take these and then I send them over to the Society of Otherworldly Investigators. That's who I work for as a researcher and hunter. I was looking for work and then I found this jackpot. I make a report of everything I find and document."

"That's interesting," Poe replied. "People that go after it all."

"They do, and I have been a part of it for a few years now, but I feel like my coming to Mock Cob has been the feather in my cap for my career. They ate this up, and I was happy to feel like I could be settled here. And here I am, about a year later."

Rex said that last sentence with prideful undertones, looking around the room.

"These monsters from below are nothing to be trifled with, trust me. You have only seen a tease of what all comes out."

He gathered all the photos together and a notebook with a red ribbon marker down the middle.

"We have to gather these notes and photos and make copies to send to the Society. And get my film developed, too."

He looked over at Poe, who found a piece of hair to twirl over her fingers, forming multiple questions in her head but not sounding any of them out yet. She told herself not to ask too many right away, and see which ones got answered first. She started with one.

"How many more pictures of things did you get?"

"Not too many, but these are from an earlier night. There's a lot more. There are some things I don't know if they will even come up on film or not."

He started packing a messenger bag with things while Poe turned her attention back to the rows of jars filled with specimens. She particularly liked a skull with wide eyes and many teeth. She did not know what creature it came from, but it looked like it was smiling ... like it was something playful and mischievous.

"All right," Rex stated. "Time to introduce you to the rest of the town."

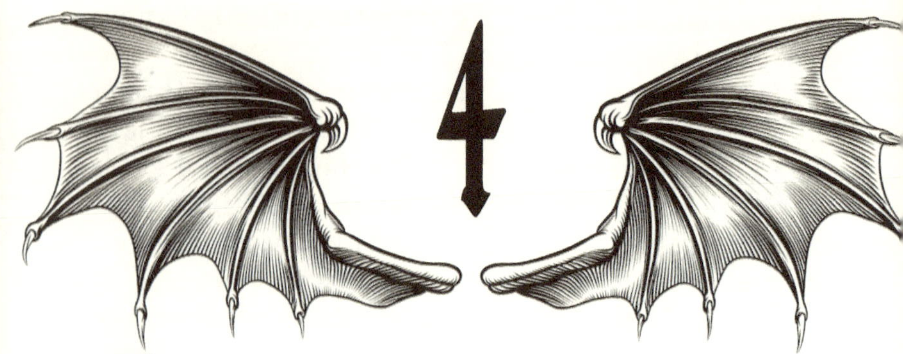

oe did not need to come out of the house all the way to see the livelihood she missed during the night. While Rex shut and locked the door, she walked down one step and instantly saw almost every house with people on the roof. They pulled up canvases covering their windows. Others were around the houses inspecting their barbed wire fences, and almost all of them were removing the giant sheets of wood over their windows.

"Welcome to daylight," Rex said. "Just like clockwork."

He joined her on the sidewalk and they walked together, Rex narrating the activity before them.

"During the day, it is safe again."

They passed a house where two men were walking with a sheet of wood, three curves of slashes visible down the front. A few carriages drove down the street with content, galloping horses, dragging behind them a net at least six to ten feet long. People bent over in their yards to pull out sharpened stakes, and some came out of underground shelters, pushing the doors open and coming out to greet the sunlight for the first time, squinting their eyes and shielding them with their arms like they never saw it before. As Poe and Rex walked down the street, she also saw people picking up broken tree branches and pieces of fencing.

"It has gotten worse throughout the year," Rex muttered. "There have been more of them."

They passed another building that still had its wood slabs on its windows. Each and every one had claw marks all over it. When they got closer, Poe could make out a dead goose lying mangled in the grass.

"The town does everything it can to protect itself … but it's not always enough. It has become a heated debate and only continues to get worse."

Rex led Poe onto a sidewalk where she could see a man and a woman bent over another dead goose. Its head was missing.

"So these … things, they come out every night?" Poe asked.

"That's right. A few come here and there, but when the veil between planes is the thinnest, they all come out full force. It is the last night of October, known as The Night of Passing, and everything imaginable comes out. Demons, monsters, and spirits. Some of them linger for another night or two, and then when the season is over, the nights end and they go back. The demons all do anyhow, some of the spirits, however…"

"What about the spirits?" Poe asked, not meaning to sound too eager. "They stay? Well, that makes sense, I guess. I've seen some before."

"You have?"

"When I was little. There was a little girl that drowned in a lake and I could see her reflection on the water when I went there."

Rex did not respond right away, allowing the crunching of grass to fill up the silence.

"And I saw her standing there before the lake once. She went away. No one believed me," Poe finished.

"I believe you," Rex answered.

They stopped at a place that was already open for business, wood slabs down, and windows clear. Rex pulled his camera out of his bag.

"Let's get this film developed first, and then we'll go to the printing press and post office. Boring errand stuff, but I figured now would be a good time to let you get familiar with the town and all."

Poe loved the photo place, the way the room was an eerie deep red and the way she could watch the pictures slowly come to focus in their trays. They left them to all develop, Rex having them make a circle around the block.

"Rex!"

A bald man in tan coveralls and dirt-caked gloves flagged them down.

"Rex, I need you!"

"Ezra, hello. What is it?"

The man's wrinkles stretched over his eyes, two worrisome pools of sky blue, looking like forever drops of tears. Poe picked up something from Rex's tone and leaned in.

"Well," Ezra started. "There's something in my garden."

"There is?"

"Well no, no, it's gone. I mean, I think it's gone, I mean, I think it might still be lingering ... and oh, who is this?"

Ezra gestured a glove toward Poe.

"I'm Poe," Poe replied. "I am Rex's new assistant."

Ezra gave Rex a curious brow. "New assistant? Rex, I didn't know you got yourself an assistant with this now!"

"I have," Rex stated, and Poe smiled. "And I got me a good one, too. This kid arrived in the middle of the night with no fear in her heart and helped me get my camera back from a Nether flyer."

Ezra's pool eyes grew. "Is that so?"

"I did," Poe insisted, and she did want him to believe them. But it was as though this man had never seen a Nether flyer for himself.

"Well, I am glad I caught you while you were out. Both of you, please, could you spare a minute?"

Ezra gestured to his house, his fence gate swinging in the wind and hitting the unlocked padlock. "I just... Come over here and tell me what you think."

Rex and Poe followed Ezra to his garden around the side of his house, rich with shrubs of green and giant red and orange vegetables. Ezra hesitated by the soft dirt.

"Do you have any of your equipment on you?"

"I don't right now," Rex admitted.

"Do you ... feel that?"

Poe did. Poe did before Ezra made any mention of a "that" and the chill went up her arms and legs and all the way up to the back of her neck. She tensed. She did not move. She cast a look at Rex, who was crossing his brow and staring at the garden as though it would reveal something.

"Try going in there," Ezra suggested. "Please."

Poe let Rex go first. They took steps down the leafy greens and budding bulbs. Poe walked next to him, waiting for him to feel it, wondering why he did not as quickly as she did. She debated when to say something, thinking that she should if Rex did not, but sure enough, he did. He stopped short and held his fingers out to his sides.

"Oooohh."

"Yeah," Ezra agreed. "Right there."

"I feel it too," Poe said.

"Something came in my garden some night and stuck around for a while. I don't know if it's still here and I can't tell. I don't exactly want to tend to my bell peppers right now."

They each stepped forward carefully. Poe paid attention to the plants and leaves, making sure they all fluttered in the same direction as the wind. Rex seemed to be watching that as well. The wind carried into a gentle breeze that passed through all of them.

"There was something here. It must have walked right through your garden. I can come back later with my equipment."

"Thank you," Ezra said with a light smile. "I am sure that others ... well ... I hope no one had anything happen."

Ezra walked them back through to his front yard and out the gate.

"Have a good day, Ezra. We'll come back later."

"Thank you, Rex. And good to meet you, Poe!"

"You too!"

Rex and Poe continued down the street, crossing a path of wild yellow flowers, also littered with pieces of broken debris.

"Yep, spirits," Rex commented. "Those are always more complicated than creatures because we can't see them. We'll be back here."

Poe did not need Rex to tell her that. She already knew, but she just had to wait to see for herself.

One after the other they pasted into the book, Rex scribbling basic descriptions of them all. They got to the one Poe took of the Nether flyer in the sky.

"They'll know what this one is," he commented. "I mean, I did get a closer one once, but that wing span is impressive."

Poe picked up one of a long clawed footprint plastered in the mud and another of what looked like a very tall person with very long arms. Long enough to touch the ground. Rex separated the photos, one into the pile he wanted to go into his collection and another to be sent off. He gathered a portfolio filled with writings and fastened it closed.

"Well, I am going to go and mail these off and run some other errands."

He reached into his coin pouch and pulled out four silver coins and five bronze ones. Poe's eyebrows perked.

"Here. When I get paid by the mayor for all this stuff I send, there will be more for you too, of course. This is a little something to start out with since you've earned it. Why don't you go out and explore the town and get yourself a little something? Do you have a watch?"

"I do," Poe said, pulling it out from a chain in her pocket and showing it off. She popped it open to reveal the ticking hands she had just recently wound up.

"Okay. I should be back in a few hours. There's a marketplace not too far from here, many general goods stores, and a bigger grocer on the other side of town. Go on and get the kinds of foods you like and we can get more later."

Poe had those coins cupped in her palm like they were all made of gold. She pocketed them while Rex packed up the rest of his bag and headed out. After lacing up her boots, she finally went out and down the steps, and she was on the town.

Poe stood there with the realization that she was meeting Mock Cob village for the first time alone.

Down the streets were some people. People out, people coming out, people in doorways and in windows. People were in carriages. High in the sky, the sun blasted upon the entire town, showing her the identities of all the places she passed by the previous night. She could see now just how ... settled everything was, with all the different layers around and all the houses that stuck out from on top as well as below. It could almost give one the feeling of being closed in, of being in the middle of a crowd where everyone could see you without your knowing. Far off came the braying of goats and cattle and the chatter of chickens. A carriage breezed past Poe and shot up the street, the wheels screeching as they turned the corner and disappeared. This breeze whistled in the tree above her, but also set the sound of different tunes. She caught sight of a shop with magenta window frames and blue wood, and hanging from the roof were differently shaped metal contraptions. They were long and twisted, many differently colored rods hanging and smashing into one another in the wind to create the song of chimes. Down this sidewalk were more buildings of different colors, and different signs advertising different things. She was too far away to read them.

Poe crossed the street in the direction of the swirling chimes, rushing up to the windows to see all the glass artwork and centerpieces on tables. She turned her head in the direction of the smells of lavender and citrus, following her nose to the shop next door selling handmade soaps and candles. The next shop appealed to the next sense, the one she wanted to satisfy more, as she watched some people come out of it scooping frozen pink stuff into their mouths. Hers watered.

Moments later she exited the shop holding a mango half, scooped out enough to hold the iced treat of the same flavor. She felt the cold rush down her throat and the frozen burn that came from it and still thought nothing of it, scooping and scooping as she walked down the street, trying to see everything at once. In stark contrast to meeting the town at night, by day it was lively, bright, and robust. Ahead of her, a woman walked two fluffy little dogs on leashes, the wind blowing their fur about their eyes so they could not see, but they still sensed Poe. They barked anxiously, pulling on their leashes with little nubs of tails wagging while the woman kept them back. Poe smiled and waved; greeting them in a soft voice reserved for babies and animals, and kept walking. The dogs insisted on giving her their attention, beating the air with their tails and barking in question even as their owner ushered them along, wondering what had gotten into them. Though not as obvious as the dogs, it seemed that some people expressed a light interest in Poe as well, giving her a moment's look before going back to minding their own business. She walked on with the sense that this town was smaller than any she'd ever been to, loving the hand-painted signs above stores with family names. Business names she never heard of, and only came from small towns like this where names carried.

Poe stopped by a trash barrel, scooping out the mango half all the way through, leaving her with the flimsy, leftover skin. She put the very last scoop of fruit and ice in her mouth before discarding the skin and spoon, listening to music playing from a second-floor window. She continued down the street on her aimless path in a sense of bliss.

"This town gets invasions from other creatures for a reason."

Poe walked down a sidewalk as a rack of clothing outside a shop swayed in an upcoming breeze, sheets of red and yellow and polka dots mixing together.

"That's because it's by a border to another world."

Poe paused, sticking a fist in one of the pockets of her messenger bag. She brought the crystal out, turning it a few times in her hand and holding it up by the sun. It remained clear, sparkles flashing at every edge and point. Poe wrapped her fingers around the shape, keeping it close by while she turned down another street.

She held the crystal in her right palm, letting the sharp edges dig into her skin, but was not sure what to expect or just how exactly it was supposed to work. Would it vibrate? Change colors?

She came across a small wood bridge over a stream. A bird hopped along the railing before taking off, right when Poe approached it and crouched down, holding the crystal to the planks. She stood up and waved it across the bridge, taking step by step, seeing it still stay the same all the way across. Something rippled in the water as she passed it, a drop of something that fell from nowhere or something coming up from below to spy above. She walked down the grass as a few carriages rolled down the street ahead of her, each curving into the bowl shape of the street and circling around. Poe stepped into an area dominated by grassy squares of people strolling down sidewalks at leisurely paces and those running at play with dogs and children. Poe came upon a sidewalk and joined the leisurely flow, admiring the fat, leafy plants outlining the sidewalks and careful not to step on any of the flowers. The trees here had thick trunks and large, overbearing arms as branches, long swaying leaves drifting in the front of them like long hair covering a face from behind it. Poe slowed down and imagined climbing those trees all the way up to the top, knowing the view must be breathtaking. She had already made the mental note to herself to do so whenever she got the chance ... when there were fewer people around or none. Poe's hand closed around the crystal, but it did nothing to alert her of her own surroundings better than her instincts did. Though the sun bore down on her enough to threaten sunburn, Poe caught a chill down her back, and then all the way down her arms and legs. She peered at the skin on her arms, fresh goosebumps making her skin look like raw poultry. As she walked, she felt no breeze, no blow of the wind ... yet something was telling her that something was there.

Ahead of her was another square that was less populated, with longer grass and plants long enough to make a nature-made fence. There was not much there, except for the one thing that stood out the most: a tree bigger and wider than any of the previous ones she'd seen, with multiple arms reaching for the sky. And something danced in Poe's stomach.

The grays in the clouds blended to a darker color that was now more black than gray, but still preparing turmoil that would be unleashed from the sky when it wanted to. The chill moved around down her back as well, and she could swear she could feel the hairs on the back of her neck stick straight out. Poe held the crystal to the square ahead of her; it seemed like she was holding a piece of blue-gray sky before a rainstorm the way it reflected it. Her eyes alert, she walked ahead on that sidewalk, taking care to notice that there were no more passersby where she was going. Most caught the signs of the upcoming rainstorm, but even those still outside were nowhere near where she was. This square was the very last one where the sidewalks ended and the backgrounds disappeared into more shrubbery. There was basically nothing there at all except for that tree. But there *was* something there. Poe shuffled her feet, wanting to act on her other instinct.

If danger you do not mind,
Then you can come.

Poe stepped into the square, the sun disappearing behind the tree so that she could see it in full focus. It was almost like a shadow itself, towering over anything that would come within a few feet of it, with branches looking like multiple outstretched arms. They were inviting, though almost too inviting, and Poe automatically got the sense to stop where she was and not go any farther. Like she did not want to wake it. The goosebumps on her arms ran all the way up to her shoulders and prickled even more at the back of her neck. She stared at a particular point by the trunk, convinced that she saw something ripple in the air. She lifted the crystal to look through it, expecting it to turn into some sort of crystal ball to reveal what was not visible to the plain eye. After a few minutes, nothing appeared, nothing except the rogue raindrops that landed on her arm, head, and shoulder. She lowered it, backing up a few feet until she was far enough away to trust to turn her back and walk away.

The wind picked up and sent a sea of cold air washing over her ankles. It was loud enough to moan through the trees, soon becoming loud enough to sound like screams. Human screams. She turned back around to where the wind picked up again, sending a blast that seemed to have come from the big tree. Poe shielded her eyes against loose dirt and leaves. It swirled around her, almost keeping her in place, the screams coming in short snippets and disappearing down the street. She looked through the blasts of wind, seeing the occasional ripple just as she saw before, but nothing else. Nothing except for the sprinkle of rain falling from the sky.

Poe watched the rain come down in light and thin slivers. The scene reverted back to something ordinary and quiet ... though for the moment Poe believed that it was not. She was almost experiencing a reflection of something that had happened there before.

On her way, she would glance behind her now and then, because the goosebumps on her arms still bubbled. The rain sprinkles continued. Poe pulled on her hood and quickened her pace.

5

oe blew across the rim of the steaming hot cup of coffee, walking to the living room to join Rex. She came all the way in before she noticed why it looked so different. For starters, she could see the couch in its entirety, cleared of all debris that used to litter it. It was blue, a cool cerulean color with an occasional stray feather poking out of the cushion. The table had cleared, too, revealing a few circular stains in the wood. Rex sat in one of the sofa chairs. He had at least six or seven books open in front of him, holding a pen, trying to figure out where he wanted to make a note. Instead, he picked up a notebook and scribbled something else. Poe sat down in the other chair next to him and took an interest in the books. One had a picture of a towering figure in black robes, with even blacker horns on its head.

DEMON LORD. RARELY SEEN.

SPEAKS THE OLD LANGUAGE.

CAN SUMMON ARMIES OF UNDEAD WITH A
SIMPLE CALLING.

DO NOT APPROACH.

Another was a small humanoid with rough, textured, reddish skin and a very unfriendly grin. It had two horns on its head that gave it a hellish profile, curved and rough. A worse thing to encounter than a ram or goat. Its teeth were so big it almost couldn't close its mouth, and its claws could almost touch the ground.

RUBRUM

FAST. NASTY. LAUGHS AS IT TEARS SKIN
OFF ITS VICTIMS ALIVE AND EATS IT

NO KNOWN WEAKNESSES

NONE REPORTED SUCCESSFULLY
KILLING ONE

Poe turned the page to a drawing of a pond, and there in the middle of it was a baby's head, barely visible on the surface. Its eyes were colored green ... and somehow it had a facial expression to suggest it was much older.

BOBBLEHEAD

MADE UP OF THE HEAD OF A HUMAN
INFANT AND FOUR LONG ARMS.

CAN MIMIC THE CRY OF A BABY AND WHEN
ITS VICTIMS GET CLOSE, IT PULLS THEM
UNDERWATER TO DROWN AND SENDS
THEIR SOULS TO THE RIVER OF DEATH.

Poe's eyes grazed over every one of them. Her mouth opened akin to curiosity and alarm.

"You don't have to worry about some of those until next Night of Passing. Some only come out when it gets closer to then. It's best to avoid things once you see them, but they're not the worst of it. The worst is what can see you, but you can't see them: Ghosts."

Rex picked up another book and turned some pages.

"Specter, spirit, wraith ... no, no, it can't be a wraith."

He glanced at Poe. "Just to be certain, when we walked through Ezra's garden, you didn't see anything did you?"

Poe shook her head. "No. It seemed a little foggy. But I did feel something."

"Foggy. Ezra's visitor might be more of a wisp ghost then. Here, look."

He handed her the book so she could see it on the page, looking like a collection of fog that just clumped together with the description:

A FOG GHOST, AKA A WISP OR A MIST
AMONG OTHER NAMES, TAKES A SHAPE
IN THE FORM OF FOG OR MIST. THEY DO
NOT LINGER LONG AND LEAVE THE AREA
THEY HAUNT FEELING COLD.

"We'll go back with the equipment made for reading energies and take pictures to see if anything comes up on film. OH! I need to show you some!"

Rex dashed with the excitement of a dog going for a walk and disappeared down to the basement. Poe, in the meantime, returned to the book and more descriptions of spirits, and how and if they manifested. There was the photo of three women in an old house, the third one slightly blurry. The description read that the two women claimed there was no third when the picture was taken. Rex came climbing back to the living room with another photo album.

"Did you catch ghosts on film?" she asked. "Were there many?"

"Not too many," Rex admitted. "But we do get orbs. Lots of orbs. And a few of the other kind of mist ghosts as well. Take a look, see if you can see faces or human-like shapes in these."

Poe took the album, which only had a few pages filled in. Sure enough, there were white and yellow spots of light that were in the background of many photos. Most were landscapes and near gravestones. Poe looked at one next to an old well where she could see the faint eyes, nose, and mouth. Most people probably just saw holey shapes, but she could make out pupils and eyelashes, and even the curve of a human nose.

"I see it."

"Yeah. Most of the time it is subtle, but when people think there's something there, they want someone like me to come and check it out, and make sure it's not a bad spirit that wants to harm them."

She kept her attention to him as he went silent for a moment.

"Have there been many?"

Something dark passed over Rex's face, almost making it sink and blend into his beard.

"A few. Some haunt old buildings and make everything break and fall apart. I know of others who have had ... well, worse encounters. And there might be many here who have."

There was a beat.

"Especially the mayor. She's mayor for a reason."

While Rex knocked on the door, Poe shuffled the weight of the bag on her shoulder. She did not get to see what exactly he packed when he filled up the bags, but she could feel how heavy some of it was. Ezra opened the door on the first knock even with Rex prepared to make a second.

"Hello, hello! Come, I must show you what I discovered!"

Ezra shuffled out of his house. He wore a very wrinkled shirt and pants with mismatched colors like he pulled on whatever he could find in haste. The green bottoms and pink, baggy tunic almost made him look like a plant himself, if there were any that were wrinkled and gangly.

"Come here," Ezra went on as they went around to the side of the garden. "I have been avoiding it for the most part and just watching out the window in case I could see anything, which I never could. Since I knew you were coming, I went out there this morning to take a look and this is what I found."

They walked through, Ezra stepping aside to let Rex and Poe make the aforementioned discovery for themselves. They were careful to step over the large, orange gourds on the ground until Ezra stopped at the place. Silently they stared at the wall of leaves, vines, and thorns and the massive break down the middle. Rex went through his bag and got out a small device with knobs and a meter pin. He turned a knob, and it lit up red and green, the meter hand dancing along the screen.

"See here, Poe." He showed her. "This is something we use to read electromagnetic waves and energies. Turn yours on so you can follow a read."

Poe did so even though she did not need the device. She knew by the way her short hair stuck out. She turned on the device and watched her own red and green lights blink, the meter hand wavering somewhere in the middle.

"Looks like it though, there's no doubt," Ezra stated. "Does that mean it's gone?"

"From your garden, I'd say," Rex replied as he moved his device around, watching the meter move more to the right. The green lights went on.

It's more than one, thought Poe.

"It's not just a spirit," Rex said. "Whatever did that was making a path. We're going to go follow it."

She nodded to Ezra like she knew that was the plan all along. Something tingled along her skin as Rex gently waved his device all over the broken thorns.

"Well, I hope you find it. Or them. Or whatever it is. So, what is it you'll do once you find it?"

Poe looked to Rex as he turned around, equally curious about his answer. Though the bag she carried had different metal things and papers, none of them were weapons.

"Depends on what it is," was Rex's answer. "But capturing anything on film is key."

Poe joined Rex at the made hole in the bush and both their devices flashed green.

"Well... good luck," Ezra said. He backed up and then turned to leave as soon as they entered the opening in the leaves, some blackened at the ends, like whatever touched them stripped away some of their life.

Poe and Rex were now on a clear path from Ezra's house, walking along a grassy knoll and little path behind other houses. Both of their devices stayed green and the meter pin jumped in the middle as they moved along.

"Spirits can sometimes have energy left behind. Sometimes people can still sense something even after they're gone."

"I can tell," Poe said. "I can definitely feel it."

"You can ... so you can feel it now?"

"It's a little chilly, especially now."

"We're right on its path."

They walked along the grassy knoll until it dipped down and continued away from the streets, taking them past a ravine and hilly area. The grass got longer as they walked, long enough to scratch the exposed parts of Poe's shins. They stopped at a place where they could hear a bit of water running and viewed a stream trickling down from something. Both of their meters stayed green and Poe's skin stayed tense. She could see the curved cylinder of the concrete and the grated cover. Only Rex bent forward to aim his device as far as he could reach.

"Seems just beyond that sewer. Floated away, probably went through that grate."

He noticed that Poe had her device down by her side and was trying to look beyond the sewer. She was looking through the grate as if she could see what was inside it ... or wanted to.

"Do you see something?"

"No," she said honestly.

Rex pulled out his camera and took a couple of shots, the flashing light revealing nothing behind the grate but a dirty sewer.

"See if anything comes up. This is the best we can do. The only thing that can go through there is an animal, anyway. Come on, let's head back and then we can go through town. I'll show you this place where we can get some great shish kebabs."

They took the side path past Ezra's house, Poe seeing that his curtains were shut.

"He mostly keeps to himself," Rex said. "Nice, quiet man. He grows the best vegetables around here. He can get them really big."

"Don't we go tell him we didn't find anything?"

"Not yet. We'll develop the photos. If anything, there might be orbs or other traces, but we don't know yet."

They crossed the street after a few carriages rolled by, and a boy on a bike rode past, ringing a bell. The sounds of the bell and the horse's hooves drowned out the commotion on the side of the street, where they could make out some people standing at the corner holding sheets of bright yellow paper and clipboards.

"Stop the massacre!"

"Keep traditions alive by keeping *ourselves* alive!"

"Motion to build underground shelters and continue Shut-In! Come and sign the petition!"

Poe probably could have walked down that side-walk unbothered and unseen, slipping between other pedestrians, but not while walking with Rex, who towered over some of them. He groaned under his breath.

"Keep walking. Don't look at them. We don't have time for this."

A middle-aged woman with a pencil stuck between her ear and red-brown hair, wearing pink glasses, rushed at them and held her clipboard out.

"Petition for Loman & Co to build underground shelters!"

"Not today, we're on a mission," Rex said in haste and walked faster, making Poe keep up. He only slowed when they turned the corner and were out of sight.

"Last thing we want to do is get involved."

"What was that about?"

Rex sighed. "The town is a bit divided. The hiders versus the fighters. No one can agree on anything."

They walked a bit more until Rex pointed out the place he mentioned to her, her mind changing gears from curiosity to hunger, and a few minutes later, they both walked out with giant skewers of roasted squares of steak with alternating potatoes and peppers. They ate with one hand while the other held bottles of sarsaparilla.

They came to a stop on the sidewalk and turned down to the right, each still eating and drinking on the go. Poe chewed through the meat and let the juice run down her chin.

"This is fantastic."

"See?" Rex said after a gulp of his bottle. "What did I tell ya? I get these a lot. It's perfect, easy food for when

I'm pouring over photos and writing up logs from when I'm out on the hunt."

They walked down the street where they could make out another gathering of people by the neighboring shops. Rex groaned.

"Great."

"More of them?"

"You could say that. Come on, let's cross this way instead."

He urged her to cross the street, picking up the pace. Poe heard the shouts of the people egging on anyone who walked down that street.

"Fight or die!"

"We will not live in fear! We will not let these monsters rule our lives!"

"This is our town and we have to defend it!"

As she jogged to catch up to Rex, she stole a couple of glances behind her. They were also carrying signs, and one of them also had a clipboard. He was an older man who could not walk as well as he used to, but insisted on it. The man next to him was quite large, wearing a leather apron.

"Sign the petition for Thisby & Koach to make advanced weapons! Either we kill them or they kill us!"

Rex rushed Poe down the street until they reached another block they could take home. Rex slowed down enough to finish his shish kebab and toss the skewer into a nearby trash. Poe deposited hers too, addressing him.

"That's what we're doing, though, right?"

"What's that?"

"We're going after them to kill them."

He looked at her with soft but serious eyes.

"Poe, listen to me."

Rex looked around to make sure no one else was within earshot.

"We don't go out looking for a fight. Our job is to go out to study creatures and ghosts, to learn about them and raise awareness of their existence. The goal is to trap them first, keep them confined, and take them out only if they threaten us or hurt us first. We have weapons, but we only fight them if we must, if they come after us, and only then. We do not agitate them, do you understand?"

Poe nodded.

"I need you to tell me you understand."

"I understand."

"You've proven to me you are stealthy. That's what I want. That's what we need to be. It is our job. Finding out how to be rid of them ... that's going to be someone else's. If it is even possible."

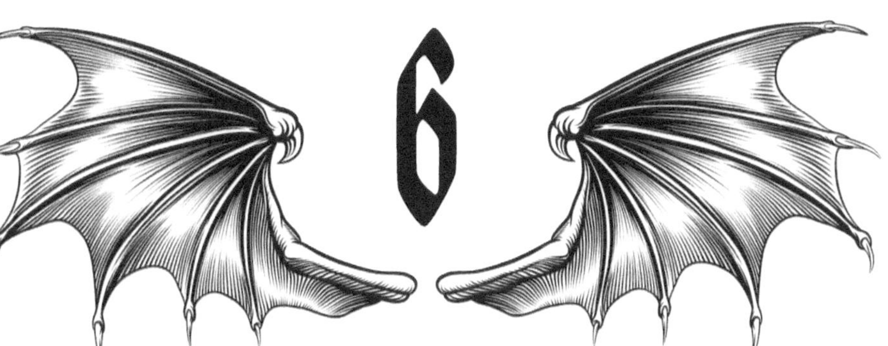

6

oe flipped the page to the illustration of the ghoul, a pale-looking humanoid all hunched over like it no longer had use of its body but kept it moving anyway. Its entire face was sunken in with blank, expressionless features. At that moment, Rex opened the front door and came in with a bundle of papers under his arm, holding one opened letter from an apricot-colored envelope. And Rex adapted the features from the ghoul, standing there holding the letter and losing all expression on his face, body slouched.

"There's going to be a town meeting," he said. He did not look up from the letter and his expression stayed the same. Poe kept the book balanced on her knees. "Things did not go so well last time this happened."

Rex came over to the living room area and put the papers down on the table, as well as various pieces of junk mail and letters from various paranormal investigators asking Rex to be their sponsor. He sighed, still holding the paper.

"Almost turned into a brawl."

"What happened?"

"Well, you saw the people picketing down the streets."

He landed the letter over to Poe to read for herself. She immediately felt the formality of it due to the thickness of the paper, the elegant flow of cursive letters, and the polite language.

Citizens of Mock Cob Village:

We invite you to a town meeting to discuss new ideas on the precautions and preparation during Shut-In, and especially leading up to The Night of Passing, including new suggestions on Night of Passing to be taken in a civil manner.

"'New ideas on the precautions and preparation?'" she asked. "'Especially leading up to the Night of Passing?'"

"That's right. This will not be pretty."

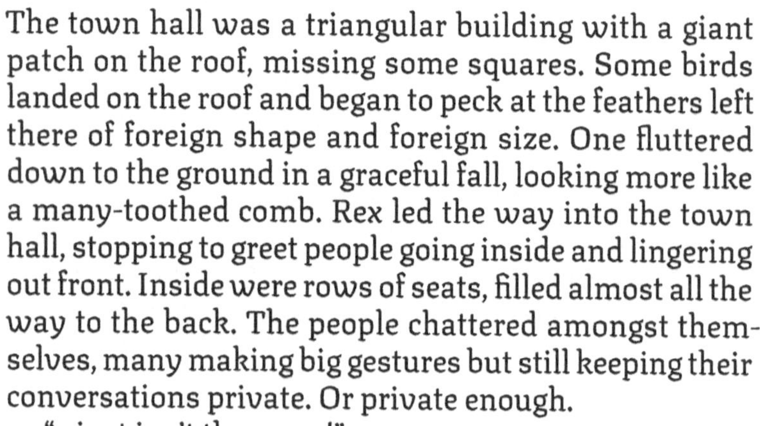

The town hall was a triangular building with a giant patch on the roof, missing some squares. Some birds landed on the roof and began to peck at the feathers left there of foreign shape and foreign size. One fluttered down to the ground in a graceful fall, looking more like a many-toothed comb. Rex led the way into the town hall, stopping to greet people going inside and lingering out front. Inside were rows of seats, filled almost all the way to the back. The people chattered amongst themselves, many making big gestures but still keeping their conversations private. Or private enough.

"...just isn't the same!"

"...worse and worse, and I don't see how we've been going on with this for so long!"

"...got to be done. This better be what this meeting's about!"

Rex and Poe found two empty seats down the row and near the wall, so they did little walking in front of others. Poe was glad of it. A discussion much more heated was happening on the other side of the row.

"Well, you weren't there! You wouldn't know! So don't stand there and act like you know what you're talking about!"

"And who exactly called *you* an expert?"

Two men of comically opposite sizes stood inches apart in the row, their voices rising with each sentence. The men grabbed each other's arms and the whole hall erupted in an uproar, many rushing to get between them and multiple voices shouting over one another.

"Order, order!" boomed a growly voice at the front. There came the sound of something hard and thick striking a podium. Poe looked to the front to see a woman standing before it, lips pinched like a schoolteacher reprimanding her students.

"That is quite enough of that! The two of you get a hold of yourselves! Everyone take their seats!" She hit the mallet on the podium again for good measure while the congregation obeyed.

"That's the mayor," Rex muttered to Poe. "Vivienne Tellenboe."

Vivienne was elderly, though young enough to have spark, with enough wrinkles in her face and hard-learned lessons in her eyes. She addressed the hall with the high energy Poe had.

"Now everyone, thank you all for coming. I know that you all have your thoughts and opinions about everything, and we will continue to address all common issues and concerns and make time for your ideas."

Poe scanned the crowd, instantly noticing the woman with the pink glasses and the large man with the leather apron. They sat on opposing sides of the room, and Poe felt a sting in her gut. Had they accidentally chosen a side? The arguments seemed to come from everywhere, so they might not be.

Vivienne straightened up behind the podium, looking through some papers no one else could see.

"I want to report firstly that this is the third year in a row where we had no casualties and no injuries."

This prompted general applause.

"This year in particular was mostly incident-free. However, we cannot overlook the sudden increase in ... company. There have been several reports of fences broken, large and abnormally shaped footprints, and scratches on trees. We want to make sure the fences and your homes in general are the strongest they can be—oh, yes? Alvin?"

The whole room looked to the back, where a large man was raising his hand.

"I..." he started. "My chickens. They got my chickens. All of them."

The murmurers increased throughout the crowd.

"I am sorry," the mayor said. "That is terrible. You will be added to the list of people who need help with stronger fencing and a new chicken coop, and we'll see to it that you get some new chickens. My condolences, Alvin."

The mayor moved the subject matter back while Alvin sat there, content, yet still holding on to a handkerchief he had been wringing. She looked through some papers for a moment when a voice rang out from the crowd.

"Guy lost his chickens, big deal. My neighbor's sister's cousin lost their kid a few years back!"

"Hush up! Have some respect!" came a woman's voice from a few rows back.

"Chickens, children, adults. Point is they attack and still will attack and devour whatever they find," another said.

"Silence," Vivienne announced. "This is the very reason why we are meeting today. We need to come together to decide on a new course of action."

"Hear, hear!" came a few shouts.

Vivienne silenced the crowd, paused for a moment, and really looked at them like she wanted to make eye contact with each and every one of them.

"I know that there are opposing views on this right now. Let me assure you, I will do everything to consider all of your concerns and try to find common ground. I know about the different petitions going around and I happen to see all sides to this and always have. Especially since we have seen this get worse. There are more of them, somehow, and more kinds of them that we hadn't known or seen before."

She paused, the whole room pausing with her, hanging on her next words.

"Now, we know that we have come to believe that there have, for some reason, been more of them."

At that, the town hall became quiet; Poe could hear the shuffling of clothes in the chairs.

"We are here to gather all our options."

"We have to fight!" called a man.

"We can't keep living like this!" came another.

This riled them all up, many now shouting things left and right.

"No, we can't!"

"We are no match for them!"

"We can't kill these beasts!"

"You, of all people, should know about our town's history!"

Vivienne squeezed her eyes shut for a minute before smacking the mallet on the podium.

"While we have come a long way since our forefathers and ancestors, and have advancements in construction, technology, and weaponry, we also have gotten some more help in learning more about these beings from the Nether realm, both creatures and spirits, that can help us figure out the best course of action. One of which is an esteemed hunter and researcher of paranormal beings from The Society of Otherworldly Investigators, Rex Arken, who joined us a little over a year ago."

Poe felt the flutter of pride to hear her new boss mentioned, and even more when many turned to acknowledge him in his seat and came to notice her.

"And he has given much information on these beings and just how unpredictable and untouchable many of them are. Now, we also have some new residents who are here to provide the kind of protective help we need the most."

This time the entire town hall turned around and Poe did too, seeing the three sitting together at the far right side: two women, one with short, spiky white hair and the other with shoulder-length black shiny hair. In between them was a young girl with long, deep red hair who almost looked down in bashfulness. These three stood out so much visually from the group and from each other that they were hard to miss.

"The Briar-Whittles are a witch family that came here from a coven all the way from Petrified Woods. They specialize in cooking and medicinal magic and are here to help with powers of protection. They own the Something Stirring tea shop. Their specialty-made teas and cakes have proven to take care of any illness or ailment you've ever had."

The two women smiled, yet the girl never looked up.

"These specialty residents have been tasked with special objectives. Our creature hunter expert will be able to tell us more about what we're getting and how to be both defensive and offensive when necessary, and our witches are working on protection and any other kind of charm work to help us. Meanwhile, we will put together a plan for our next course of action. And it will be something that we can all agree on and work on."

The mayor looked at the whole hall, adjusting her glasses.

"It is with our experts that we will decide what to do next, and I assure you, we will be doing something about it."

The room clapped, group outbursts and chatter lasting until long after the meeting ended. Many stayed standing in the aisles talking with one another, all breaking off into separate private groups.

Poe followed Rex as they made their way through huddles and out the doors. They passed through people standing around on the stairs outside.

"That's why we need to make better traps! We trap them, we kill them!"

"The whole town should just be one big trap!"

"If there's more of them now, we can't just sit around and do nothing!"

Poe was about to ask if anyone had ever killed one when she stopped, catching sight of the girl with the deep red hair, long enough to graze her waist, standing nose-to-nose with a boy. Her hands were in fists at her sides.

"Well, aren't you?" the boy taunted.

"I said, shut up!" the girl cried.

"Isn't it your job? Isn't that what witches do? So why don't you just make them disappear already?"

"You know absolutely *nothing*."

"I know freaky things go together."

The girl exhaled sharply and stepped closer to the boy. "Take that back."

"Or what?" the boy half-laughed. "Are you going to do something? Go ahead!"

Poe saw the girl's fists shake by her side. Sure enough, the white-haired and black-haired women went rushing to her side. The boy stepped back and lost his bravado.

"Harassing our daughter, are you?"

"That will be the last thing you ever do."

The two of them escorted the girl away, and just when they were far enough away, the boy muttered to himself.

"Witches are bitches."

The girl spun around and ran back to him before the other two could stop her. She ran right up to him, just as the two women grabbed a hold of her and fought to hold her back, just as she raised her finger to the boy's face.

"May your face erupt in boils!"

The black-haired woman grabbed her wrist and pulled it away, covering her finger like a discharged weapon. The white-haired woman kept her hand on her back while talking to her as well. Even from where she stood, Poe could see that the young witch allowed herself to smile a sly grin. The three of them hurried away from the crowd. Rex, having noticed Poe lingered behind, wove his way back through the crowds to retrieve her. She noticed him, but she was too busy watching the boy putting careful fingertips to his cheeks.

"Come on," Rex said.

Poe followed, but she could not help but turn around. And then her stomach dropped to the ground. The boy's fingers danced across his face as his breath came out in short, whimpering panics. His face was now covered from forehead to chin in blusterous red bumps, large enough for shiny pus-filled whiteheads. His punishment for crossing a witch.

"Keep walking," Rex urged her. "*Keep walking.*"

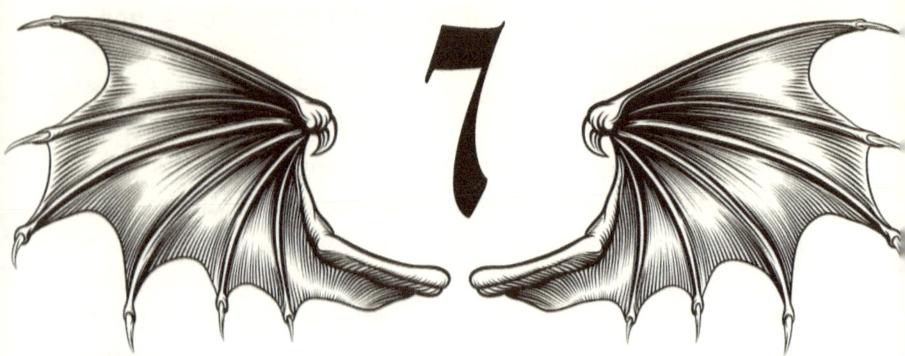

7

oe tried all the drawers, finally finding scissors with splotches of rust on the blades, but they were better than nothing. She would find the better one eventually, but this one would have to do for now. She held her pants across her lap and attended to the holes, stitching with the needle carefully to try to make a clean job. Rex knocked on her open door.

"Come in," she said without looking up.

Rex came all the way into her room. He watched her sew for a moment, opening his mouth and closing it like he did not know what to say.

"Do you need clothes?" He blurted out.

Poe pulled the thread and looked up at him, chuckling. "I can get some more. I just like the ones I make myself the best."

He sat on her bed, bending down to get a better look. "You made those?"

"Yup. Or just took something and made it into my own. I never really had much."

She closed up one hole and then moved on to another, this one right above the knee she got when they were crawling through the high grass.

"I never liked the outfits they put me in as a kid, so to really become my own person, I revamped them and made them my own. Once I worked in a tailor shop, and got to read different things in books. I make things myself, but I mostly just make it up as I go along."

Rex brushed the pants, feeling the ends with his thumbs. "You're going to need some warmer things. It's going to get colder now this time of year. Do you know where some clothing shops are? You can find a bunch of stuff in there."

"I will," Poe promised.

Rex got up and let her to it. "Maybe you can make me something."

Poe perked up and smiled at the new spread of warmth in her stomach. She watched him, secretly letting some ideas come to her. She stopped herself from giggling, deciding she would rather surprise him, and somehow already knew that he would love anything she made for him.

"There's one where you can get some better sewing supplies too," Rex said. "And different colored thread, not that random red I have."

"Where is it?" Poe asked. "I want to go."

"It's down the street on the right. It's called 'Sew What' or something like that. You should go visit it ... before or after I send you on a little mission."

"What kind of mission?" Poe asked, intrigued.

Rex paused again.

"Well, I've got to go over to the blacksmith and meet with him about swords he wants to make—"

"Neat!"

"Yeah, but it's not neat yet, not until he makes up his damn mind, otherwise he is just gonna be very chatty and chew my ear off. I thought you could take care of something else."

"Okay..." Poe prompted.

"Go get yourself acquainted with the Briar-Whittle family. Find out what they're brewing. We want to be able to find out whatever we can about their insight into that world."

Poe felt a different spread of something all up and down her skin. She sat up. "You want me to go meet the witches?"

"I have a feeling you will quite like what you see. Even though I only passed by a few times and never really talked with them. I, well, I wasn't always so sure. But no better time than now when we're all supposed to be working together. The shop is called 'Something Stirring,' or something like that."

Poe already got up to get her cloak and bag, giving it a cursory search to make sure her coin pouch was in there.

"Um, be careful," Rex blurted out. "Just in general."

Poe was out the door; Rex was right about the weather. As she stepped out, she felt a breeze tickle her nose. She fastened clasps on her cloak and set out.

The sewing shop was easy to find first, not at all surprising given that it easily fit in with the other shops along the sidewalk. Poe had to stop herself from wanting everything in it, only getting the pools of thread, scissors, and pack of needles she needed ... and a few yards of fabric for later use.

A bird sang in a tree above her. A gust of wind blew some shutters against a house. The sun pierced rays across her eyes the minute a cloud passed and she shielded them, making out only abstract squares and rectangles on either side of her. Through the wind, she could hear the rise of chimes, of decorative metallic rods hanging from above doorways, and then the smells hit her: Something herbal, and something spicy, where one inhale was enough to awaken all the senses in one simultaneously—all five, and enough for a sixth one. Poe felt this all up and down her skin, smooth and inviting, and yet there was no mistaking the prickle of a warning. She found herself walking on tip-toes, gently up on the pads of her feet. She saw it once she turned the corner.

For all the square and rectangle building shapes, this more abstract shape was surely out of place. It was more rounded, but with windows here and there like a creature with many eyes. Its build was out of place as was its position. It looked like a cottage built by fae and plucked from the woods to just perch right on the corner of that street. The prickles on Poe's skin increased. The smells of spices made her eyes water, and before she could think she found herself inching closer and closer to get inside that tea shop.

Poe pushed on the door, leaning into it and turning to the side from its odd shape. It was about the shape of a coffin lid, slanted and narrow like all visitors were expected to enter alone. The creaking of the door was enough to announce the arrival of a visitor, and yet the bells above the threshold still did their job. The first thing that she noticed was how much darker it seemed, all daylight blocked out with the walls bathing in amber light from the lanterns. It was lit enough to be seen, yet covered in darkness enough to make one feel engulfed by it. Poe took a few steps in, realizing that the dim and darkness felt like a comfort. The place seemed to have two major colors: brown and amber. The dark brown of the walls and cases and shelves and signage, and the amber light and writing etched onto things, of every-thing likely created out of nature itself, a secret place inside a large tree.

Poe scanned it all, filled with awe at something that could have doubled as a museum or curio shop. Much like Rex's basement laboratory, shelves lined the walls filled with various things in jars, most so old and opaque with dust she could not tell what was inside. There were sealed frames of dead insects pinned spread-eagle, bones of various sizes, and collections of crystals and jewelry behind glass cabinets. The shop opened into an oval to feature the centerpiece: a countertop covered in giant ceramic jars. No one was behind it. Poe could now smell more than one kind of herb, and she liked every one of them. She did not know what to look at, from the plants at the back to the different things that hung from the ceiling: branches of dried plants and woven baskets. The books on the shelves had a broken spiderweb in between them, where someone had quickly grabbed one of them, a thin line of web hanging over the edge.

Poe caught a faint purple glow out of the corner of her eye to her right, and when she turned she saw a narrow hallway where a violet light was flickering against the wall. She focused her ears and kept still. For now, she could make out the soft crackle of a flame. She walked down the hallway, treading carefully with the idea that this came from an area that wasn't supposed to be seen. The purple haze brought her to an open area where she saw the flame, all by itself, on its own table. The flame itself was almost as long as its candlestick, thick and towering like it wanted to reach the ceiling.

Poe approached it, watching it move. The flames danced near the top, blinking.

Did it just wink at me?

"Get away from that!"

Poe jumped out of her skin to the voice that rang behind her, shrill and angry, with a mane of fiery red hair to go with it. The girl's face contorted into a piercing scowl.

"Sorry, sorry!" Poe said, backing away. The girl walked right up to the candle and cupped a hand around the flame for a second before turning back to Poe, still keeping her hard defense.

"I was just—"

"You were just *what*?" the girl demanded. "You think you can touch things that don't belong to you without knowing what they are?"

"I wasn't—I'm sorry!" Poe said again. The young witch, the very one from the other day, stood before Poe and stared at her intensely. She did not blink nor break eye contact, and as loud as her hair was, her eyes were the opposite of a cool brown, deep like they were reflecting the darkest parts of her. Subtle freckles on the girl's face mingled with other splotches that were not so subtle. Green and black speckles of something exploded all over her, from specks on her chin to the splatters on her blouse and skirt, still fresh and dripping dark droplets on the floor.

"What are you even doing back here? This is a private area and you shouldn't be here!"

Poe remembered the boy with the boils, knowing that the wrong words and wrong move could earn her a similar fate. She kept her hands out at her sides, and she could feel this girl visibly reading her, from her choppy unkempt hair to the quirky handmade tunic and fur cloak she wore. Poe made the motion of backing up toward the main part of the shop, a part of her knowing that she should tail out of there as fast as she could, but also knowing that it would be unwise to make any sudden moves.

Poe was saved by the budge and creak of the shop door opening and its accompanying bell. She felt a rush of relief at no longer being alone with the young witch and backed up to the shop. The young witch followed and once the coffin-shaped beam of sunlight cast inside, that relief diminished. Two women entered, each carrying what looked like gnarly vines or roots that curled all around their arms so that they looked like extensions of them, each with long, claw-like nails. One had short, frosted white hair, and the other had flowy, black hair, just as recognizable as when Poe first saw them in the town hall. When they walked in, their expressions of content turned sour. Poe cringed, believing that they not only witnessed her coming from their private area but the girl would now rat her out. She bit the inside of her cheek as their attention simply glossed over her for a second before turning to the girl.

"Oh no, now what?"

"What happened?"

They rushed over to the girl and fussed over the splotches all over her clothes.

"It's nothing," the girl started.

"It's not *nothing*."

"What did you use?"

"It doesn't matter. I'll clean it up!"

The women regarded her in reprimand.

"Obviously, it didn't work. I'll take care of it, okay?"

"We're sorry." The woman with black hair instantly turned to Poe. "She just gets wrapped up in whatever she's doing, and doesn't pay attention to the rest of the world, especially when she is supposed to be watching the shop."

The girl took the roots they were holding and walked away with them, pretending that their encounter did not happen. She went behind a counter and put them away in a cabinet before looking around inside others.

"You're new around here," stated White Hair.

"I am. I work for Rex Arken."

The two exchanged glances.

"Yes, we thought you looked familiar," said Black Hair. "You were at the meeting."

"Bern, this girl works for the creature hunter." White Hair gestured to Poe.

The girl regarded Poe, the angst fading from her face and softening to curiosity.

"She—hey, I am sorry, I don't believe we caught your name," remarked White Hair.

"I'm Poe."

"Poe, I'm Ivy, and this is Emme," Ivy jerked her chin toward her black-haired partner.

"And this is our daughter, Bernadette."

Bernadette stood there letting her eyes roam all over Poe, trying to be subtle, and not doing a very good job.

"She's fifteen."

"I'm fourteen."

"Oh, close in age."

"Well, welcome to Mock Cob, Poe," Emme said.

"Thank you."

"You seem like someone that would fit in," remarked Ivy.

"I, I do," admitted Poe. "I think I really do. I have only been working for Rex for a little bit, but I already feel that way ... That is actually why I came... because Rex says that you're both here to learn more about these... things and that you are working on ways to be rid of them."

"That is true, we are," agreed Ivy. "We only just moved here a month ago, so we're still getting used to things and learning everything that we can."

"Do you see anything?" Poe blurted out. "Have you?"

"A few, yes," stated Emme. "But these creatures are not of this realm. They are proving to be more difficult to deal with than we imagined. We are studying them and researching older types of magic. We're trying new things for the shop. Simple things at first, and we're going to move our way up."

"Speaking of which, Bern, did you get more elixirs made?" Ivy asked.

Bernadette spun around from the open cabinet, her look telling them what the answer was.

"We're all out in the shop! We told you to make more!"

"I'll do them, I swear, I was just—"

"You were just messing around with other things."

"I was *not* messing around! I was trying—"

She cut off with the reminder that Poe was right there.

"I would, but I can't find any of the quartz crystals. Anywhere."

"No quartz crystals?" asked Emme, confused. "I thought we had a bunch."

"Well, I can't make the quartz-infused elixirs if I don't have them!"

Poe blinked, the penny dropping. She made to shove the right part of her long cloak aside so she could access her messenger bag. She dug past some pens before she found it, crystal clear and ready for the moment.

Bernadette half stepped back in a look of either amazement or suspicion.

The three of them stared at Poe holding the quartz. "I've got one! Here. You can have it!"

Bernadette just stood there. Ivy, being closest to Poe, reached out to take it.

"Well, thank you … You just happened to have a crystal on you, huh?"

"I, yeah, I … tend to collect things," Poe answered. She thought back to her rendezvous on the train, deciding that mentioning it would invite questions she did not have the answers to.

Ivy and Emme exchanged glances, still holding the crystal, until Ivy handed it right over to Bernadette. Bernadette took it like it was nothing and walked back around to the back room where she was before, not saying anything.

"It must have been fate then," Emme stated. "That you're here."

"I think you're going to fit in here nicely," added Ivy.

Poe could not help but turn to the hallway to the back room.

"Don't worry about her," Emme said. "She's … distracted, yet hyper-focused, if that makes sense. She gets like that."

"How would you like to try our new tea today?" Ivy asked.

"I love tea," Poe blurted out. "I would."

Poe found herself completely entranced by these two women, giving in to their magnetic pull. They were stark opposites in looks and personalities; the way Ivy had white hair chopped even shorter than hers looking like frost on grass, and Emme had black hair that billowed around her shoulders like a cape. Ivy had a fiery demeanor and Emme was calm and cool.

They walked behind another corner where in the corner sat a big cauldron cooking something on a low fire. Poe instantly felt the warmth of the fire, however so small, and the warmth that came from it told her that she could trust them.

"We've got the variety. This one's a new apple spice tea with cinnamon."

Ivy lifted the lid and Poe's mouth watered at the smell that escaped.

"Ooooohh."

"We make it all ourselves," stated Emme. "Now, how about a sample ... on the house?"

Poe's warm instincts burned. She knew exactly where she was, and just who she was with, and the words that came out of her mouth were, "Yes, please."

So the two women team worked fixing a cup of their specialty brewed tea, the smell of fresh apples and cinnamon filling the room and surrounding the cup they placed on the counter before Poe. She carefully pulled the handle and let the steam tickle her face and make her pores sweat. She blew on the top, the liquid a light brown color. As she blew, she could make out tiny bits of things floating around, things swimming around in a boiling pool. Poe slurped a sip and then slurped another and made a small noise at the scalding of her tongue.

"Wow."

She blew again and took another sip. "This is fantastic. I have never had any like this before."

The women smiled at her compliment, and even more so at her. Just like their daughter had done before, they were both reading her.

She took another sip.

Poe drank her tea and only just noticed that they did not hear any activity coming from the back part of the shop, whatever activity Bernadette was a part of. Poe's cup, now empty, passed back and forth between each hand. Emme reached over the counter.

"You done with that?"

"Yeah, thanks."

"Have you seen our loose-leaf collections?" asked Ivy. "Why don't you go pick out one you like and we'll give you a welcome-to-town discount?"

"Okay," said Poe. She was happy to browse more of that selection, even though she caught on to the real reason why. She made a show of looking through tins and even opening some of them to inhale while overhearing:

"...something, yeah."

"where did she come from?"

"don't know, but..."

"...interesting."

"And you can tell?"

"Oh yeah, can't you?"

"I can."

Poe turned around just as the two witches were putting away bags of leaves and clean mugs. "I'll take this one," Poe said, holding up a bag of vanilla rooibos pyramid bag tea.

"You got it," replied Ivy. "I'll ring you up over here."

Poe followed her over to the register by the front, her legs getting tickled by an overgrown plant.

"Three bronze coins."

"Wow, thanks."

Ivy put her purchase in a small paper bag. "You come back and visit us, all right? We especially would like to be in touch about the things you find."

"I will, and I want to know more about you as well."

She turned to leave, seeing Ivy go to the back room to attend to Bernadette and her earlier fiasco, and whatever current one. Before she could get to the door, Emme, swept in from her side and halted her in place

"Hey Poe. Really, you will come back, right?"

Poe regarded her. "I sure will."

"Oh, we hope so. Listen, we are in positions to work together when needed, when the time comes. But also, we would like you to come more often, for Bernadette's sake. She ... she doesn't have any friends. She didn't back home in Petrified Woods, and she doesn't here. She has a hard time. We really think that you would be the perfect companion for her."

Poe smiled, not breaking eye contact with Emme, whose eyes were a soft hazel color, the color of tea swirled with honey.

"I would like to get to know all of you," Poe answered honestly.

Emme's happiness radiated from her face, which did not have a single wrinkle. A mother to a fifteen-year-old, and yet, how old were they?

"Thank you, Poe. We look forward to seeing you again!"

"Thank you, too!"

Poe pushed on the coffin-shaped door and stepped out. When she turned to close the door, she instantly noticed a single letter in the mailbox, the familiar apricot envelope from town hall. In big, handwritten letters were the words: *To the Briar-Whittle family: Important town meeting, by invitation only.*

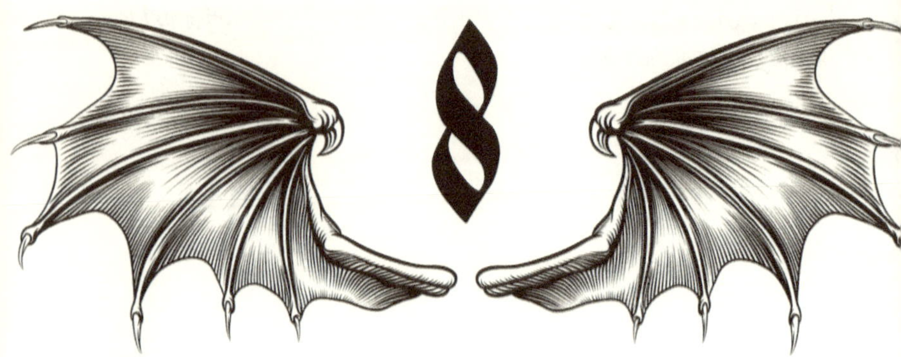

oe walked through the front door.

"Rex?" she called, walking through the kitchen, and then to the living room to see them both empty. She went to the basement door to find it open, but the stairway was dark. She circled back around, about to head upstairs, when the back door opened and Rex stepped in from outside.

"Hey kid, thought I heard you."

He held a bag of a handful of dirt, while Poe held an envelope in hers. She gave it to him.

Rex read where it was specifically addressed to him in handwriting.

"It was shoved in the door," Poe explained. "And the Briar-Whittles got one, too."

"Oh! That's right. How was it? How are *they*? What did they say?"

"They're really charismatic and really nice, and they said they haven't been here very long but they have this amazing shop! The whole place has interesting and weird things in it you would like. They said that they are researching old magic."

"I believe I would," considered Rex. "So, old magic."

"That's right. They have to study these things, too, they said."

Rex allowed himself to get lost in his thoughts for a moment before turning to the envelope in his hand. He began tearing it open and pulling out the letter, dog-earing the corner.

"Well, this is it then."

"What is?"

"The 'official' meeting between the involved parties."

He read a few more lines. "They want to talk about the new course of action and how to band together. For us, we have to put together some visuals of the things we've encountered so far and share what we know about them. So we got one, the witches got one ... pretty sure we know who else."

"How many meetings does this town have?"

"Not as many as we have been having. Usually, they have been every first of October, and then another one in late November. Now, it's more than that. This year's Night of Passing is going to be worse than it has ever been. I guess that's what we're all trying to get to the bottom of. Most of the pressure is on me. And us."

"But why would it be on you? I mean us, that is."

"For my knowledge."

"Knowledge?" Poe was shaking her head. "They live here, though. Why wouldn't they have the knowledge?"

"Well, it's like having bears invade your area. You may know what bears are. You have seen bears before, and you know enough that they're dangerous and you should keep away. But you're not going to know what to do if you encounter one, right? And then you get wolves that come, and coyotes, and lions, and tigers, all at once. Wouldn't you rather get an expert to come to determine how to keep them away altogether, but also individually?"

"Yeah."

"That's what we're doing, even though a lot of locals think they're the experts when they're not, and go after things they don't know a whole lot about and end up getting killed."

Rex put down the envelope on the counter and held up the bag for Poe.

"Speaking of which. Gotta check this out."

He jerked his chin toward the basement, motioning for her to follow.

Rex flicked the light on and they sauntered down the steps into the triangle of light. Rex brought the bag over to a corner, where another flick of the light revealed a table small enough to be a shelf. He put the bag down and opened it, pouring the dirt onto a cloth.

He and Poe peered in.

"Any guesses what it is?" he asked her.

She frowned, leaning in close but seeing nothing but the dirt. She had the idea to stick her finger in and poke about until she found something, but something told her that it was not ordinary dirt. It was darker than normal and perfectly rounded ... unlike most clumps.

"Is there something in the dirt?"

"No," Rex answered. "Because it's not dirt. It's eggs."

Poe leaned back. "Eggs? Of what?"

"I may have my theories. Went out with the electromagnetic device in the prairie and it went off. Some mama laid her eggs and took off ... and it's time to figure out what it is."

Rex pulled over a small wooden box from a shelf, complete with a built-in light. He placed the eggs in and flipped on the light.

"We watch them ... for a while. But for now, how about we go outside tonight and see if anything hatched?"

"Got your lantern?" Rex asked.

"Yeah," Poe said, holding it in one hand, while the other played with the straps on her rubber leg covers. Rex did not fasten them tight enough, and they were still so big on her shoes. Big as they were, they were even more difficult to walk in. She walked stiffly like a toy made of wood.

Rex put his hood up, revealing a jacket brown and faded with a big tear down the side. Poe made a mental note to herself to fix it for him, putting up her own antlered hood in response.

They exited the house silently into the night, as per the routine Poe was no stranger to.

They walked along, keeping their lanterns to the ground, and keeping quiet.

The night remained still and silent, not even the sound of a cricket, nor a blow of wind scattering leaves across the ground. Even though their focus was down on the ground, Poe could not help but cast an eye to the sky now and then to see if anything flew across. When they entered the prairie area, the tall grasses whipped against their leg covers, and if anyone—or anything— were even out, they could hear them from a mile away.

"It was about ... here. Somewhere." Rex scanned the grass with his light while holding onto his device.

Nothing beeped, or lit up, not as he circled around the area bent down.

Poe stopped to scratch an itch on her wrist. After Rex walked on a couple feet ahead of her, she turned down another path to see if there was anything there. She scanned the grasses with her light, not even sure what she was supposed to be looking for even though she thought that she would know it when she saw it. Poe walked on, waving the lantern this way and that into the grass on either side of her, but then had to stop to scratch another itch on the back of her leg, already bothered by the tall grass. She caught something big and thick in the middle of the grass and the lantern revealed it to be a tree stump. Up close, the wood gnarled into rot, its spiral lines deep enough to be canyons with mold growing in every crevice. Though old and of no significance, Poe wanted it to be, peering at every piece of broken bark, expecting something to come out of it.

Poe's hand flew over to another itch on her arm, and fixing her hood once it moved down, only to have another itch form by her neck. She scratched here ... and then there, and then there, on her neck and arms and back of her legs. Poe put the lantern down on the stump and pushed her sleeves back with the force of panic: And there they were, what looked like hundreds of tiny black balls the size of peas rolling up and down her arms. She cried out and scratched them away, rolling up her sleeves more to brush off a few more. She did the same with her cropped pants, the ends barely swaying on the ends of the leg covers and just enough to cover all of her. But they still got in. Three or four or five or fifty rolled on her thighs until she shoved them away and scratched her legs, seeing pinpricks of blood form. She grabbed at her neck and scratched at her face.

"Rex!" she called. "Rex!"

She was relieved at the second light that came rushing back from the grass, just as her hands flew all over her body. Just as she threw off her cloak and scratched at her arms, legs, neck, face, and from what she could reach on her back. The little creatures, whatever they were, crawled and bit the more she thrashed around.

"What is it? What happened?" Rex rushed back.

"Help!" she cried, with her arms in a twist at her back. "I'm covered in ... something. They're biting me!"

Rex took her arm, flipping it over and seeing all the spots of blood that formed there until one decided to show itself for Rex. It crawled down and revealed two spiny legs. Rex cursed and flicked it off.

"Come here!" he said, dragging his lantern over to hers for more light. Rex looked at her face and brushed off one with his thumb, pinching down to catch it before flicking it away. He reached into his bag and pulled out a can of something he sprayed all around Poe, her gagging once the mist reached her face. First he sprayed his hand and plucked one off of her neck, holding it out in front of him and then bringing it over to the lantern on the tree stump. There he inspected the parasite while Poe anxiously kept pulling up her sleeves and pants and then lifted her shirt a few more times. She touched all the bite marks, all clumps of freckled sores, all over her stomach and abdomen just as she spotted them on her arms and legs, and, no doubt, face and neck. She coughed at the smell of the spray and how sticky it made her skin.

"You all right?" Rex asked, with his back still turned.

"Yeah, yeah," Poe said, pulling her shirt back down. "I think they're all gone now."

She slowly went to join him by the tree stump, holding her arms. Rex held the thing pinched between his thumb and forefinger by the light: It was like a little black puffball, though it was not fluffy. Its ends were spiny and moving on their own, all independent probosces. It had two thread-thin legs that kicked about and fought to either bite Rex or get out of his clutch.

"Vampire burr," Rex stated. "Nasty. These legs are tiny but they pack a powerful jump. They wait for prey to walk by and then leap on and roll around to drink their blood. When they reach adulthood, their legs break off and turn into wings. So then they can fly around and land on whatever they want."

Poe's fingers scratched the tops of her arms, still holding herself. She couldn't help but shudder. She reached back and began to scratch the back of her ear. What started as a small scratch turned more vigorous.

"They'll itch more. But just like anything else, you don't want to scratch too much. And don't worry, I have something that can take care of those. Come on, let's go take care of you. Now we know what those eggs are."

"Are they in my cloak?" Poe pointed. Rex took the spray and covered her cloak in a misted shield. He picked it up and brushed it a few times.

"They won't be hiding in there, don't worry. It looks like a living thing because of the fur, and that was what attracted them in the first place, probably. But they took off when they realized it wasn't an animal and found you underneath it instead."

He handed her the cloak, and she took it but did not put it on. They walked back through the prairie, holding their lanterns down.

"I'll get more of that stuff and just exterminate the area. Not that big a deal."

Poe scratched behind one ear, and then the other.

"Hey now, try not to scratch."

"I can't help it. This is worse than poison oak!"

"Yeah, it is, but I got this mud that will cure that in minutes. Don't worry."

They walked on with Rex scanning the area while Poe twitched and moved her hands to scratch before stopping herself. Rex seemed like he was trying to hold back a smile.

"So giant flying demons don't bother you, but little bitey bugs do."

"They were just all over me! They came out of nowhere, and all at once."

Rex nodded sympathetically. "Not that I blame you. You're still one of the bravest people I know. I've seen grown men scream and then throw themselves on the ground to roll around. They didn't know that actually made it worse, and they became one big blanket of a feast."

They got home. Poe inspected her cloak now that she had better lighting and from what she could see the furs were all unbothered. She hung it back up on its peg, imagining that anything still rolling around looking for flesh to prick would fall off and die of starvation. That was the goal, at least.

Poe held her arms out and looked at the damage: tracks of blood marks from the little spikes that rolled all over her. Some were smaller than others, others bigger from where she flicked them off and interrupted the gentle pierce to instead become tears in her flesh.

Rex was looking at her arms as well, and after a moment, disappeared to the kitchen. Poe looked at her stomach and legs, daring to touch the marks and feeling the instant sting of itch. She gave in and scratched her legs, going all the way up to the knee as much as her short nails could muster.

"Quit scratching," Rex said. He held onto a container with words in another language she did not recognize. "So here's what you do: Go on and take a bath, but be as gentle with your skin as possible. Wash your hair, too. Then when you've dried off, take this stuff and put it all over the marks. Brush it through your scalp, too. When you go to bed, it will start to harden ... and you will be bed-ridden for a while."

"Bed-ridden!?"

"The mud needs to remove the toxins, and you will not be able to move."

Poe's mouth opened to a scowl, and her arms folded. "What do you mean, I won't be able to move? For how long?"

"Maybe a day. So you can just relax."

Still frowning, Poe took the container from him, looking at all the foreign descriptions.

"What is this stuff?"

"It's a special kind of mud for any minor bites from ... well, creatures that are worse than mosquitos. I got it from an occult shop years ago. It never expires."

He looked toward the basement. "I am going to go downstairs and check on those eggs."

Poe looked up. "Do you think they hatched? Are you going to kill them?"

"No, they wouldn't hatch. They need good land to do that. I think they can be sold to those that would want them … for a nice price."

He smiled, and she did too at the understanding.

They parted ways for their separate tasks for the night, Poe pulling herself up the stairs with the stuff that was going to make her stop itching. Every step she took, she had to ignore the burns of attention all around her body. Rex was right. It did get worse. She clenched her teeth when she got to her bathroom to get that bath going as soon as possible. It felt like they were biting her all over again, like hundreds of them were on the floor and were leaping onto her to make a meal of her once more.

Sinking into the water was an instant relief, and she usually hated baths. She sank in it until it was all the way up to her ears, ducking her head under and just letting the water cleanse everything and anything it could. She opened her eyes under the water, viewing her body from a slightly murky vision. The red marks stood out in clusters of constellations, and she touched them lightly to see some of the itching was still present. Touching them also caused the blood to leak, the further damage she made by scratching, tendrils of red diffusing in the bath water.

Poe surfaced and lathered up the soap, a pleasant-smelling lavender with matching shampoo, and took to washing herself. She added extra shampoo, worked her fingers through her scalp, and scrubbed the base of her neck. She soaked for a bit longer, surprising herself that she wanted to stay in the bath a bit longer. The time came to put on the mud when she got out, towel-drying her body and hair and opening up that container.

The mud looked like lavender as well, a light and pale purple that was the same color as the suds of her soap but did not smell like it. It did not smell like anything at all when she smeared it all up and down her legs, stomach, arms, and wherever she could reach on her back. She stood before the mirror now seeing her face and neck trekked with ugly red holes akin to sores. She scooped out a chunk of mud and smeared it all around those areas. Lastly, she finger-combed it through her hair, watching the ends slick back and looking like she now had a head of plaster. Her entire body was now a mold of wet plaster—thick and smooth purple paste with very little flesh showing through. She could immediately feel every inch of her start to tingle, something cool blowing into her pores, getting cooler and cooler so much that she started to shake.

Poe put on her pajamas, choosing a loose pair with a short shirt and shorts, thinking she wanted something longer but knew that the mud needed air. She walked over to her bed and lay on her back, thinking she was just going to read for the rest of the night and most of the morning. But as soon as she was settled a ringing sounded in her ear, and an ache started to form at the base of her forehead. She rubbed her eyes, unable to block out the ringing or do anything about it. The ache started to spread, and she pressed her fingers to her head. Her mouth felt like she stuffed her towel into it and dried that, too. The only relief she got was the sound of Rex coming up the stairs and rapping a gentle knock on her door.

"Yeah," she grumbled.

He came in carrying a jug of water and a plate holding a large hunk of meat.

"You dizzy?"

Poe groaned. "Yeah."

He put the water on her nightstand and handed her the plate. The meat was blood red like it was just pulled out of the animal and thrown on there, juices sloshing all over the plate and staining the accompanying mashed potatoes next to it.

"So glad I picked this up at the butcher during the day. You need the iron."

She sat up and began to cut at the meat, barely needing the knife. She forced herself to take a bite, and her tongue tingled. Her pupils may have even dilated. She wasted no time cutting another one.

"You just take it easy and rest up."

Rex left her to it. The more she ate, the more she felt like some of her energy was coming back, though not completely. The pain in the center of her forehead still throbbed, and when she took gulps from the water, she actually felt like she could rest. She fell asleep soon after, dreaming of giant black clouds rolling across the sky.

oe's eyes opened at the tittering of birds, though their song sang in her head a while before then. She blinked a few times, no sleep dust lingering in her lashes to give her the groggy release from slumber. Instead, she was instantly awake and alert, and the first thing she noticed was that she could not move her arms.

Poe tried to lift them, but she stopped when tried to bend them to feel her face and found that her elbows were completely locked. It was useful in that she slept on top of the covers and she could see the aftermath for herself. She had gone to bed with a cooling, light purple scrub and now woke up to a dark gray, almost black paste hardened on her skin. It looked like the tar that dried on the roads. She moved her arms straight up at the same time she worked to sit upright. Poe pivoted and stood on her legs without bending those either, hanging onto her bedframe for balance and teeter-tottering. She kept up the teeter-tottering to her bathroom, each step feeling like her legs were two planks of wood.

Poe saw the creature of cracked mud in the mirror, her hair completely flattened down on her head but still sticking up in places. Her eyes stood out, wide and green with blood-shot tree branches stretching from the corners. Poe tugged at her pajamas the best she could, glad that they didn't stick, resting comfortably on the parts of her that were safe. She sighed, touching her thighs to find the texture rough and unbreakable. It would not come off for another day. She did not even remember what Rex said about how it would come off.

She turned and went back to her bedroom, now glancing at the clock on the nightstand to see that it was two in the afternoon. She stopped at the nightstand for relief, then teeter-tottered over to the windowsill and pulled back the curtains. The sun was unusually bright and people were out and about as per a normal routine. Just as she thought she had no idea where Rex was, she heard his footsteps coming up the stairs.

"Yeah, come in!" she said.

Rex pushed open the already open door to find her standing there.

"I heard you get up. How you doing? You look like a mud monster."

Poe teeter-tottered back to the bed as Rex held out a hand for support, his other underneath a tray.

"Brought some food. I got ham and made omelets with ham and cheese."

He put the tray down on the bed, a plate with a large fluffy egg log with melted cheese leaking out the side. There was also a slice of buttered toast and a handful of blueberries. Next to it was a steaming cup of tea.

"Thanks," Poe replied. "And I feel all right, I guess. Just ... stiff."

She sat down the best she could with her back to the headboard, using the fork with effort to dig in.

"You itch still?"

"A little bit," she answered with a full mouth.

"You feel tired?"

She shook her head. "So, do I just take a bath now and get this stuff off?"

"Not yet, I'm afraid," Rex answered.

Poe blew on the teacup. "So when do I do it?"

"Well, it can't come off yet. You have to wait another night."

Poe stared. "Why?"

"Because your wounds need to heal, kid. Those things are tiny, but they bite deep and drain you. That's what they do. You can wash it off tomorrow."

Poe just kept eating.

"Look, I am going to be out and about tonight. I need to go check on a nest of something living in someone's mailbox and then a possible spirit that spooked someone's horses. I'll come by later. Don't you go anywhere."

Poe took a big bite of toast.

"Hey, promise me."

Poe looked at him, suddenly having a flashback of her former employers at the orchard. They had their ways of keeping her in when she had the urge to wander, to roam, to sneak. Rex would not board and bolt her window ... ironically, even in that town where it was common for a different reason. But would she, even if she wasn't in a body cast of healing mud? She smiled and wiped her mouth.

"Okay, I promise."

Rex seemed satisfied with her answer. He left, and she took to enjoying the rest of her breakfast, or lunch, or whatever meal it was, drinking the hot tea that made her wish she could be back at the witches' shop.

Poe turned the page, her elbows aching at the slight bend she was forcing on them. She kept a good grip on the book, although it was so old the spine was broken in places. This book was about a brother and sister believing there was a ghost in their attic, disappointed to find that it turned out to be a bird that flew in and kept flying around and knocking things over. She frowned at the reveal, imagining it to be a previous owner who just never left.

Instead, the jolt of anticipated fear came from the sounds she heard outside.

Poe picked her head out of her book, listening to the scratching coming from the side of the house. It was subtle at first, but then the scratching continued. Poe looked up to the ceiling as they now came from above her in a series.

Scratch, scratch, scratch.

Her thoughts immediately went to a bird ... but knew that would be the culprit in a book. Not here.

Poe got up, forcing her legs to cooperate.

The scratching turned into something that was now moving, moving across the ceiling.

Scratch scratch, thud thud thud, scratch scratch.

Poe teeter-tottered over to the window and gently pulled the curtain. She knew that she would not be able to see anything outside late at night, and with no lights. Instead, she tuned her ears to determine where it was coming from.

Thud thud, scratch, thud thud thud.

Poe jerked her head to the ceiling, staring at it, imagining that whatever it was, was a few inches from her on the roof. Her hand rested on the latch, pulling it up and out without a sound. She pushed on the window just enough and stopped when it betrayed a light *creeeeek.* Poe froze, leaning to the skinny gap of outside air. She held her breath, not letting a single puff reveal she was there and alert whatever else was. And she waited. And waited. After another moment of silence, Poe braved the window open just a little more, just enough to try to get a peek. She curved her head toward the roof, peering at the triangular shapes in the dark to see if there were any abnormal shapes perched there. She did a cursory scan of the entirety of the roof from her room, not seeing anything at all in the darkness.

Thud thud thud thud SCRATCH.

Poe retreated back inside just as whatever it was sounded very close to her, too close. She moved to shut the window before it showed up, but the inability to bend her legs, her torso, anything at all, took her balance. She fell backward in one straight fall before she could even try to get a grip on the curtain. The sound of her crash thumped in the floor, and she lay there as the impact throbbed through her stiff body. Poe's face scrunched into a grimace as she turned her head, watching the disturbed window push more, more and more, and all the way, exposing the rectangle of the open night sky.

Poe remained still, though getting a grip on the floor with her palms and heels. There was nothing she could do but stare at the open window.

She listened, her body stiffening even more with the tension she felt. She worked her palms and heels to move her away.

Thud thud thud.

She felt her palms slip on the floor, and she allowed herself to look away from the window, only to scan her room for anything she could use as a weapon. There was the lamp on the nightstand, her knee-length steel-toe boots, and some thicker, heavy books. She shook these thoughts and instead pushed her body closer to the window. Closer; the scratching intensified as no doubt the discovery was made. Poe scooted closer and closer until she could lift her legs and reach for the window latch with her feet. She stretched and arched her foot until she found it and pulled the window shut ... just as she could feel the vibrations of something crawling across the roof. She kicked the window curtains over to cover as much as possible, and then she kept still, very still. Poe exhaled in puffs of heightened fear as her feet held the window closed in a death grip and stayed like that for quite some time, even after the sounds on the roof went around the corner and then stopped completely. Poe lay on the ground, wide awake as the hue of the outside went from black to blue. The only sounds that came after that were the songs of birds announcing the arrival of morning.

Poe remained still, almost feeling her heartbeat pulsate through the floorboards. She took deep breaths, and then and only then did she lower her legs to the floor and let her eyes close.

Her neck hurt when she woke up, and at first, she thought it was because she dreamed she was being eaten alive by some gigantic fanged creature. She even reached up to touch her neck, feeling the hardened paste cast that brought her back to reality and why she was on the floor to begin with. With effort and a series of groans, she worked herself to sit up, scooting over to use her bedframe to hoist herself up. So far, the chipper morning birds were the only sound she could get from outside, and nothing on the inside yet. As she moved, the paste on her skin crackled, some of it even flittering down in a flaky snowfall. It crackled more and more until the flakes that fell off were bigger puzzle pieces and her muscles erupted in newfound freedom. She felt the intense sensation as she bent her knees, getting up to head to the bathroom to run the shower.

The water ran down her skin and she helped scrape off the remaining mud paste in the tub, watching it dissolve from her body and melt away into wet clumps. The water ran over her body and she turned the knob to make it hotter, letting the shower needles inject healing into her throbbing skin. She just let it run down her skin for a while until she could not feel it anymore, only picking up the soap when she was completely paste-free.

Poe got out of the shower still blinded by the steam that permeated the bathroom, wiping the mirror to see her reddened yet smooth again face. No more pock-mark bites, aside from the microscopic ones of her pores scrubbed back to freedom. After dressing in her room, the first thing she did was pull back the curtain and open her window. She pushed the window open all the way and climbed out, working her muscles to remember how to move and ignoring the leaf that crunched under her foot. The roof remained intact, with no disturbances. She crawled along, scanning the roof, looking for signs of claw marks or footprints or loose feathers or anything, anything at all. But she found nothing. Unsatisfied, she backtracked to her room and made her way downstairs.

Rex stood over the kitchen table spread out with clear, plastic slides of illustrations. He considered one after the other and looked up when Poe joined him.

"Well, good morning, or afternoon," he said. A glance at the clock told Poe it was after 3 p.m. He left the table and came to examine Poe closely, and she could smell a strong smoky smell wafting off his clothes.

"Looks like you're all healed up."

He gently took her arms. "Some skin irritation is normal, but you'll be back to good in no time. How do you feel?"

"There was something on the roof last night."

Rex's eyebrows twitched at the turn of topic, but he considered it.

"I heard it crawling along, and it almost came into my window. I stayed up making sure it didn't."

"Did you see it?"

"No."

"Would you like to?"

Poe perked, Rex recognized the expression and led her toward the basement. Rex's enthusiasm made him thunder down the stairs with Poe's newly awoken legs struggling to keep up. As they inched toward the center, Poe smelled more smoke. There, under the swinging light bulb, was a large barrel with some spilled drops on the floor around it.

"Go ahead, take a peek."

Poe approached the barrel and leaned in, seeing the ripple of water and the hollow animal skull resting just under the surface. However, the longer she stared at it, the more she saw it was not a skull. It was an almost wrinkled red-brown texture.

"What...?" Poe started.

"It's a smolder salamander."

Rex went next to her and reached into the barrel, grabbing onto something and pulling it up. The animal had been petrified in a U shape as it righted itself to try to escape from the barrel when Rex dipped it in the first time. Its tail looked like a fishhook holding bait, writhing, twisting, and mouth popping open. Poe wondered what noises it made. It probably screeched. She saw the way the claws curled and how thick the tail was, imagining it crawling across the roof over her head.

"They're made of molten magma," Rex continued. "And live down in the fiery depths. I'm glad this sucker didn't get any closer. It heats up when it gets agitated. I saw it last night and put it out with the hose, shot it with a stun gun, and then stuck it in the barrel. It went out almost immediately. The Society is going to go nuts when they see this!"

Poe stared at the petrified salamander as Rex lowered it back into the barrel.

"I'm going to bring it, along with the other stuff. This is great. I've never seen one of these before, and no doubt, no one else has."

"You haven't?"

"No, and that's just the point. None of these things can be defeated the same way."

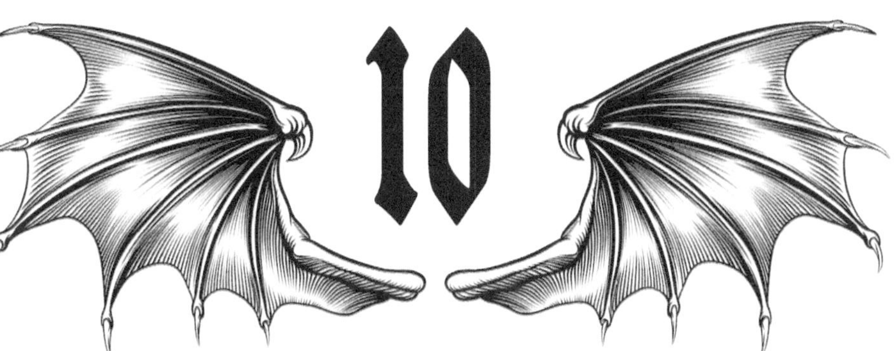

he once bustling town hall had a smaller gathering this time around, smaller, yet bigger. The tension in the room could cut through brick and the energy filled to the ceiling.

This time, Rex and Poe chose seats near the aisle for reasons they both knew. Rex held on to the long envelope in his hands while Poe held on to a smaller one, knowing all of them by heart and ready to take out whichever one he asked for.

At the front was a table of officials with Mayor Vivienne Tellenboe in the middle, her head turned in private conversation with the woman next to her. Poe looked around the room, searching for the only others she knew that would be there. Sure enough, the Briar-Whittles were all the way to the wall, present yet inconspicuous, but it was only two. The third member was not present, and although a little disappointed, Poe figured it was not her problem.

Mayor Vivienne addressed the room.

"Good afternoon, everyone. It seems like we have everyone here that we want, and we can get started. Just a reminder, we are here to receive some ideas and information, as we seem to have different ideas about the same information. That is why all of you are here today, so thank you for coming. You will all have the chance to have the floor and tell us what you got. We're going to start with Babs Loman of Loman & Company. Babs, come on up."

Poe saw her, the woman with the pink glasses, who ran after her with a clipboard. Babs sat with a group of people dressed in tan coveralls and bright, reflective vests. She wore one as well and carried a large roll of parchment.

"My team and I have been putting our heads together on different projects for the town and how they can overall contribute to the safety," Babs began.

"I have here our blueprints for underground shelters we want to build, at least a few to start. We have gathered signatures of those who stand by our idea that better protecting ourselves against unpredictable and dangerous forces is the best action."

She unrolled the parchment, revealing lots of blue lines in different shapes and positions.

"This is what one can look like. It will be large enough to hold ten people maximum, and here are the separate individual rooms for sleeping. They will have a common area for sitting and eating and separate toilets and such. They will all have a padlocked door that locks from the inside."

The mayor studied the blueprint.

"And that is definitely an idea to consider. We would need the right amount of time for planning and construction."

"We would bring in outside labor," Babs immediately said, "to speed the process along and get some finished as soon as possible."

"Thank you so much for your ideas, Babs. I will put this down."

Vivienne wrote some things down while still looking at the blueprint. Babs rolled up the parchment and took her seat.

"Next is Carl Thisby of Thisby & Koach."

Poe instantly recognized the tall and bony old man as he got up from the front row. From the way he carried himself, it seemed that he was not as old as he seemed to be. As much as he hunched over, his steps were springier than those younger than him, and he walked with a definite sense of purpose. He was hairless except for the whiskers above his eyes and sticking out of his chin, straight and straw-colored like the end of a paintbrush.

"My guys and I also have been collecting signatures," Carl began. "Of people that are willing to band together and go and fight these things. And I think I am not the only one here who thinks we need to. I was there thirty years ago during the time of The Great Battle."

The room stiffened. Someone sat up in their chair, making it creak.

"Even though they were ordered to obey Shut-In, they made a plan to go out and take care of it for themselves on the Night of Passing. They fought. They killed some of the demons. Yes, many did not make it back in one piece, and there were many who did not make it back at all. But they took some of them out with them, didn't they?"

Carl paused.

"That was thirty years ago when they had simpler weapons and tools. The point is, we have advanced things now. We have better tools and weapons and firearms. Anton and I learned the trade from our fathers, and we have improved our materials in the years gone by."

Carl gestured to the other familiar man who was sitting next to him, who rose and joined him. As thin and brittle as Carl was, Anton was the opposite in size. He towered at about six feet with a burly build. He had a tail of charcoal down his back, which matched the various smears across his shirt.

"My father taught me to make my first sword," Anton started. His voice was low enough to thump in the deepest parts of anyone's gut. "And I know what we can make some big ones. Suitable ones. I can make a double-edged sword that'll chop one of those demons in half. We also have guns."

"Before that happens, Anton ... and Carl, we need to know just what will do the trick and with what," stated Vivienne. "And that is where Rex Arken comes in."

A man from the table got up and went to get a projector near the wall. Rex was already out of his chair, going to the front with Poe when the projector was being set up. They turned sideways to face both the table and the crowd.

"I've been with the Society of Otherworldly Investigators for about eight years now. I've studied and hunted cryptids of all kinds, and plenty of spirits, but this town takes that all a step further."

Rex took out a clear plastic slide from his envelope and placed it on the projector. The sketches were simplified, but they were enough for the townsfolk to recognize. Tiny demon creatures, imps, goblins, and the slightly larger rubrums with spade tails. Poe wondered just how much they had seen, or how many had never seen any at all if they were always ordered into hiding. Surely, they were curious enough to peek out through their curtains once in a while.

"So, many of the Nether realm demons are corporal, solid, but many are not in the cases of shadow demons and spirits. Many things are considered 'undead' and cannot be killed with a simple gunshot, and many undead things do not just fall over when they are hurt."

He gestured to Poe to place another slide. This one had blurred, black images. One was a sketch of something tall with horns and wearing a robe.

"I believe these are among many of the things that come out."

"Hold on there!" cried one of the men near the front. "That looks like the Devil himself!"

"The Devil?"

"It is the Devil!"

"Order!" called the mayor over everyone starting to talk at once.

"It's a demon," said Rex. "And from what I've read, a demon lord. Said to be intelligent, appearing from smoke. I don't think a double-edged sword is going to do anything against this."

Rex reached down into his bag and pulled out his ace card, needing both hands. There were a few gasps from the audience. The bone was still polished with dirt and dust so it was not naturally white, though would not have been the same shade as a creature from Earth. It was its own sickly yellow-white, darkened all the way down to the full set of almond-shaped sharp teeth.

"This is a hell hound," Rex continued. "Some look a little worse than mangy junkyard dogs. When you kill a hell hound, it reanimates as an undead skeletal figure. They come back meaner and faster, all bent on destroying anything in its path. Especially if it finds whatever killed it in the first place. I learned this the hard way."

He held up the skull, and a hush came over the room, especially the way the jaw hung open like it had been in mid-attack before it was finally defeated. The men with the weapons leaned on their seats, waiting for Rex to continue the story.

"So how'd you kill it?"

Rex held the skull like a prize trophy.

"I dug a trap with long spikes on the bottom. It fell through, the spikes impaling the ribs, and it got stuck there. I then took my iron sledgehammer and put the damned thing out of its misery."

There was general unsettlement and excitement among the crowd, and mostly pride with Poe. She smiled a smile that told the audience that she, too, participated in such activity. She almost wanted people to ask her.

"There's another," Rex said.

He put away the first skull, reaching into the other bag for the other one. He had wrapped it in newspaper, and, unwrapped, it looked like it was made out of clay with lumps all along the edges. Though slightly smaller than the hell hound, it still generated the same size response.

"This is a smolder salamander, and one of the smaller ones actually as they can get about three or four feet long. You're looking at something that comes from the fiery pits themselves. It needs to be put out with water in order to weaken it. Poe here heard it crawling around on the roof over her head."

It was Poe's moment to nod to confirm Rex's statement. Just another encounter with a vile creature that they took care of. She was glad he did not mention her treatment for the vampire burr bites.

"This is the first time I've seen one of these in person," Rex continued. "We can encounter something new at any time and not know what to do about it."

He put up some more slides. Dark blobs, whitish orbs. Smoky things taking no form.

"And then there's ... these."

"Spirits," someone said.

"That's right. They can't physically hurt you, but you can get pretty cold when they confront you. Like your soul itself is going numb inside you."

"I've felt that before!"

"Yeah, me too!"

A few from the audience voiced this.

"Have you seen a lot of ghosts?" someone asked Rex.

"I've seen many kinds of forms here. Spirits themselves can take many forms. There are different ways to deal with different things," Rex continued. "I am using my own experience and technology to seek out spirits that linger and drive them away. Same thing with monsters. Since I have been here, I have also been creating different types of traps. It's more effective to trap these creatures and stop them from doing harm than to go out and try to fight them on the loose. We don't know what we're getting into."

"Aren't you an expert?" called out Carl, voice dripping with snark. Rex addressed him with a straight back.

"Yeah, I am. An expert in knowing that these things are unpredictable and some of them are just as smart. Which is why I have been working on trapping them, so they can be studied. And killed if necessary."

The mayor thought for a minute. The way her eyes blinked showed how the gears were switching in her head. She was looking from Babs to Carl to Rex again.

"Well, that's exactly it then, isn't it? Babs, how about building different types of traps to place throughout town? Carl, you get with her and help with the kinds of materials. Rex, you'll get with both of them with your knowledge of everything and what has worked."

Babs considered this, turning in her chair to converse with the people in her group. She turned back to the mayor. "I think this can be doable."

"I'll say," added Carl.

"Can do," Rex said, nodding.

"Thank you, all," said the mayor, with a hint in her tone that she was pleased. "We shall revisit your progress in a few weeks."

Poe saw her watch Rex put away his slides and go over to join Babs with a light smile tugging at her mouth. Poe tried her best to listen to their talk but diverted her attention once the mayor called the Briar-Whittles to the front. Emme and Ivy came to the front carrying various jars, holding substances of various colors. They set the jars down on the table and the room quieted again, a combination of revered awe and terror. They also reached down into their bags and pulled out the funny bundles of sticks that were shaped into little dolls, placing them more or less in front of the jars. Some people shifted in their seats, already believing these little dolls had eyes and were looking at all of them.

"We have plenty to offer in terms of protection," said Emme, gesturing to the jars and the strange stick dolls. "They can be used on the person or for the home, outside and inside. Your basic salts can keep spirits away, and we've got plenty here you can put outside your homes and businesses."

Ivy held on to one of the stick dolls, twirling it in her fingers. "This is a protective talisman, made with locks of witch's hair. They can scare away evil spirits, creatures, or even persons with evil intentions, as it makes them feel the magic presence."

They spread out the jars on the table so everyone could see them, along with the smaller ones in the front.

"Today, you can all take home a small jar of salt and a talisman ... on us. We'll have more of them for sale in our shop, along with other things," continued Ivy.

"We're working right now on creating things that could do greater levels of protection," added Emme. "And we're doing as much research as we can on things that are not in this plane."

"Like why more are coming out?"

"Yeah, who opened the door to Hell?"

"Someone opened it, and they opened it all the way. Can you figure out why?"

"I saw a ghost a few years ago, a lady walking down the street wearing all white and then disappearing, but it was closer to the Night of Passing."

"There's been more walking around *now!* I swear I saw a guy running down the street by the square. You know, where they used to execute people, running clear as day with a rope around his neck trailing after him."

"That just goes to show you that something happened because there are more ghosts! And none of this white-orbs-of-light-in-pictures nonsense they're actual ghost forms!"

They all started talking at once, about things they'd seen walking past their houses and things they'd heard in the night.

The mayor hit the podium, calling the others to quiet down. The way her brow furrowed, the way her mouth pinched, Poe could see that she was tired. She was more than tired.

"This is why we're here," she repeated, trying the patience in her voice. "Our experts here will help."

Someone muttered something in the audience that made the mayor jerk her head. Poe didn't think she could hear it, but Poe could. Someone said, "Like last time." It was an older man sitting between Carl and Anton, arms folded and looking down. Poe instantly wondered about all the meetings they had before, of all the things they tried before that failed. She also thought of the creature hunters and witches and whoever else that came before them, and what had become of them.

"I have to finish those designs," Rex said, moving her along. "And bring out the new cage trap I made out of iron that I will have to tell Babs about now. And the blacksmiths, too. They are going to have to make every-thing out of iron from now on. There are a lot of things that are weakened by iron, like fae, ghosts, and other creatures, and I need to get more of that. They were probably all using stainless steel, and that doesn't do anything but how would they know—"

Rex was indeed walking faster the minute they left the town hall. Though Shut-In was hours away, he wanted to get home as soon as possible. Poe turned around to see if she could see the witches, but they had long gone, along with the others.

"Rex," Poe started.

"—because rope nets aren't going to work on those, they've cut themselves out with their claws—" Rex went on.

"Rex, were there other hunters here before?"

"Other hunters, before me? Well, no, not exactly. I heard that there was a guy a while back who came here proclaiming himself to be this big, important professional ghost hunter. He did all this fancy-pantsy stuff, and everyone ate up every word that came out of his mouth. He was apparently very convincing, but it turned out that he was a giant fraud."

They passed a house with something dangling from the tree in the front that was easy to spot: the doll made of sticks and twine, hanging from a branch and swaying in the wind. Just like a hanged corpse. Poe also saw the strand of black hair mingled with it. Would a demon or evil spirit stop in its tracks and flee, or go right past it?

"—smoke-and-mirrors junk that so called 'magicians' do on stage, but this isn't for show, this is for real, and we're not playing around here. No phonies here."

They got home, Rex kicking his boots off at the door.

"We'll show them, and they'll see what we can do will work. It will. You, me, and the witches."

Poe slid her shoes off and gave the envelope with the slides in it to Rex. She saw the drawings on the living room table they had been looking at, the ones Rex worked to mimic. They were sketchy outlines of humans—wavy, heads with misshapen arms and bodies.

Rex joined her at the table where they both left off and now both lost in thoughts.

"I'm no phony, but ... there is something I have to confess."

Poe looked at him.

"I've never actually seen a full-form ghost."

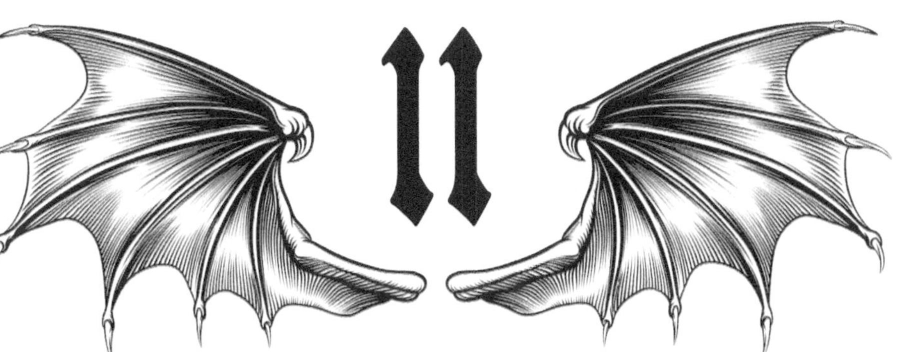

Poe wrapped up her purchase bag to stuff in her own messenger bag, careful that the needles wouldn't poke through. The sky still had the dreary gray color to it, like all the clouds just merged together into a smoked canopy and there was not a single hint of sun anywhere. Though the atmosphere screamed rain, Poe could already feel it in her skin that it was coming, but not yet, as she usually knew when it did. She kept her hood up, fastening the clasp by her neck.

As Poe walked down the sidewalk she already had the idea that she did not need to go home so soon, even though she told Rex she just needed some more sewing needles and thread while he was going to make dinner. This gave her the freedom to stroll through the town with no particular direction, with no real motive but to roam.

The house that appeared around the corner looked very ordinary, and it was actually too ordinary. Not a decorative flower pot nor garden sculpture in sight, and the lawn was maintained enough to prove that someone lived there. It was the color of old slate, plain and hidden in plain sight, but something was giving Poe a funny feeling that it was in fact hiding something. Poe's curiosity peaked, as that prickling sensation started on her arms and made the little bumps rise. She scanned the area first, turning on her senses, but not picking up on anything. As she walked, a cloud passed to cast a shadow over a section of the house like a shroud or a curtain meant to conceal something.

Fat drops of water fell onto Poe's eyes and blinded her for a moment, blinking away tears of the sky subjected to terrorizing weather. The clouds lingered and merged as more drops splashed onto everything and created a cacophony of drops, falling against the houses, sounding as hard as stones. Poe wiped her face, and the hair from her face, blinking into the torrents and seeing something through them in the topmost left window of the house. It at first seemed like a curtain, pure white though with an aged tarnish, but when her eyes came to focus, she could make out the form that was not a curtain at all. She saw the face as a glimmer in the window, but seeing the eyes that were not drops of rain on the glass made it clear. Wide, round, pale as a fog light. They were a part of a very pale face, too pale to be human, small and round. Like a child. And as the rain fell faster and harder, Poe could only wipe her eyes again to see that the figure was gone within seconds. There was nothing there but the curtains of the room hanging there as an afterthought. Poe stared at the window, waiting five, ten, fifteen, twenty seconds before holding her hood in place and turning in the direction of the rain to rush home. She looked back only a few times, but nothing reappeared. She figured that it would not. This was something that no doubt had often appeared in the window a few times, but it just might have been the first time it was seen.

Poe raced home, almost slipping as she shut the door and stomped her feet on the carpet, leather boots squishing in excess water. She unbuckled them off as well as her cloak, placing it on the hook and shaking through her hair. She ran around the house to find Rex, crashing into him in the kitchen.

"Where have you been? You're soaked!"

Outside, the rain pattered against the windows, followed by the flash of lightning and crash of thunder loud enough for Poe to feel it in her gut.

"Rex, Rex, I saw one!"

"You saw what?"

Poe ignored her hair dripping all over her shirt. "I saw a ghost. A full human ghost with a face and everything! Not a wisp!"

Rex's eyes widened, the lightning catching the flash of interest across his pupils.

"Are you sure?"

"I am sure," Poe nodded. "It was very real. It was a kid, I think, I couldn't really tell, but it was really pale, and it looked like the curtains, and then this face just *appeared* and it—it flashed for a second and then it just vanished."

Rex considered her. "Where was this?"

"Some random house by Peach Street. I'll know which one. We have to go back!"

Rex already rushed past her to go to the closet. He came out with his rain galoshes and a large raincoat. He tossed them on the floor before going back to get another raincoat.

"This will be big on you."

Poe didn't hesitate to put it on, the two of them dressing themselves in all kinds of gear by the closet before going out into the storm.

Rex turned on his meter reader the minute they were out the door, although it was not yet necessary. Poe waited until they walked down the sidewalk a bit for her inner reader to kick in, for the slightest tickle or brush on her skin that wasn't the on-pour of rain.

"Up here," she told him. "It's this way!"

She and Rex jogged down the street as they got pelted with rain drops and stepped in already-growing puddles. She brought him to the very corner where, in full view, was the house, plain as a stone yet grand enough to be an artifact.

"Okay, this is it," Poe said, turning her focus on the window and not taking her eyes off it. "It appeared right up there."

Rex turned his device to level it with the window. They shielded their eyes against the droplets falling from their eyelashes.

"We have to get closer," Poe stated, tugging on his arm. She led him over to a few spots, trying to pinpoint the exact one she had stood on, never looking away from the window.

"See the curtains?"

"Yeah," Rex said, steadying his device. The red and green lights stayed on, the meter pin not moving.

"It was there, it appeared there."

The device remained steady, no waving pin, and no blinking lights.

Poe frowned. "You have to move closer."

"Well, not too close. I don't want to spook whoever lives here."

"Or whoever used to live here."

They waited. Rex raised his device as high as he could to get even with the window. Poe was screaming on the inside, urging it to appear. She willed those curtains to form into the shape of the ghost child with wide, dead eyes. Lightning flashed behind the house, illuminating the window, revealing nothing but the curtains.

"There's nothing here," Rex said, lowering his arm.

"No, there is!" Poe insisted, holding his arm so that he could keep it there. "I saw it! It's there!"

"Well, it's not picking up anything," Rex said gently. "I think it might have moved on."

Poe looked from him to the window and back, the image printed on her brain. It was so clear and so real. This did not make any sense.

"But then, why can't you pick up any traces of it?"

"It's probably too high up," Rex answered. "And with this rain, it's not picking it up. The device is getting soaked."

Poe, after a moment, let his arm go and he lowered his device. That feeling she had was still there ... and stayed there.

"I don't understand."

"Maybe it was just a person," Rex offered. "You saw a person."

"No. That was no person. There was no life anywhere on that face. It was haunted, pure haunted."

"I believe you," Rex said.

Poe appreciated him, but she still wanted one more minute by the window. The curtains remained still. She did not blink.

"How about we pencil this location in for now? We can always come back later! It's pouring buckets and kind of hard to see. We'll have better chances later."

"All right," Poe surrendered.

Poe finished another chapter in her book and then debated whether she wanted to start another or start on another clothing project. There was a collection of scraps of fabric littering the floor she meant to make something with but could not decide what. Rex had given her a book of paranormal encounters that she could browse through again. It was in her best interest to create disguises that were realistic, especially after her recent encounter. She put the book she held down on the sill and instead stared at the moon, the perfect circle standing alone, no star or cloud near it. The clock read a little past one o'clock in the morning and although comfortable in that window nook, Poe never dressed for bed. She did not intend to so early.

She unfastened the window and pushed it open, meeting air that felt more refreshing than cool, even though she reached for her cloak by default. Poe crept along, her feet moving rhythmically to the new roof they had become accustomed to. Of all the different roofs she climbed in her life, she liked this one best. Probably because the buildings in Mock Cob were so grotesquely fastened together like the odds and ends of formations that were lying around, giving Rex's—and her—home a smooth surface with square and triangular edges. She found the corner of the roof where the drainpipe was and slid down, landing in damp grass. Some nighttime bugs chirped in the grasses, happy and peaceful little creatures with nothing to fear. Poe walked along the grass with the moon staring right at her, beckoning her, welcoming her to the night, the one true thing she called home her whole life. Poe kept to the darkest parts of the sidewalks, walking along the shadows of houses and trees while she let her senses do the navigating for her. Fully tuned, she wandered with the intent to let them pull her in any direction, though she knew she was aiming for a particular one. With the rest of the world asleep, this time was when all were in the deepest state of sleep common for dreams to occur, to keep an audience captive enough to not stir at the sounds of night creatures out and about, especially this one in the tattered, stitched-together cloak.

She strolled along the streets until she found the one. Of all the houses darkened for the night, this one wanted to be the darkest. She stood before the window again.

"I'm alone again," she whispered. "You can come out now."

Even standing there imploring for something to manifest, no such face came back to the window.

When Poe finally accepted defeat, she turned back, crossing over a small stream and taking a shortcut. She walked past other sleeping giants with no activity … until something stirred on her skin that made her stop. It was subtle enough to feel like a tickle, a light brush of electric charge, and it was pulling her off her path from home. Poe turned and followed her senses, keeping her eyes and hearing sharp. She already knew where it was coming from before she got there. And when she did, she immediately saw the faint light that was coming from the basement of the witches' tea shop.

Poe sauntered along, moving quicker but keeping low. She made sure she did not break a single twig or leaf on the ground and her steps in the grass were delicate enough to barely touch them, making her steps almost the same as tiny leaps. There, in the basement window, was a light that was dim enough to be inconspicuous ... but enough to light up late night activity of someone else who liked to claim the night as their own. Poe was down on all fours now, the basement window low enough for those to see out, but not quite for those to see in. Poe crept closer, and the flash of something red made her almost lose her balance. Smoke tinted pink clouded the window and as fast as it swirled together, it already started to evaporate. The window cleared enough to reveal the activity and the one performing it. She was anxiously waving away the smoke with her hands, holding an empty bottle in one and a cork in the other. The swirling smoke matched her hair in both color and temperament. Poe could see that she was wearing striped pajamas similar to a pair she owned, but her own did not have stains of brown and green here and there.

Poe watched Bernadette put down the empty bottle and stir something in the cauldron before her, mumbling something to herself. Even though Poe could not hear them, she knew that they were not ordinary words. Bernadette took a stick of something and put it in the cauldron, stirring away as the stick became thinner and thinner until it dissolved. This time, the cauldron bubbled, and she blew on it. Poe instinctively leaned back, expecting another explosion, but instead, Bernadette looked up and made direct eye contact with Poe.

Both girls' eyes were stunned and frozen open. Poe remained rooted to where she was, though right as she blinked, she saw that Bernadette disappeared from the scene. Poe scrambled up, not bothering to brush the grass from her knees. She turned and jumped a mile in the air at Bernadette standing right behind her, so startled at her sudden appearance she almost fell out of step. She could not figure out how she got out of there so fast, and without making a sound. Poe held herself and tried to look as innocent as she could.

"I thought that was you."

"I, er, uh—"

"Why are you spying on me?"

"Well, I saw a flash of pink smoke and I wanted to come and see where it was coming from. And it just brought me here, that's all."

Bernadette regarded her. "You must be out on a hunt, then."

"I am," Poe truthfully answered. "I came out to check on a ghost I saw before."

"Where?" Bernadette asked with a hint of interest.

"It was on the top-floor window of a house, and the first time I saw it, it was raining but it appeared right in the window, and it was a fully embodied person."

"Did you see it again?"

"No," Poe answered, allowing her guard to come down a bit. "I came back, but it wasn't there again."

There was a beat of silence as they both stood there, both apparently not sure what to do about the other. Bernadette turned her head back to wherever she came from and said something Poe did not expect.

"I caught something, but I don't know what it is. You might. Do you want to come see it?"

Poe felt all the disappointment of the night disappear and in its place a wave of warmth she did not prepare for. "I would!"

"Okay, come on."

Bernadette turned and walked through the grass to the side of the house where a staircase hid in plain sight: dark and descending somewhere darker where there was no telling how far they went. Poe followed the young witch back to her basement lair, right into whatever configuration she was cooking up so that Poe would get questions answered. Bernadette walked down those stairs without light and Poe's only choice was to follow blindly with nothing but the sounds of the guiding footsteps ahead of her. The steps were short as Poe's feet found straight ground and she heard a door open. Poe walked a little more before a rectangle of light revealed the basement lab. She was expecting it to mimic the shop upstairs and Rex's basement, but this was no such extension of the upstairs. While there was still clutter of mason jars and boxes, it was only a storage room. Boxes and containers lined the walls and shelves against the wall. The room had nothing else but a table and chair with a single light on and a few small cauldrons, bottles, and jars.

Bernadette brought her over to the table where Poe could see what she had in the centermost jar: It looked like a single puff of black smoke, darting around, angrily hitting each glass wall. It opened a mouth and snapped what looked like needle teeth.

"Hey!" Poe said. "You got a snapping shadow."

"A snapping shadow? Okay." Bernadette rounded the table so Poe could be nearest to it. "So, what does that mean?"

"Well," Poe said, peering at the jar with an air of expertise. "They hide around in the grass and shadows on the ground and like to bite things that pass. Though their bites are more like a sunburn. I caught one with Rex the first night I got here, actually. They're mainly just pests. They disappear in the daylight."

"Everything disappears in the daylight," Bernadette said matter-of-factly. She turned the jar around, watching it swim around in the air. "It is a shadow, but I wanted to see if it took a solid form. You know. Like it would if it were in Hell."

Poe let that thought roam, peering at the jar. "You think it does that where it comes from?"

"It's possible," Bernadette answered. "I thought you were an expert."

"Well, I'm still learning," Poe said coolly. "There is so much, and I see new monsters and spirits and things all the time." She looked at the cauldron near the jar, where pink foam was still sticking around the rim.

"So what were you trying to do with it, exactly?"

Bernadette was leaning on a book on the table, and at Poe's question, she picked it up.

"A spell to see if it would take another form. It's really complicated with otherworldly things. Like things on the Earth realm, no problem. This, not so much."

She had a few pages marked, and she skipped over all of them but the last one.

"There's another one I want to try."

Poe forgot her cool manner. "Can I watch?"

Bernadette smirked, keeping her face down to the page. "You can, but I doubt anything will happen. Besides, we already have this in common anyway and—"

She stopped herself from saying something.

"And we're all learning these things."

Bernadette ran a finger down the page of small print words. She reached over to a jar next to her for a dried plant with no more color. She crushed it in her hand and sprinkled it over the lid holes. Poe leaned forward as much as she could, but then thought she was too much in her way, so she went to the other side of the table. Bernadette said some foreign words, waving her hand over the creature in the jar.

The snapping shadow froze and turned a blazing white as though encased in ice. Bernadette seemed taken aback, and Poe had no idea what she was trying to do, but this was not it.

"It's ice?" Poe blurted out.

Bernadette scowled and picked up the book and scanned the page she was on, turning another and scanning that.

"Well, no, it's probably not supposed to be."

Before anything else could happen, Bernadette waved her hand and spoke in a clear tone.

"Go back as you were before. A spell undone, and nothing more."

Poe felt a vibration that passed through the air and felt like it passed through her as well. Her nose tingled, and she reached up to scratch it. Meanwhile, the iced snapping shadow turned back into the little black shadow, now thrashing around in the jar and snapping its mouth more aggressively.

"What was that?" Poe asked.

"Nothing," Bernadette stated. "It was a reversal spell."

"I felt it."

Bernadette shrugged. "Well, you felt that I did a spell."

Poe scratched her nose.

"Relax. It's not going to do anything to you."

Bernadette shut the book and picked up the jar. "Guess I didn't get anywhere with this."

"It was cool to see some magic, though."

"Uh-huh."

Bernadette stared at the creature. "Should I just let it go?"

"Yeah."

Bernadette turned, and they went back up the stairs into the night. She waited until they were a few feet on the grass and then opened the jar. The snapping shadow floated along the grass until it disappeared down the road somewhere.

Bernadette stood there for a minute, not saying anything. Poe adjusted her cloak.

"Well, I should probably get going. Thanks for inviting me in and showing me that."

"Sure," Bernadette nodded.

"I ... I would like to come back to the shop sometime and have tea with you and your moms again. I really think it's interesting, and they're pretty cool."

Poe swore she caught the first smile on Bernadette's face.

"Yeah, okay."

"Well, good night," Poe said, not wanting to overstay her welcome.

"Good night."

Bernadette turned and went back downstairs to the basement while Poe went on her way, considering the outing to be victorious in the most surprising way possible.

oe opened her eyes and sat up in bed, rubbing her face where it had been smashed into the pillow. When her eyes adjusted she stared at nothing, really, coming to terms with her thoughts and trying to determine her sudden urge to be awake.

She sat all the way up and listened to the outside, clean and quiet. The clock on her nightstand said it was almost 4 a.m.

The night was about done, but not quite.

For some reason, this thought was something that grabbed Poe's insides, filling her with a sense of urgency she did not know she had.

Poe got out of bed and immediately got clothes to change.

There had to be something out there, and close by. What else would explain it? She must have picked up on something and she had to act on it.

Poe grabbed her long jacket and put it on, securing the hood and going over to the window. She opened it slowly, sticking her face out. Outside she could hear the chirp of crickets and the drip-drops of leftover rain falling from the gutters. She crawled out, shutting the window behind her and scaling the roof.

Across the horizon, the sky remained black but bled blue on the edges. Poe slid down the drainpipe with ease and let her feet hit the ground, startling a grasshopper which pounced away. As she walked along, there was nothing else hiding in the grass, and from where she could see, nothing else hiding in the shadows. Poe took a deep inhale of the freshly misted grass as she sauntered over the sidewalk, keeping her hood secure about her head, knowing to blend in the shadows herself. It was all leftover rain in her nose ... until it wasn't. Poe paused and turned her head. Two houses stood almost adjacent, with their roofs forming a triangular shadow on the grass and something fluttered inside of her. She crept toward this area, catching the scent and pinpointing that it was exactly where she thought it was.

And what she thought it was.

Whatever did it was long past, leaving the remains where they were, but the blood and torn meat were still fresh enough.

She could not tell what it was, or what it used to be, for it was so well mutilated it left nothing but its mangled fur and bones in the grass. Poe hovered above it just to casually look for clues, if there would be any. Whatever did this wanted a snack and got one. There was no doubt that it was still close. It was still fresh. She hunched down, crawling across the grass and hiding behind a tree. Above her, a breath of wind blew through the leaves, though it could have been more. With the smell of wet, mangled meat in her nose, she trailed down the street as she tried to pick up on anything else. The streets remained quiet. Not a shadow passed the ground nor in the sky. The threat of dawn sent most creatures of the night away, but Poe knew that not all had gone just yet. The further she walked to nowhere, finding nothing, the more her mouth dried up. She could feel her tongue rough as sandpaper against the roof of her mouth, and the new smell infiltrating her nose that made her want to sneeze.

The dire opposite of the smell of rain and grass moist with blood and dew, it did not make sense. Her nose, mouth, and throat felt like they just inhaled a dust cloud. She felt scratched, parched, and chalky. Poe resisted a cough, scratching her nose as she worked to pinpoint where it was coming from. She expected to find a pile of meat, a carcass meal finished off. The more she pictured it, the more it made sense, especially once it made sense to her nose. She nearly gagged once that musky scent kicked in, the kind that could only come from bones long dead. This lingered like it wanted to stay, or wanted to be found. Poe could feel it all the way down to her own bones, the magnetic pull she had for seeking it out. It was strong now, stronger than ever before, she just had to focus on it. Poe followed her nose all the way down the street until her eyes found it, stark white against the dark grass. She stopped far enough before the pile in the grass, arranged as a full intact animal crouched on the ground. Poe was close enough to see this, and when she went to get a better look, her alarm stopped her in her tracks. Those bones were not supposed to move.

The legs pushed up, the entire form coming to a standing position, all the bones in perfect skeletal assembly. It moved just like any living creature would ... but it was not. It turned the way any living creature would as well. The eyes and nose were empty hollow sockets, but there was no doubt it could both see and smell Poe. She stayed frozen in place as she stared into those eye sockets, full of nothing but seeing everything, just as its entire body tensed back down to a crouched position. The kind reserved for attack.

Poe forced her feet to cooperate and back up just as the face skull opened to reveal its animal teeth and a growl in the lowest octave ... the one that almost sounded like a regular sound, but slowed down to only resonate in the deepest cavities of the brain, a sound deep enough to churn the mind into unease.

Poe scrambled into a run just as the beast charged at her, the growling turning into barking from an undead hound from hell. An undead hell hound. That was it, from its appearance to sound to the way it ran in pursuit of the chase. Poe darted behind buildings and leaped onto a pair of garbage bins before a lower section of a roof. She crawled across this one to scale the higher one while the hell beast circled from below, agitated from its miss and trotting away. Poe let her breathing out in short, controlled spurts. The sky all around her now leaked a dim blue with the promise of the dawn light, the best weapon against the monsters of the night. The only time for Poe to catch it at its weakest.

She climbed down without making a sound, half wondering if she should whistle the thing, for it seemed like the threat of dawn may have sent it scurrying to a heavier shadowed area. She backtracked the same path and even went around the bend to a trio of trees with shedding leaves. The musky smell nearby revealed where the thing was pawing at a tree. Poe marched along making a lot of noise, just until that head perked up to snarl. And then it gave chase. Poe leaped up the second tree and grabbed a branch, pulling herself up just as the pile of bones snatched at the bottom of her jacket.

She pulled it up, not without hearing the dreadful tear and feeling the fight from below. Poe lifted her jacket end with the newly jagged piece as the hell hound jumped up to try to reach more. She held herself on the branch as she watched this creature, jaw opened all the way as empty as its eyes. It growled and snarled, and stood on hind legs and sounded its promising bark to Poe, a promise she knew would not take place. She stayed comfortable on that branch, holding on to the only part of her that suffered damage as she looked to the horizon. The hell hound snarled and snapped its teeth, hard as walnuts. Poe watched ... watched as the first leak of daylight touched the grass. The creature still growled and then suddenly yelped, the dust across its bones floating in the air. It pounced on the trunk, its jaw unhinged to the oncoming anguish. Poe watched the bones crumble as the creature collapsed, falling to the ground in a chalky heap. The skull remained on top, hollow eye holes spreading bigger and bigger until the shape was all gone, gone into nothing but dust.

Poe climbed down.

She bent over the bone dust with scientific observation, lightly brushing a finger over the remains. What would Rex think? What could he know about bone dust? And what of the witches? She let her hands scoop it up and pour it into her pocket, filling as much as she could before zippering it shut. She turned on her heel to make it back home, giddy in her hunt, and found that almost took no effort at all.

I'm getting good at this! I'm getting so—

Poe nearly tripped over herself at the sound of familiar growling. She pivoted to see something that only seconds ago dissolved into nothing, now running and barking at top-notch. That tree where she had hidden blocked the horizon and was large enough to cast a shadow for this thing to still be there, and still be after her. How foolish of her to think there would only be one.

Poe felt the wind knocked out of her as that full skeleton leaped onto her and she crashed to the ground, crying, rolling over with as much defense as she could. She grabbed the skull before it could open and close on her face, its muzzle digging into her chin as her fingers scraped the nose hole. She kicked, and she thrashed her head back and forth as she struggled to keep her hold on the beast, its bony nails digging into her chest. She pushed and grasped on the ground, fighting to get a clear shot of light blocked by the tree. She tightened her grip and rolled with all her might, slipping in the grass to get just an inch out of the shadows.

The bone creature shifted its weight on her chest and she kept her knees up to keep it away, all the while craning her neck to will the sunlight to come through. She pushed and pushed until she got the creature where she wanted it and kicked it out. She got up and ran out from the shadows just in time for it to pounce on her again, pinning her to the ground and going for her throat. Poe grabbed the jaws... right at the same time she could see the new pinks of the sky fill the sides of her vision. She squeezed the jaws, already feeling them crumbling, and squeezed as the bones became chalk and the whole thing cascaded onto her in a dusty snowfall.

Poe threw back her tension to the grass, laying there with her arms spread out. Now the dust cloud filled her senses, making her sneeze. She lay there for a moment or two collecting herself, wondering just how many more things across the town were disappearing and just how many exits there were.

When she got home, she went to the kitchen table to sit down and wait. Rex was only a late riser on nights he was out all night on an active chase, and considering his only active chase was to the bakery, she expected him up within a couple of hours.

And she sat there for a few hours, maybe even more, never nodding off or blinking the slow and heavy blink. Poe kept her jacket on and her arms on the table and made sure all that she was sprinkled in stayed on. Soon the pinks and oranges of the sky graduated to a full-blown sun, waking up cheery birds who fluttered around with no idea of what used to prowl around stalking what was up those very trees.

Poe heard the water running upstairs and the eventual creaking to the downstairs. He came down in his usual heavy sluggishness, wearing his usual terry-cloth tunic and pants, bearing a look of surprise at the unusual that greeted him.

"You're up early."

Poe waited while he let his morning eyes and mind adjust.

"Or ... up late."

"Yup."

"What happened to you?"

Rex came over to the table and observed Poe, head to toe and staring at her hair. He looked like he wanted to touch it, but decided against it.

"You went out alone."

"Only a little bit, I wasn't—"

"And what are you *covered* in? What's this dust?" He gestured to the particles that ran down her arm and settled on the table.

"It was an undead hell hound."

"What happened? How did you find one? Did it go after you?"

"Two, actually."

Rex raised a brow.

"And actually I went after them. I went out, okay, only a little while ago before the sun came up. I don't know why exactly, but I just woke up and saw what time it was and thought to myself that I really needed to go see what was out there at the last hour, you know? Like, I had a really strong feeling, and I saw those bone hounds and I knew that they were going to disappear soon, so I sort of just teased them a little bit and they attacked me. I just held my ground until the sun came up and then BOOM they completely turned to powder!"

Rex just stared.

"I ... I just ... I really feel like I am starting to get really good at this!"

Rex blinked a few more pulls of sleep out of his eyes, a smile forming. He ran a hand through his hair.

"I figured you would want the leftovers for like, observing and stuff," said Poe, holding out her arms. "I've got some more in my pocket."

Rex sniggered. "First, coffee."

He went over to the counter, Poe carefully taking off her jacket and setting it down on the table. She noticed and remembered the tear, taking it in her fingers. She got up to the kitchen herself to rummage through a drawer for a needle, thread, and scissors and sat back down.

"Close encounter..." Rex observed.

"A bit. I climbed a tree."

She took to sewing the end while Rex set the pot. He leaned against the counter, not saying anything, just watching her sew.

"You're really good at a lot of things, Poe."

13

Poe carried it in her arms as she thundered down the stairs, having a hard time keeping it together as it was so big.

"Are you ready?"

Rex appeared around the corner with two thick clubs. He already wore black pants and shirt and gloves for the added chill. Poe already had on her long black robe of scrap fabrics, mimicking the feathers of a bird. Her hood looked almost like a beak, as if she, herself, could be a bird of prey. She held out the fold of black material to Rex.

"Try it on!"

Rex put down the clubs, regarding it with amused interest. He opened it up to reveal a large jacket made from some animal with wild, scruffy black hair. And its hood had ears and a handmade snout as well.

"It's the size of a bear! Where did you get it?"

"It's furs from the textile shop. I just made it look like a monster on top, kind of like a big wolf. I almost picked brown, but it needed to be black to match your hair and beard!"

Rex was already putting the thing on, long and furry, the sleeves fitting over his own. Poe smoothed the fur down for him and pulled the hood over his head.

"It fits perfectly," she said.

He went over to the mirror in the hallway, at once fingering the ears and snout she made.

"Incredible," he chuckled. "You made this."

"I used one of your jackets as a guide for your size. It looks great on you!"

Poe stood by him in the mirror with her hood up, her creature disguise, next to Rex and his.

"Look at that," Rex said. "We really do look like the things that came out of the dark." He turned to her with a smirk. "No wonder things don't notice you."

He walked back to the foyer and scooped up the clubs, handing one to Poe.

"It's going to come in handy to look bigger and meaner."

She picked up her lantern.

"What exactly are we going after?"

"Not quite sure. Some people put in a call to me about their garden and yard getting destroyed and new holes in the side of their house. They've patched up everything, scared something's going to get in. This could be anything."

Rex opened the door to a blast of cold air and they set out, lighting their lanterns as beams of guidance. Poe adjusted her coat and hood, and the beak sat close enough to her nose to pass as one. She loved the new sense of power and adrenaline it gave her, especially during her advance in hunting. It made her feel like she had a better chance of catching monsters if she looked like one ... and felt like one. Rex walked in his new ensemble, the ears on his hood giving a monstrous silhouette against the sky. She wondered if it would give him the same confidence if he would now display more aggression in his pursuit. The way he walked made it seem so the way he was holding his club and bag in firm determination. She loved the way his beard blended in with the fur so much that she could not tell where one ended and the other began ... a creature newly made in the moonlight.

They rounded a bend and followed a sidewalk for a while, all while keeping ears pinned to the scene around them. Quiet and still as it was, that either meant that something already passed or had yet to. Poe felt the prickle on her neck long ago, though nothing lingered.

"Okay, up here," Rex instructed.

They found the house and the damage instantly: the scratches and gashes in the fence, the turned-over and broken flowerpots, and the piles of dirt and upturned plants in the garden. Rex and Poe approached the fence with the broken pieces. He bent over to the ground to look at the tracking in the dirt to try to find a footprint while she lifted her head to the house. She could not hear any activity around the outside. Perhaps there was activity happening on the inside. Something pushed at the back of her brain.

Rex overturned flowerpots and walked over to a tree with a metal cage door wide open and empty.

"It got the bait," he stated. "Got the bait and managed to get out."

He kept his lantern on his arm while he got out his electromagnetic device to scan. Poe did so with her eyes, ears, nose, and all senses. They both turned to one another, coming up short.

"I'll have to talk to the owners about more effective traps and if they saw anything at all."

"But, what is it?" Poe asked.

"That's the trouble. Can't really protect against something unless we know what it is. At least we know it's not a spirit."

He inspected the cage and ran his light over the lawn and marks in the dirt.

"We're going to have to come back. There's nothing here."

Poe crossed her brow. She saw nothing, heard nothing, but she felt something.

"I think that there is."

"What do you mean?"

Poe pivoted around the yard. "Something is still here. I can sense it." She paused. "I think I can even smell it."

Rex kept his lantern even as though something could jump out of the grass at any moment.

"Smell it?"

"Yeah, like ... old mold."

Rex inhaled. "I don't smell anything."

Poe turned her head to the section behind the house, the part of the house that was a separate greenhouse.

"There."

Rex raised his lantern to the greenhouse, where they both saw the doors padlocked and the whole thing covered in a protective tarp. The bottom flap of the tarp waved loosely in the wind in what had to be a brand-new tear.

"There. It's in there."

Before Rex could say anything, Poe moved down the lawn, past the house, and to the greenhouse with careful steps.

That old mold smell invaded her nose.

She crouched down to the torn flap, Rex bringing his light just close enough to see it. The gashes and holes looked like it took multiple attempts before finally succeeding. She carefully took an end and lifted it, exposing the newly made hole in the side of the greenhouse. Rex said nothing, but Poe looked up at him with the suggestion he did not like to hear.

"I can fit."

"Listen, be careful, it—"

"Don't worry."

Poe put down her light, crouching down on all fours and lifting the flap more. "I just know."

And then she turned and crawled right inside that hole, squeezing perfectly in the jagged mouth and disappearing into the dark interior. The only thing she heard was the increase of Rex's footsteps by the greenhouse, anxiously pacing the outside to try to find his own way inside, but only if the situation called for it. His footsteps stopped right where Poe went in, and where she would come out.

Poe stayed low, creeping on all fours and using the dark to her advantage. Her eyes soon adjusted and she could make out the shapes of the troughs of plants all around the greenhouse and the rows they were arranged in. Her hearing and her smell sharpened, picking up on the wind outside and the mint plants inside. She watched for any irregular shapes crouched down as well. She moved along on the pads of her boots, stopping at the sound of something scuttling behind her.

She heard the scuttling again, this time closer and faster. She stayed low and ducked behind some plants.

To her right was a mostly empty shelf, and she climbed it without a second thought.

Below her, the scuttling continued, quick and scratchy. Poe positioned herself at the edge of the shelf and picked up that old mold scent, right on her radar, the shadow revealing a silhouette with tiny horns.

And then she saw it, small and humanoid but lumpy. Its skin was the dirtiest gray that could be green or yellow or a mixture of both. It made a gagging, snorting sound as it looked left and right, knowing that Poe was somewhere. She made her way down the shelf, carefully balancing. She could see the flowerpot and where it was positioned, and there this thing was standing just close enough. It stopped sniffing the air and instead diverted its attention to something on the ground it started to snack on, nibbling with added crunches that could have been a worm or bug. Either way, it was distracted enough to not notice Poe pick up the pot and hold it straight out in front of her. It did not know the flowerpot would land on its head.

Poe sank back just in case, checking again to see the creature lying in a heap on the ground. She climbed down and immediately threw netting to wrap it up, not sure if it was completely knocked out and for how long.

The look on Rex's face when she crawled back out was a mixture of surprise and irritation.

"Good ... catch. Goblins. Great. They're annoying. How'd you do it?"

"Dropped a pot on its head."

"Nice save. Give it here."

Rex took the netted bundle, and they set off. Rex talked about traps and goblin teeth and claws, though Poe did not listen to too much of it. It was that hunch.

She listened to it and it had been right, yet again. They passed some more houses and one of them had white curtains, long and thin, reminding her of a ghostly figure.

14

ex was going to dig traps, according to him. Poe was going to roam, according to her.

She had excuses ready, having told him that she learned that goblins tend to travel in groups and even if they appear solitary, there are plenty not that far away. He seemed impressed that she did research and only by this agreed that they should split up and cover more ground. Even though Rex warned her not to stay too long so late by herself and meet with him soon, she had the notion in her mind that she planned to, and would, end up doing so. She was just too anxious.

She did not tell him she had somewhere specific in mind, just watched him round up his shovel and bag, listening to him talk about how nasty goblins were, and the sooner they got rid of them, the better.

He made her at least carry one weapon and wear the most concealing cloak, a long, dark one. Poe and Rex went their separate directions, the sun already sinking into a reddish-orange hammock. Poe walked quickly, her legs moving at a determined pace. She picked up on something lingering around the house down the street, making fallen leaves dance up in an updraft, but she ignored that one. She was aiming for a particular house, and would not stop until she found it.

It looked the same, except for the umbrella resting against the front porch. Somebody was here. Maybe they knew about what was upstairs, in that window, maybe they did not. But Poe did know. She slowed her pace down to something more casual. Her heart skipped a beat as that feeling came back, that very one. She made her way to the window now, expecting those curtains to come alive at any moment. The setting sun behind the house cast an orange-blue to the sky and a shadow over the lawn to make it look bigger than it was. Poe felt the prickles on her legs, arms, and back as she stood at the window and saw that it was open. There was just enough to let air in, but not much else. Someone had been in that room. Poe gained confidence and walked right on the lawn to the house to confront the window face-to-face. It was there, whatever it was, and whether or not the living of the house knew it. Poe sauntered over to hide in the bushes for the moment, waiting for that time clock to sound.

The chimes sounded one, two, three, four, in the melodious call to lock up. She crouched low, the evening still light enough for her to be seen. The chimes repeated their chorus for the final warning as the daytime light waned. The streets were already empty and quiet ahead of time, the clock of warning finalizing the day and sealing it to a close.

Poe kept her gaze on the window at the way the curtains were spread out a little more than they did before and the slit of fresh air they welcomed in. It was welcoming enough.

She got up and walked across the grass, creeping along the side of the house once she saw exactly where the edges were, the gutter she could climb, and the part of the roof she could safely perch. So she climbed the gutter all the way up, and all the way up to the edge by the window. It was just enough for her to lift her face and inhale ... and it caused her to double back so abruptly that she almost lost her grip. She held her nose, suppressing a cough. She had never been inside a hospital or mortuary, but she knew what one would smell like, and this was it. It smelled of a room of death.

Poe crawled further down on the roof, the lowest she could go. She made it to the window and placed her fingers there cautiously, peering inside while holding a deep breath inside her chest. She immediately saw the bed and saw what was on it.

It had a single white sheet completely covering what was underneath it. The shape was human, from the straight legs to the torso to the head lying perfectly still. Poe staggered at the window, looking at the source of the smell, noting the strength of it, and wondering just how long it had been there. She saw the spirit, what, a week ago? Rex might have been right about it taking off, but it left behind its shell. Poe's mouth was so dry she could not swallow, could do nothing but taste the equivalent of milk froth. But, someone opened that window. Someone knew that it was there.

Poe leaned back from the window with her mind racing and the desire to run and tell Rex immediately. She worked to get her feet to cooperate and move her from that gruesome scene in the window when something stopped her, freezing her in place. She squeezed her eyes shut and opened them, refusing to believe that she just saw the sheets move. She peered into the window, her breath leaving a small patch of fog. The creases in the sheet folded as something turned, as two arms bent and the corpse reanimated. This reanimated corpse pulled the sheet away to reveal the face, the face of something that did not wake up the same ever again. It was the one she saw all right, with eyes as ghostly orbs locking right onto hers and widening, but only a little. Whatever it was remained under the sheet for a moment, but when it sat up, the sheet fell away and revealed itself to her.

Poe was right that it was a child. Or, had been a child, for any youthful sparks or signs of any life had been stripped from this face, leaving it as an empty shell.

The child raised an arm and a small hand reached out to her and started beckoning, and beckoning.

Poe's fingers slid under the window and she pushed it up enough for her to slide in, slowly, still keeping her eye on the figure who made no other movement or expression. She stood up in the room where the death took place, right before the figure that experienced it ... a figure of living death.

"Are you a monster?"

The voice was a light and scratchy whisper, like someone who had not had a drink of water in years.

"No," Poe responded. "Are you a ghost?"

"I should be," the child said. "I don't know how, or why, I'm still here."

Poe braved a couple of steps forward, feeling some of the tension falter. The child had the palest features, from opaque skin to light peach fuzz hair that was so thin it was almost not there at all. Poe could not tell if they were a boy or a girl.

"Are you dying?"

Poe could smell that the most, like she could actually smell parts of the body that expired, or were about to. The child's eyes sank into their face so much they could fall into the cranium.

"I did," the child croaked. "I died already ... but I guess I didn't stay dead."

There was a beat before they spoke again.

"I thought you were one of the beings finally coming to take me back."

Poe felt the stillness of the room and the way the child's voice hung in it. She then recalled the first time she saw their face in the window and the expression of recognition and what they thought they saw.

I died already.

So, she was not entirely wrong about what she felt. But she still felt bewildered. Here was a body of flesh, and not of vapors.

"I'm Poe," Poe blurted out without knowing what else to say.

The child shuffled to sit up some more. "I'm Caleb."

Boy.

A boy who looked like he was made out of porcelain. Not real at all.

"How old are you?"

"Thirteen."

"Thirteen, oh! I'm fourteen."

Poe did not want to admit that she thought he was much younger.

"Why did you climb up to my window?" Caleb asked.

"Well, I am not a monster, but I hunt them. See, I hunt for beasts and ghosts and ... well, I saw you from the street and I thought you were a ghost."

Poe by now was close enough to the bed to lean against it, just a little.

"You saw me too."

Caleb's eyes flickered. "I did. I did see you. You looked like a monster, but one I haven't seen before."

"Do you see many of them?"

"I do. Whenever I feel okay enough to get up, I go to the window. I see all kinds of them. Sometimes."

Poe could hear a faint excitement through the fatigue.

"You're a monster hunter," Caleb whispered.

Poe was all set to unleash a couple of bragging stories when a noise from downstairs made them both stop. Poe turned her head and Caleb sank back down on the bed.

"You better go!" he hissed. "My mom might be coming up soon to check on me."

"Okay."

Poe made her way to the window, turning for one last look at Caleb.

"Well, it was, um, nice to meet you."

She barely got one foot out the window when she heard his voice again, farther way, but still carrying.

"Will you come back sometime?"

Poe paused in mid-climb and smiled.

"I will. I'll tell you about things I've seen ... and then maybe you can tell me about the things you've seen."

Poe departed with the knowledge that his list would be longer than hers. There was something about him, she did not know what, but there was something there that told her there was so much more to Caleb.

Poe made it back home quick as a whip, not stopping nor in pursuit of anything else, even though she did hear the shriek of something in the distance catching prey. She dismissed it as an animal, not caring, only caring about her own "catch" she had to get home to tell Rex about right away. When she got home she had to determine if Rex was home or not.

She followed the light on in the basement and galloped down. Rex was bent over pages and one photo he had stood up on the table.

"Guess what I just saw?"

He turned around.

"Was it a soul collector? Oh, please don't tell me it was a soul collector!"

"No, no," Poe answered. "Soul collector? What's that?"

"You don't want to know."

"Is that what you saw tonight?

"No," Rex said, sitting up. "But someone else did, describing it to me and I told her that it was way too soon for those, but people have been saying things are coming out a lot more for some reason, and—so wait, what did you see then? Did you find more goblins? Because I didn't even see those."

"No, no, it wasn't goblins!"

Poe went over to the table where he sat and leaned against it.

"Remember that time I swore I saw a ghost in the window, but when we went there was nothing there?"

"Yeah?"

"Well, I was both right and wrong, because I did see someone and I went back to the house and climbed up to the roof—"

"Poe!"

"No, no, it was easy and slanted and the window was open a little, and I saw a boy in bed, and he invited me in because he thought I was a monster. We talked, and it turns out that I did see him and thought he was a ghost because he told me *he's died before!*"

Rex processed it. "Died before."

"Yeah, he's super sick, so it's sort of like he was a ghost because he died. But instead of turning into one, he came back to life for some reason and he looks like a living corpse."

"His window was not only unbolted but open?"

"Yeah. And I think he did that himself. He says he thought I was something coming to take him back. Like, back to the afterlife. Like ... he just sits there and waits for that."

Poe finished that story and Rex sat with increased alarm. He reached for a book on the table and picked it up, leafing through the pages before stopping on a picture of a skeletal figure in a shawl so torn it looked like cobwebs.

"This," Rex said.

"What is it?"

"It's a wraith. People only see them when they are about to die."

Poe shook her head at the picture.

"You didn't see anything else around the house?"

"No."

Rex folded his arms and looked at a random spot on the wall. "So he died, but came back..."

Poe thought the shawl the wraith wore could have looked like the black cloak she wore, though not as shabby. It was just pieces of different fabric. It was raining, and she did have the hood up.

"Someone or something decided it wasn't his time yet." He darted his eyes to her. "Well. You watch that. Something will come back. We need to watch that house."

Rex then diverted his attention to a mason jar on the desk with things that were claws, or teeth, or both.

"Well, at least we got the one goblin. I dug some traps and told the homeowners about the greenhouse. In the meantime, why don't we go and bring what we got to the witches?"

Poe felt the elevated excitement of another outing, and the company of others she found exhilarating. He gave her the jar for examination, and she could see some leftover gums and blood around the teeth where they were removed.

"What came of it?" she asked.

Rex snickered. "Well, you got it good. It had a small crack in the skull, so it was already gone. I got the teeth and the claws, and you know they'll want those for something."

They set out for the witches' house, but not before Rex got his fur jacket off the hook once again. Poe held on to the jar as they made their way out like the claws and teeth could come back to life and try to scratch their way out. The image of Caleb's face flashed in her mind and she pictured what he looked like at the window, and then what he looked like from his bed. He thought she was a monster. He also seemed to act disappointed to find out she was not.

Poe's nose picked up the smell of burning leaves, and she wanted her sense of smell to pick up any brewing of tea, hoping that their delivery would turn into being invited in for a drink and to see what they were working on. The last time she saw Bernadette was when she caught that snapping shadow. Had they caught other creatures on their own, taking a claw here and a piece of hair there, to run various experiments?

They got to the house without a scent of herbal refreshments in the air and without much interior lighting. Even the basement was dark with no activity, though there was something. Poe did not know what it could be. Without questioning it, Rex started to walk right up to the door with Poe behind him, and the force of something throwing them back sent their alarms spiking. First Rex stepped back, hard, pushing into Poe and almost knocking her over.

"Whoa, whoa!"

"What is it?"

"I don't know," Rex stated, holding out his hand. They stared at the house, and with the glint of light, Poe could now catch the glint of something else, a kind of bluish reflection, like the walls of a glass dome.

"There's some sort of force field," Rex concluded. He kept his hand up and pressed against it, and they both watched the wrinkles form in the air and then release in a wobbly sheet of gelatin.

"That is so weird," Poe said, reaching out her own hand to touch it. She pressed harder than Rex did and tried to push in further, feeling that gelatin wall squish in between her fingers as far as it could go before she pulled away. She and Rex watched the handprint she made thin out and the wrinkles straighten back out to the invisible wall.

"That's one protective barrier they are testing," Rex backed up on his heels and turned around, and Poe felt the drop of disappointment in her gut.

"Looks like we'll have to catch them later."

ex and Poe pushed on the doors to the town hall to find the rest of them gathered there, turning around to see the tardy party.

"Sorry, so sorry," Rex said. "We were tracking a spirit in an old well."

They both stopped for a moment to catch their breath, the congregation staring at them. Poe spotted Emme and Ivy Briar-Whittle right away, looking at them curiously. In fact, the curious looks were on all of them. Poe thought that maybe they all wanted details of their adventure as to why they were late for the meeting. But why would they? A spirit haunting a well wasn't new to the town. Just how much did they shelter themselves?

Why are they staring at us?

"Those ... are some outfits!" Mayor Vivienne said.

Oh.

Everyone was looking at a giant wolf man and bird girl.

There were murmurs of interest as well as disturbance. Rex and Poe remained rooted to the spot.

"—look like monsters," Poe heard someone mumble.

"Oh, yes," Rex started, keeping his tone professional. "We wear these out, especially at night. It helps hide us from the beings," Rex explained. "But they're also good against the cold, on days like today. Poe made them." Poe stood up a little straighter at the sense of pride in his voice. The others in the room, the blacksmith and his companions, the contractor and her team, and the two witches exchanged glances while the mayor leaned forward from the podium.

"She did?"

Rex nudged her.

"Yeah, I did," Poe answered. "I love to make different outfits, and always did."

"They certainly come in handy!" Rex added.

"Do they?" the mayor asked with increased interest. "So, you're saying you wear those out at night and blend in?"

"Yeah, that's the point," he said. "We do."

The mayor leaned to her associate to whisper something, the associate nodding.

"How effective is it? Against the ... beings?"

Rex gestured to Poe. "She's brilliant. She makes us look like them. It's like we're in disguise. And it makes it easier to go out at night and do our jobs."

"Things don't notice you?"

"Never!" Poe said. "It's almost like they think we're one of them."

The mayor studied her.

"Could you make more of them?"

Poe perked up.

"For more people?"

"I, I think I could."

"Right, because you know we have some groups of people willing to defend the town. That could be helpful."

The groups in question in the front row started to rouse at the revolutionary idea, the blacksmiths pointing at them and pointing at themselves. The civil engineers talked among themselves as well, considering Poe and Rex. Babs tugged her glasses off and mimicked putting up a hood. The mayor went through the paperwork until she found a scrap to scribble on.

"The way we think the Night of Passing will go this year, it seems like we'll need every new idea we can get."

"Surprise attacks," blurted out Carl in the front row, his eyes gleaming. "We can attack guerilla style."

"You can make us look like the monsters?" asked Anton, turning to face Poe.

"Can it really protect us?" asked Babs. "When we go out to set the traps?"

Soon, everyone was chiming in.

"I want to look like one."

"I want to look like a demon with horns!"

"I want to wear a long dark robe, and get a big scythe."

"This is something we will look into arranging," the mayor said.

Poe felt a new wave of warmth wash over her as everyone was talking at once. They believed in her. Her. A simple girl who knew how to make clothes and made what she needed before she started to make what she wanted. Rex and Poe moved down the aisle and found seats among them.

"We'll get with you on that, dear," the mayor continued when Poe sat down. "Let's check some other things off this list. Anton, Carl, what do you got?"

Anton and Carl stood up, each holding long and thick weapons with saturated edges.

"We made these big ones for big things, and with long range," Anton explained. They flipped them around so that everyone could see every inch.

"The key is to make everything out of iron," Carl said. "Because it repels things, especially ghosts."

"Iron, really?" someone said from the crowd. "I didn't know that."

"Yeah, everyone knows that," said Carl with a smirk, presenting the weapon.

This made Rex utter a low growl. "You didn't know that until I told you," he muttered.

"Have they been tested?" asked the mayor.

"Well," Carl said, holding the weapon. "No ghosts or nothin' have come near me yet and they aren't going to!"

The blacksmiths expressed vocal agreement and patted Carl on the back, which made Rex sigh and look at the ground.

"Excellent," Mayor Vivienne said. "Babs, let's see that thing in the wagon."

Babs stood up and pulled a wagon near the front with the help of an associate. Murmurs started in the crowd, the wheels squeaking as the tarnished gadget came into view. It looked like a deadly chandelier. Instead of lights, it was lined with spikes all around the lower rim.

Babs pushed it with ease and held on to the sides in pride, or steadiness.

"Here is one that we think can be best against smaller things, and this trap is best hidden in shrubbery to camouflage it, but it does the trick once something triggers the rope from here."

She reached over and flicked something, the rope flying out and that spiked chandelier coming down in milliseconds and creating the sickening THUD that echoed in the town hall.

"We are at work at larger cages and spiked fences that can be made to go around whole areas too if needed."

"Very good," Mayor Vivienne said with a nod. "And it has been tested?"

"Caught a goblin already," affirmed Rex. "And the bigger ones ... we believe that the same kind of fencing will work on keeping out just about anything. Solid and not."

Babs agreed, grinning at Rex.

"Okay, yes, you focus on building what will keep the most things out and away from homes."

She turned to another part of the audience.

"Emme and Ivy? What have you made?"

The witches stood up.

"We tried a barrier spell recently, testing it around our house," started Ivy.

Rex and Poe craned in their seats so much their vertebrae could have detached. Now that they could see them better, the two looked wet, like they were slick with some sort of gelatin covering.

"It was a more advanced spell we attempted," continued Emme, something dripping from the ends of her hair. "If anything, all it could do at best was slow something down, though it was still penetrable. This will not work."

Mayor Vivienne leaned forward. "This the barrier spell you tried on the town line?"

The sentence hung in the air, especially with a hint of anxiety in the mayor's tone. Poe noticed Emme and Ivy stagger to keep patience.

"As we said before, that has been difficult," started Emme. "We find that it could only work against any living creature that cannot pass through the realms. So, anything other than what we're trying to keep out."

Mayor Vivienne nodded.

"We know this is why you wanted us here," said Ivy. "But it's proven to be very hard to figure out how to keep things from getting in."

The next gust of silence was so uncomfortable Poe heard a ringing in her ear. She scratched it for something to do.

"But we *can* protect the town," started Ivy. "And we will. This is why we are all here."

"Yes, we will," Mayor Vivienne agreed. "We will get ahead."

She reached out to the witches first.

"So, you'll brew up the protective potions and make talismans and sell them in your shop."

"Yes."

"Should have a full stock soon."

"Good. And you—"

She gestured to Rex and Poe.

"Continue the hunts. In the upcoming month, there will be more of them, and more until the Night of Passing when we all get the full swing."

She turned to Babs.

"You and your team finish as many contraptions as you can. Only build on them during the day for the time being."

"And you." She turned to the blacksmiths, particularly the ones holding weapons. "You keep your promise and *stay in* until proper arrangements are made for your protection. No hero stuff, do you all understand? Leave the late-night hunts to the experts here. From now all the way up until the Night of Passing. Understand?"

There were murmurs of obedience.

Mayor Vivienne did not blink.

"I will not allow ... anything to happen ever again. Our cemetery can wait."

Bobblehead

Fractured shadow

Harpy

hell hound

Nether flyer

Smolder salamander

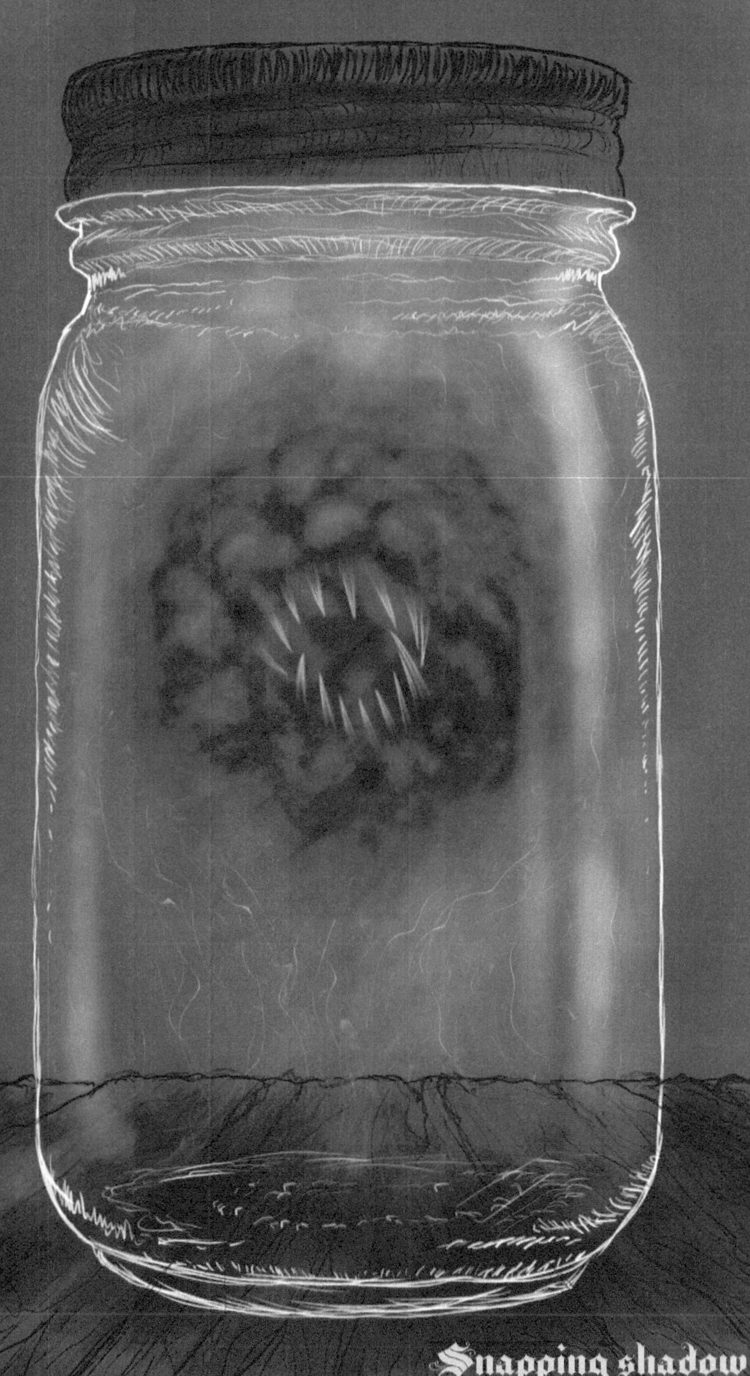

Snapping shadow

Vampire burrs

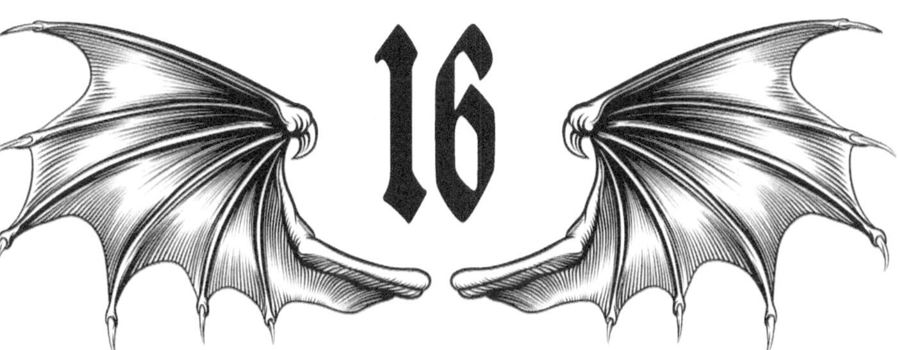

16

oe felt it in the deepest cavities of her gut, jolting her awake. It sounded from somewhere far away, but close enough to carry over the buildings and to her ears. She sat up, knocking over the book she was reading before she fell asleep to the floor and ignoring the KER-PLUNK. The sound echoed behind it, a moan that was not quite a cry, but more like a song. Her senses alert she threw herself out of bed to go listen by her window, curtained and locked, taking extra care to undo all of that just to stick her face out to hear—and possibly—see. She only opened it an inch, keeping the curtain to conceal most of her face. She shut and locked it again when the gruesome song sang across the sky, now closer.

She went down the stairs in the hopes that Rex was up.

How could he not hear that?

Standing in the middle of the downstairs, she tuned her ears. Things were shuffling through the trees. Things in flights. As if on cue, she heard a door open and Rex thundered his way to the living room. He met her with crazy eyes and hair to match.

"Did you hear that?"

"I did!"

The two stood there with an equal amount of chaos to their hair, pajamas, and moods.

"It can't be what I think it is!" Rex shuffled his feet and rambled. "No, no, it can't be what I think it is."

"Are we going after it?" Poe decided that was the question to ask first, already reaching for her shoes, not caring that they would look stupid paired with her pajama pants.

"No, no," Rex said curtly. "Not like this. Not if it is what I think it is. Come on, let's ... let's see."

They went to the front door where Rex mimicked the same activity Poe did with her window: unlocking, opening carefully, and standing to the side just enough to hear ... and possibly see. Both Rex and Poe stuck their heads out. She had so many questions but knew better. Sure enough, it sounded again, sending a vibrating wave to their ears that tickled, itched, itched like a rash would. Rex shut the door and bolted it.

"Impossible," he murmured. "Too early. It's too early!"

Poe waited before he turned to her. "They don't come out, and when they do, it is not until the last days of October for the Night of Passing."

"What?"

"A demon lord."

"demon lord..."

Rex started to pace the room, picking up book after book on the tables to try to find the right one. "demon lords are the things that come out only at the Night of Passing when the veil is thinnest ... so that they can call out to the rest to come out and join in the havoc of collecting souls ... and enjoying feasting on flesh."

Rex put the book down and ran his fingers through his hair, talking to himself or her or both. "Not supposed to be here already. Not supposed to be here at all. Why is it here?"

"Will other things come?" Poe asked. "It's out there calling for more to come out, but can they too?" She still held on to her shoes by the laces. Rex raised his head as though trying to listen. Poe did not hear anything and knew that there was nothing out there anymore.

"I don't know," Rex surrendered. "I don't even know for sure. It's my best guess that's what it is, and I hope I'm wrong. No, Poe." He eyed her shoes. "We're not going out to that. It will alert everything in the Nether realm, even if it thinks we're from the Nether realm. No. We need to know for sure. We need to know if anyone spotted it."

"Why if they're so rare? What does that mean?"

"It means that the mayor was right...the veil was opened bigger. Tomorrow we ask around. I don't know anyone that would have seen it."

"I think I do," Poe said.

Poe finished breakfast, lunch, whatever meal that was, while Rex flipped through books. Her eyes stung with the sleep she wished she held on to, while Rex's remained open and bloodshot, having not slept at all.

"Some have decent photos, others are just sketches," he stated. "But, here." He showed her the page of the best-illustrated photo: the long dark robe billowing around on the ground with the grayish-red skeletal face in the middle.

"This one. I am going to ask around those I know. Do you want to bring this with you?"

"No, I think I'll be good. I am going to stop by the witches' first."

"Good idea. Catch you later."

The sun was out all the way, providing beams of warmth to the still air. Poe buttoned up her raven jacket and set off.

When she got to the witches' place, she paused, sticking a hand out to check on the invisible barrier. Her hand met open air to her relief, and it occurred to her that it would not be there during the day, when they of course held business hours. She went up to the door but hesitated before knocking, immediately picking up the sounds of disturbance inside. She heard voices sound and raise, though she could not hear exactly what was being said.

"I *know* that!" came Bernadette's voice.

"And we know that you know that, which is why you need to do a better job of using your head!" came Emme's.

"I *am* using my head, that's the point! How am I supposed to know what something is unless I try it first?"

"You need to be more prepared!"

"I am just so sick and tired of it, and it's never going to change!"

"Yes, it will!" came Ivy's. "You need to stop working harder and start working smarter!"

Poe couldn't make out everything, but she wanted to. She moved up and pressed her ear against the door.

"...when we were your age."

"Don't you get it?! I'm *not* like you! I'm different from you, I'm different from everybody! And nothing ever goes right for me! This is … this is just too…"

Someone shushed her, and they all did. Someone said something about a "visitor."

Poe jumped back from the door just as a pair of footsteps approached the door and opened it. Emme stood there with a pasted smile on her face while Ivy and Bernadette lingered in the background. Ivy put on a smile as well, but Bernadette did not.

"H—hello," Poe said. "I was just about to knock."

"We knew company was calling," Emme responded. "How are you? Won't you come in?"

Poe stepped in. "I came by because Rex and I were asking people if they saw anything last night. Heard anything."

"No, I don't think so."

"I didn't hear anything."

"Well," Poe said awkwardly, reading the room, dripping in discomfort. She could almost taste it like bitter drops of something were landing on her tongue. "So sorry to bother you, it's just that Rex thinks it might have been a demon lord and we need proof since it would be proof that the veil opened bigger. Anyway, I've got to go see someone that I think did see it. Um, thanks. Have a good day."

Poe gave a little wave and turned.

"I'll go with you."

Poe spun around, just as surprised at Bernadette's declaration as her mothers were.

"You'll…?"

"Yeah, why don't I do that? I can help find out more. Because … I just have so much to learn anyway, so I might as well." Poe picked up on the scorn in her tone but did not question, just stood there as she gained an unexpected companion. Bernadette gave a half a wave to her mothers, and they shrugged and gestured as to say, "All right, go ahead."

"So, demon lord," Bernadette started talking right away. "Interesting."

"Yeah. They don't really come out, and when they do, it's to call all the other demons to come out. We think we heard it last night. You sure you didn't hear anything? It sounded like ... singing almost, in very low tones."

"No. I was too busy wasting all our ingredients on spells that didn't work."

She seemed like she was going to say more, but did not, and Poe did not ask. She just followed Poe without a care.

"So, where are we going?"

"To visit someone. If anyone saw or heard anything, I think it might have been him. He's sick with something and stays in bed all the time. And when I first saw him in the window, I thought he was a ghost. He might still be one because he told me he died and came back."

Bernadette's red eyebrows jumped.

"I think he's seen lots of things."

"What?"

"He lives right down here."

They turned the corner of the street. The house was in the state of quiet stillness in the day as it was at night. The windows were bare yet open and empty, like the lifeless eyes of a corpse, oblivious and nonexclusive to any activity around them. Poe led Bernadette to Caleb's window, shielding her eyes from the sun's rays.

"I don't know much about who is around except for his mother, but it never hurts to check. He told me to come back and visit him, anyway. I think he gets lonely."

Poe started to climb up the drainpipe.

"Wait, *wait*," Bernadette interjected. "What are you doing?"

"I, well, I just climbed up to the window," Poe explained. "I'll get him to come to the window and then you can talk to him then, okay?"

"You climbed to the roof? Are you *nuts*?"

Poe didn't dare say Bernadette sounded and looked like Emme just then.

"Yeah, I do all the time! Don't worry."

Bernadette stood there with her arms folded and made an exasperated scowl and gesture.

"Well, what am I supposed to do?"

Poe was already halfway up the house, catching on the lower roof to hoist herself up and crawl to the window. Below her, Bernadette paced a few steps while watching cautiously, like she expected her to slip. Poe went to the window, peering in. Caleb was sitting up on the bed, legs folded underneath him, leafing through a magazine. She waved, hoping that he would catch her shadow before she could tap on the glass. He looked up, only slightly startled, then unfolded his legs and stood up to get to the window. Poe watched his movements, slow and easy like his legs could break with each step he took, yet there was a new light to his face. He was pleased to see her. He opened the window up, all the way, letting her in.

"Hi, Caleb!"

"Quickly," he said. "So no one sees you."

The room smelled of something minty, and it automatically made her think she could taste chewing gum.

"My mom is out," he explained. "But I never know for how long."

Caleb still looked pale, the bags under his eyes deep and blue, though his voice sounded less parched than when she first met him.

"How are you?" Poe asked, not knowing what else to say.

"Okay. I am walking a lot more today. I ... I am glad you came back."

Poe let that moment linger, offering a smile.

"Of course! I brought a friend with me. She's just outside. We're out asking people about monster sightings. Did you see any last night?"

Caleb stood with an interested and thoughtful look on his face.

"I always do in my dreams. But, they're always ones I have seen before in real life ... or just that I saw for real. I thought I saw a big demon a while back."

"What did it look like?"

"Like it was made of smoke, dark red smoke, and it had horns. Maybe. It was for a second and it floated away in the sky."

At that moment, Poe and Caleb saw something else red and floating in the sky, right at the window. Bernadette's full head and face rose at an unexpected position, hovering all the way up. She *was* floating.

Caleb moved back in surprise while Poe stammered.

"Hey! Did you ... did you... How are you...?"

Bernadette came all the way up to the window and revealed that she was sitting on a tree branch. She floated into the room and landed on her feet, holding the branch at her side.

Both Poe and Caleb simply stared.

"That was, *wow*! How did you? You flew on a tree branch?"

Bernadette stood there holding the branch like a powerful staff.

"Levitation spell," she said like it was nothing. She and Caleb glanced at each other.

"Okay, well, this is Caleb," Poe started. "Caleb, this is Bernadette, and as you can see, she's a witch."

Bernadette simply regarded Caleb as a foreign specimen while Caleb stood frozen in awe.

"A witch," he breathed. "I never met one before."

The three of them stayed in that shared energy of one another: new, different, and all-around intriguing. Poe thought she was the one enjoying it the most, looking back and forth between these two interesting individuals, knowing that they were as well. Even Caleb, who was at once frightened and excited to have not just one secret company in his room but two, and one a witch who just used magic to reach his window. Even Bernadette, standoffish and cold, was clearly also enjoying it.

"Um, so I am studying monsters and ghosts and stuff, and Bernadette and her family are working on new potions and spells to try to protect the town from them. I'm looking for something in particular, something that can help us. It's like this big skeletal thing with a long robe."

Caleb crossed his brow. "There are a lot of skeletal things in robes."

"They're called demon lords, and they're higher up," Poe went on.

The look in Caleb's eyes told Poe what she expected. "I know those."

"Did you see it?"

"Long robes. Tall. Horned. Human, almost, but mostly not."

Poe looked at Bernadette. "They think this means the veil has opened bigger."

"My moms said the same thing."

Caleb reached out to his bed like he needed to steady himself.

"We've only been here for a little while," stated Poe. "Both of us are new to the town, so we have not actually experienced a Night of Passing before. Have you?"

"Yeah. I have lived here my whole life. And whole afterlife, now."

They waited. Poe and Bernadette regarded Caleb as some sort of seer or oracle who could give them all the answers they needed.

"What's it like?" Bernadette asked before Poe could. Caleb looked at the two of them like he did not know how to word it.

"It's not like a regular night when they are around randomly. It's everything that just comes out at once. Everyone puts up more protection on the houses and boards up the windows completely. Mama puts a sheet of wood on mine and makes me keep all the lights off as soon as it's dark, and hide in my closet and not make a sound. I've snuck out sometimes to peek. I always do now. I watch big things with big wings fly around and things just through the streets. Sometimes things land on the roof and I hear their claws walk across my ceiling, but that's it. I hear things scream. Things scream and shriek all night and it's hard to tell what it's from. There's just … a lot, I guess. It's like one big invasion. One big outing."

Something passed over Caleb's face, some sort of inner light that made his expression more vibrant and alert.

"I see them all through my window, but I have seen all of them in person in their natural habitat. I was there … when I went. It felt like a dream, but I could see them."

Bernadette side-stepped from the window. "Speaking of window, someone's here. Walking up the driveway."

"Mama!" exasperated Caleb. His murky eyes bulged, and he gestured to the two. "Don't let her see you! Get away from the window!"

Bernadette and Poe stepped away from any view while Caleb went to the window, acting like he also did not want to be seen. He sighed, the two girls not seeing what he was seeing.

"She's got my medicine, and I have to take it now."

"What's—"

"You have to go," he interrupted Bernadette. "I'm not allowed to have anyone here."

Bernadette held the branch and waved her hands over it while Poe ducked out the window, listening for the front door to open and close.

"Come back," Caleb said. "But come back at night. If you can."

She scaled the roof and drainpipe just as Bernadette was gliding down at a delicate decline, defying gravity like she owned it. She tossed the branch on the grass by the tree she took it from. They both rushed to the sidewalk and power walked back where they came from, each looking back at the house.

"What's wrong with him?" Bernadette asked Poe. "What does he have?"

"I don't know. I honestly just met him."

They passed people coming out of the neighboring house and avoided eye contact.

"He told me that he died and then came back."

"I can tell."

Poe said it low. "So could I."

"He's going to be important ... to both of us. We're going to want to have him around. I can tell that, too," Bernadette stated.

"You can?"

"Yeah," Bernadette paused. "The same way I could tell that about you."

Poe tried not to react to the compliment. The first nice thing that came out of her mouth.

"Me?"

"Yeah ... there's something about you. I don't know exactly what it is, but I can sense something strong that says I can trust you. There's something ... peculiar, but comfortable about you. My moms sensed it too."

Poe smiled and did not say anything else as they walked back to her home. Bernadette lingered by the door for a moment.

"Well, see you around."

"Okay ... and thanks."

"Sure. Bye!"

Bernadette turned her back, and it was only then she smiled, but it was enough for Poe to see. She did not care, as long as it was there.

"Now, up here," he said in something louder than a whisper, his chin almost low enough to touch his chest. "I'll bet there is some evidence up here."

They crossed to where the grass was shorter, where it stepped-in more. Rex stopped before it and peered down, passing his light over to prove it was just that.

"Do you see?"

Poe aimed her light to where he was and saw for herself the deep groove, and how it had the right kind of dent. And shape. Her lantern traveled up the groove to see how it ended ... in forked points.

"Big ones, aren't they?"

They.

Of course, they would follow suit in a pattern, continuing down the trek through the marsh. Rex bent over to brush in the mud with his fingertips.

"This one walks upright. Probably about six or seven feet tall."

"You know what it is?" asked Poe.

"A type of demon I saw a few months ago."

At that, Rex stood up to follow that very set of prints. Poe fixed her hood inching to slide off her head, keeping it up and secure. Though no breeze passed by, not an exhale of anything, she knew what the chill down her back was. She stepped in line with Rex, making her steps as careful yet determined as his. The footprints continued in a regular, widespread pattern to show just how large it was. Accompanying them in the mud were brushes of something that dragged along.

"Clothing," remarked Rex.

Whatever they were following must have had wings, for Rex shined his light on one and came to a complete stop. He lit the rest of the surrounding area, taking care to look into the trees to see if anything perched in its branches, waiting for them to come closer. Poe scanned the trees then, only seeing pairs of lights glow for a minute and then disappear the second she looked at them. They could be fireflies, but they seemed to be too big and too close together to be going out at once. Rex had started to move forward again, although silently, while Poe still stood where she was. She wondered if he had the same chill go down his back as it did hers, and that he walked that line of danger on purpose. But, if he did not, perhaps she should ask him...

The minute Poe joined Rex on his trail, she heard a swooping noise behind her that was close enough to make her jump, make her duck, as something dark passed over the sky and blocked the clouds. Rex cried out as it passed, spinning around, but his lantern was too late to catch it. They both tried to find it with their lights, each time hearing it but seeing nothing. Rex held his spear at the ready. He signaled for Poe to keep quiet while he steadied the things in his hands.

SWOOP.

Before anyone could react, something zipped past them so fast it almost caused them to lose their balance. Rex cursed and ducked with Poe along with him. She kept still while Rex kept up his jerky stab motions. She heard the swooping sound again, but this time it landed with a huge THUD only a few feet away from her, heavy enough for her to feel it in the ground. Poe's heart raced as every hair on her neck stuck straight out, looking at the dark mound very close to her. That was all it was, or all it seemed to be, something that almost took no real shape at all but was one ambiguous mass. All black, all things even darker than black, like it was formed out of pieces of darkness itself. Or, just all of its very worst parts. It moved now, fully aware of Poe next to it ... and perhaps it landed there on purpose. It turned its attention to her, even for her to see it did not have wings, but rather its whole self could open into some kind of parachute. Poe and Rex both stayed low, not making a sound, as that parachute opened and soared over them, folding back into nothing.

Rex got up and searched the skies. Poe joined him, scanning everything he did.

"What was that?"

"Fractured shadow. It can take different shapes, whatever necessary, to swallow something whole. You should see the inside, or what is the inside of its mouth. Doesn't really have teeth, just these nubs for holding its prey in place."

Rex looked around again and cursed. "Where did it go? Not knowing where it is is a problem. Stay down, stay quiet."

Rex and Poe crawled now. Though Poe kept her eye trained on the clouds, none of them moved to reveal themselves to be this fractured shadow. The land they were on now curved upward and the only thing Poe could really focus on was a gnarly tree with many open branches stretching down into a valley.

"Maybe it flew down there," remarked Rex, partially reading her mind.

Poe turned to talk to him, not losing her view of the tree.

"I can look," she offered. "I can look from that tree down there."

Rex considered the tree and looked back at her.

"All right. Just go as high as you can."

"I can go all the way up."

Rex followed her to the base of what was a small incline, and Poe set down her lantern. She secured her cloak and moved up the incline, coming into view of a small patch of moonlight to give her a frightening silhouette to anyone who would see her, a creature with horns stalking along the ground.

Poe scaled the tree with ease, with barely any pause in between steps. Through the tangle of branches, she could make out the stars and how spread out they were, all of them clearly visible. No such dark shroud disturbed any of them. She pulled herself up to a higher branch and rested upon it, holding on to another for balance as she surveyed the scene. The only shapes present were houses, all dark down the rows without a single light. Before Poe could blink, she both heard the SWOOP above her and felt the gust of wind it made and nearly fell back at the weight that joined her in the tree.

Poe flattened herself against the branch as she heard Rex gasp. A few leaves fell from the weight of the creature and rained on her head and shoulders, and as Poe made sure her hood stayed in place, she peeked to get a good look. It could have been a blanket that got torn into a thousand pieces and sloppily put back together, for the edges looked almost sharp. Jagged. She made a tunic like that once, one of her first, and it was easy for it to come apart. Just like it was easy for the fractured shadow creature. It fell upon the branches and folded itself over them, making them vanish under its heavy canopy. And through the branches, somewhere deep in its cavity, Poe could see those little nubby teeth Rex described. They formed out of nowhere.

"Give it something!" Rex screamed from below. "Anything, anything to distract it! Throw something in its mouth!"

Poe rummaged through her bag, her hood falling off her head and a leaf falling by her eye. This only gave the thing more interest at the discovery of the human company. Poe had a notebook, a multi-purpose knife, and a coin pouch until her fingers found something that crinkled. She paused around it, determining its shape and what it was until it felt less crinkly and more sticky. Of course. She had forgotten the taffy candy she got from her train there. She pulled them out, disgusted at first that they had melted, but the sticky stretching instantly gave her an idea. The fractured shadow now morphed every one of its parts into sharper and sharper ends, including the teeth that somehow grew longer. It moved in on Poe. She held the taffies and waited.

"Poe!" shouted Rex.

She focused on the nubby teeth and waited for them to reveal the part she was looking out for, and sure enough, there it was. It was a groove with a shiny-slick lining and it was enough for her to toss the taffies right into the contracting orifice.

The nubby teeth wavered as they immediately took to exploring what they just caught. The more the teeth stuck to the taffy, the more the taffy stuck to them, smearing into a melted mess. However jagged the fractured shadow was before, it became more sharp and jagged now, its shape stretching and shrinking in panic. The entire form pulled and pulled as it all suffocated in a batch of pink tar, and the blanket folded in on itself.

Poe climbed back down the tree and met Rex standing by the trunk, who looked like he either wanted to grab her away or hug her in relief.

"Kid..." he said, squeezing his spear so tightly she could see the whites of his knuckles. Poe could see the tension in his forehead and answered the question she knew he wanted to ask.

"It was candy," she said. "Taffy candy that melted. It just ate them up and got stuck."

Rex put a hand out as though he wanted to touch her shoulder but did not, guiding her away from the tree and the thing in it. They both watched it from a safe distance, where the ever-changing black mass kept swallowing itself until it shrank down into a pulsating knot, falling out of the tree in tangled twists.

"Should we go kill it?" Poe asked casually.

"No, it seems to be taking care of that by itself."

Poe picked up the lantern and staff where she last left them, standing by and waiting for Rex. She watched that wavering figure writhe on the ground, its pixelated blanket tentacles curling up and shrinking. A hissing noise seemed to come from all of them as they shrank, the knotted mass oozing leftover pink tar. The look on

Rex's face was something Poe could pinpoint as either fear or worry ... or something to that of intrigue.

"The pantry!" Rex called to Poe.

"I've already checked it. I didn't see any!"

"Try the little compartments on the bottom. There has got to be some there!"

Poe sighed and went back to the kitchen without shouting back, not understanding why he thought he would find anything in the basement. She opened the compartments on the bottom, pushing aside napkins and some small paper plates. The next one had bags of dried apricots and apples, and then a bag of milk chocolate balls. She considered the bag, pressing on it even to see that it had a decent amount in it still. It had to be better than nothing.

She took it down to the basement to see if Rex found anything better, which she already knew he did not.

"What did you find? Oh!" Rex took the bag. "These, yeah, good to suck on, but too hard to chew. Almost broke my teeth. They might be a little harder to melt, but..."

"Witches can melt bones," Poe stated.

Rex gave a little shrug. "Might be easier to melt bones than these jawbreakers. Anything will help."

"So, nothing else?"

"Nope," said Rex, as he led them on a defeated walk back up the stairs. "I thought I had some chocolates down here too, but I must have eaten them all."

They went back to the kitchen to ultimately add the last of their search party to the already gathered collection: some gummies in a partially opened roll and a few stray mints.

"It's a start," Rex stated. "They might have more over there. We will have to get more, anyway."

"How *much* more?" Poe asked, eying the little mints. They could only be enough for an afterthought after a meal to cleanse one's palette or freshen breath. What if only certain kinds worked? How many concoctions would they create until they had just the right recipe—spell—for disaster? Even more important, she tried to imagine what the witches' responses would be to their request. Ivy and Emme at worst would hesitate and then tell them it might not work. Bernadette might just laugh at them ... and then she might not take Poe seriously ever again.

Rex gathered the gummies, mints, and bag of chocolate balls together.

"Well, they're witches. They probably have a spell to ... multiply something. Make things bigger. You know. It's all we can go by right now."

"Can't we just get more?"

"There's not going to be time," Rex explained, the strain in his voice not hard to miss. "We have to give them something now so they have something to work with."

With the collection in tow, they set off. Rex's pace moved faster than normal. Down the neighborhood, Poe saw a man and a woman wearing blue coveralls lifting up metal rods to add to an assembly of more metal rods, arranged with pieces sticking out. Near them, Babs was bent in a box holding a blueprint.

"...got to be larger!" she was saying. "We've got to expand it so it can hold it!"

It, whatever it was, was big enough to have destroyed the tree nearby with slash marks, and gotten away to do more damage elsewhere. Poe imagined a giant creature enclosed in such a cage, thinking about how they were to come up with all kinds of ways to trap something. And here the two of them were now, out with their own idea no one ever saw coming.

The shop was empty of customers and at first, looked like employees were nowhere to be found.

"Hi!" called Emme from above. "Be right down." Rex and Poe came all the way in to see her levitating up to high shelves on the wall, going through boxes. She was sitting on a box, her skirt a black waterfall trailing off of it. Poe watched as Emme floated down on the box like it weighed nothing.

"H—hi," Rex started. "We ... we came here with an idea we need your help with."

Emme walked over to them, sparks jumping off her shirt like static cling, and then they were gone.

"Yeah, hang on." She went and stuck her head down a hidden hallway. "Hey, Ivy, Rex and Poe are here!"

She turned to them. "She was just talking about you two the other day. How goes your endeavors? What did you find?"

"We had an interesting encounter the other night. Or, I should say, Poe did."

Emme's eyes twinkled. "You did?"

Ivy appeared in the shop. "Interesting encounter, huh?"

Poe wondered if the third witch was going to appear as well and waited a second.

"Poe here single-handedly outsmarted a fractured shadow the other night."

"Fractured...?" Emme pondered.

"Oh, I think I know that one," Ivy said. "It doesn't really take a solid form."

"That's right," Rex continued. "Poe was with it up in a tree and she managed to distract it and trick it into eating some melted taffy candy which made it sticky and indisposed. It's like it wasn't trapped in a trap, it was just trapped itself. Anyway. Made me think that maybe we can make something that we can use on all of them. Well, most of them. Maybe all of them. We want to know if you can ... create something."

Rex pulled out the chocolate ball bag, gummies, and mints to show. "We brought some. I mean, all candy can melt, but like, I don't know. Can you melt these into ... something? Something that will be strong?"

Emme and Ivy seemed to think for a minute, looking at the candies like they were already brewing possibilities inside their heads. Poe felt a sliver of warmth as her doubts drifted away. Of course, they could come up with something. They could do anything! They were both smiling now, at the prospects and whatever private thoughts they were having that Poe suspected they could share with only one another.

"You want to do a binding spell, then," started Emme.

"Yes," Rex answered like he knew what she was talking about. "Right, a binding spell."

"They're pretty simple," added Ivy. "Though we have done so with different materials. This could be interesting. But doable."

Poe saw Rex exhale with relief.

"We'll be happy to test it out, too," added Poe, imagining a giant net made of gooey mixture stretched over a demon howling on the ground, glowing with magic, a net that would not break. She waited a second before she blurted out, "Where's Bernadette?"

"She's out today," answered Ivy.

The witches paused, either waiting for the other or waiting for someone else to change the subject.

"Oh," Poe responded. "I thought maybe she was going to help."

"She will," said Emme. "In her own way. She just … she needs to hone her skills, that's all."

"She prefers to be alone," added Ivy. "But she'll help out too. We just have to do it first."

"Do us a favor, though. If you happen to see her out, don't tell her about this yet."

"Oh … all right."

"She'll take it personally."

The Briar-Whittles considered the pieces of candy on the counter, the items in a science experiment.

"Well, we'll call on you later."

18

Poe opened the door to Ivy and Emme, rushing in from the gust of wind that blew them both into the house. Their cloaks blanketed around their legs like pairs of wings settling down after a flight, something that Ivy and Emme could have very well done. Their hair was in disarray and sticking up in different direc-tions. Ivy even finger-combed a leaf out of hers, making Poe believe that they actually did fly to their house.

"We got it," Emme said.

"You *got it!*" Poe repeated. "Rex! The Briar-Whittles are here with the mixture!"

She turned back to the witches. Emme was holding the small cauldron, covered with a black cloth that was too coarse to be cloth. Fur? *Skin?*

"We tested it," Ivy said. "Just a little bit on a goblin we caught."

At this point, Rex joined them in the entryway. "How did it go?"

"Like a charm," Emme said with enough charm in her voice. "It's loose enough to hold, and it will bond to whatever it lands on, then it becomes hard as tar. Our little goblin test subject was practically rooted to the ground."

Rex and Poe let that visual form in their minds.

"And then what did you do with the goblin?" asked Poe.

"Nothing, really," said Ivy. "We sprinkled that stuff ... if you could call it sprinkling. After a few seconds of finding its target, it goes to work. It hardened, and it caused the goblin to slow down enough to stop moving. That was all it did, but that was all we did. We watched it for a while, to see how long it would last. By the morning it was gone, but the point was, it held."

"Fantastic," Rex said, eying the cauldron.

"This is just a small batch," said Emme, offering the cauldron. "Until we get more."

"We'll work on getting some, but the problem is getting a large amount. We can only get so much from shops in town that sell candy. And buying a big supply would be expensive," explained Ivy.

"We'll get what we can," offered Rex. "But in the meantime, we'll practice this. Tonight."

Emme finally surrendered the cauldron to Rex, who held it as delicately as a baby or small animal. He peeled back the covering, revealing contents that were not quite liquid, and not quite solid. It really did look like black tar with smears of pink, green, and yellow in there, the crystals of color leftovers from whatever sweets they came from. Poe stuck her head in further, entranced by the sweet smell it still had.

"It's almost like I want to eat it," Poe said.

"I wouldn't recommend that," Ivy said. "Your jaw will stick shut, and then we'd have to melt it off with blue fire."

Poe could not decide if she found that horrifying or interesting. "Oh. Right."

"We best be off," Emme stated. "We're going to go look around for candy ... if any shops sell large amounts."

"Good luck. Thanks," Rex stated, covering the cauldron.

The witches opened their door to another burst of wind whistling through the air. After Rex and Poe shut the door, all Poe saw was the flutter of their cloaks in the wind, and believed they must have flown after all.

The cauldron sat on the counter for the remaining daytime hours, given no real instruction except to use it when needed, and even that did not have much. Poe peeled back the covering and dared to touch it, just a little, feeling the squishy texture of the tar and the way her finger sank all the way through to the bottom like it was air. She pulled her finger out and examined it, expecting it to be covered in the stuff and forming around her finger like a cast. There was nothing there except for small leftover crystals sparkling on her finger, making playful winks to prove the magic was there.

At sundown, they barely waited for the curfew chimes to sound. Poe and Rex walked down the street just as the last set boomed across the town, Rex holding the cauldron against his chest.

"They said we can just scoop it out and throw it like it's sand or powder or something," Rex said to her. "And then it will work instantly, turning sticky and solid. We should test it on something small first."

They walked down the street in the now Shut-In hours just waiting to see whatever would come out first, or whatever they would encounter first, and Poe had the thought that they would not really get the choice to use it on something small first. She thought of seven-foot-tall demons tall and thin enough to lurk behind trees. When Rex headed toward a woodsy area, Poe felt a pit drop in her stomach, and she hoped her instincts were not telling her just that. The sun was disappearing behind houses, leaving a faint orange glow akin to a candle that was getting ready to go out and leave them in the dark. Poe put up her hood with the jackalope antlers in the event that she would be meeting something else with horns.

"Where do you want to look first?" She asked Rex.

He smirked. "You know I was going to ask you that first, Miss Instincts."

Poe trod lightly. "Here."

"Here ... what's here?"

Poe jerked her head up to every tree they passed, hearing that subtle swoop of something in flight. She saw a few leaves fall in the disturbance, but nothing else. She naturally turned right to continue into the wooded area and not the street of houses that would more likely have things clawing at the windows to get at the living prey hidden inside.

"Something airborne and small," Poe answered.

Poe heard and felt the SWOOP near her ear and she swiped at it, catching nothing, looking for the source with her hand still raised.

"Bat," answered Rex, pointing.

She followed his finger to the cause of the swooping noise, the light squeaking across the trees confirming its identity. She spotted it, but would not have recognized it if Rex hadn't said something. Poe crossed her brow.

"What ... kind of bats are those?"

Their wings too leathery, their skin so thin across their bones, it was as though they were skeletons dipped in wax. One turned its face enough, red eyes beaming through its head. Poe tried to make herself look smaller. It could see her, whether or not it already knew she was there.

"There's more," Rex added, pointing to the trees while cradling the cauldron in his other arm. He cupped his fingers over the rim. "Come here. We have to get them to fly down."

Poe side-stepped to Rex, watching one leathery winged creature from the next in the branches. She knew that there were more in the trees behind her that did not fly off. She could feel each pair of red beady eyes at the back of her head. Sure enough, she heard the whipping of the leathery wings and thrust her hand into the cauldron. The stuff, the mixture, whatever it was, clung to her skin at first. She pulled out a handful and held it cupped in her hand, the sweet aroma of the candy still there, though with a hint of something older, like a trap that would be used in a dark and musty basement. She spotted the undead bat before Rex did. Before Rex could alert her, it was there and she threw the mixture as it swept over to the nearest tree.

The bat fell against the tree, its wings folded flat against its body and unable to move. It fell to the ground in a light crash. Poe and Rex rushed over to it as other bats flew around in the trees, unalerted to their fallen comrade. Rex leaned in, first keeping a hand in the cauldron, while Poe just stared at the creature. It lay with its wings wrapped around itself, a self-made trap, while its mouth hung partially open to reveal the vampire fangs that wanted to bite and lost the opportunity. It was as still as a statue, a gargoyle frozen on top of a temple.

"It ... worked," Poe said, simply. She made to nudge it with her foot, even just a gentle tap to confirm, in the hopes that a touch would not break any binding the spell held and send the creature flying at her face.

"Careful now," Rex warned. "Come on, this means we can test it on some bigger things." They darted between trees to avoid any more bats. Poe followed along but could not help but look behind her, wanting to test it on more of the bats, especially should any of them follow them out. She stayed close to Rex and the cauldron of magic at the ready.

Rex's hood slid a little as he power-walked, and he pulled it further over his head, the handmade ears flopping just like a curious creature's would, alert in its surroundings.

"We're going to somewhere obvious," Rex said with a smirk and an air of confidence. When Poe recognized the path they went down, she felt the stone drop in her stomach. The gate lined the sidewalks, tall with sharp design if anything to look sophisticated, or threatening. Though how sharp would they be to keep out anything wanting to fly across, or anything that wanted to climb out?

Or perhaps find other ways in. Like the silhouette of whatever stood in there now.

Whatever it was, it definitely was not human, the way it stood slightly hunched over, proof of something that used to have a living, working backbone.

"That," Poe hissed to Rex. "That's not a person."

Rex shook his head. "Ghoul. I usually don't go after these. I think that now might be an okay exception."

They approached the gate leading into the cemetery with Poe realizing an obvious factor. She saw the padlock, twisted around the gate with a chain so thick she could not even see where it began or where it ended.

Rex cursed. "I forgot about this." He even reached out to tug on the padlock in vain. "It wouldn't be open in general. Why would it be?"

They both stared through the black bars of the gate at the only thing that was in there that found a way through other means ... other means that were not clear. It was immobile for the most part, hunched over a gravestone, though they could not see what it was doing. The fog settled on ground level so thick it gave the illusion of there being no ground at all, just a figure hovering. Poe stood by Rex at the gate, her eyes wandering for the alternative that she knew she would be taking. She thought that Rex knew, too, by the way he turned to her.

"There's a tree over there," she stated.

"Yeah."

Rex wiped his face. "I just don't like it."

"Don't worry. I can do this."

"They have a strong sense of smell," he warned, his voice raising. "You'll barely be over and then it will come—

"So do I," Poe answered. "And it smells like mothballs."

Rex snickered. "Yeah. They do."

He held out the cauldron. "Well, put some of this in that pouch on your belt."

Poe filled her pouch, scooping more handfuls than she should before leaving some for Rex, whom she wasn't sure needed more than her.

"Make it quick, don't linger, don't give it a chance to even try anything. They're slow and stupid so you just be faster."

"I will," Poe said, already making her way to the tree to climb it. She scaled it, seeing over the gate at the gravestones of different lengths and sizes and the figure, the thing she wasn't sure was facing her or not. She climbed over and jumped, landing on a soft spot of soil. Poe stood, raising herself up enough to see but not be seen. The figure was tall and lanky, though large. It looked human, though she could tell through her senses it was not. Mothballs was an understatement by the way the smell hit her, her nostrils flaring. It was very dead. Its body was barely together in one piece, and yet it moved. Poe walked toward it, her pouch of power powder at the ready. She could see Rex positioned against the gate to see her and watch his back, not sure which to do more of. Poe got to the section of gravestones, close enough for it to notice it had company. And then that hunched form stood up and showed Poe its face.

With all the life drained from its face, sullen and gray, Poe felt all the life drain from hers the minute its eyes looked into hers. The eyes held only enough life left in them to be alert and to make decisions. The ghoul looked humanoid, though this thing was formed out of grime and grit itself, molded from filth into something that could never be a human. It went after humans ... the aftermath of humans, really. It had dug and dug at the gravestone for its prize but was interrupted by the living human who stood a few feet away from it.

The undead man-thing opened its mouth and let out a wail Poe felt in the deepest cavities of her gut, watching the jaw almost unhinge itself from its head.

From where she stood she could now see where it had been hunched over and why, for the hole dug showed it got close to the casket but not close enough to access it. Its attention was now on the flesh right in front of it, fresh and alive, and so close.

Poe opened the pouch. The ghoul moaned and lifted a hand to reach out to her, just as she tossed the mixture at its face. She threw another and another, not sure how much to use for a bigger target, already seeing the witches' magic work for many beings. She stopped as the stuff flew at the monster like powder, but settled on it like tar. It spread instantly and froze it into a statue, its arm raised in mid-air and its lower jaw hung open. Poe stepped back, watching the effect. It was still alive, of course, just in a petrified state. She watched the dead-staring eyes to see if they would twitch, to see if they could still see her and were helpless to do anything. The only thing that gave any signs of life was the mixture itself, a shimmer or two of pink and purple from the different colored candies used.

"Poe!"

Poe spun around and ran back to the gate where Rex had his big hands wrapped around the bars. "What's it doing?"

"Nothing," she answered. "Just a couple of scoopfuls, and it worked."

"Just what we want. We don't know how long it lasts, so you better get out of there."

Poe turned and climbed back up the tree, moving at a quickened pace with the idea in her head that the mixture would wear off and it would go after her. She came down at ease, spying through the bars as she met with Rex.

"This is exactly what we're looking for," he said. "That's all the time we need to slow them down and possibly take them out. Come on, let's head home."

They walked back down the sidewalk, every once in a while catching glimpses behind them to see if the thing was still immobile, a grotesque statue guarding the graves.

oe and Rex walked along with a quickened pace, combined with adrenaline and satisfaction. Rex cradled the cauldron in his arm with the cloth cover halfway across the top.

"...have to remember what we gave them, and if it matters," he went on. "And to see what works better, taffies and gummies of course, though it looks like the chocolate worked in it pretty well too. They're amazing, aren't they?"

"Have you never seen witchcraft before?" Poe asked.

"No!" He turned to her with a curious eye and tone. "Are you saying you have?"

Poe realized she did not have an answer. Instead of telling him no, something in her gut was telling her that was not so. It felt like she had before, but could not quite remember. She was just as entranced to meet the witches and see their craft ... but her exposure to the magic did not phase her like she had seen it before. She let that question hang until Rex nudged her.

"Have you?"

"I ... I don't know," she said honestly. They walked past a house with a shadow gliding past a window. The chill Poe got told her it was not a person, but that was not what made her go numb. The witches. She warmed to them quickly, just as they had warmed to her quickly.

"We think you'd make a suitable companion for her."

"Are you all right?" Rex prompted. "You look a little pale. Did I ... bring up something?"

Poe shook her head. "No, it's ... no. It's just that..."

They walked on, Rex feigning interest in the shadows on the next house, even after they rose up and disappeared.

"I don't really remember much," Poe admitted. "My entire childhood is kind of hazy."

"You said you were an orphan," prompted Rex.

"Yeah, sold to servitude, at some point. I just don't remember anything before that. I don't even remember my family ... if I even had one. I have no idea where I come from."

They passed a quiet neighborhood, Poe dwelling on her last sentence, the most truthful thing she admitted to Rex and out loud to herself for the first time in a long time. She walked with her face lowered to the ground, praying for Rex to bring up a different subject and start talking about anything. Anything at all. She wished some giant demon beast would come out.

"Kid," Rex started, putting a hand on her arm to stop her from walking.

"I don't—"

"Shh!"

Poe forgot her moment of insecurity as it seemed her wish had come true, though now she stood there with regret at the sea of fog forming before them. She even could see her breath now, exhaling in a light puff, adding to the fog to make it thicker.

"You feel that," she said, not a question.

Rex, still holding her, pulled her back.

"This ... this is bad..."

She followed his lead as he urged the two of them to walk back, though the fog now seemed to surround them. It blended with the night just enough to erase the line between the sky and the ground. Poe could see something through the fog ahead of them, something moving, and moving quickly.

"What's that?" She pointed. "Look, it's—"

"Duck!" Rex cried, pulling Poe to the left and ducking down by the ground. In a flash, they both saw the thing that was racing down the street, or rather, gliding. The transparent outline showed that it was a human or in human form, the way its arms stretched out ... but its legs were straight out behind it. It flew at them so fast that its clothing whipped behind it like it was flying at a rapid speed, though they did not know how. Its arms stayed ahead of them, with one still and stiff and the other desperately grabbing at the air. The figure, male, turned its head and looked directly at Poe and Rex. They could hear the wailing that came out of its mouth in a permanent oval of terror, and as it rushed past them, it reached out to grab Poe. Rex pulled her down just as the figure passed over them and almost through them. Poe hit the dirt and felt the dust of the dirt go up her nose at the same time she felt the ice brush across her back. For the moment, they were both clouded in the fog that brought the temperature down around them and then it was gone. Poe raised her head as the flying ghost continued down the street ... only now she could see the ropes that were tied around its ankles, dragging behind it in afterthought. The ends were frayed, cut in haste from wherever they were tied, or possibly torn away. The figure still reached out with its one arm, wailing, trying to grab anything, all while its other arm stayed straight ... still attached to whatever it had been attached to in life. Poe watched it as much as she could until it was gone. For a moment, they stood transfixed to the scene, listening to nothing but their breath, and then Poe listened to Rex's increase.

"Geez, did you, oh my Lord what! Did you see?! Did you see *that*?! A full one, a *real* body it was!"

Rex was pacing and running his fingers through his hair and through his beard.

"Ghost!" he cried again, extending his arms to his sides. "Ghost, ghost, ghost!"

Rex rummaged through his bag to pull out his electromagnetic device, turning it on. The red and green lights flashed, the green ones blinking while the hand in the middle waved back and forth. Rex looked from the distance to the device to back again, his mouth opening and closing like he could not decide whether to shout or stay quiet.

"God all mighty," was all he said. Poe was still looking down the road, just as the fog was starting to thin. She squinted her eyes like she wanted to see it again.

"There was something ... familiar about that," he said. "Like something I've seen in one of my books."

Poe kept her eyes trained, the fog staying fog until it became nothing but air.

Rex turned his head down the streets, scanning all of them. He tugged his hood further over his head. "Let's head home, now."

They disappeared through the fog, hearing the sound of howls in the distance, and the occasional squeaking of bats through the trees. Rex took them off the streets and down the sidewalks in power walks, although it was clear that he did not put away the electromagnetic device. To either his relief, or disappointment, the lights stayed on red all the way home.

Upon entering their house, Rex wanted to head to the basement to look for the particular book he mentioned.

"I'll show you, as soon as I find it," he stated. "But it's the exact same clothing, exact time period."

He ran downstairs and to the shelves, scanning the spines until he found the one.

"Here," he said, opening it and flipping the pages. He stopped at the very one and held it so Poe could see it.

"Those are the early colonists," Rex stated. "The ones that fought in the battles I told you about."

Poe pulled the book a little closer to her, peering at the men in the photo, standing together as soldiers. Poe especially saw the ones at the end, the ones in the puffy shirts with long sleeves, trousers cropped at the knees, and the shoes. The shoes with the square buckles were a dead giveaway. But she still did not quite understand.

"It looked like him," she said. "Wearing something like this. But ... I don't understand how he died."

Rex took the book and flipped a few pages. The next photo Poe saw was the dire opposite of a group of men looking proud. One man was standing with his arms bound over his head, tied to the tree branch above him while his legs were tied to a stake in the ground. The illustration showed that it was nighttime, and from the looks of a sketchy shadow, about to get a visitor.

"This is a part of the town's history," Rex added. "Let's just say we know where the vengeful spirits come from."

Poe looked at the picture now with her own replay in her head: something coming to claim this live bait and tearing it from its bounds, dragging it away down the street while it did nothing but scream of its horrible fate.

"They were criminals, or people accused of being criminals, forced to carry out a drastic sentence. But a lot of the times, it was just a sacrifice." Rex turned more pages, and they looked at more pictures together: executions in public, sans the public, all safe and sound except for the condemned. Figures stood together, as many as three tied to the same tree, all wearing the same white cotton gown, already looking like they were dead. Poe felt a jolt of realization that she knew exactly where that tree was. She stood in that very square, looking up upon it live and in person, as it had its own way of telling her its significance. She could feel it again now, remembering the way it looked like something was moving in the air, now realizing it was those three empty ropes.

"This one and this one," Rex said, putting down pictures of humanoids with horns. "Oh, and plenty of these."

He held the pictures of flying skeletons over trees, wings spread and outlining every detailed bone. They looked like angels of death. Poe figured that was what they actually were.

"Right," Rex went on. "What else?"

Poe searched through her own pile of photos. "Well, we have the Nether flyer, the vampire burrs, the wailing ghosts we saw..." She added her collection to Rex's.

The knock on the door made them both gather their photos in a hurry.

"Coming, coming!" Rex called.

He answered the door to Mayor Vivienne wrapped up in a colorful wool coat and matching hat.

"Hello!" he said.

"Hi Rex," she responded while stepping in. "Thanks for having me stop by."

"The pleasure is ours."

Vivienne came into the living room with an automated interest in the mess of photos on the table.

"So, here's what we got," Rex began. "This group over here is confirmation of what we saw. This middle pile here is what others saw and gave to us, and the rest are ones that were just seen before in general but not recently. Some we photocopied from books."

Vivienne took up the pile of confirmed sightings, flipping through each one and nodding nonchalantly. "More of the usual," she said. "But, more in general at any given time."

"Yep," agreed Rex.

"I could hear a poltergeist making noise the other night."

She put the pile to the side and went to the middle one, viewing each one after the other. Some she looked at for only a few seconds and others she looked at longer, imagining seeing them for herself, but it seemed like those were the ones she had seen for herself.

"Yep, there definitely have been more of these out," she said. "That we know for certain. You're doing a tremendous job. Both of you."

Vivienne added a grin to Poe, who beamed.

"Our plans are coming together and I think we can be prepared. We have to do our best."

"And we will," Rex replied.

He talked about the past years and the things of things he saw, rambling a bit, but the mayor did not seem to be paying much attention. She was picking up pictures and illustrations from a section of the table that could have been in one pile or the other. She would give each one a look before moving on to the next.

One she picked up caused her to gasp, dropping the picture. Rex stopped talking. She swallowed a large gulp, and for a minute she did not blink. She only came to when Rex said her name.

"Mayor Vivienne? Ma'am?"

"Oh," she replied, giving a little shake. "I'm—I'm sorry."

"You just—what were you looking at?"

"I ... I..." she stammered. "No, it's..."

The mayor gestured to the table, and Poe and Rex remembered which picture she had. Poe picked it up, and they observed it. It was a drawing as detailed as it could be, which was not much, but had enough color, shading, and lines. The figure was the shape of a man, though hard to tell if the figure was a living man or just the spirit of one. He looked ... crooked, almost hunched over. The sketch made him seem like he was made out of the amber light fumes from a weak lantern, there but not. His face was too dark to have any features except an uneven, toothy grin and hollow eyes that almost seemed to glow. Almost. What did glow, almost indefinitely, was what he held. It was a decayed head. It was lumpy and misshapen, small enough to be a child or humanoid with big eye holes and a wide mouth with uneven teeth ... holding the same uneven, toothy grin the holder had.

"Have you seen *that*?" the mayor asked.

Poe looked at Rex for signs of recognition, though his brow remained crossed.

"Either of you?" she tried again. "Ever? Have you seen that?"

"No," Rex answered. "I have never seen that before."

Rex shrugged and looked at Poe, who shook her head. Vivienne seemed a little relieved, if not still alarmed.

"What is it?" Poe asked.

Vivienne came around the coffee table, arms crossed tightly at the elbows.

"This is an old legend," she started. "This is a man who was known as 'Stingy Jack.' He was a trickster, and he tried the devil many times. When he died, he was not admitted into Heaven and the devil did not want him in Hell, so he cursed Stingy Jack for eternity. He gave him a lump of burning coal to light his way through the night. See this here?" She pointed to the head the man was carrying. Poe knew exactly why it looked so disturbing. The lump of burning coal was inside the head, hollowed out, and used as a lantern.

"It's a … turnip," Vivienne said, like it was worse than a human head, and what Poe did not expect.

"A turnip?"

"Yes … it was a turnip, though people believed it was a real human head and it very well looked like one, but he took it and turned it into a lantern of sorts. He made it look like a face to scare off demons…"

Vivienne's voice broke off, and she stared at nothing and nowhere for a minute.

"I've—I've got to run," she said, handing the photo to Poe. "I just remembered something. Sorry."

"All right, Ms. Mayor, thanks for stopping by," Rex stated as she turned and left without a second's delay, leaving the two of them with blank minds and expressions. Rex held on to the picture as though he were trying to see what she saw.

"What was that all about?" Poe asked.

"The turnip face," remarked Rex.

"What?"

"The mayor actually has an irrational fear of turnips, and now I know why. She's not as bad as she used to be, but one time one of the farmers told me a story about how he was trying to sell them at a market day event and she saw them and apparently almost fell over and made him get rid of all them."

"Really?" half-laughed Poe.

"Yeah, really. They're banned in this town."

Rex put the picture back on the table, prompting Poe to revisit the image with a new perspective. The head did look like a turnip, and the turnip did look like a head. If Poe saw a hollowed-out thing with glowing eyes and mouth there's no doubt she would also think it was a real head.

"Vivienne is not afraid of anything. I bring her dead imps I found in the garden and undead demon skulls and she doesn't blink. But she sees a picture of a carved-out turnip and she forgets how to breathe."

"Stingy Jack" and his turnip-head lantern stared up at Poe, his face so dirty and gaunt it could have been all skull and teeth. No, the only face that looked human was that supposed turnip, and the shape of smooth, aged flesh, its eyes and mouth open holes wailing its last wail while the embers of the coal burned through.

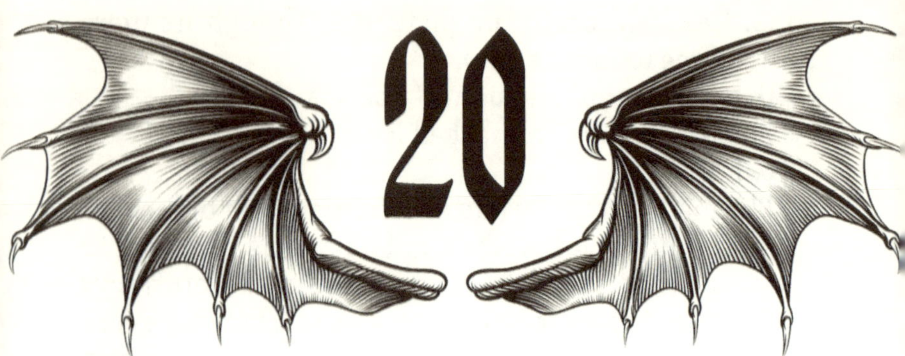

20

oe had to pull the wagon a bit more over the uneven sidewalks, and then up the pathway to the front door of the town hall. Heads all turned as they rolled in, even more so with anticipation as to the contents of Poe's wagon.

It was Anton and Carl who came down the aisle first, quickening their steps once they saw what Poe had in the wagon.

"They're finished?"

"Let's see!"

Poe set the wagon down to dish out her creations, specific ones for specific people. These were a bit like Rex's, one large coat of furs and one heavy cloak with a long hood. Anton tried one on, a giant hairy beast, while the one Carl picked up made him look like a Grim Reaper, especially with his size and skinny frame. Poe grinned as the men pulled out their coin pouches and handed her bunches of coins.

"Brilliant! We look just like the demons of the night," said Anton.

Carl tried his on, snickering. "What do you mean? We're going to be scarier than demons of the night. They'll run from *us*."

Poe took out the rest of them for their friends and colleagues, all the equivalent of long, black cloaks with horn-shaped hoods, four each. The men put them on with pride and joy, maybe even feeling a little devious themselves. They fit perfectly, as she knew they would. She sorted out the others: the jumpsuits, the ones that were darker than what they would typically wear, with strips of torn fabric. Light, gossamer, so when the wind picked up they would float, looking like the movement of a many-legged creature running at full speed.

Poe picked up the one for Babs as she came down first, her team behind her in equal enthusiasm. They all had hoods too, of course, covered in clean chaos of torn and layered fabrics. Babs picked up the garment and held it up to her, playing with the loose pieces of tulle.

"Oooo," Babs said, her eyes big behind her glasses. "Look at this. It almost looks like it has multiple legs. Like a spider! I'm going to look like some big monstrous spider thing!"

"That's the point," Poe reminded her with a grin. Babs returned one of her own, holding the outfit against her chest as her colleagues picked up their own altered many-legged jumpsuits. One by one, they handed Poe more coins, her pouch feeling just a little heavier.

Poe watched the recipients of her creations, imagining each one as her creations out in the streets at night, all out after Shut-In, all to feel the night air just like a night creature would.

Someone else entered and interrupted all of them, someone who also pulled on a wagon holding some kind of important contents. Everyone raised a curious and confused brow. The mayor walked in first, holding a medium-sized pumpkin in her arms, the stem curling around her as though it wanted to have a tight grip on her, or her on it. Behind her, her assistant rolled in this wagon full of more pumpkins. And behind her rolled in Ezra, the man who once had a spirit in his garden. His wagon was the fullest, and so was his grin.

"My apologies for being late," Vivienne called out. "I have more matters to discuss!" She stopped short at all the people either wearing their disguises or trying them on. She looked them up and down before nodding and smiling at Poe.

"Very nice."

She cast a look at Poe that suggested she was more than pleased. The smile in her eyes told Poe that she was impressed but also hopeful. Throughout her time as mayor and lifetime in that village, any new idea might be a good one. Her look had hope.

"They'll blend in."

"They sure will," Poe agreed.

"And that's because *you* can."

Poe felt the tickle in her stomach. It had nothing to do with her, really. She could not turn people into other things ... she wasn't a witch.

The mayor and her assistant went to the front of the hall, where Ivy and Emme Briar-Whittle stood near a cauldron.

"Now," the mayor began. "Aside from everything else we need to go over, I have something new to bring. I was over at Rex and Poe's home recently where I was viewing pictures of demons, creatures, and spirits, and I saw one that prompted, well, an old memory. And it gave me an idea." She held up the pumpkin for everyone to see, and then she slowly rotated it to show what she really wanted everyone to see. Poe was taken aback at what the mayor created, at the last thing she expected her to re-create. She stared at the holes cut into the gourd, though triangular shaped, it was obvious they were the eyes and the nose. The large sideways oval was the mouth, cut big enough to show the empty inside.

"There is a legend of a spirit, long ago, who was doomed to wander the earth by the devil, given a burning coal to light his way. He carved out a vegetable and placed the coal in it to make a lantern." She paused.

"And in the darkest nights ... it looked like a human head." She held up the pumpkin, smoothing over the front part.

"I knew that our friend Ezra Stimola here had a hefty crop of pumpkins this year with no use for them, and I believe I can help him out with that. We are going to make our own lanterns. Everyone can get a pumpkin, carve it out completely, carve a face in it, and put a candle in it. We can all put them in our windows, on porches, on doorsteps, and they just might help scare away evil beings. They certainly look frightening..."

The mayor's assistant held a small candle and lit it. The mayor lifted the top off of the pumpkin, already cut out so that it functioned as a lid, and placed the lit candle inside. The tiny flame did wonders for the hollowed-out gourd as instantly the face appeared, the holes for the eyes and mouth illuminated, enchanting the room.

There was a murmur among the group of everyone at once, ecstatic and entranced. The mayor held the pumpkin head for all to see and placed it on the table, like some malevolent beacon to worship. Ezra immediately picked up a large pumpkin for everyone to see with another face carved in it, eyes shaped like almonds with pupils and all, and an open mouth with teeth. He placed it on the table and lit a candle for this one as well, joining the other. Surely, hundreds of those all around the town would do something to let the demons of the Nether realm think that perhaps there was more than what it seemed.

After the meeting, Rex wasted no time telling Poe they were going on another excursion that night.

"People have been telling me things," he said in a low tone as they were leaving the town hall. "Of something seen wandering around the edge of town. All black-robed, hooded, couldn't see its face, but it was speaking in tongues. Could be some sort of evil spirit. It's not a demon lord, but I think it is something trying to open more portals. It might be the very thing that has opened more portals. We're going after it tonight."

"What do we need?" Poe asked. "The ghost hunting equipment?"

"Not sure. This is something new."

That evening Rex made a nice dinner of chicken with rice, the white meat plump and satisfactory with Poe getting her fill. It occurred to her that something happened during her time in her new home. She remembered when she first came, back when she walked into Rex's life and his life of bachelordom, of eating out of cans and using all of his living space as garbage space. She hadn't seen garbage in weeks and noticed how Rex would be up before her to make sure there was a meal for both of them. Her meals used to be whatever she could scrounge up, and whatever was left over for her to pick on. It occurred to her that having a fresh, hot meal was a luxury, and it was something she could not get enough of. All of a sudden it became the new normal for the two of them, for whatever reason. She sat back in her chair feeling satisfied in being full, something else that had become her new normal, and would have liked to rest off the digestion for a bit if Rex hadn't already gathered the plates. Outside, the chimes went off, and a carriage charged down the street of someone wanting to get home in the nick of time. Poe took the last gulp of milk as Rex put a lid on the pot.

"You ready to go after this hooded spirit thing?"

Poe smiled and sat up. "Yeah, gimme a second."

Rex chuckled. "I think I am starting to spoil you."

They put their shoes on and went over to the peg on the wall for their jackets. Poe opted for the raven one, observing the fabric fragments that got a bit torn during their adventures, and made a note to herself to fix it up and add more. Rex adjusted his wolf hood in the mirror, letting his beard out over his shirt. They left the house with the bags of equipment ready by the door, the carriage well gone, along with everyone else.

"It was last seen..." Rex started. "Er, back behind the nursery and preschool building. Someone saw it out of their window and cornered me when I was out, bringing someone a trap one time. It could have been wearing all black or something just made of shadows. Spooked them right off."

Poe did not catch a feeling of anything near them as they walked along, even looking around very carefully to see if anything would form out of the dark. Rex was doing the same, until at one point, he rushed the two of them behind a building.

"Shhh."

He motioned to Poe to stay flat against it, keeping his hand up in a stop sign, but she got the confirmation in her gut already. At Rex's signal, they peeked around the corner at something a few feet away, moving past the houses. Its back turned, all it looked like was a piece of darkness itself moving on its own.

"I think that might be it," Rex mumbled. "Let's follow it."

They trailed the thing, leaving enough space between them and their subject. From the distance it stopped, turning side to side as if to decide on a direction, ultimately picking one that led closer to the entrance of the town.

"Where is it going?" Poe asked.

"I don't know."

They ducked behind a house, narrowly avoiding the rope traps set at the front, which were still undisturbed. The dark figure raised its arms, waving them in any general direction.

"It is true, then. It seems to be a demon that is doing something. Summoning more demons. Opening another portal!"

Poe already got a container out of her bag. "Well, no better time than the present!"

She looked to Rex for his signal, for his cooperation, and he was already inching along on the grass. "Come on," he said to her in low tones.

Together, they crept along. Rex moved like he was in a hurry but did not want to make any noise, and was challenging with his thick boots and overall large build. Poe, however, trod along as though she could make herself weightless, a surprise to both her and Rex.

"How are you doing that?" whispered Rex, as he winced at the light crunch of a leaf under his shoe. Poe's footsteps seemed to bypass any leaf, stone, or twig completely.

"Skill I guess," Poe answered.

They both stopped talking when they were near enough to the figure, near the front gate welcoming or warning entrants to Mock Cob Village. They were close enough to see this particular demon was not very tall, but thin enough to possibly be made of just bone, and to hear a low voice murmuring words neither of them could make out. Poe and Rex stood still, feet arched, so that they were almost on their tip-toes, as the figure continued to chant. The figure stood with its arms frozen in an extended position. Before Rex or Poe could do anything, its head turned, the tip of its nose pointed right in their direction. They stood there ready to run while the figure removed its black hood and pieces of dark red hair fell down.

Rex and Poe fell into relief, if not still confused.

"Oh!" Rex exclaimed sheepishly. "Oh! Uh, er, sorry. Thought you were a demon. I mean, you do look like one. Sort of."

Bernadette smirked, making casual eye contact with Poe.

"What are you doing?"

Bernadette cringed at the question, knowing that she was going to ask it. Poe just knew that she was not expecting anyone to see her out there.

"I've just been out ... trying to find it," Bernadette answered in a small voice. "The opening."

"The opening?"

"To the other side. To the Nether realm. I feel like we need to attack within, and that's the only way to solve all of this. If I can find the opening, then maybe I can close it."

Rex and Poe's eyes were equally wide.

"I mean, not completely," Bernadette rushed. "Just enough for the dead to be able to pass when it's their time, but I am talking about the other stuff. I am trying to find it so I can seal it off from the other stuff."

Bernadette brushed off dirt and whatever dust and magic powder was on her sleeve. They missed the rod she held in her hand before, thin enough to hide in her sleeve.

"Do you think you can find it?" Poe asked with interest.

"I'd like to. I am trying. It's ... it's almost impossible. This is not something that can be seen with the human eye, that's for sure. It's complicated."

"Well, we're glad you're not a demon trying to do anything else," Rex replied. "We'll leave you to it and make sure there are no poltergeists around or anything."

"Right. Happy hunting."

Rex and Poe turned to leave, only getting a few steps before Bernadette blurted out.

"Wait."

Rex and Poe turned.

"Please don't tell my moms you saw me out here."

"No, we won't," Poe answered for the both of them. "You got it."

21

Notice:

The communal collecting of meltable candies and sweets will take place leading up to and during The Night of Passing by select individuals, on a special mission by the mayor for the purpose of a solution made by our resident Briar-Whittle witch family. The candies are crucial ingredients for the protective mixture, and any and all kinds are needed. Please be advised that visiting candy collectors will all be disguised to conceal themselves as demons and might easily be mistaken as demons, so please do not be alarmed. Your cooperation and contribution are much appreciated at this time.

Thank you,
Mayor Vivienne Tellenboe and
Mock Cob Town Hall

They had the notice taped to their refrigerator, as a reminder, as a token of pride. Every time Poe approached it to get a drink or something to eat, she felt that ping of pride, though at times, she was also contemplating how that notice would read to others. Would they be accepting and welcoming to disguised visitors coming to their doors? Would any of them carry a weapon, just in case? She pulled out a bowl of fruit to snack on something, something to occupy her while she stayed busy. Up in her room, she had almost everything laid out on the floor, even some clothing pieces to mix and match with other clothing pieces for visual. She had a book or two for reference and some folds of new fabric sitting still unused. She held the bowl of fruit and popped a few berries in her mouth while looking at all of it from a bird's-eye angle, hoping for any new ideas. Rex's footsteps sounded ahead of her.

"Hey, how is it going?"

"All right."

He saw her fashion floor layout. "I thought you were going to go all out and make something new."

"Well, that is what I am trying to do," Poe explained. "I am just not sure what to do and with what."

Rex leaned against the doorframe, reaching over her shoulder to steal a strawberry.

"You said you were going to do something insane with big horns and a long tail and stuff."

"Yeah," started. "But, like I don't want to just make something up. I want to look like them. Like something real."

She scowled while scanning her inventory. Aside from the crow-beaked hoodie and the cloak with the jackalope antlers, everything looked human. Strange aside, just still human.

"You did amazing with those fur jackets and hoods," Rex suggested. "They look like wolves or hell hounds. Especially mine. It looks like it is a part of me."

"But that doesn't fit my body type. It fits yours, and Anton, and those big guys. I am just having a hard time figuring out what I could be. It has to be believable."

Rex scooped another handful of fruit. "I'm sure you'll figure it out. And whatever you do go with, it will work. You're a natural. I am going to head out and run some errands. Need anything?"

"Nah."

"All right. I'll see you later."

Rex left and Poe continued with what she was saying to herself. "I feel like I need to be something I have seen before."

She went and sat down on the floor, putting the bowl in her lap while picking up a nearby book. She flipped through those pages again, eying the illustrations and the garments spread out in suggestion. Sure, there were robed demons, but real demons were taller than her. There were horned imps, but she did not have anything red. There were goblins, but she was too tall. She dug around in the bowl where there were slices of apples and crunched on one. The next page in the book showed skeletal beings, things that used to be animals, or just undead things that looked like animals. There were the bats she saw, and the hounds she saw as well, both encounters not too far from one another. Poe looked at the photos of those she had not seen before while she reached into the bowl for apple slices. While holding the slices, she saw the way the bones were shaped, and the idea sparked. She looked up, getting the visual in her head, before scrambling on the floor to look at her piles of outfits. Poe had plenty of black, sure, including black leggings and tops that were tight enough to be a bodysuit. She went over to her closet to look in the box again of unfinished projects, looking for that one black hood she had that had not attached to anything yet and pulled it out in glee, knowing that it was big enough, for she did not get the chance to shape it on her head just yet and was glad of it. It was going to shape around something specific now. She gathered these items and placed them on the floor next to the fruit bowl in front of her, from hood to long-sleeved shirt to leggings. Poe pictured this now, in pure perfection in her head. Now, it was a matter of fabrication. Still holding the apple slices, she placed them on the shirt strategically before plucking more out of the bowl until she formed a complete set of ribs.

Poe then made her way out of her room and downstairs to the basement, thinking of what she saw in those boxes. Foam-padded sheets, sure, but they were white and probably easy to cut and shape and get the look she was going for. But how much was in those? And did Rex even need them? They were packed covering glass picture frames that he already put up on the wall, so it wasn't like he needed them anymore. Poe found the boxes and pulled out the foam sheets, as well as the picture frames themselves, which would be plenty to work from. She excitedly pulled out a few more sheets, her fingers grazing the edges, already imagining how she would make the shapes. She held the pile in her arms while she thought about what the next thing would be, the thing that would be more of a challenge. Over by the cluttered table and shelves were the jars of different specimens. Poe walked up to the shelves to browse, going straight to the big ones with different-sized skulls. She did not think Rex had any of normal animals, but she wanted to base it off something close enough. At least with the teeth and jawline. She picked up one that was similar, or very close to what she had in mind. The teeth looked about right; the structure looked like it could pass. She could make something like that and even look up real photos of any animal skull she wanted for reference. She held the jar in front of her and stared into the eyeless holes, trying to imagine what the creature looked like in life. No doubt, covered in glossy black fur with amber-yellow eyes for seeing in the dark. That alone felt right.

Rex and Poe's hammering drummed to a single beat, almost as one. Rex went faster than Poe, making sure the stake was all the way in the ground before tying the rope around it.

"Okay, this one's good," he stated. He tugged on the rope leading to the net trap, spread out and covered in leaves. Poe tugged on hers as well, still bent over. She stood up and put her hands at her waist.

"So now what?"

Rex headed over. "We go inside."

"What?"

He eyed her. "You heard me."

"But the chimes didn't even go off yet," Poe declared.

"That's the point." Rex surveyed the area of their work one last time, squinting at the upcoming sunset.

"This is our last chance to test everything. And to do that, we have to stay in and watch. Just to be sure."

Poe let the hammer slide in her hand but did not drop it right away. The first set of chimes went off, and like clockwork, Rex gestured to Poe to follow him inside.

"If you thought it was bad before, wait. It's go time, kiddo. You don't know what you're getting into and I don't want you out in this right away. Do you understand?"

"Yeah," she answered.

They were careful to step inside the house, tiptoeing over the threshold to not disturb a single grain of powder out of place. It was pink, so it was easy to see, but last time Poe accidentally scuffed some of it away it made Rex panic. He had sprinkled more in the area, gently patting it as though he were trying to make a perfect line. "If you mess with that, then spirits will be able to enter the house. Be careful!" he had warned.

Poe followed Rex into the house. He went to the curtains to close them enough, though still wanted a small view out. The chimes sounded a second time as Rex went to the kitchen to get matches. Poe noticed he did not clean up too much of the pumpkin guts. The majority of them were still slathered all over the newspapers on the table, some if not most of them still holding seeds. Rex picked up the behemoth he carved, complete with slanted eyes and eyebrows and a wide, jagged mouth. Poe was too busy watching Rex carve his to have made one of her own, taking too much enjoyment out of the way his tongue stuck out a bit as he traced lines with a marker and then looked it at to make sure it was just right before carving. He lit a candle and placed it inside, the wicked eyes and open mouth sure enough to scare anything.

"I know just where this baby is going," Rex declared, bringing it over to a stool he had by the window and putting the curtains around it. "See look, it's like it's looking out the window!"

He then reopened the front door he had just locked and Poe's jaw dropped open in protest.

"I will just be a second. Stay here!"

Rex scampered outside, sidestepping all net traps across his lawn. He backed up enough and went to the side window, where he made a facial expression that was more than pleased. He bounced up and down on his feet and pointed to it in the window to Poe, who had her hands on her hips.

"It looks fantastic," Rex said as he came back in and bolted the door like nothing had happened. "And at night, it will look even better."

The candle flame flickered inside the hollow gourd, the carved-out face reflecting off of the window. It was casting a wavering orange glow that could give the impression that this face was emerging from fire. Rex adjusted the curtains around it before stepping away from the window.

"Now we just wait, I guess."

He headed into the kitchen, groaning at the mess of pumpkin guts he had neglected, and started pulling at the newspapers. "I'll soak these seeds and bake 'em for later," he commented.

Poe left him to finish plucking seeds from the orange slime, going up to her room to check on her work. They were all folded into separate piles on the carpet, one for each person, things going with each item. All were done, except of course for her own, the one she needed more time to get each and every piece exactly right, all the right shapes and everything. Poe went over to the windowsill where she placed it to the side, leaning in to observe the pieces on the outfit to see that some were still sticky with the recent dabs of glue she'd applied earlier. Leaving it be, she instead looked to the window at the premature darkness starting to spread. She frowned. It had only just turned dusk.

Poe pushed on the window with care, looking across the roof to a sky of a deepening blue. Her ears perked, maybe even moving an inch to stretch to try to pick up hidden sounds. She went out on the balls of her feet and the tips of her fingers to scale the top of the roof, keeping low. *Was that thunder?*

She stayed near a point where she could see most of what was below ... and it was not much due to the growing fog. Something must have punctured a hole in a cloud somewhere because the fog was filling up the ground like a running faucet. It rushed through the ground below, surrounding the houses to create a bottomless sea. The thunder sound grumbled in the sky, and the pit in Poe's stomach told her it was too animalistic to be thunder. She looked at the clouds and began to visualize pictures from the shapes, a habit of anyone looking at them for a long time. It was easy to do so. For many times, one's brain could make the clouds into anything they wanted, and they stayed that way the longer one looked at them. Poe distinctively spotted one that started its own cloud formation, one standing out from the rest in a different darker color, much like a malignant spot appearing on the skin among freckles. It formed from an oval-shaped cloud and dropped to a narrower oval, with smaller cloud bursts coming out of it to make points that were to make new shapes. It curved and curled, the four points sticking out looking like four legs. And then, the top formed to a head, a head with a long visage and pointed ends. Two dark holes appeared in the right places, dim enough and narrow enough to be a predatory gaze. As the shape sharpened, it grew in size, the legs getting longer and skinnier, the back end with a tail swishing in the middle of a run. The formation darkened as it only grew bigger, bit by bit, right in front of Poe's eyes with the realization that it was moving down from the sky at a rapid speed. It was as big as the house now, the legs now moving fast enough to be galloping, the form now the blackest storm cloud taking over the entire sky. The face became clearer now, though still dark it was enough to make out the long face and points that were ears. Tiny puffs of cloud exhaled from its nose, a creature on the run, its dim glowing eyes reddening to a bloody pink.

Poe threw herself down on the roof as the creature from the sky darkened her entire surroundings. The massive shadow passed over her, coming low enough for her to feel the breeze of it dashing by. She made herself as flat as possible while the chill went from the base of her neck to her tailbone. Once the breeze passed, she allowed herself to turn her head. She saw nothing, but down below in the streets, she could hear the continuous galloping of hooves. Poe brought herself back to a crouched position to view the town as much as she could. The fog still moving, she could make out a few shapes lingering and making their way around. There was the occasional flap of wings and a screech or two coming from the wooded areas. Wherever that cloud steed was, it was gone. Poe made her way down the roof, all the way down to the storm pipe, wrapping around it and scaling down. From down there, the fog was not too thick, and once her eyes adjusted to it, she could see all right. She turned the corner, not wanting Rex to spot her from the window, though she did not want anything else to spot her either. She peeked out to the streets, where in the distance she could see some sort of goblin with a long, forked tail crawling out from the fog. It disappeared behind another house, tail sticking up in glee or discovery that she did not want to know about.

Poe still stood stiffly, not making any quick movements, trying to let her own ears pick up anything. After a while, she moved back around to the side of the house with the storm pipe and climbed it with the speed she did not have on the ground. She crawled back onto the roof and did another scan of the area, especially looking back up at the sky at the clouds. They stayed stoic, not committing to any other shapes.

22

oe rushed down the stairs with an armful of outfits, folding up the fabrics she was almost tripping
over. She found the wagon where she left it by the door,
piling it all in and then heading out.

The sun blasted through the leaves of each tree on
the sidewalk, making their already changing colors
appear brighter. As Poe rolled down, a few bursts
of wind blew a fallen collection at her legs, leaves as
orange as though the sun were responsible for staining
them in the first place. She noticed other orange things
that lifted her spirits, and although a grotesque nature,
made her smile. There were already a few houses that
had them, that made them, and although made crudely,
it made them all the better. One sat in the window, a
small plump one with two big holes for eyes and then a
sideways oval for a mouth. Simple enough, but with a
candlelight in it, it could very well be the face of a fiery
demon in the night. Another had a larger one right on
the porch, impaled on top of a post to create the right silhouette. Poe rushed down the streets and onto the one
with Something Stirring, just as she watched the smoke

rushing out of the chimney. She leaned in to knock, fist paused in the air as she listened.

"...could have helped, you know!"

"Hon, it wasn't that much. We just managed to put it together."

"Sure, when I wasn't around! How convenient!"

"Bernie, would you just—"

Poe jumped back as the door opened.

"Hey, look, Poe's here," Bernadette said, opening the door wide so she could come in.

Poe came into the shop, rolling in her wagon and seeing Bernadette spy its contents.

"What do you have?"

Poe rolled the wagon all the way in where she could see Ivy and Emme, and they could see it too.

"Hi Ivy, Emme," Poe greeted.

"Hey there."

"Hi Poe."

"I came by with some things. I had a feeling you would like them," Poe said. She rolled the wagon over so that she could see it, right on top, sitting straight up with its odd shape. Poe kept the smile on her face as Bernadette bent down to peer at it.

"What is it?"

"Here!" Poe cried, lifting the object and placing it right on Bernadette's head. Bernadette allowed her to, feeling the brim and the cone shape and then walking down to find a mirror. Poe followed in glee, watching Bernadette's reflection and her initial expression.

The hat fit her perfectly, as she thought it would, and though the brim was wide, it gave the perfect balance and shape. Poe was especially excited about the shape. The tall cone she fabricated gave Bernadette's head a pointed head. And the colors. The mix-match was glorious, with all the black, orange, green, and purple fabrics complementing one another. Poe was already holding up the cape and held it open so Bernadette could try on the whole ensemble. She stepped back as she tied the strings while still standing in front of the mirror. Poe was beaming. Bernadette looked at herself like she did not recognize herself.

"Poe, this is..."

"Do you like it?"

"It's—it's incredible. You made this?"

Poe grinned. "Yeah. I know you like purples and blacks, and I found some more fabrics that go with those."

Bernadette could not stop touching the hat, feeling from the brim all the way up the odd conical shape.

"You made this for me?"

"Yup."

"Why?"

Poe eyed her mothers, who each had a smirk at the side of their mouth so that they formed one long smile.

"I have been making some ... disguises, some altered outfits to make it so some people can go out at night. When they do. When they can. Like now."

"Bernadette," started Emme. "What we were trying to tell you before is that you *will* have a special part in this. We made the solution, but we are going to need more ingredients, especially for the Night of Passing. We want you to be one of the ones tasked to go out and collect it."

Bernadette looked up. "I can?"

"Yes," Ivy continued. "In disguise. Many will be. We need you to not only get what we need from all the neighbors and residents as you can, but we also need you to use the solution."

"Against the beasts."

"To stop them."

"To test it, to use it, as much as you can."

Bernadette had a new sparkle to her eye, her face lighting up, so much so that Poe could have sworn a few new freckles popped on her face.

"So I can go out and use it?" she repeated excitedly. "I can go out and fully experience this 'Night of Passing' and see ... everything?"

"Yes, you can," Ivy and Emme said.

"Don't worry," Poe added. "You weren't forgotten."

Bernadette turned back to the mirror, biting down on her lip. She kept adjusting the hat, holding the rim, and touching the long shape.

"This is ... strange. I have never seen a hat like this before."

"I got the idea from a photo of a demon with a long horn, and I had a thought. This sort of makes you look like you have one big scary one coming out of your head. In the dark, nothing is going to mess with you."

Bernadette swished the cape around her.

"You really made this for me."

"I did, and it looks great on you!"

Bernadette allowed a small smile. "No one's ever made anything for me before," she admitted.

They made eye contact in the mirror, Poe standing next to her friend. "Well, now someone has. And oh, check this out!"

Poe pulled at the rest of the stash in the wagon, taking out two more hats in a similar style, but both solid black, and showing them to Ivy and Emme.

"I had extra, so I made two for you as well."

Ivy and Emme each took one.

"Look at this."

"It's neat-looking."

"You have black robes, right?" Poe asked.

"Oh yeah, yeah, plenty of those!" said Ivy.

"We'll match perfectly," added Emme.

Both Ivy and Emme tried them on, rotating the brims and feeling the cones.

"These are one of a kind," Ivy said. "And you made these?"

"I did."

"Well, thank you so much, Poe."

"We love them!"

Ivy and Emme looked to one another and to Bernadette with their new items, temporarily forgetting about their work until Ivy broke the ice.

"The new brew is coming together," she said. "I used more heat this time. We had some candy with caramel in it, very sticky. It needed to melt more. But we think it makes it better."

"All right, excellent," Poe stated. "Do you think we'll have enough? Do you think it will be enough?"

"We will soon find out," Ivy answered. "But I think we got this."

Emme smiled at her and the girls, turning her head down just enough so that the brim of the hat covered all of her face but her devilish smirk. "We'll have enough of the solution to give out in the nights to come, for any and all who need it. We're ready."

Ivy motioned to the cauldron behind the counter, letting the girls go over to it while she lifted the lid. The steam greeted Poe and Bernadette as they peered in, inhaling the sweet aroma that was almost like candy soup. Poe watched Ivy stir it with the big wooden spoon, stained with mixtures of greens, blues, pinks, and reds.

"This is our more complex batch," Ivy explained. When she lifted the spoon, it fell as a thick waterfall of colors, folding on itself over and over again. "We see the colors brighten when it thinks it comes in contact with something, and then it will start to work right away."

"Faster than the stuff we used before?" asked Poe, going to stick her finger in before Ivy stopped her.

"Don't, it needs a bit more," she said.

Emme joined them behind the counter, holding a vial of something that looked like dry, old grass. She took some out and crinkled it in her fingers, letting it sprinkle in the mix while Ivy stirred it some more. The mixture bubbled and rose, almost boiling over, and as it fell back down, Poe could make out bubbles that looked like eyes and a big gaping mouth.

"It will be," Emme answered. "We tested a bit of it last night."

"Did you go out?" asked Poe.

"Just a little," Emme said, eying both Ivy and Bernadette.

"Well, *we* did," Ivy said, gesturing to her and her wife before Bernadette could say anything. "We did. We had to test everything out, and that included the protection potion we sprayed on ourselves."

"It was brief," added Emme. "But we went down the lawn to the sidewalk and then we saw a spirit standing in the middle of the road. We stayed quiet and then tossed some of the mixture on it and it froze right then and there! The spirit turned like a glossy pink, almost enough to be solid, but it didn't move."

"It works on ghosts?" asked Poe, incredulously.

"It does!" answered Ivy. "We were hoping it would! Spirits were one of the biggest challenges to get over as they're not tangible, but we still can't have them causing trouble and getting in the way."

"And there will be more of them. But now, I think that you'll be ready."

Bernadette looked like she could not make up her mind if she was excited or irritated.

"Especially now." She turned to Poe. "Poe, why don't I show you the outfits I have that can match this?"

"Okay!"

"Thanks for the hats, Poe," Ivy added. She and Emme pulled the rims, smiling, the hats looking equally good on both of them.

Poe followed Bernadette, it dawning on her that this was the first time she was being invited to Bernadette's room ... and seeing the personal domestic lives of the witches in general. She followed Bernadette up a hidden flight of stairs and through a regular-looking door. They were now in a kitchen area that had a mostly normal layout if it weren't for the stacks of cauldrons and mason jars by the counter. Poe caught a whiff of something cinnamon in the air but could not tell the source, and did not have much time to look.

"Come on, this way," Bernadette said. "My room's over here. Forgive the mess."

She opened a door and led Poe inside, flicking on a light that only confirmed what she said was a warning. Piles of books, clothes, cardboard boxes, papers, tote bags, wicker baskets, and bags of things filled Bernadette's floor. There was a string of purple lights along her window that gave the room a soft glow, making it look like it could always be nighttime. To the right corner was Bernadette's bed, a tangle of blankets, and some pillows that never stayed in the same place. To the left was something Poe took a liking to right away: a wicker chair on a stand with its own pillows.

"That's my favorite chair. You can sit in it if you want."

Poe obliged. "Wow, you got a lot of stuff in here."

Bernadette flopped on her bed and gave a little shrug. "I guess. I like messes. I know where everything is. My moms never stop flipping out about it. I just tell them I can't perfect a cleaning charm just yet." She snorted.

Poe swiveled in the chair, allowing her feet to come off the floor. "This is so cool."

Bernadette got quiet, watching her swing. "This is actually the first time I've ever had anyone come over."

Poe looked at her. "Oh. Really?"

"Yeah, well. I don't get out much. Homeschooled mostly and whatnot. Been looking forward to doing something like this for a long while." She looked at Poe. "They wouldn't let me go test everything with them last night."

"They wouldn't?"

"No," Bernadette said a little too harshly. "They still treat me like a baby sometimes. Told me I wasn't ready and blah blah blah."

"Rex wouldn't let me go out last night either," Poe stated. "We set traps and then the chimes went off and he scooted me inside. Well, I mean, I sort of did sneak out."

"You did?" perked up Bernadette.

"Yeah, I snuck out on my roof."

Bernadette laughed.

"Yeah, I ... well..."

Bernadette's smile faltered. "What? What did you see?"

Poe kept swiveling in the chair, listening to the rhythm of the squeaks. "Something came out of the sky. Some cloud that turned into this giant horse that ran or flew over me and then went somewhere."

"What..." Bernadette muttered.

"I went to try to find it ... it was like it raced through the town and made everything go still. Like some sort of weird horse spirit that came out of nowhere. I have no idea where it went, but it made it feel like time just stood still."

Bernadette shuffled the pillow in her lap.

"But that was it. I didn't see it again, and I didn't see anything else."

"It came from the sky," Bernadette repeated, more for herself.

"Yeah," Poe said. "I still sit out on my roof from time to time. I have to watch and see where everything comes from. I guess I will have to put on a disguise to do even that."

Bernadette got off her bed and opened her closet. She pulled out a black dress with ties on the front and long, flowing sleeves, holding it up to her.

"Well, this would look really good with that hat."

"It would!"

"I've got more. Hold on."

Bernadette then pulled out black and purple striped leggings and a pair of boots with curling toes.

"Those—those shoes are neat! Where did you get those?"

"These are customary style for ancient witches, actually. They're not worn that much anymore except sometimes for special occasions. I wore these to a cere-mony honoring a friend of my moms' who passed away, but that's pretty much it."

"They look like ... wow," Poe repeated. She got up to see them closer, marveling at the shape and the style. "These are such a strange enough shape. You'll look like you have curled feet. Very strange!"

Poe could not hold back her enthusiasm. Bernadette smirked.

"Then that's what I'll put on tonight. My moms will have me put on protective jewelry and stuff too, no doubt. What about you? What are you wearing?"

"Oh, it's neat. You'll see. I'll be as undead as they come, and nothing will want to eat me."

"Hopefully nothing will want to eat me either."

"Nothing will! This will work! I just hope we'll get enough," Poe commented. "I mean, I am so glad you and I are going to do this, and I know that some of the others are going to be out too, but it would be helpful if we had another one, you know?"

"Who else is going to want to go out during the Night of Passing in disguise from monsters and wicked spirits?"

Poe's expression changed, and from Bernadette's reaction, she already knew what she was thinking.

***

"Come on, let's go!"

Bernadette mumbled something, but Poe could not understand her with the food still in her mouth. She wiped her bread crumbs off her shirt while Bernadette put their dishes in the sink.

They went back down the stairs and Bernadette casually called to her mothers that she was going out. Busy with customers and pouring protective brews into bottles, they gave the girls a wave and went back to what they were doing.

They still had plenty of time outside, though they knew that they would have all the time in the world later. They jogged down the street, passing all the people making preparations to their houses with traps and boarding up all the windows. Poe was pleased to see many making use of the barrier powder that the witches made. She tried to catch Bernadette's expression to see if she noticed, but she was too busy trying to run faster.

"What's the rush?"

Bernadette didn't answer.

When they made it to their designated house, Bernadette stopped and cursed.

"Dammit..."

She looked around.

"Do you see any tree branches or anything around? I thought I tossed that big one in the bushes last time."

Poe searched the grounds. "No." She did see something else that was close enough. She walked over to the side of the house, nearly by the front door, and produced it for Bernadette.

"How's this?"

Bernadette stared at Poe standing there holding a broom.

"That's going to look ridiculous, but it will do."

"I'll go up first and make sure the coast is clear, and then I'll signal you."

"Okay."

Poe scaled the storm pipe and then crawled her way across the roof to the window. It was not conveniently cracked open like the last time, and to Poe's distress, it looked like something was barricaded across it from the inside. She pressed on it with her fingers, noticing the section to the left that had a hole big enough to see inside. Outside. She peered in, jumping back at the shadow that instantly joined her. Someone removed the board and the ghostly face appeared in the window with a grin. He opened the window.

"You came back," Caleb said with a clear voice, no longer as raspy.

"We did," Poe said. She turned behind her so that they could see each other, giving Bernadette the thumbs up. Bernadette awkwardly put the broom under her legs, trying to sit on something that was not meant to be sat on.

"Can we come up?"

Caleb answered by opening the window all the way and Poe climbed in. She noticed the piece of wood he held in his hands and how easy it was for him to remove. Caleb put the piece down as easily as it would be his thousandth time doing it, the window bare and exposed. Poe stood before Caleb and tried not to determine if he looked better or worse. His voice sounded better, though his visage was still pale and horrendous purple-black grooves caved in under his eyes. In moments, Bernadette joined them in the room, the bushy end of the broom brushing at the floor as she landed. Poe and Caleb stared at her.

"What? It works."

She placed the broom by the window and acknowledged Caleb.

"I am happy you both came back," Caleb said. "My mom is in the bath, and she brought wine and a book so she'll be in there awhile."

"How are you? How's it going?" Poe interrupted Bernadette.

"I'm all right. Bored mostly. Are you hunting the monsters?"

"I am," Poe answered. "And Bernadette and her moms made all sorts of protection potions and one that can freeze them in place. And it works."

"Do you know the notice that went around?" asked Bernadette. "About going to houses to collect candy? That's about us. That's what my moms are using to make the potions."

"It is?"

"We're going out tonight. To collect as much as we can to stop as many as we can."

Caleb thought for a minute.

"I wanted to ask you something, actually," Bernadette started. "When you say that you died, and ... you went somewhere, were you able to... see where you went? Like, what it looked like?"

Caleb's face stayed blank. "It was bright at first. Then, it got dim but was still clouded almost. I didn't really see ... how. I just woke up feeling like I was in a dream."

He was silent for a minute, in thought, then turned his attention back to the two of them.

Bernadette was studying him, even looking back to his bed to see if that would offer any clues.

"We're trying to get any information we can to help when the veil thins," explained Poe.

"It has already," Caleb answered. "There were more of them around last night, and the last few nights, I think. I've seen tall hooded demons disappear in the shadows, and Nether flyers fly across the sky. But ... so far, nothing came this way."

Poe did not say out loud that he sounded disappointed. He looked back at the window when something flew past, but it was only a bird.

"You want to see them for real?" blurted out Poe.

Caleb stared.

"This mission we're going on tonight ... we could use a third. Think you would and could be up for it?"

It took some time for the smile to form on Caleb's face because it was the first one that was genuine in a long time. Poe watched how his eyes turned into tiny lights and the crescent curled his mouth.

"You mean you'll help me go out?"

Poe felt the flutter in her stomach hearing that. She watched how Caleb seemed to stand a little taller. It was faint, but she heard the tiny pops that came with him straightening up. There was something else on his face, too, something that worked his muscles to make him look like he was thinking carefully.

"My mom takes sleeping pills every year and goes to bed early. I don't."

23

oe pulled on the leggings first, pulling them all the way up and seeing how the bones all matched up in the same place as her own. Next she put on the shirt and stood in front of the mirror, holding the head and mask. She put the mask on where she could line it up perfectly, although a larger version of the skull would get the message straight across. Poe backed up, looking at her entire self in the mirror and not recognizing herself. She moved her arms and legs, looking at each bone piece, and touched the carefully crafted skull that was on her head. The tail wavered behind her, gravity swishing it side to side, just like a living animal would. A living dead animal. She ran out of her room and sprinted down the stairs to show Rex and Bernadette, who were impatiently waiting in the living room.

Poe entered the room just as an animal would, first coming in on all fours, arching her back like she was going to pounce. She raised a hand, showing them exactly where the claws would be, pretending to strike at them. She crawled toward them with Rex chuckling.

"Don't tell me you're going to walk like that all night!" exclaimed Bernadette, though she showed amusement as well.

"This is brilliant, kid," Rex said as Poe stood up. "What is that? What is that made out of?"

"Foam!" she said proudly. "I made the whole skeleton out of foam pieces I found in boxes in the basement. I found pictures of different animal skeletons and just mimicked them to make it look like one thing. It was pretty easy. And this is how it turned out."

She moved her hips so the tail behind her would sway.

"I had to be some sort of undead thing. This will blend in the most!"

"I should say you do," said Rex. "You look great!"

Bernadette smiled from the sofa, dressed in the black dress with a lace tied on the front. She stretched her legs out, clad in black and purple leggings and the black, buckled, curled-toe boots. She really did match the hat and cloak that Poe made for her, folded up neatly on the table and ready for wear. Poe liked she added dark makeup to her eyes, lips, and under her cheekbones, no doubt blending into the dark. She seemed to have done some more to her face to give her more shadows, though it was hard to say how. Poe continued turning to give them a good look at her work, swaying her hips to move the tail she made. Behind her, she heard Bernadette let out a little giggle, and out of the corner of her eye, she saw her moving her finger at Poe.

Rex gasped, and Poe turned to watch her cloth creature's tail lift from the ground and animate like a worm. It waved and swayed, the tip curling by her back.

"Hey!" Poe cried, turning around, the tail following. "Thanks!"

The tail seemed to move of its own accord, yet follow her movements.

"Yeah, no problem," said Bernadette, hiding a much bigger smile. She picked up her hat and cloak and went to the hallway mirror to put them on. Poe waited to see if she would cast anything to herself, but she did not, adjusting the rim almost over her eyes and letting her hair trail down her back. Her eyes caught Poe's in the mirror, a look that had a sharpness to them, as though the mirror would reflect the true happenings of her mind. They flared, sending Poe a message.

"We should get going," Poe stated.

"Right," agreed Rex. He got off the couch, going straight to the pegboard where his fur jacket was waiting. The two girls were ready to go out the door first, both faces hidden or mostly hidden by way of a hat or skull.

"We'll ... see you about," Rex started. "Now remember, don't try to be a hero. You use the stuff the second you think you have to, and don't stick around for long, or try to do anything else. Understand? And go and get as much as you can. We'll all be on standby, on the lookout. Keep your wits about you."

"We will," Poe said, with Bernadette nodding. Rex turned to gather a few things from the closet, sorting staff weapons and knives, both long and short. Poe led Bernadette out the front door, closing it behind them and standing on the step.

The oncoming evening already pushed out the afternoon, turning the soft blue to the burning orange. The horizon line was already getting darker with the promise of what was to come, what was already coming.

Poe felt the prickling on her skin, starting on her arms, going all up her legs and up her backbone so intensely she felt it arch. She exhaled, almost thinking she could see her breath, but why would she be able to see her breath? She cast a side eye to Bernadette to see that she was doing the same.

"You feel it," she said.

"Yeah," was all Poe said.

"Well, you feel *them*, I guess … I can feel them too."

Bernadette turned in different directions, staring out at that dark line in the distance.

"I wonder where they come from."

Poe shook her head. "It's just … all over. We don't know for sure. They just appear."

The girls stood on the step, hearing nothing but the scatter of leaves across the ground. Even they wanted to flee.

"It's almost time," Poe noted. "But we know it's time already. We have to go now while we can."

She took off first. Bernadette stepped in beside her, though she noticed she hesitated just a little. She kept her arm arched around her messenger bag, the grip tighter than she wanted Poe to see.

Poe started to trot, her tail twitching behind her, acting almost as a wind-up to stir her into action. She almost went to walk on all fours. It was as though her disguise was to become real and make her into the creature, and Poe thought the more to blend in, the better. Bernadette tipped her hat, so the rim was just above her eyes, slightly slanted, the cape draped around her shoulder just as mysterious as a figment created from shadow. They passed some places where mostly everything was boarded up, everyone was in, except for the small group of people near the end of the street with a giant metal sculpture made of different bars, with some thin wire netting spread across them. It was invisible until the moonlight hit it just right, revealing the secret trap of the trap. The smaller and heftier person had bunches of bushy hair sticking out of her hood, holding a wrench in her teeth as she held the bars together. Poe grinned behind her mask, though they could not see it, offering a wave as they passed so that they knew it was them, and would know when they encountered them again that night. They were all dressed in their garb, their black jumpsuits with some extra fabric for legs sticking out, giant spinners weaving nets to trap. The girls passed them as they made the finishing touches on the structure. Babs took the wrench out of her mouth to tighten something and then bent over to kick a lever, forcing the entire half of the structure to fold down in a monster-sized cage, giving it its one last test run before the night came.

Poe and Bernadette got to his house, the streets completely empty with no sounds but the galloping of their footsteps across the street. Poe immediately leaped onto the storm drain, climbing up with ease as though she were weightless. Her enchanted tail actually helped her with balance, giving her the support she did not know she had while she climbed. When she got to the roof, close enough to the window, she saw Bernadette float up beside her on the same broom as before. They stayed at the window, both peeking in the section with the missing wood. Sure enough, two small fingers pulled away the wood and revealed Caleb at the window. He seemed more surprised than startled at the two beings, things not of this world, though he knew who they were. Caleb still wore his white nightgown, and from the gray-yellow stain on the front of his collar, it was evident he did not have good health that day. He opened the window almost all the way.

"We're busting you out," Poe said. He gave a little smile and opened the window some more to let them in.

"I was waiting for you," Caleb declared. He shut the window all the way but did not put the wood piece back just yet, looking down at the streets.

Poe was glad to be wearing a mask, for the mixture of smells ranging from medicinal mints to human bile was off-balanced.

"Mom's in her room. She won't come out again."

His voice was back to scratchy and weak, though spoken with the strength wanting to push through it. Bernadette seemed like she was studying the bottles of pills on the tray next to his bed while Poe was studying Caleb.

"So you said you had … something."

Caleb retreated to his closet and came back with a single white sheet. Or, one that had aged to an eggshell color.

"That's it?" Bernadette said.

Caleb looked at the floor. "I mean, I don't have much."

He opened it up so the two girls could see where he cut two holes. He pulled the sheet over his head, moving the holes in position. The girls stared at the flowy white thing with two eyes popping out of nowhere. No body, no face, and from the length, even no feet.

"Hey," Poe said. "That works."

"Yeah," said Bernadette. "Not bad."

"I am a spirit," declared Caleb. "It's fitting and easy. And this way … in case my mom looks outside for whatever reason, she won't know it's me."

"Do you have something for collecting?" Poe asked.

Caleb moved over to his bed, the sheet dragging behind him on the floor that gave Poe a start. It really did suit him. He took an extra pillow and pulled the case off of it, holding it open toward Poe and Bernadette and standing there as nothing but an opaque form.

"That ... yeah."

"Works," finished Bernadette.

Poe's tail moved and Caleb stepped back in surprise. "How ... how are you doing that?"

Poe grinned. "Bernadette enchanted it for me!"

All Caleb did was stare at Bernadette through the sheet. His face disappeared behind a shapeless mold. "Wait until you see what else she can do."

"I, no, it's nothing," said Bernadette. "So anyway, we should really go over our game plan."

"Right," said Poe, going over to peek out the window, where the crimson sunset was deepening to brown. "It should be happening any minute now. We figure we'll just start in this area. Now, we have enough of the stuff to sort of start with, but we need to keep collecting, and then we need to bring it over to Bernadette's family's shop so they can keep making more. People are going to expect us and answer the door, at least they should, and there's going to be others out and about to fight these things if necessary."

"Last time. Are you sure you're up for it?" Bernadette asked Caleb, a bit more harshly than Poe would have liked. She turned to her, and to Caleb for his reaction. He kept his attention on them without blinking, never making even a ripple in the sheet.

"I am," Caleb said, simply. "I very much am."

Poe wanted to say to Bernadette that it had probably been a very long time since Caleb left his room ...

but thought it did not need to be said. She gestured to the two to the window just as the first chimes went off.

Don, don, don, don.

The three of them watched the sky change, the black washing through the watercolors of sunset that seemed to darken everything in their sight, starting at the edges of their eyes and leaking toward their pupils.

Don, don, don, don.

Something sounding like a static charge zipped through the sky, and for a moment nothing, nothing until the shuffling of a creature running on all fours somewhere below and then in the distance, a high-pitched cry ranging from torment to glee to both.

"I'll go first," Bernadette said in a low tone, starting to open the window.

"No, no, I will," Poe insisted.

"It's *my* formula."

"Well, *I* am the creature hunter. I have to go first."

Bernadette scowled, but Poe ignored her, pushing the window up carefully and sticking her head out.

"Wait, how am I—"

"You're going to come with me," Bernadette interrupted Caleb. "Sit on the bristle end."

Caleb stared.

"Will you relax? I like to think I know what I'm doing."

Poe stepped out on the roof and let the two of them deal with each other, crawling on her hands and feet back across with ease. She adjusted her mask, still able to see—and smell—just as well. It almost smelled like rain, except muskier, muggier, and moldier, like she just landed in a damp cellar. It was that strong, and she almost gagged. She climbed down the storm pipe just as Bernadette and Caleb drifted down on the broomstick, a bit shaky, but still landing smoothly. Bernadette dismounted as though it were a horse, whereas Caleb slid off and landed in the grass with a thump, bolting upright like it was a sea he could drown in. Poe was standing very still, letting only her head turn this way and that, her fingertips waving as though she could catch a feeling of something. She stayed still when the other two joined her, Bernadette in front and next to her holding the broom like a staff, and Caleb a little behind the two with short, hesitant steps.

"Cold," was all Poe said.

"It is very cold."

Caleb said nothing.

Poe took a few steps and turned her head to the right. "This way is safer. I don't … feel anything there."

Bernadette and Caleb followed her, the three of them creeping in the night and trotting through the grass. They circled a house with a giant, glowing, grinning pumpkin face on the front porch, eyes cut into slits like they were half open and sneaking a mischievous peek. There was no mistaking the giant iron fence that staked in the grass, going all the way around with only a small gate at the front. A draft of wind passed through, sending skittish leaves at their feet and a chorus of chimes that sounded from the porch. The gate door opened, unlatching from the lock and inviting just enough space for them to pass through.

"Let's hit it," stated Poe.

The skeleton, the witch, and the ghost approached the house. The pumpkin greeted them with its flickering squinted eyes and wide grin, but the house itself had boarded-up windows and a deadbolt on the door. Poe tentatively raised a fist and gave the door a gentle rap, and the three of them stood still. They froze at the sound of oncoming footsteps, and then, to their surprise, a loud CREEEEK came from below them as the mail slot opened.

"Who's that?"

They jumped back.

"It's ... just us!" Poe said. "We're here to collect the candy."

The mail slot closed, and then a moment later opened as a waterfall of candies poured out.

"Hey, thanks!"

They gathered it all and put it in their bags, Poe with her messenger bag, Bernadette with her drawstring bag, and Caleb with his pillowcase. They rushed over to the next house over, narrowly avoiding the holes dug in the lawn, not sure just how deep they went. This one had a lit-up pumpkin face as well, although smaller and more of a joyful face, emitting playfulness. This time it was Caleb who knocked on the door, the nub of a bed sheet that was already a part of him. They waited for a moment or two, no activity coming from inside. Caleb's nub for an arm lingered for a second knock before there came the shuffling of steps, and the door opened.

It looked like a pile of rags that answered the door or someone that put on every single piece of clothing they owned. A woman's face stuck out in the middle of it all, clutching something in her hands.

"We're here for ... candy," Caleb said as the three of them held out their opened bags. The woman did not say anything, just scanning the three like she wanted to be sure. Then she tossed a few pieces of sweets into their bags and quickly shut the door. The three scampered off just as quickly, prancing down the sidewalk and narrowly avoiding a jagged fence that looked like it was made of barbed wire.

"Watch it," Poe warned. "It's sharp."

The fence stretched down the sidewalk, wrapping around the gate to the next house. Poe could make out bits of reddened fur stuck between the barbs, imagining that whatever ran through it and suffered had done so only recently. They opened the gate and advanced, making sure their knocks were gentle. The man who answered the door wore a cloth covering pulled down on his head with the holes cut out by his eyes. His own mask. He quickly gave them three candy bars.

"Stay safe," he said before shutting the door and deadbolting it shut.

They came to a street that curved in a bend, a path moving away from homes and into an open and unprotected area. Poe clutched her bag at the sound that echoed in her head.

"Can you hear that?" she asked the other two.

Bernadette looked first to where it was coming from, followed by Caleb. The galloping thundered in her ears just as a shape in the darkness moved toward them down the street. It was almost made of smoke ... or a storm cloud that fell down from the sky. Poe stepped back at the red, glowing eyes and the long face, grabbing at the other two to pull them away.

"Hide!"

They ducked back by the side of the house they came from as the galloping figure flew down the street.

"It was..." Poe started. "It was going so fast it looked like it was going to run us over, and I don't even think it was solid. I don't think it's the same thing I saw in the sky, is it? I don't know it—"

"night mare," said Caleb.

Poe and Bernadette jerked their heads toward him. "What?"

"night mare. They charge through everything, picking up other demons and creatures on their way to and from levels of Hell, and take them there."

Poe opened her mouth and closed it.

"I-I right," she stammered. "Of course. I've seen that in one of Rex's books, we study so many. You, uh, you know the name?"

"I've seen them," Caleb answered. "I've seen them before." And he left it at that.

"We're ... going to see a lot," was all Poe said.

Bernadette held her bag by her side with a grip on the clasp. "It was going too fast to try, anyway."

The three stuck their heads out and made their way back onto the street, Poe trying to concentrate on her surroundings and trying not to look at Caleb. *He spends most of his life in his room,* she thought. *He probably reads all day. And he does see things, looking out, all the time.*

Something flew above their heads and interrupted her wandering thoughts, and it nearly knocked them over. It was something with large red wings that sailed through the rooftops and disappeared into a cluster of trees. They made their way through the grass as what looked like tiny fireflies bounced off the grass blades. Up ahead, they heard a commotion: the struggle and fight of human voices.

"Hurry, it could get out!"

"The ropes are thick enough!"

"Look at those talons, they're bigger than an eagle's!"

"I'm trying, hang on!"

The three rounded to the house in their path to see three people in black hooded jackets and cloaks surrounding something in a net trap, something also in a black cloak, though its face was hidden in the shroud.

"I got it, I got it!"

The woman nearest them pulled on the rope to tighten the net, struggling a bit with the black mask she had on her face, enclosing the shroud and causing its talons to stick out of the holes. The thing hissed.

"Come on," Poe urged. They stuck to the direction they were heading. "They're catching them. The others are catching them!"

They reached the next house where no residents were occupied with anything on their front lawns, a home shut up and boarded up so much it could have been abandoned.

"I don't think anyone lives here," said Bernadette.

"No, someone does," Poe insisted.

Bernadette scoffed. "I mean, it doesn't look like it. How can you be sure?"

"I can smell them."

Though she could not see Caleb's reaction, she knew it had to be just as perplexed as Bernadette's.

"I don't know ... how," she explained. "But I do."

"What ... what is it that you smell?" Bernadette asked.

Poe lifted her head in the fog. "Rotten. Something rotten. Something *rotting*."

"Like food?"

Poe shook her head, not knowing just how she could explain it to them. Instead, she walked forward, urging them to follow her and follow along. She reached up and knocked on the door, and they waited.

The door opened at a glacial pace. The creaking was a long and drawn-out cry. An old woman stood in the doorway before them, stoic as a statue in both expression and stance. They doubled back in alarm at the person that was all skin and bones, the way her face looked so serious, her gaze at them almost challenging. Poe did so as much for that stench. The woman looked at the three of them, then half of her face formed a smile.

"Come for me?" she asked in a dry voice.

"No, we—"

Bernadette's voice trailed off as the woman stepped over the threshold past the three of them at a solemn pace. Poe watched her walk, trying to figure out how to tell the others what she thought, what she suspected, and what she knew. Before she could say anything, Caleb chimed in.

"It's her time."

Poe wheeled on him as Bernadette did as well.

"It is!" Poe said. "I can tell that! How could you—how could you tell that too?"

"How could *either of you*?" Bernadette asked, looking back and forth between the two of them. "You both are something else. How? It doesn't make any sense."

Neither Poe nor Caleb answered. Ahead of them, the woman still walked down the street through the fog, into the void of flapping wings.

"So then, where is she going?" Bernadette asked in a small voice.

The fog thickened, and the night darkened in due time, though it seemed it did so more on this side of the town. At some point they lost track of the woman but continued going straight, following Poe's senses.

"I just smelled ... death," Poe said stupidly. "I don't know how else to describe it."

"Okay, that's a whole different story to unpack. What about you?"

Caleb was pretending to adjust the sheet around his face. "Well, I know what a person looks like, and can feel like, right before they ... go."

They passed a ditch littered with bones, though none paid that any attention.

"The body starts to shut down. Slowly," Caleb explained.

And things start to shut down on the inside, Poe thought.

"This lady knows it."

"Okay, you, with your amazing tracking, where did she go?"

"Still going straight," Poe answered. She only just noticed that her enchanted tail twitched more than usual, curling around at her back in anticipation. She stuck her nose up in the air while the other two kept up with her.

They stopped short of something moving ahead of them: something large, hunched over, and bumpy, as though it were a mob of people gathered together. The three of them slouched down.

"What is that?" Bernadette asked, reaching for her bag.

"I don't know," Poe answered as her skin prickled.

They moved to the side where they could conceal themselves by a house with a garden, ducking among the leaves. The horde, the mob, the bumpy thing merged from the fog now only a few feet away. Poe's stomach flip-flopped when it came into view, where the idea of people lumped together wasn't exactly incorrect. The heads were separate but still attached, somehow, sticking up and out all over the thing like they were kept in pockets. But they were skulls, or mostly left as skulls, things that used to be human faces with nothing left but empty sockets. Empty holes that glowed with the orange of burning embers. An arm here and there stuck out as well, pulling at them, pulling at nothing, at anything left over stretching jaws without teeth, eye sockets without eyes. They were just close enough to hear the low moans coming from it, different voices, the desperate cries of the damned.

"That..."

"It..."

It looked like a shroud covering leftover mangled pieces, pale sickly green and blue mixed with the black of death. And it moved down the street like it could have had hundreds of legs stuck on the bottom, but there were none. All it was doing was gliding weightlessly. The three could do nothing but stare at it as it slid down the street, its decayed gaps for mouths opening and closing and the hands pulling at the eye sockets. Occasionally, trails of smoke came out of it from somewhere, shrouding the dead in gruesome veils. Caleb's knees were buckling behind the white sheet.

"Ohhh that. I've seen that before," his voice managed to make him say.

Poe considered him.

"You have? What is it?"

Bernadette touched Poe's arm. They watched one head turn in their general direction, then two, then three, and then more. The eyes all slanted a little as though they were peering at them, and then suddenly the whole body positioned itself toward them. And then it started to move again.

Caleb staggered. "We have to *go! Now!*"

He pulled the other two, just as this thing started to fly toward them and breaking into a run before anything else could be said. They dashed down the street and ducked behind trees and bushes. They kept low and ran around houses, moving faster when they noticed the fog start to grow around their ankles. The fog rose, making them wade through a flood of old souls. They had their backs against a toolshed behind a house, watching that fog dance around up to their shins. Their breath came out in quick puffs, looking like misshapen little ghosts.

Poe did not want to peek around the corner.

"It's close, but not gone," she whispered.

Caleb adjusted his sheet, putting the eye holes back all the way.

They heard the moans coming from behind them, multiple voices in multiple ranges. Poe heard another voice too at the same time her nose met the familiar smell from before.

"She's out there," Poe said.

She urged the others to move around the house to a different angle. She peeked around it, her skull's maw only barely sticking out.

"There she is," she said. "Look."

The old woman stood in the direct path of this thing, facing it, chin down in acceptance and submission. Her nightgown flowed beneath her knees in a gentle wind, though there was no wind. There was something else about the woman that none of them could put a finger on.

"It's like she's in a thicker part of that fog," Poe declared. "But she's..."

"Waiting," Caleb finished.

"For..." Bernadette started, though already knowing.

The shroud of undead faces, now all the faces emerging from their pockets all over its hunched back, mouths open in silent screams, and the arms and hands flaring and reaching. The thing moved faster down the street in a glide toward the woman, her arm outreached.

"We have to get closer," Bernadette urged. "We have to see where it's going to—"

The girls inched closer, with Caleb hesitating, staying behind. He held on to the sheet covering him, holding it around him like he was in bed. They could hear little moans coming from it as it drifted down the street, and an outburst of smoke that seemed to surround it. More and more, the woman seemed to dissolve to become part of the fog, her hair and nightgown fading as some invisible vacuum seemed to be pulling her in. In a swift passing, the shroud floated past the woman, with all the heads, hands, and arms thrashing and moving, and then a new cloud of fog formed around it as it moved. It then dissolved into the fog itself as it went through it, disappearing.

Poe and Bernadette were shoulder to shoulder as they tried to see where it went.

"So it just disappeared!" Bernadette exclaimed. "Like, into nothing and nowhere."

"It..." Poe shook her head. "It has to go *somewhere.*"

"Exactly the point. Could that be it?"

"I don't think so. It can't be. It's just in the middle of the street. That doesn't make sense."

"I have to go see." Bernadette took off before Poe could protest, though she did want to see for herself. It wasn't until they reached the street did they notice that Caleb stayed by the side of the house.

The street was empty of everything. No such beings, living or dead, or extra patches of fog or smoke filled the area. Poe felt, heard, and smelled, nothing.

"So, what, they come and go as they please ... they can just travel between realms at will?"

Bernadette had both her hands stretched out like she was trying to feel for something invisible. "There is no actual entrance or anything?"

Poe scanned her area with her own senses. When she pivoted around, she saw plainly and clearly the ambiguous shape of the boy under a white sheet standing on a lawn.

"Not for spirits," Poe concluded. "I suppose."

The ghost boy moved a part of the sheet that could have been a hand, wavering in the dark.

"Caleb wants us," she said.

The two ventured back to join him, now away from the house and into the open area. When they got closer, they realized he had not been facing them, and instead, his back was turned. He only turned back to them once they approached him.

"At first I thought it was coming for me," he admitted. "Like ... it knew I got away."

Poe tried to swallow as he pointed in the distance.

"I think ... over there," he mumbled.

Poe and Bernadette exchanged glances. Then it was Caleb's turn to lead an expedition, already walking in that direction and having them follow him without asking. It was something to be shown, not told.

"You saw that, then," Poe prompted Caleb. "That thing, what it did, that it disappeared."

The top of the sheet ducked up and down. A nod.

Caleb led them to a square around the corner, one with thick trees and a park bench with someone sitting on it. The person was still and leaning back against it.

Caleb's steps were purposeful, yet obligated. He got to where they were close enough to view the bench and stopped, waiting for them to get it.

Poe saw the form, instantly recognizing it. Slumped and empty now, she looked more like a model of clay that melted in the day and now stuck to the bench, already starting to gray to match the nightgown. Her eyes were still open, though now with a peaceful glaze over them.

No one said anything.

No one did anything.

Not until they heard the scuttle of something running in the square. Of more than one thing running in the square. The horde was small, full of small things. Fast things. Things that were small enough to be children. They ran excitedly, silhouettes of long, curving horns on top of their heads, spikes on their shoulders and all down their backs, and pointed tails swishing behind them. The three friends could hear the sounds of their long claws clicking together in excitement, their teeth gnashing together ... and it was enough to make them turn heel.

All three of them cried out and stopped short at the other horde that was coming up behind them, and they could see them up close for what they were. The rubrums' skin were deep, dark, and speckled red like they were splattered with blood, and they smiled with needle teeth. The little demon creatures squawked at the three of them and at one another, acknowledging them with interest, but their interest was in what brought them to the square in the first place. The two hordes met as one as they engulfed the bench to enjoy the new meal they smelled from miles away, nails and teeth digging away and tearing into something that was still very freshly dead.

"Go, go," Poe urged. "Come on, let's get out of here!"

She jumped back with a light yell at what leaped down from the tree, wings folding behind its back. This Nether flyer saw Poe as what she was, an undead skeleton thing, bypassing her as it went to join the others. Poe stayed still as the two did the same behind her, or so she wished. As the Nether flyer made more menacing steps, Poe heard the cry of Bernadette as she made the swift throw from her bag.

Bernadette screamed as she tossed the formula, as the Nether flyer froze in place and crackled into a statue. Poe realized that the hordes they saw were not the only ones as Caleb then did the same to more rubrums. Poe maintained a defensive stance as the three of them became surrounded by rubrums and a few more Nether flyers that flew down to join the scene. They threw their dust, handful after handful, to learn that it was all it took to turn all the incoming creatures into sticky statues. They stood with claws and wings, half-extended, with the solution dripping off of them in gobs.

"Go *now!*" Poe hissed. "Now, while the others are occupied!"

They fled the square, the circle of statues in various positions of attack, while the living ones engrossed themselves with the corpse, their nails and teeth strung with shredded flesh.

Poe, Bernadette, and Caleb ran down the street, no longer caring about stealth for the moment. They went into another square after scanning to see that the coast was clear, each holding onto their bags.

They stayed where they were for the moment, catching their breath, and processing everything that had happened in those couple of minutes. Caleb coughed a few times and bent over in the grass, lifting his sheet to spit.

"You okay?" asked Bernadette.

"Yeah," came Caleb's rough voice. He wiped his mouth and fitted the sheet back over it, no doubt glad he could hide how his face looked. "That was close."

Poe faced behind them, where they came from, continuously watching to see if any imp-sized shadows ran down the street.

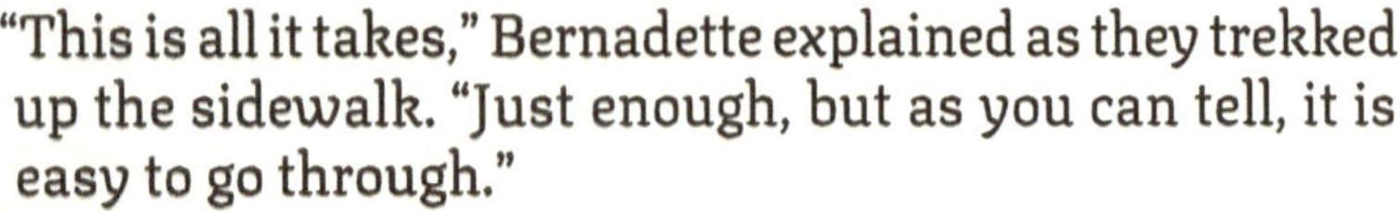

"This is all it takes," Bernadette explained as they trekked up the sidewalk. "Just enough, but as you can tell, it is easy to go through."

"I've got some left," Poe said. "Good enough for any others."

"I still have more," commented Caleb. "I didn't use as much."

There was another block of houses, some partially hidden by the fog that was down there.

"Should we really go into that blind?" Bernadette pointed out. "I mean, there could be fifty there for all we know."

Poe jerked her head to the tree next to them in the square, and her twitchy tail wiggled by her head. "I can check."

Poe leaped up the tree with ease, grasping the branches and knobs in the trunk and matching her speed with her agility. She did it all in one breath, the pads of her hands and feet forming minds of their own as they took her all the way to the top. She did see Bernadette clench her broom, but she and Caleb stayed put with their heads tilted up to where Poe was in between a "y" of the topmost tree branches.

Poe almost had the thought of lifting her skull mask to see better, but saw the scene before and below her as clear as though nothing covered her eyes. The scenery was sharp, as though no fog permeated the air, or her vision was just sharp enough to see through it. The buildings and houses stacked like irregular blocks in the pueblo-style land, and in between them were dashes of things running here and there. Humans—in disguises— holding spears. There were other things, not so human, and not so disguised. She saw someone do as they did and throw their own magic dust, some demon turning into a melted glob, and the human turning their spear to it. She crept back down the tree, and when she was a little more than halfway down the branches, she pushed off and landed right on her feet in front of Bernadette and Caleb.

"Geez," Bernadette reacted.

Poe shrugged. "It's nothing. I've been climbing since I could walk."

"What did you see?" asked Caleb.

"Some of the others are using the stuff to fight off some demons in that neighborhood. There are definitely plenty more down there, but the one next to it is empty. We should go there next to collect. And help out."

The others agreed, and they carried on mostly in silence, rushing up to the first house on that block, which resulted in handfuls of taffies just like the ones Poe got first. They continued on, going from one house to the next, only slowing down to go around traps decorating each lawn. And each time, the door opened slowly and carefully, each adult or child that answered the door looked upon them with fear. But each time, they filled their bags. The three, not able to help themselves, each felt the weight of their bags and stole a peek at them.

"We certainly did get a lot, didn't we?" said Poe.

"Unbelievable. I can't wait to show my moms. They are going to make so much of this stuff we'll have leftovers to sell it all and we'll be rich!"

"I have never seen this much before," said Caleb, peering into his bag. He rummaged through it, picking out a wrapped chocolate ball and studying it for a moment before feverishly unwrapping it.

"Hey, what are you doing?"

Caleb took the unwrapped chocolate ball and tucked it under his sheet. Poe and Bernadette watched the sheet move as his mouth moved.

"Hey, stop! We need that!" cried Bernadette.

Caleb was already searching for something else to unwrap.

"I have never had candy before! This is amazing!"

Poe and Bernadette stared. Caleb ripped off the wrapper of a taffy, his sheet now lifted to his face and shoved it in his mouth.

"You never had candy before?" asked Poe.

Caleb shook his head. "I was never allowed," he said with sticky teeth. "But if I didn't stay dead before, this isn't going to kill me now."

He shoved something else in his mouth, a low groan coming from somewhere inside him, something inside him waking up.

"Come on, don't eat it all!" exclaimed Bernadette. "That's our main ingredient!"

"Just ... let him," Poe said. Caleb's lips were covered in chocolate, the foil wrappers falling at his feet.

"Chocolate! I finally know what chocolate tastes like! This is the best night of my life!" Caleb declared.

Poe made the biggest smile under her mask neither of them could see. Bernadette looked down and sighed.

"Well, then I guess we have to go get a lot extra."

Down this next street, Poe could see it, almost as big as the house.

The dirty gray made it look like old bones or rusted metal, or maybe it was supposed to look like both. It looked like something built to hold flapping laundry drying in the wind, or catch flying demons atop its spikes.

"Oh god, what is that?" Bernadette asked.

They walked past the skyscraping structure, built quickly, but effectively. The flapping laundry turned out to be the wings of the creature, the wind moving them as they no longer could on their own.

"Some flying demon," muttered Poe.

They walked past it, trying not to stop to stare at it too much, only enough to see that the spikes impaled in more than one place the way it lay at crooked angles.

"Another trap," she said. "And one made of iron."

They moved on to an area with more open fields, deciding to take a shortcut by the pond. The pond surface was as clear and reflective as a mirror, showing the half-sphere of the moon directly underneath the horizon line. It did not draw the same attention as the other half-sphere that sat atop the surface did, causing the three to stop and peer. It was too smooth and too round to be a log or a rock ... and too buoyant. Poe peered from a safe distance, her mind retracing the things she read, while Bernadette, the most non-trusting, stayed further back with her brows crossed. It was Caleb who came around the two of them, his steps quickening to urgency.

"Caleb, wait," Poe started.

"No, look," he said, pointing to the pond.

"Yeah, we see it, and it doesn't look like anything that we—"

"No, look," Caleb cut off Bernadette.

The thing bobbled in the water, causing only the lightest of ripples that barely washed over cattail leaves. It was turning, rotating in the water just enough to reveal the line of a mouth and the nostrils of a very human nose.

"Oh, my god."

"It's a baby!"

"Still alive?"

"Wait, wait, *no!*"

Poe reached for the two of them, but they were already rushing to the edge of the pond, standing just enough to bend down.

"Don't!" Poe cried. "Don't go near it!"

"But it's a baby…" Caleb said. He leaned in, the edge of his sheet almost grazing the water. "Is it still alive?" He looked around for a stick or a cattail long enough.

"It's not a baby!" Poe answered.

The head turned all the way now, soft blue eyes staring helplessly up in the sky and water moving underneath it, no doubt treading to stay afloat.

"What do you mean?" Caleb asked.

Something that looked like a stick rose to the surface and within seconds a long, lanky arm ending in claws shot out of the water, heading straight for Caleb. He screamed and ducked out of the way at the same time Poe and Bernadette rushed to pull him back. Its claws stabbed through the end of his sheet, ripping four tears. They pulled Caleb out of the way as the baby's head angled in the water to see all of them properly. The helpless blue eyes now hardened to frost white. The water was now right under its nose and going inside it, though it still flared its nostrils impatiently. Then came the other arm, shooting out from the left side and almost scratching the tops of their feet.

"Bobblehead!" Poe cried, dragging the two away from the pond. "They pull you in and drown you!"

She managed to shove them away while she reached into her bag and scooped out a handful of the dust, throwing it over the claw reaching for them with an open hand. She tossed another over the head in the water just as the claw weakened and stiffened onto the ground like a frozen branch, the head floating now. Just as a rotten egg would.

"Caleb, are you okay?"

He and Bernadette bent to his sheet, the front part ending in a few distressed fragments.

"Yeah, I'm all right," he answered.

They did not say much else as they moved away from the pond, but huddled together to walk as a single unit with three pairs of legs. They each looked in their candy bags in relation to their magic dust bags.

"Let's head back to my place," Bernadette said in a hurry. "Let's give my moms what we have. They might need more supply. And I think we'll need more of the stuff."

efore they could even get to the door of Something Stirring, it opened and three people in Poe's fur jackets came out. They stiffened when seeing them, but only took a minute to know who they were.

"Hey, it's the kids!" said Anton. "You're doing all right."

"We are," Poe answered. "We've got more candy here to make more of the solution."

"It's working," Anton stated. "It's working so well. We're getting them. We can stop them at least, even if we can't kill all of them upfront. But anything that wants a fight, we give it to 'em."

"Good, I knew it!"

"We came to give my moms more candy. Are they close?"

"They are, and my god it's working. Like a charm. Where were you witches before now?"

Bernadette beamed, her chin angling at a higher level than before as they walked into the shop. There, they saw the hustle and bustle of people in different disguises in the shop, all lined up with bottles and mason jars. Poe recognized a few more of the blacksmiths in the black furs and hoods with horns. She also saw the black jumpsuits, the spider creatures that made up the civil engineers. Poe immediately saw the pointed cone tops of the black hats moving to and fro behind the counter. They approached the counter with their bags just as Ivy and Emme poured lime green and pink liquids into vials and took turns stirring what was in the cauldron behind them with the high flames.

"Good, give us more!" said Emme enthusiastically. "This is starting to get low."

She scooped up the melting mass of brown, the wooden spoon making a scratch on the bottom.

Ivy secured a vial for the last customer and sent her on her way before turning to the three.

"The protection potions we made are going like hotcakes as well. They must be working. Most people wouldn't even dream of being out like this after Shut-In, let alone the Night of Passing." She peered at them.

"Well, Bernie, you look absolutely terrific. And Poe, my god, that's you, isn't it, under that skeleton animal? So talented. And—"

She looked at the one completely draped on the end next to Poe, the one that hadn't said a word the whole time. Emme joined them with equal curiosity.

"And who is this?" Emme finished.

"This is Caleb," Bernadette said, gesturing to him. "A new friend."

Caleb moved so that he could see both Bernadette and Poe through his eye holes like he was looking for a prompt or clue as to whether to lift the sheet and introduce himself.

"Hello," he simply said. Just like regular people, Poe figured that this was his first time meeting witches.

"All right then, collectors, give me what you got," Ivy said, leaning across the counter.

The three opened their bags and dumped the contents, spreading out a collection of gummies, chocolates, wrapped hard candy, taffies, gumdrops, and more. Emme ran fingers through the load like she was trying to read them like Braille marks, and then she scooped them into a basket and tossed them into the cauldron, wrappers and all.

"Good work," Emme said. "You taking care, then?"

"Yeah Mom, we're fine," Bernadette answered. "It works instantly, and Poe's outfits make it even better."

"Have you seen Rex?" Poe asked, the idea coming to her as she just saw Anton and his crew.

"Rex, yeah, he was here a little while ago to get more," Ivy answered as she sprinkled something into the cauldron. "He loves the stuff, too, talked about how he used it on a few things in traps and he bragged about being able to kill this one demon with big teeth. He asked about you and said he was going to look for you at some point."

"We'll find him," Poe said. She could imagine him doing just as they were, just as he had always done, but now it was better and easier because of them.

It did not take long for the solution to be ready, Emme collecting their little compartments and Ivy filling it as quickly as it went from melted liquid to dry powder.

"Be quick, as always," Emme said.

"And don't be quick about anything else, Bernie," Ivy warned.

"I know, I know," Bernadette groaned. "Thanks, Moms, we'll see you later."

She urged Poe and Caleb on their way, shutting the door behind them and standing in the safety of the shop front for a moment.

"How much more do we need to collect?" asked Caleb. "How many people are out fighting these things?"

"As much as we can," Poe answered. "And there's a few. Not too many. We need to be able to hold them off."

"So how long we keep going like this? All night?"

The three looked at one another.

"I want to stay all night. I don't care. Whatever it takes," stated Bernadette.

"Me too. I couldn't sleep if I wanted to. I feel like—I feel like it's my duty to do something about them," admitted Poe.

"Me too," stated Caleb. "I don't want to go home. I finally get to be out and I feel ... I feel more at home out here, actually."

Poe and Bernadette let that sentence linger between them.

"We all have our reasons," Bernadette said.

"And you've got one too, a very specific one at that," Poe said. "Do you really think you can find it?"

"That's the goal," Bernadette answered. "And I won't stop until I do. It would only be visible tonight, of all nights, and I just have to know. And I feel like the two of you are the ones that can help."

Poe felt that in a part of her gut she didn't use, a sixth sense of sorts, something that told her that Bernadette was right.

Caleb was doing a scan of the horizon, his head stopping back to the two of them.

"I'm trying," he said. "I just—"

"Trying what?" asked Poe.

Caleb shuffled in his sheet. "I am trying to see if I can find it."

"Well, that's the goal," Bernadette said matter-of-factly.

"No," Caleb stated. "You don't understand. I thought I would remember what it looked like."

Poe and Bernadette waited.

"I thought you said you didn't remember," Bernadette recalled.

Caleb paused. "I guess I came out here because I thought I would know it when I saw it. I thought that it would be easy for me. Easier. I thought it would... I thought it would open up for me." Caleb coughed, clearing his throat. "I feel more alive out here than I ever have, out with the undead, and that's kinda funny. And all I want to do is explore."

"We'll be able to do more exploring," Poe stated. "Later. And afterward."

"Afterward?" Bernadette asked.

"After they all go to sleep. The grownups. Those out fighting them, setting the traps, all using the formula, and those waiting behind doors with the candy to make it. Until then, we go collect and trap and fight. And then, the rest of the night will be ours."

Poe quickened her pace at what she saw ahead of them, an outline of a large being with short ears atop the head.

"That!" cried Caleb. "That looks like a wolf beast!"

"No, I know it," Poe said, running a bit and forcing the other two to keep up.

The wolf being was crouched low in a defensive stance, and in the dark, it was hard to tell which way it was facing. The ears on top of the head moved as Poe approached, and this being stood all the way up.

"Poe!"

"How goes it?"

The others joined Poe, at once taken aback and relieved.

"You nearly had me throw the magic dust on you!" Rex said as he adjusted his hood, wiping his forehead. Poe stared at the scratch above his eyebrow, still fresh with a red shine.

"Your face! What happened?"

"Nothing," Rex insisted, though Poe kept trying to get a better look.

"Something got you?"

"It was nothing, some demon, dumb as bricks. It didn't get me that close, but enough. I should be more worried about you. You all okay? Bernadette, you, and— who is this one?"

Caleb held on to the inside of his sheet again.

"This is Caleb. He's a new friend. He—he knows a lot of monsters. He's seen them from his room. And ... we've been doing all right so far. We got plenty of candy already and headed to the Briar-Whittles for them to make more solution. It's working."

"You're darn right it's working," Rex said. "Saved my life. You know I would have had a mark much worse than this one ... if I had a face left at all."

The three, now four of them, made themselves still at the sound of the roar from across the town, a growl from something that was not a bear. They turned their necks, keeping themselves motionless with their feet firmly planted. The roaring sounded again, a rumbling that Poe could even feel with her feet.

"Back there," Rex said through his teeth. "Up that way. Quiet."

Rex had his spear and bag by his side and led the way, all of them also holding onto their bags. Poe could feel the change in the air of something diffusing through it that hadn't been before. She strained her eyes, trying to make out what was forming in the dark, of what could possibly match the noise that was coming from below. From below.

"Rex!" she whispered. "It's ... it's underground! It's under us!"

Bernadette and Caleb took this news with shock, stepping back and looking at their feet.

"How do you know?" Bernadette demanded.

"Where?" Rex cried, aiming his spear at the ground.

They all looked down, every which way, but saw nothing but dirt and gravel.

"They're..." Poe started. "They're not exactly solid."

There came a gasp from Caleb as he stumbled backward, nearly tripping over his disguise. He landed on his behind and scooted back in alarm as the shadows bled over his white sheet like dark liquid, though they were irregular and looked like they kept changing form.

"Fractured shadows! A horde of them!" Rex said, rushing over to Caleb. He picked him up and kept his light pointed down, the others watching one or two or three black amoebas spill out of the ground. The way they were changing and constantly shifting shapes made it difficult to count.

"Will these work?" Bernadette asked.

"You have to get it in their mouth," Poe said, already digging through her bag for the container. She pawed through the solution as the entire ground beneath them turned into a swirling black sea of things that were stuck in a tar pit and flailing around as to try to get out.

"There's so many!" she cried as Rex pulled all of them back. They picked their feet up as a jellyfish-shaped shadow floated nearby. Poe waited for it to open up, to stretch what would be its mouth, recognizing those nubby teeth when she saw them up close and personal and tossed her handful at it. The dust fell and settled on it, immediately melting back into the sticky tar-like substance that made it stop moving. Now, the creature looked like it was stuck with tar, trying to open and close its mouth but causing it to stick to itself even more. Bernadette got her own handful in, though Caleb in the back struggled to get a good shot and got help from Rex. They each froze a few, at least, though the ground was nowhere near as solid as it used to be.

"Come on, you can't get all of them!" Rex cried. "Save your stuff from things you can't get away from!"

They ran from the area, Poe leading the way with Rex and not turning back until they were a few feet away. Caleb nearly collided with Poe when she stopped and realized there was one missing.

"Bernadette!" she called. "Come on!"

Poe jogged back a bit to motion to her friend, standing still and straight in the middle of the place they had just come from. She stomped one foot on the ground in one area and then stomped the other on the other side.

"Come on!" Poe tried again. "More of them could come out!"

"Yeah, that's the point!" Bernadette called back. She bent down, doing something with her fingers and murmuring something that Poe could not hear from there. Rex eyed Poe.

"What is she doing?"

Poe shook her head, her tail twitching anxiously. "It's ... that's ... that's not it."

Bernadette stood back up, tossing another handful of solution to a shadow that looked like a long hand. It closed into a fist, fingers curling to the middle and flopping onto the pavement.

Bernadette jogged to catch up to Poe, and since Poe was masked, she did not see the face she was making.

"No Bernadette, it's not ... it wouldn't be there. It's in the middle of the street."

"But it could be anywhere," Bernadette argued. "Because they come out of everywhere."

"They always have," Rex stated when the girls joined them. They looked to him, resting his spear on his shoulder. "Guess what? They also come out of the sky. Doesn't matter. Don't you try to go after them."

It was like speaking the word "sky" prompted something, for Rex instinctively ducked at whatever passed the moon, the outline of wings over them. They saw nothing but the small cloud patch next to it, though after a moment Poe saw something stretch out on the cloud, spreading a wing made out of the cloud itself. It took off, leaving a puff of air in the sky, ducking all the way down to the ground to greet it with a shadow of its own.

"Like some spirits," Rex finished. "They tend to cause havoc when more are together. You keep your wits about you."

In the distance, they heard a shrill shriek, followed by another that matched a human cry. Rex angled his spear.

"Better go after that," he said. He got a few feet before he turned and put a hand out to the three of them.

"Don't you dare. You go keep collecting the stuff, use it only when you need to, and then get out of the way. Understand?"

The cries intensified and so did the shrieks, higher and happier, a predator catching prey.

Rex took off, dashing down the street with his chin ducked and his hood ears pointing straight.

"Come on," Poe urged, keeping her ears in tune, as far behind her as she could, not feeling satisfied until the shrieks subsided.

26

hey walked around the bend, following the dirt path around the fence that would no doubt lead them to the next house. There was one they at first thought was a place of business by the way it stood out on its own, taking up a corner of the town like a guard always in position. When they circled around the fence, they could see the mailbox ... all tied up with bright pink yarn. They came to the front of the house and saw it was not the only thing, for the entire home was wrapped up and decorated with colorful trinkets and ornaments and reflectors that looked like the inside of a giant kaleidoscope. They stood there frozen to the spot, wanting to view it long enough to try to come up with an explanation.

"Like they needed those pumpkin faces," remarked Bernadette. "All the rest of this is scary enough."

The pumpkins lined up the pathway up the house, each stationed on each stair of the porch, all had mismatched holed faces. The candles that flickered behind them suggested that some had been burning longer than others, and some that were threatening to go out altogether.

"Well, I hope this could only mean they'll have some candy," said Poe.

The three walked up the pathway, watching the trinkets and things hanging from the house move a little in the breeze, or perhaps move to alert that they had company.

"I recognize some of these," Bernadette said. "Some of these look like protective charms."

"There sure are a lot of them."

"There's more than a lot of them! Look at those Magic Eyes all tangled together!" said Bernadette, pointing to the stringed ovals with gems in the middle. "They're supposed to change color when something is present. They're, well, all sort of pinkish bluish."

"Who lives here?" Poe asked. Her question dreaded the answer.

They stood before the front porch, the nearest pumpkins with an ember glow so faint their faces were barely visible in the dark: the different-sized eyes and wide stretched hole for a mouth, the faces carved in a hurry so that many could be made. The three had one foot forward like they were ready to knock on the door and find out, but one back in hesitation. Bernadette stepped forward first and Caleb, his bag already open, followed her. It was Poe who kept rooted to where she was, staring at the door like she was trying to see through it.

"Something ... something doesn't feel right," she said.

The other two turned to her.

"What do you mean?" Bernadette asked.

Caleb turned so his sheet eyes could see her. "Is there something here?"

Of course, there was something there. In this town, at night, there was always something somewhere, but especially on this night. Poe felt it the minute they were in front facing the house and it could have been a spirit passing through the air above them aimlessly, but once that passed the feeling would pass and this feeling did not. It grounded her; it grasped her heart and did not let go.

"Yeah..." Poe finally answered. Her feet made the decision to walk up the porch steps and lean an ear against the door. The other two crept behind her. Bernadette looked up, around, and every which way while Caleb simply stood with his chin up, like all he could do was be ready for what he would encounter. They both jerked their heads toward Poe as she knocked on the door, her ear still against it, and her tail swaying behind her like a broom trying to sweep up their tracks. Poe's breath was so silent she did not hear it bounce back against the door, but she could hear Caleb's infirmary wheeze and Bernadette inhale sharply through her teeth. Poe was barely on the door, but her touch caused it to open. It fell away from the doorframe and opened noiselessly to the inside of the house.

The three stood for a moment as the house revealed itself to them: a foyer of seemingly normal décor, with striped maroon and beige wallpaper, and a table with a vase of fake flowers on it. And unlike the outside, with the clinking of trinkets together in the nightly breeze, the inside was quiet. There were no oncoming footsteps to greet the secret visitors. Whoever lived in that house probably did not know they had visitors, if anyone was home at all. Caleb muttered something about that, but Poe contradicted him right away.

"Someone is in there. And something is very wrong with them ... I ... I feel strongly about it."

Poe stepped into the foyer and the other two followed, the door wavering back and forth until it shut on its own and caused them all to jump.

"Just the wind," Caleb tried.

"Yeah, sure," scoffed Bernadette. She had her hand around her bag to reach for something, anything, in there that she would need. Poe even saw her muttering something under her breath, as though she could conjure up some sort of spell of protection or revealing. Poe led them into this foyer that opened up into a larger entrance accompanied by a curving staircase. The same wallpaper continued, though covered by symmetrical pictures mounted on either side. It was hard to see in the covered darkness, and so much so that Caleb occasionally bumped into one of them.

"Will you stop that!?" Bernadette whispered in a hiss.

"Sorry!" Caleb whispered back. "I can't see anything."

"I can," Poe suddenly said. "It's not that dark, and I can make it out."

"What, so you have night vision now?" asked Bernadette.

"I don't know," Poe said. "I could okay before, but now I really can. Like, I really can. Does the veil thin out the air here too, or what?"

"Who's got a light?" asked Caleb.

"No, don't do that," Poe insisted, her voice softer than his now. "Whatever's here, we can't let them know we're here until we figure out what's going on."

"And we're going after this because ... why?"

Poe positioned herself to the left, toward the staircase; her toes attached to a compass and her gut attached to a fishing line.

"Because I think someone is in danger."

She led them toward the stairs. Bernadette feverishly dug through her bag until she brought out pendants and necklaces she threw on over her head, squeezing them and muttering things under her breath. Caleb held the sheet against himself and shuddered a little, walking with stiff movements as though trying his hardest to actually pass as a spirit himself.

Poe kept climbing the stairs, both hands out to her sides like she was expecting something to leap out at them. Like the people in the picture frames along the wall, posed in stoic formal poses, suggesting older time periods. As the three passed them all up the stairs, if they had any light at all, they would have seen things change in the pictures. The eyes woke up and noticed them, each face in the pictures following them as they climbed the stairs and their mouths stretching open the higher and higher they went. As though they were surprised to have visitors or calling out to them to warn them not to go any further.

Poe's tail twitched when she stopped, curling at her back in the shape of a question mark as she considered the room next to them on the left that was partially ajar. She pushed on it and brought them into a room that was even darker in the moonlit house.

"Now I really can't see," hissed Bernadette.

"It's okay, there's a little lamp here, hang on."

"Are you sure that's—"

Poe pulled the little chain, and it made a clicking sound before creating a little beam of light. The light revealed a small study, one that would just be used as a memorabilia or trophy room that is there for show. Or to preserve. Poe coughed in a bit of the dust ticking her nose even through the skull mask, likely from the bookshelves at the rear of the room covered in dust, as well as the desk that sat in front of them. It, too, looked like it had been preserved in time and untouched, with the exception of a stack of letters that sat on it.

"So this is someone's office or something," declared Bernadette.

"Someone important," Poe agreed.

This room had pictures as well, and when the three noticed them, they saw they ranged from different time periods. They looked at one nearest to them that was probably the oldest of all, in black and white, depicting a large group of people wearing similar clothing. Robes, tunics, or religious gown garb of some sort. They stood in the middle of one of the squares in town, and Poe recognized it as the one with the biggest tree she visited. She stared at it, knowing the significance of that square and tree, but trying to figure out what could make the people in the photo have different facial expressions. Some looked happy, prideful, while others looked serious and threatening, almost. All were adults, with the exception of one little girl standing by the woman in the middle, most notably a mother-daughter pair. The girl looked much younger than them, about eight or nine, and other than her age, the only other difference was she did not wear the same garb. Poe fixated on the kid's face. Her expression was a curious one, trying to make herself as small as possible. It was clear she was there out of emotional obligation to whatever group this mother was a part of. She turned her attention to the ones occupying Bernadette and Caleb, both staring in recoils of disturbance. Poe saw the old photo of three men kneeling, their heads downcast, arms tied around their backs. The ropes behind them were

attached to something, possibly to stakes in the ground. Next to it was one of the photos like Poe saw before: five people, three men and two women, their arms tied above their heads. These were secured to the great big tree that was in the square, and the photo was taken far enough away to see that other spectators were at the scene. Watching the scene. Enjoying the scene as though watching a museum exhibit, documenting their own photos. These five all wore similar garb, but bright white like they were ghosts. They did not stay white for long, for they all had been drenched in something that was poured over their heads and spilled onto their garments. Although black and white, Poe could guess well what it was. It was not paint.

They looked at the next one, which was a grainy and dark photo of a large group of people in the communal garb. They were gathered in a circle, surrounded by candles and a few books. In the middle of them was a platform with more candles and a pile of human bones. The same woman who seemed to be the mother of the little girl inched a bit further into the circle, as though a status symbol.

Down the wall were more, and the pictures seemed to be in timely order. Poe did not understand how or why they were important, but they were. The next one showed the same people from before in another group shot, mostly, as most of the older ones were gone. The girl was older now, about teen-aged, and the mother had gone.

"Look," Bernadette pointed to the photo she was looking at that came out of a newspaper article. Poe joined her to see the growth of the girl into a woman, surrounded by a new group, and the garb had gone out of style. This had a caption read: *Tellenboe family, Mock Cob Crier, 4th Annual Spring Picnic.*

"Tellenboe," repeated Poe. "We're in the mayor's house!"

A shrill cry interrupted the silence, sounding like it was coming from the far right of the hallway toward the right side of the house.

"Is that—"

"That might be her!" Poe cried. "Come on, let's go after her!"

Poe skidded out of the room, the other two in tow, though not as eager. Poe sauntered down the hallway with ease, the lamp they left on helping them see a bit more. They came to a small railing leaning over a sitting room on the floor below them. The cry sounded again, louder and more agonizing.

"It's her!" Poe said. "It's her all right!"

She led them down the hallway, all rooms on either side with closed doors. Poe thought to run past the doors that were closed, not believing that a monster would come into a house if it actually could open a door, and then shut it ... unless it was not a monster... She kept going and they turned the hallway again to another one with a few more rooms, and sure enough, the one at the very end was ajar. A soft light sneaked through the open crack.

Poe kept one hand on her bag, Bernadette held on to her necklaced items and her bag, and Caleb hung on to his sheet. Poe rushed down the hallway with her back arched and low enough to the floor that she almost ran on all fours, and could have, making her go faster.

She charged through the door to see the mayor with her back turned, though she could not see what was in front of her.

"Mayor Vivienne! We heard screams! Are you all right? What got in?"

The mayor stood still, not acknowledging Poe at first, but then slowly turned to meet them.

They gaped at the face that was not hers ... hollow and static, frozen into an expression of sheer terror just like the faces carved into the pumpkins. Though, hers looked less like a pumpkin and more like the original turnip face: gaunt and pale and drained of color. Her lower jaw hung unhinged into the last scream it made and seemed to just stay there. The three of them became rooted to the spot as she took a couple of steps toward them, and they could finally see what was wrong with the rest of her expression. Her eyes, normally gentle brown, had clouded over to an opaque white and looked like eggs once they became hard-boiled. But she could see them.

"M-m—Mayor Vivienne?" Poe tried.

Bernadette clutched her necklaces and said some words under her breath while Poe made like she was reaching for the solution ... though the next movements made her stop. At that moment the mayor suddenly lifted herself up, so that she was up on the tips of her toes, nothing but the pointed sickle boots touching the ground, and then she flew at them with the speed and drive of a winged predator that found its prey. And then she unleashed a scream that sounded like it came from anywhere but her—something low, deep, and angry.

The three of them screamed at once and ran from the room, tripping over themselves and each other. The sound of the ear-splitting cry filled the hallway and almost paralyzed them as the thing that was Mayor Vivienne dragged itself across the carpet, arms outreached. It could not be possible, but somehow it looked like her arms and legs stretched longer.

"What the—"

"It's not—"

"She's possessed!" cried Bernadette.

Poe made to reach for the solution the same time the others did, the same time the mayor hovered over them like she was about to fly, or already was. Poe reached into her bag, a sickening drop in her stomach when her fingers scraped the bottom.

"I'm almost out!" she cried. "I've got, like, none left!"

Caleb and Bernadette reached into their bags.

"Me too!"

"I've got only a little bit!"

"Quick!" Poe ordered. "Give her all you got!"

Poe and Caleb threw their handfuls at once and watched the shimmering pink and blue and green catch onto the abnormally long arms and legs, melting onto them and stopping them long enough to be able to get away. They ran down the hallway and made their way over to the stairs, though behind them they could make out the tearing noises of the mayor pulling her feet from the candy-cemented carpet.

Thwunk. Thwunk.

"Move! We've got to get out of here!"

Poe could hear the tearing noises continue and increase, and at the same time, Bernadette was reciting words she could not place. She held on to her last handful of solution, saying them more and more aggressively as the possessed mayor practically broke her own bones to release herself from the magical bond. They heard the crunching and the snapping that no human could perform, let alone withstand. The thing that was inside the mayor twisted her body, stretching her arms, legs, and even neck and face. It unleased another cry that was sharp enough to break glass as one leg broke completely free from its hold. Bernadette's back was to Poe and Caleb, facing it and reciting her words louder and louder until the lone scoopful of dust in her hand started to glow bright green, then bright pink, and then Bernadette threw it with all her might as the mayor screamed and flew at them.

Something else happened that Poe did not expect and could not place at first, seeing the flash of pink practically blind her, then seeing that it was surrounding them completely. Bernadette was heaving in and out like whatever she just did took all the energy out of her. Poe regained her senses and let her eyes adjust, the little gasp coming from her inaudible to anyone but her.

Pink stuff plastered the entire house, covering everything on the walls and strung across the light fixtures on the walls and up on the ceiling. It coiled around the floor but missed their ankles. Bernadette intended the aim to be away from them. She made her aim. The thing that was the mayor hung drawn and quartered from thin shreds hanging from the ceiling and spattered against the walls, holding an arm and leg each. One piece fastened against her face, covering her mouth and whatever kind of monstrous noises she was making.

"Bernadette! Bernadette, what did you *do*?"

Bernadette turned around with her hands covered in the pink sticky mess, her face twisted in shock.

"I ... I made more."

Caleb was nudging a pile of the mess with his toe while Bernadette urged Poe to get away, watching the mayor in her trap.

"It's not going to hold for long!"

She urged them to move while they could, running down the stairs. They would look back to see if she got loose, and that was all they looked for. If they looked at the portraits lining the walls, they would have seen all of them in expressions of fright, covering their mouths with their hands and following them as they fled down to the first floor. The solution mess continued down there, stretching along the stair banister and across the walls. And across the door.

Poe threw herself at it, pulling the knob. She made to swipe with her fingers, though the foam-made claws on her full-body suit could not sever the sticky mess. It absorbed into the crack between the door opening and the threshold.

"It's stuck!"

"I'm sorry!" cried Bernadette. "I didn't mean to! I didn't mean to make so much and such a mess!"

"Don't worry about it now, just—"

The three of them turned around, searching for another way out. They instead heard the tearing and the high-pitched screeches coming from upstairs. They could not help but stare at the thing that somehow turned a human into a monster. It was the way the mayor-thing pulled away from the candied restraints, and the way that its head could roll about like it had no neck. It stood before the base of the stairs, its eyes blended in with the paleness of the skin, and its mouth warped into an uneven shape as it locked onto the three of them, standing there trapped. The body twisted itself down to all fours, back arched into a bend as the arms and legs extended themselves into gangly daddy longlegs. And then it crawled down the stairs at rapid speed.

Poe and Caleb bumped into each other trying to get around, trying to find another door, or anything. Her head swam and poured thousands of thoughts, none of which would form a coherent sentence or idea.

"This way, move!"

Poe urged them down the part of the house to the right, finding a kitchen with no doors and a closet full of clothes and boxes.

They ran around a corner toward a big open room, following the light glow that was coming from there, and seemed to be calling to them. They found themselves in an open sitting room. A big ornate couch curved around the fireplace. Its flames were dying and small, but still enough to light the room.

"Is that a door?" whispered Caleb.

They flew to it, the fire flickering as they entered the room, and disturbed the serenity of it. Poe grabbed the handle and heard the agonizing click. They could see through the glass window that it led to outside, to some outside area, and would have been their saving getaway.

The gangly shadow spread at the door and across the room. The fire flashed in and out as the shadow grew taller and closer, now standing upright. Poe turned first and faced it, standing there, reaching an arm out to them. She saw the fire pokers by the fireplace, keeping her thoughts on them while anticipating the moves of the monster.

"Don't move yet," she whispered to her friends.

Caleb said something, but she did not hear him. Instead, Bernadette was rapidly spewing out another series of words in another language.

"Wait, no!" hissed Poe.

Bernadette shook her head at her but did not snap at her like she thought she would, keeping her full concentration and sticking her hand out. She kept it up as the mayor-thing entered the room, its head jerking from side to side and mouth twitching open and close. It moaned, it screamed, and then it screamed louder. It half-walked, half-crawled, hunching over, then standing upright again. Poe inched by the fireplace and grabbed a poker, and then another to give to Caleb. Bernadette spoke louder this time, opening her hand and aiming her palm at the possessed woman like she was trying to make balls of flame come out at her. Bernadette stuttered, her breath getting shorter, repeating the words, just as the mayor stopped short of not quite past the couch. She let loose another scream and both her hands flew to her face. Poe and Caleb held the pokers in tight fists while Bernadette paused, hesitant, looking like this was not the reaction she had been expecting. Bernadette stayed still while Poe kept her poker raised in defense. The mayor rolled her head all around her shoulders, and they saw the way her fingers were digging into her flesh like she was trying to make her head stop. Something flickered in Poe's gut.

That's it.

The mayor pulled her head to the left, and then again to the right. Her legs stepped in place and then stepped back, wanting to move forward, but at the same time not wanting to move forward. She let loose a series of yells as her body wobbled and twitched. She pulled at her face, and all three of them heard the sickening ripping that sounded like canvas being torn. Not flesh. Her hands pulled down to the left, while her face moved to the right. Her whole body moved to the left at the same time struggling to move itself to the right. The canvas-ripping sound intensified ... and then they saw the mayor split in half.

What they really saw was the ghostly outline come out of the right side of the mayor's body, another face with equally big eyes and mouth. The rest of the spirit came with it and seemed to be stuck as the fight to separate continued, for the moment looking like conjoined twins, until the mayor let out another grunt and heaved herself to the side. And then that spirit peeled off of the mayor's body in one long phantasmal mess and did not stay, dashing through the wall and disappearing. The mayor fell to her knees, rubbing her eyes with her fingertips before succumbing to the ground, and laying still.

<h1 style="text-align:center">27</h1>

"Mayor Vivienne!"

"Mayor!"

Poe dropped the poker, rushing to the lump on the ground. The mayor was steadily breathing, though she still had a lack of color in her face.

"Someone go to the kitchen and get a wet towel or something!"

Poe saw Caleb dash away and she bent toward the mayor, gently putting a hand on her shoulder.

"Mayor Vivienne?" she tried again.

The woman's lips were moving, but no words were coming out. Poe leaned in, waiting for them to form. Bernadette came close but stood at a distance, stiff as a board. Caleb came back with a wet dish towel, splotches of water all across his ghost sheet. Poe folded the towel up and placed it on the mayor's head. After a moment, her eyelids fluttered, learning how to work themselves again, and they opened to see the three things standing above her.

The mayor gasped and jerked up, making both Poe and Caleb back away.

"It's okay, it's us!"

"It's us!" Bernadette said, putting herself in front of them. "It's us, Mayor Vivienne. It's Bernadette, Poe, and Caleb!"

Poe lifted enough of her skull mask to reveal her human face. Caleb lifted his sheet over his head and kept it there like some sort of holy garb. Vivienne looked at them all and then exhaled in relief, rescuing the wet towel from her shoulder.

"Oh, thank god," she said in a short breath. "Thank god. Are you all okay?"

"We are."

"Yeah."

"Are you okay?" Poe asked with more urgency.

"I am now."

She looked around the room for a moment, at the walls and up at the ceiling. She sat up and Poe helped her to the couch.

All four of them sat down before the fireplace, the still-burning embers crackling in each log. It only took a few seconds to learn there was still warmth and still could be, even if a fire seemed weak or small.

"I was fighting it," Vivienne started. "The whole time."

The fireplace cracked and a little spark rolled into the ashes, pulsating a bit before dying out.

"It overpowered me for the most part. I knew that you were here when you came, that someone was here because it got excited. And I knew that I had to fight harder once it wanted to go after you. Especially once it knew it had you trapped."

Vivienne wiped her face with the towel and placed it on her shoulder, now acknowledging them with equal parts amusement and surprise.

"But, you're here... What made you come to my home and come inside?"

"We were out collecting candy, as you know," Poe started. "Of course. We were walking past your house, and I sort of got this really bad feeling, like something was wrong, so we had to investigate."

Vivienne smiled. "Well, you must have really good instincts."

There was a beat.

"I'm sorry," Bernadette said in a small voice.

They turned to her, sitting at the end of the couch with her head low.

"I'm sorry, Mayor."

"What for?"

"Well," Bernadette shifted to face her. "I didn't mean to make it worse when I was trying a spell to pull that thing out of you. It was just really powerful, and I had a hard time with control and all, and—"

"No, that's all right."

"Well, it was fighting me."

"That's okay," Vivienne said in an encouraging voice. Poe caught the undertone, though, the one that suggested that the actual exorcism did not have the aid of magic. She was not sure if Bernadette knew it, or maybe she did, the way she needed to provide defense.

"And—," Bernadette continued. "Um, I am really sorry about the mess upstairs."

Vivienne crossed her brow like she was trying to recall something that she did not see.

"I'll just do a cleansing charm on it, okay? And then it will all be gone in seconds. Sorry about that."

They shuffled on the couch, making themselves comfortable, finally feeling like they could be safe in that moment. Poe had the moment to ask the burning question when Caleb beat her to it with context.

"How did that spirit get in here?" he asked.

"It didn't get in here. I stepped out, knowing the risks … I do every year, even just for a moment. Sometimes I want to see if a spirit will visit me. Not one like that, of course."

"That was an angry spirit. It targeted you. Why did it target you?"

Vivienne squeezed her eyes and sighed at the question she was expecting, though not in such detail. "How did you know it was angry and targeted me?"

"I've seen them," was all Caleb said.

Vivienne took another breath. "It's because of my blood. It would come after me because of my family history. And since I'm the last living Tellenboe, well … that's all they would know."

"Your family history?"

The mayor nodded.

"My family ran this town for as long as it existed. The Tellenboes were the early settlers, ones who founded the town. They knew where it stood in regards to the planes between worlds and wanted it to be a secluded and sacred place. So, the entities from the other planes were things that were worshipped and respected. And, well … they were worshipped in harsh and extreme ways sometimes. Back in the day, criminals were executed, and they were done so by sacrifice to the entities that came out to visit at night, especially the Night of Passing when more came out."

Poe was picturing the old photos they saw, and the tree in the square she saw in person.

"Have you seen the old jail cell?"

Poe nodded. Bernadette crossed her brow, and Caleb stayed silent.

"Criminals were sentenced to death, sometimes even for things not worthy of a death sentence. Just so that the beings would get their offerings. They would stay in there, and then be brought out to the square. They were basically presented to the Nether realm beings as entrees on a silver platter. It was so common. Everyone was made to believe it was for the greater good, to have them take the bad ones so they would leave alone the good ones."

Vivienne's lip twitched.

"Not always the case, of course. We still had the Shut-In, but there were ... accidents, of course."

"Is that why more of them are coming out?" asked Bernadette. "Because the town is not giving them 'offerings' anymore?"

"Sort of. I am the one who put a stop to the live sacrifices once I became mayor. I was very young, but I fought for it. I fought to make it seem like there were no people here anymore and they were going to have to find their own victims somewhere else. But ... they still came. The vengeful spirits haunted the town and would continue to come to haunt the town and the family that made it happen. And then, at one point, more of them came out. More spirits, more demons, more monsters. Like they all caught on or something. We've seen a surplus over the last year or so."

Caleb turned his head to look around him like they could be right behind him.

"I'm the last one. I was the one to correct all of my family's mistakes and put a stop to it. To figure out how to put a stop to it all. If possible."

She looked at the three sitting on the couch by her, smiling. "I think I did a good job getting a supernatural being hunter, and his assistant now, and then, a family of witches. And three brave young people going out into the night to help me on this."

Vivienne gave her eyes a good rub, stifling a yawn, while her company let her compliment comfort them.

"It must be so late," she continued. "You three should get on now. You should get home, get back to your families and get to bed. You shouldn't stay out all night for this."

"I am used to being out," Poe commented. "Besides. It's my job."

The words tasted like pride on her tongue and she beamed. Poe could hear those words, and say them as often as she wanted, and it would still have the same effect. She was a creature hunter. She was, she just never knew it before. And here she was, mayor-approved.

"Well, don't stay out too much longer," she insisted. It was amusing that adults tended to act on parental roles for children no matter the relation. Still, the mayor was more on their side. "You keep it up, though."

Bernadette got up first. "I'm going to, uh, take care of the mess." She left the room while Poe and Caleb stood back up, the mayor taking her time.

"Are you going to be all right?"

Vivienne gave her a knowing grin. "Don't worry about me. I'll be fine. I've been around for a while, remember?"

She escorted Poe and Caleb to the foyer, and Poe cringed at what her reaction would be to the pink webbing all over the walls. Bernadette was standing by the stairs of the room completely back in order—no trace or speck of the sticky mess anywhere. Poe blinked, unable to believe it. Moments ago, it looked like a giant bubble gum bubble popped and now, there was no proof of anything that had happened. They came into the foyer where the pictures in the picture frames were clean of anything, even dust, and were still and unmoving as pictures should be.

"Thank you, again," Vivienne said. "For coming to my rescue."

Bernadette tugged at the things around her neck, pulling out a rose-colored crystal on a velvet cord.

"Here," she said, presenting it to the mayor. "Take this. It's for protection."

Vivienne cupped the crystal in her hand and put it to her chest. "A real witch's talisman, huh? I've never had one before. That's very thoughtful of you, Bernadette. Thank you!"

She walked the three to the door and opened it, inching just enough to see the outside. All they heard was the light screeching of the front door, and a few stray leaves running across the street with the breeze. Just as the fire in her fireplace stayed alight, all the pumpkins down the steps kept their little flames, the wicks protected by their hollow holders. Poe stuck her head out first, immediately pulling the animal skull back down in its place. Caleb pulled his sheet back down, matching his own skin tone, and only making his glass gray eyes appear bigger with the sheet holes. Bernadette looked up to the moon resting on someone's roof, aging into an amber color so dark with flecks of orange it could have been becoming a pumpkin.

"Be safe, you three," Vivienne said. The three exited down the steps, with Poe giving the mayor a final look.

"Thank you. You too."

The door shut, sending a puff of air big enough to blow out the candle in the pumpkin closest to the door. Though as the three left, the fire circled back around the wick and became taller, brighter, showing off the toothy, triumphant grin.

Poe arched forward and held her hands out with her fingers curved into claws. Her tail seemed to get the signal, waving at her back and knocking into Caleb and Bernadette. She pointed her face upward to hear, see, or smell anything.

"You're really getting into that," Bernadette remarked, though she wrapped her cloak all the way around herself and pulled the brim of her hat down.

"Remember, we're Nether realm beings ourselves," Poe pointed out. "We've got the keep up the act without any protection until we can get to your place."

Caleb let his sheet billow around him, the long length looking like he had no feet.

"Does anyone have any idea what time it is?" Bernadette asked. "I mean, I know my moms will be up. That's not an issue at all."

Poe and Caleb answered that they did not.

They went back down the same path, down the sidewalk, down where they would see something running on all fours in the distance and disappearing. Poe kept her head up, walking slightly quicker and in front of Caleb and Bernadette.

"There..." Caleb started. "There's another one!"

They stopped. Poe scanned the streets to find out what other one it was.

"Where?" she whispered. "What?"

"A spirit," Caleb answered, shuffling his feet back.

"But I don't see—"

Poe lost the rest of her sentence when she did, in fact, see it. Out of nowhere, floating down the street, going in the same direction they were going. The spirit that possessed the mayor was hazy in sight and in memory as it was gone the moment Vivenne exorcized it, but this one appeared sharper. It was sharper than any spirit Poe had ever seen, the fine detail drawing coming out of a sketch.

"I can see it!" Poe pointed. It was clear, as monochromatic clothing on a person, drawn in chalk against rough concrete. Walked like any other person would, though the tendrils rising from all around it told otherwise. Poe reached up under her mask to rub her eyes, adjusting it back down, and it was still there. It was in the shape of a man, tall and wearing a nightgown, looking like someone sleepwalking.

"I can't see anything," Bernadette declared. "Where?"

Poe turned to her and pointed. "Right there! The one walking down the street. Right in front of us."

"Yeah, he almost looks like a regular person!" commented Caleb.

But Bernadette scowled, squinting her eyes in the darkness and then back at the other two.

"You can't see it?" Poe realized.

Caleb went back and forth between the two. "But you can?" he asked Poe.

Bernadette huffed. "Well, that doesn't make sense."

"It's gone now," Caleb said. The streets now held only the light aftermath of fog, and nothing and no one else.

"Then it probably went behind a house or something," Bernadette said defensively.

"Sometimes they come in and out like that, and are seen just at random different times. Other times, you can see them the whole time. Up here they can look just like regular people," said Caleb.

Up here.

Poe regarded Caleb. "So, you know what they're like then?"

He gave a curt nod. "I can see them as clear as I can see anything, now. But, but you can see them," he turned his attention to Poe. "Why can *you* see them?"

"Yeah, why can you?" Bernadette rounded on Poe. "Did you die too?"

She said it curtly, but it might have partially been a real question, as they did not know. Frankly, Poe did not understand where that came from.

"No!" she declared. "I didn't die and then just come back to life! Pretty sure I would know if I did!"

"Then what is it?" Bernadette demanded.

Poe suddenly felt like she was shoved under the spotlight between a boy who had been a spirit himself and a witch who had indeterminate and unpredictable powers.

"I—I don't *know*," Poe said, honestly.

Bernadette did not take her eyes off her, studying her again, like when she first met her. Poe had the feeling she had been doing so from afar for so long. She felt exposed, but of what, she had no idea. Poe was saved from coming up with an answer when they heard moans high in the sky, and then the burst of more foggy entrails.

"More spirits!" Caleb said. "The flying ones, the not-nice kind … like in the mayor's house."

Just as Caleb announced it, they came and came in hordes, and the very description of "not nice" Caleb labeled. Poe's adrenaline from the recent events up until then kept her body active and warm, but at that moment she could feel each and every bead of sweat chill on her skin. The figures rose ahead, swarms of fog and smoke forming the shapes of hands with long fingers, and heads with long faces. She did not want to look up at them for long. They kept running down the street with the shadows on the pavement below them. They heard the moans sounding across the sky.

No sooner did they escape down one street when they cascaded into each other, Caleb being the door-stopper blamed for standing in the middle of the street. The moans were closer this time, and not so much in the sky as they were on ground level … but still high enough.

"It … it…" Caleb pointed, stammering as a broken record.

It moved with the grace, with purpose, knowing exactly what it was doing. The silhouette stepped out from a tree, equal in height and arms as skinny as branches, waving its even longer fingers as it sounded its call. It sounded the low melodious moan again, spreading its hands out before it, conducting the sound. It turned its head to the new sound, answering its call, revealing the thick horns curling out of the side of its head.

WOOSH. WOOSH.

And then they all heard things flying above them at once, dark things that blended into the night, dark things that could very possibly see in the dark.

"Don't make quick movements!" warned Caleb, his words coming out as quick movements. "Stay quiet, and still. Move slow. Turn your head down, Bernadette. You need to walk slowly and look like you're a monster that just got here and is taking its time learning where it is!"

He fluffed his sheet to make it look like it was flowing. "Follow me. It's our only hope of getting by unnoticed."

They started their solemn march down the street, Bernadette keeping her head down but once in a while trying to steal glances of the giant horned man. Poe took a few steps on two feet, then bent down and walked the rest of the way on all fours. Her tail positioned itself above her like it was natural, and her legs moved in place like they were even more natural. The horned demon sent out another call, walking out into the street now with various things soaring over its head. Poe dared a peak, noting the long robe it wore that gave it its intelligence and status. She wondered how Rex would react if he saw one up close and personal.

They continued down the street, turning down another one at the sight of an enormous dog down at the other end. It sat with its backside down, positioned alert and on guard. Its front legs were so muscular they curved inward, paws ending in nails that put hawk talons to shame. One of its ears twitched. With Caleb's urging, they turned away from it and headed down the next street. Poe's sweat stayed cold, in tune with everything in surrounding, prickling under her bodysuit and going right through her disguise. Now out into the street, the demon lord unleashed another call, ringing into their heads.

Down this street, the trees and houses blocked out the moon, giving it the sense of concealment, that somehow the bleak darkness would be a comfort to conceal them, though it could also mean that it was concealing other things.

"I ... I don't sense anything," Poe declared, and thus they took her word for it. Had to take her word for it. Poe wasn't sure if she was the leader on this expedition, or if she was supposed to be. The pressure had been on her full swing, a pressure pushing at the back of her head, one that told her to make all the decisions. But Bernadette and Caleb walked beside her, side-by-side in pace, and had been equal in making decisions themselves. They were the dark horses coming up by surprise with special knowledge, personal to them. But there was still so much Poe did not know. *What interactions had Caleb had ... during his time? How long was he there and what did he find out?* And the one that stuck to her, something unpleasant she could not wipe away: *What knowledge, and thoughts, did Bernadette have?*

"My moms' place is up there," Bernadette stated in authority. "If we just go down this block, we should make it there soon." She quickened her pace, certain of that finish line and not bothering to know if there were any obstacles in the way. There were.

"Wait..." Poe started, seeing the shadow, and smelling the scent. "Wait, we can't go this way."

"Why not?"

"What's there?"

She could make out the shape, ambiguous except for the two points atop its head. It was low enough for Poe to figure that it walked on four legs, and guess what it would be.

"It's closer," she said. "Than the last one."

"Than what?"

But they all saw the shadow thing move, the way it turned its head, and twitched the pointed ends on its head. Ears. Ears listening, and ears that heard something. And then they saw the glow of two orbs coming out of the shadows, dim and subtle, and slanted in malice. The growl traveled down the empty street. Poe, Bernadette, and Caleb turned on their heels to go around this street, and would have, if it was not a direct mirror scene from the previous one. This next creature advanced silently, eyes more slanted but still glowing more fiercely, the muscular legs moving in unison.

"It—"

"Told the other one?" finished Caleb.

"That's not possible," said Bernadette. "How? They're too far away!"

Poe's feet shifted the more and more Bernadette's sentence became untrue, and they did not have time to delay. The first one growled, and then the second, and then they both charged. The beasts pranced across the gravel like they were hovering above it, like they were barely touching it at all and therefore it did not slow them down. Poe, Bernadette, and Caleb ran, skidding to a jerking halt when another one appeared right in front of them.

They stared at this animal, dark as a shadow, but was as solid and real as they were. Its black coat was so thin it gave it the appearance of skin, showing its knobby joints. The beast scrunched its muzzle into a snarl, teeth never before seen on a domestic dog, long enough to hang over its bottom lip. A line of drool escaped down its maw, yellow enough to be sickly mucus. And those eyes, amber and pupilless, burned.

It barked, starting its chase. And then it was nothing but a set of teeth gnashing inside a giant black blur.

Poe, Bernadette, and Caleb felt the gravel below them as they pushed against it, working their feet to will it to a treadmill to move them faster and bring their assailants further away. They barked, all three of them, all ... four of them? Poe could hear the call of the hounds as they all understood the same discovery, and all came to pursue them for themselves.

"Anybody have any solution left?" Bernadette asked the others.

"I don't!"

"I don't either!"

Bernadette cursed. "We have to really book it to my place!"

Poe felt herself running faster. The very tip of her tail lit on fire, and she could actually feel it running down along her spine. What else could be making her run faster? She allowed herself a peek behind her at the pack on the chase, the barking and thundering legs catching up.

"Let's split up!" Bernadette said.

"Are you nuts?" Poe cried.

"What?" Caleb cried.

"Just do it!" she said again. "Our chances are better!"

Before either Poe or Caleb could protest again, Bernadette took off on her own down another street. Caleb made his own detour and cut between houses to throw them off. The hounds made like they did not know who to follow at first, but as Poe ran, she realized more than one of them was sticking with her. She kept going straight, seeking on the very thing ahead that would be her strength. The tree's branches were open arms, and she ran into them, pouncing off of the trunk and making her way up them with that burning speed. Below her, she heard the barking and snarling of the hounds, jumping up at the base of the tree but unable to go any further. But she did, catching branch after branch until she was as high as the roof of the neighboring house. She crawled out on all fours across that branch, feet curved against it and pushing it away from her until she met the roof.

Poe sunk down and allowed herself to catch her breath. The hounds continued to bark, even running to circle the house to see if she had landed there. She steadied her heart as well as her breath, thinking of Caleb and Bernadette, and wondered where they had gone and if they were safe. Somehow, an idea at the back of her mind told her that they were. She imagined Caleb hiding in the bushes. Even with the white sheet, the monsters would pay him no attention. They would not smell him out, for he smelled like death, and they would pass him up. Bernadette, now she was clever enough to have a spell she'd have conjured up to slow them down or distract them. A spell she could do better on her own and not distracted by the three of them. So, she thought better when she was on her own and did not have to worry about the others. Bernadette would be all right. But Poe could not leave them by themselves for long. She crawled across the roof, making no sound, and gratefully so, less she frightened the owners of the home to think a monster was crawling around over their heads. She went over and slid down slanted triangles, perching at the pointed edge where she could gaze across other houses and view the streets below. They were out there somewhere, and not too far away. She knew she would have no trouble finding them, though it also meant other things could find her. Poe stared at the slants and points of the roofs, the tips of her fingers and toes tingling in a way she never felt before. She felt it in a cavity in her waist, a strange pull at her center of gravity, urging her to do something that her brain fought against, but the more she thought about it, the more appealing it was. So, she backed up a little, putting one foot behind her and keeping her balance. She raced forward with all her might, pumping her arms and imagining them giving her leverage and she leaped right off of the roof, soaring through the air and landing on the next roof without fail. Her blood pumped, sending white-hot shots of adrenaline through her veins and she continued onto the next one. Poe moved with equal parts speed and grace, feeling a bit weightless herself, almost believing for a minute that she could fly. She leaped from one roof to the other, relinquishing in the rush and the challenge of the different shapes she landed on. The last house she stopped long enough to calm herself down and try to collect her bearings, forcing herself to get back on track. She had to go find them.

Poe peered down to the streets from where she perched, feeling the advantage this gave her to oversee everything. No more creatures lurked in the shadows of her surrounding, but that did not mean they were not out there. She had to go find them. Her senses tingled with a different sensation this time, the kind she felt the first few times going out into the night with Rex. The time came for her to go on the hunt.

28

oe could smell them as she slid down the storm pipe. She knew where each one was and knew that they would not be able to hide. There came other scents, too, all of them and any of them coming and going, but she just had to pick the ones to concentrate on, the ones to seek out. The two of them. But that had become challenging. She felt pulled in many directions and felt like she could potentially go to all of them. She just had the strong urge to go to them ... but of what she would do when she caught them wasn't known. Poe kept low as she stalked through the grass and around the corner out to the street. The fog hung low, illuminated via street lamps, hiding anything that could be below it. Things on four legs, most likely, or things that were on two crouching down below it... Poe's skin prickled, more than tingled, and being alone meant that she had only her senses to listen to. She felt her mouth water all of a sudden, as if thinking about what could be hiding in the fog excited her ... excited her in the only way a predator would feel about catching its prey.

Poe stalked, silent and stealthy, running her tongue over her teeth many times. Her tail now wavered behind her, the one in charge, the one she took cues from. Bernadette really did enchant it to make it a part of her, or maybe she was more a part of it. She jerked her head to a light tapping sound.

Tap tap tap tap.

It sounded like someone impatiently tapping their fingernails. When she stalked around the corner, she confirmed the sound to the hound dog pacing back and forth in front of the road, moving this time with less stealth and more angst. It kept its head high while marching in place, no doubt waiting for her to show herself again. She left the area before it would notice her, tuning her senses to focus on the other scents. The ones she wanted to find the most.

They were close, and she was going to find them first.

She smelled them, one and then the other, and she salivated. She stayed low enough to the ground so that she could practically slither through it the way a snake would, all the way out and over to the second sound of something moving with less stealth and more angst. Poe spotted the silhouette of the long-pointed horn and the direction it was going, and her spirits lifted. She trailed it, turning down another street and ducking by houses to try to catch up. While in mid-run, she heard another angry bark that halted her in her tracks, coming from somewhere outside her radar, and she had to change course. Poe had the sudden wish that she could make some kind of deadly sound that would send it a message. Poe saw the pointed head and the cape swishing and did the only thing she could think of: run faster.

She got closer to Bernadette now and could hear her cry out, pivoting in her run to notice behind her. Before Poe could do anything she saw a flash of something bright green, and then she felt hundreds of tiny crystals stick all over her ... and then melt into a cold, wet, sticking substance. Poe felt her entire body stiffen, her muscles harden akin to bone, just the like bodysuit of pretended animal bones.

Poe tried to blink, her eyes not only under the mask but now clouded with some sort of crystal covering. She could still see, see enough of Bernadette to see her reaction when she threw the solution on her. Her stare was pointed and pierced, and less out of concern. Moments later, another figure appeared behind Bernadette, his white sheet billowing in the breeze.

"It's Poe!" he cried, clutching both his pillowcase bag and messenger bag. "It's Poe, you did that to Poe!"

Bernadette didn't say anything, staring down at Poe with a mixture of shock and alarm, and what Poe almost thought was suspicion. She kept that gaze on her, Poe unable to look away.

"Well, she makes it kind of easy to scare us like that, doesn't she?"

Bernadette waved her hands over Poe, softly reciting,

"Go back as you were before. A spell undone, and nothing more."

Poe blinked first, seeing tiny crystals pop before her eyes before feeling them pop all over her body, releasing warm streams of air. Her muscles and joints woke up from a groggy sleep, remembering how to move again. The last thing that woke up was her mouth, lips parting and partially tearing from being chapped.

"B—B—Bernadette..." Poe started. "Why—w—why did you...

"Why are *you* running on all fours?"

Poe could now stand up all the way, though her legs still wobbled.

"You were acting like an actual demon thing and you were almost too good at it!" Bernadette spat. "You can't blame me because you were running at us and I naturally thought that you were a monster coming to kill us! So what gives?"

"I was running from the hell hounds!" Poe explained. "I got away by climbing a tree and onto roofs. I got back down and just kept low to keep myself hidden, to try to come and find you guys."

Poe stared at their bags, both Bernadette and Caleb holding them in front of them like shields.

"You got more."

"Yeah, we got back to my place and managed to get the rest of the solution ... of what's left. It has to last us the rest of the night, and I already wasted some of it on you."

There was a moment of pressured silence. Bernadette focused primarily on Poe and Caleb nervously looking back and forth between the two. Bernadette finally handed Poe another container.

"Well, here's yours."

"Thanks," Poe said quietly.

"Did you see any spirits?"

Poe blinked, still trying to get herself straightened out. "No."

"Caleb did, and we want to trail them."

"They were walking," Caleb added. "Looked like people, just regular ghosts, and not evil entities. They could go somewhere." He turned. "Up there, I saw a few."

"Yeah, so now you both can ghost-hunt," Bernadette said. "Come on."

She spun around and continued back to where she came from, walking closer to Caleb and leaving Poe to walk behind them. She whispered something to Caleb, and Poe's tuned hearing made out her saying, "...want to watch her."

Poe's body still tingled with the aftermath, though now with a new sensation she did not like very much. *What does she mean by that??*

They went down a street with flickering, burning pumpkin faces on windowsills and porch steps. Some had more detailed and more creative faces than others, from people who were naturally artistic, or people who wished to scare away monsters more than others. They passed a house with a pumpkin looking more like one of the creatures themselves, with slanted, egg drop eyes and triangular teeth mapped around it. Another one had one similar, though with two small cones at the top. Horns. The glowing, decapitated head of a demon, from someone who spied one from their window and replicated it.

"It must be very late, now," Poe broke the silence.

"I think it's closer to midnight, or maybe after," Bernadette answered. "I didn't have the time to check the time."

"Most people will be asleep by now..."

"Right. Which means we're not going to get any more candy. We have just what we have now."

Bernadette turned to both of them, Poe catching up enough so the three of them formed a single line.

"The later it is, the worse?"

"Not always," said Caleb.

"Yeah," Poe stupidly agreed. She did not know what else to say.

As they walked up this street, Poe felt it before she saw it. The man walked ahead of them, a slow steady walk similar to sleepwalking. The fog materialized around him to make him more solid, and then he looked like an average man walking down the street as if it were regular hours. He even wore a brimmed hat for the sun.

"I've seen him before," said Caleb.

"Do you know him?" Bernadette asked.

"No, I've just seen him walking down the street out my window. He comes and goes like he is someone that once lived here and just likes to take walks once in a while."

Caleb pointed ahead of them. "He goes up there and disappears."

Bernadette nodded. "Then that's where we'll check!"

Poe watched the spirit just as Caleb did, the swirly outline sharpening to make him look like an actual man. And then blurring a bit to look like a ghost. *What for? Do they fade in and out, or was this new ghost vision fading in and out?* Poe reached up under her mask to rub her eyes. Too many things ran through her mind, and none of them made sense. It was strange how quickly her mood changed from euphoria to anxiety. She couldn't wait to tell Bernadette and Caleb that she leaped across roofs and that she felt invincible, but now, it seemed like it should be the last thing she should tell them.

You were almost too good at it.

Poe was good at hunting creatures, but how did she become good at impersonating them?

They left this last neighborhood altogether, now past neighborhoods and the downtown area in general. Here, the fog sat above the lawns in the squares, blanketed around the base of trees, and stretched across the woods ahead of them. There was somewhere else where it clouded together, a little thicker and a little deeper. Poe mostly kept her attention on the ghost man that would materialize in and out as they walked along the tall grasses and scattered trees. At another point, she saw another one, that of a woman with a long dress and even longer hair. This one was farther.

Poe and the others stopped once they reached an open field, at the spot where more would flash in and out, seeing not all of it was field. In fact, where they were, it was not a field at all. The fog gathered here and made it hard to make out. The glaze gave it a murky look, especially at the place where the grass ended and the mush, and water, began. Something about the water was off to Poe. She could tell by the way the ripples moved. Normal ripples would start as small circles and then work their way out as bigger ones, usually caused by a fish or small bug. Something was in the water that was not a fish or a bug...

Poe leaned forward a little, just enough to see small holes appearing, things in the water opening and closing. Eyes...? mouths...?

"Watch it," Bernadette warned, pointing to the sign. Poe and Caleb saw the distressed wood sign with the remedial drawing of a monster with big teeth in a red circle with a slash through it:

Dreadmoor Lake
NO swimming, at any time
NO feeding, of anything
Avoid at night at all costs

The three of them peered at the lake as something opened up a hole in the middle of the water that did not make any sense. More and more, these holes opened up and closed all over the surface of the water, making it look like anything but a lake. Lakes did not have holes.

"They look like ... mouths, or eyes, opening up in the water, don't they?" Poe said. Caleb was next to her, studying them as well, but he made no indication that he knew what it was. He and Poe both looked up at the same time to something, someone, materializing. A woman, hair tied into a prim bun, not paying them much attention. She walked all the way down to the lake like she knew it was there and intended to go for a swim. Except she did not swim. She walked right into the lake and descended into it like she was walking down stairs, the water almost sticking to her like it was not water and giving her hazy outline a greenish, bluish tint. She sank down and disappeared.

Poe stared, Caleb stared, and Bernadette turned to them.

"Okay, what happened? Something happened. It looked like it changed color. The lake. It got greener."

"A spirit," confirmed Caleb. "A spirit came, a woman, and she just went down into it."

The lake rippled, dark greens mixing with the blues, the hole in the center opening and closing. Like a mouth.

"It ate her," Poe said.

The lake closed, and the ripples calmed down. They watched something surface and open its mouth again every once in a while, in different spots.

"I've never seen this before," stated Poe. "I'll have to ask Rex about it."

"It's an undead sea," Caleb said. "It ... I saw one before. When I was ... there. It ... it looks like it just rose up from down there. And then they come out. Or, they come up as close as the surface. This is all regular lake until about ... there," he pointed. The water was still, for the most part, running through and over the little disturbances.

"So then it will go back down in the morning," Poe declared.

Caleb gave a little nod. "And that spirit went through it. Like it was using it as transportation to get back to the spirit realm."

"That's it, then!" Bernadette stated. "It's a portal!"

They peered into it now, all three holding themselves, wanting to see but too afraid to fall in. It looked just like a regular lake surface, though murky and holding things underneath. Things that were moving around enough to make it look like the water was moving... to make it look like it was even water from the surface down.

"I mean, it might be," Caleb countered. "But it might not be. It might just be for spirits to go through. It is water, after all. Mostly."

"What else is there?" Bernadette asked.

Caleb leaned back when something bubbled, going back down seconds later.

"It's like ... a sea of energy. Dead energy. Not quite touchable, but you can feel it. But it's a heavy kind of energy. It wears you down. It's like invisible molasses or something. In water. I don't know."

"You've been in it?"

"No. Just ... close enough."

And that was all Caleb said on the matter, ending his sentence in a rush and just watching the lake. They all did for a while, noting the unnatural way the waves would roll like a creature crawling underneath a carpet.

"Anything else go in or come out?" Bernadette asked.

The other two said no. Poe could hear the cawing of some bird of prey far off in the woods, but it was too far away to care about.

"So you're saying it wouldn't hurt you to go in it, and it's not all water?"

"I guess, but, you're not—"

Bernadette leaned forward.

"No!" Caleb said. "Stop."

"What if it were?" Bernadette wondered. Her next question made Poe's spine freeze worse than when she was under the formula.

"Well, Poe, can you swim?"

"What?!" Poe exclaimed. "Are you insane?"

"Well, you can do everything else! I just want to know if you can go in and see if you can ... find anything."

"No!" Poe cried. "I can't!"

Even with a part of her brain toying with the idea, just to see, all her instincts came back as a hard no. "I can't swim," she said, now certain.

"Have you ever tried?" Bernadette pushed.

"I'm not going to!" Poe snapped. "What, you think it's okay for me to jump in a lake of undead things that eat souls?"

"I just thought ... you know. That you could."

Poe's insides bubbled. No one could see the expression she was making under her mask, but she made it with such firmness she was clenching her teeth. She unclenched them, trying to steer her thoughts. Obviously, Bernadette thought so highly of her that she of all people would be able to swim in an undead lake without a problem. *Did she think that? But why would she think that?* Poe had no idea what went through Bernadette's mind.

"Why don't you try using a spell to see what's down there?"

"It doesn't work that way," Bernadette answered curtly. "That's complicated."

"So, why do you want me to do it?"

Poe wasn't expecting the pause. She looked to Bernadette now, crossing her arms.

"Because it's been clear from the start that you fit in too well out here. When they come out. You became a creature hunter and do so good at it. You can stalk, and hunt, and you're swift and sneaky. Your eyesight and hearing are super sharp and you act like you have no bones in your body. Now you can run on all fours and, for some reason, you can see other supernatural beings. And those hell hounds weren't chasing us, they were chasing *you.* I figured that out when it was my idea to split up. They were smelling *you.*"

"What are you talking about?"

Bernadette stared. "I thought this for a long time and now I think it's true. I think you're one of them."

"What!?"

Caleb jerked his whole body to Poe. He looked back and forth between the two but mostly kept his attention on Poe. His face also hidden, she wondered what expression he wore.

"No, it makes sense," Bernadette continued.

"No, it does not!" Poe argued. "You're crazy!"

"You said you don't know where you come from, right?"

"Pretty sure I didn't come from the Nether realm!"

"Listen, you've ... changed since you've been out here. There are things about you that come out the more and more time you spend out here. Like it's because you're spending more time in your element or something. Didn't you notice that? Didn't you notice some new things about yourself since tonight?"

Poe instantly thought of jumping across the roofs, and she put her hands to the side of her head.

"Your senses became sharper."

Able to smell death on the old woman. Hear monsters farther away from them. See ghosts. Feel... everything.

"Your body can move in ways it couldn't before that no human can."

Crawling under the fog. Moving on all fours.

"You changed."

Poe kept her hands at her head, adding pressure to make it stop. To make her thoughts stop, and to make her ears stop hearing everything Bernadette said.

"Poe ... I ... I want to ask you to take off your mask."

Now Poe's hands came down.

Bernadette took a step toward her, with Caleb backing away. Poe could see him clutch his bag, holding the new container of solution that hadn't been opened.

"I just want to see something."

"To see what? You think I'm a monster?"

"No, but I will be able to tell if more of you changed."

"And then what?"

"I'm going to help you," Bernadette said with authority. "I can and I will."

Poe didn't move.

"And you know if I can't, my moms definitely can."

Poe put her hands back on her mask, pressing all over to see if she could feel anything different through it. If she grew anything in the whole time they'd been out there. Her fingers traveled over to her forehead area, almost expecting to feel the sharp probe of horns. She exhaled when she did not.

"Poe, please," Bernadette tried again.

Poe reached both hands under her mask and pulled it off to reveal her face, looking down and not at the two of them right away. She cringed, expecting gasps or screams, but neither came. Both her eyes squeezed shut, she opened one and saw Bernadette and Caleb standing side-by-side and studying her. Bernadette did not look like she was looking at anything gruesome or terrifying, but she was definitely looking at something with interest. Her eyes opened just a bit wider.

"What?" Poe said. "What is it?"

Bernadette beckoned Poe to come closer. She reached in her bag, pulled out a small compact mirror, and handed it to her. Bernadette stepped back by Caleb and they both waited in silence as Poe opened the mirror.

Poe saw her normal green eyes and little button nose. She opened her mouth and saw that all of her teeth were the same size and shape, and moved the mirror all around her face to see that it was still perfectly normal and the same color and nothing—

She stopped, holding the mirror at the side of her head while the other hand slowly went to move her hair. That wasn't a normal shape. She parted her hair more and more to get her ear into view, alarmed to see that this was not an ear she recognized. Longer, to be exact, and sharper, ending in the perfect point. The more she brushed her hair out of the way, the longer the ears revealed. They sat at the sides of her head, giving her a horned silhouette, cone-shaped just like Bernadette's hat, and those just like the hell hounds and the rubrum demon horns.

"I knew it," Bernadette said quietly. "You're not human."

Poe dropped the mirror, hands covering her mouth, and took off in a run.

29

oe disappeared into the woods with short, panicked breaths. Behind her the others chased after
her, but she did not answer them or slow down. She ran
until she could find somewhere, anywhere, where she
could just be alone. She skidded her run when she found
a tree big enough to hide behind, then Poe pulled off the
skeletal gloves and unzipped her bodysuit, pulling the
whole thing off and stepping out of it in her undershirt
and underwear. She checked her hands, arms, legs, feet,
and back, touched her neck, and removed the under-
clothing, too, just long enough to look before pulling
them back on. Poe held herself as she steadied her
breathing and allowed herself some tears. Shivering in
the October chill, she hastily dressed again, plopping
herself down and resting against the tree trunk. She
hugged her knees to her chest and focused her thoughts.

I'm okay. I'm okay.

It had to be a mistake. Maybe Bernadette did it by
accident. Maybe there was something in that solution
that did it by mistake. That had to be it. Something had
to be it. Everything that Bernadette said made no sense.
And yet, all of it did.

She braved her fingers to touch her ears before bringing them back down, her chin touching her knees.

There are things about you that come out the more and more time you spend out here.

You changed.

I think you're one of them.

I knew it. You're not human.

She had been out countless times at night, out on hunts with Rex and nothing ever happened. They even had nights where they stayed out just as late as she was now, and nothing happened. She wasn't a monster. If she was, then it would have happened sooner, right? But why had it happened now? And what was it?

What am I?

She heard the snapping of twigs a few feet back, followed by the light crunch of leaves. She knew it was them and knew when they came close to see where she was. It was Caleb that pulled and urged Bernadette to stay back, so they backtracked to where they came from.

You said you don't know where you came from, right?

Poe touched her ears again. They were still human-like, still made of cartilage and not of fur or hair, just bigger, longer, and triangular. She even found the inside hole to be bigger, with what could have been tiny thin hairs coming out. Nothing else. Nothing else anywhere on her body.

I am going to help you. I can and I will.

Poe made herself stand up. She turned from the tree and walked to where Bernadette and Caleb were awkwardly standing around waiting for her to come out. They were talking, and Bernadette stopped them once she got close enough.

"Hey," Bernadette started.

"Hi."

"Are you okay?"

"Yeah."

Caleb shuffled closer. "Are you sure?"

"I guess." Poe looked at her feet, forgetting to be proud that the little toe and foot bones she made all stayed glued on. She stayed together all on the outside, while on the inside she was falling apart. "I ... I don't know what's happening to me."

"I am going to help you figure it out. I'm sorry I scared you."

"It's okay," Poe responded. "Because I scared myself."

Bernadette and Caleb looked at her, but they were not staring anymore.

"I don't ... feel like a demon," was all she said.

"I don't think you are a demon really. Not like an evil one or anything. But ... you're just not..." Bernadette started.

"I don't think you are either. Evil, I mean. You don't look or act anything like them. You didn't try to eat us."

Caleb's words were blunt enough for both of them.

"The Night of Passing must really be bringing out your natural ... characteristics," said Bernadette.

Poe considered that.

"Will I change more?"

They both had softer voices now.

"You might."

"But, you haven't. Not too much."

"You're..." Bernadette paused. "A being. Of sorts."

Something else caught Poe's attention, and she tilted her head to listen to the tops of the trees. Bernadette and Caleb said some more things, but she did not listen to them. Poe felt the muscles move against her head, realizing she could move those ears.

She was listening to something else.

"Poe?"

"Do you hear that?"

Now Caleb and Bernadette looked at the trees.

"No."

"What?"

Poe was already slouching down. "They're close. Or ... they just might be getting close."

Those ear muscles flared, free-moving appendages perking up in alarm and defense.

"No, they're coming, they're coming now, we have to go!"

"What's coming!?"

Poe didn't answer Bernadette and urged the two to run. She led them down the woods, in neither direction of the lake nor the town, which surprised and alarmed everyone. Even herself. They caught up as she ducked around trees and stumps, and instead of escaping out to the rest of town, they found themselves deeper into the woods. The trees multiplied and stood closer together, tall figures watching them and judging their activity. Poe kept her head up to the trees, to the sky, taking her cues from the shrill cries coming from somewhere above them.

Poe stopped, studying each branch. She searched all the holes between the tree leaves and the sky.

"Poe, what do you...?"

"Shh," Poe said, silencing Bernadette. She jerked around to something from behind them, up above, and not as far away as she thought. A shriek sounded that pierced the inside of their heads. They cowered and ducked as the source rustled and crashed through the trees on wide wings. Bony wings. It flew above them and made its way down to their area of the woods. They wanted to run, but all three stood paralyzed in terror. This creature looked part human and part bird, bones and skin were so dirty they looked like they had been submerged in charcoal. It had long, stringy hair covering its face and when the hair moved, it revealed a beak. The wings were leathery wide and long, though stringy with leftover leathery cartilage still covering them. The entire thing had some covering, and they all wavered in the wind the faster this thing flew at them. Poe, Bernadette, and Caleb tripped over leaves and sticks as they ran.

"Duck!" Poe cried.

She pulled them away as another one of these bird-demons dove, shrieking at them. They ran past some smaller trees and half-jumped, half-climbed over a large log. She heard the shrieking tickle the tops of her ears, letting her believe that these were sounding from afar. They ran through a thicket of bushes with the weeds long enough to tangle in their legs. Something landed in the tree in front of them, opened its wings to make itself seem bigger, and let out a cry sharp enough to pierce their eardrums. They backtracked against the weeds, thinking that it was going to leap down and attack them. The wings flapped against the tree with only its torso showing. As it hovered, they could all make out the vertebrae ending in a stub below the ribs. The thing opened its beak as far as it could go and screeched at them the same time they heard another pair of wings FWOOP down behind them. They jumped back at the full form standing on its legs, flapping its dead wings with its long hair hanging in clumps over its face.

Poe, Bernadette, and Caleb all grabbed handfuls of solution and threw it at the thing, the ice-green stuff crystalizing as it froze those wings in mid-flap. One by one the things dropped from the trees, clouds of bone dust erupting all around them. The three pivoted and hit all the targets, watching the claws suspend in mid-air that failed to scratch their faces off.

"We have to go," Poe said. "There's too many of them."

"What do you mean?" Bernadette shouted over an incoming screech.

"Many," Poe said, shaking her head. "An entire horde. We have to go *now*."

She led them down another section in the woods, keeping her head high. Her ears perked, catching those shrill sounds from miles away, and piling on to one another. She couldn't count them, but "horde" was the best way to number them. They tore through high weeds and low-hanging leaves until the trees thinned and they were out of the woods. Open air was simultaneously a relief and a new fear. The cold, empty air hung in silence as they walked out of the woods. No more twigs or leaves to crunch under their feet, as now they stood on untouched grass, exposed. Above them, the moon faded to a darker amber, an aging lightbulb threatening to go out. All they could hear were the sounds of their own breath as their bodies caught up to themselves. All they could see was the lineup of houses stacked up on irregular grounds.

"Are they gone?" Bernadette asked.

"Not quite, but we did lose them," Poe confirmed. She turned back to the woods, hearing each flap of wings, each brush of trees, and each cry of lament at losing fresh targets. "Well, I've never seen those before."

"Harpies," answered Caleb.

"Do they come out a lot?"

"No. Not really. You usually can see them before you hear them. Their cry is deadly and often paralyzing."

The other two kept looking behind them, though staying put like they were waiting for a signal from Poe. They trusted her, at least.

"If it weren't for you, we would have probably been bombarded by a ton of them," Caleb continued. "So, you saved our lives."

Poe let herself make a small smile.

"Yeah," Bernadette said. "That supersonic hearing of yours. It did it."

There was a beat of unspoken understanding as Bernadette and Caleb stood by Poe. No one said anything for a minute, but Poe could feel it. Her insecurity diminished a good deal, especially by the way Bernadette looked at her. It was no longer out of scrutiny, but of interest. It could have been something else, something akin to sincerity.

"You really are something," Bernadette concluded. Poe smiled all the way now. "I don't even know what that means, but I can't wait to find out."

"And you said you can help me?"

Bernadette nodded. "Yeah. And you? You can help everyone."

The fog lifted from the grass and took up in a current, washing over the ground. It did not create any new forms, though passed through everything in its way like it did not matter what was in its way.

"We still have work to do," she finished.

Caleb inched forward with something he had been holding that Poe forgot about: the skull still intact, jaw open, black cloth ears on top of it to give it its identity, as Poe had hers. She took it from him, and then put it back on over her head, feeling complete again with the rest of her disguise. A disguise that was roguish enough, mysterious enough to give her a shot of confidence back, and help her think better. She immediately looked to the dark, beyond the neighboring houses and buildings of the town, orchestrating her next move.

"Let's get back at it."

"I've tried the town borders before," Bernadette commented. "But it meant nothing. I didn't find anything, feel anything. My charm spells are really useless against anything that isn't of this plane. I don't even know how to find the plane."

They walked past squares of lone trees and empty park benches. Caleb took it upon himself to enjoy more of the leftover candies in his bag, no one stopping him. He lifted his sheet just enough to eat a piece of chocolate and still keep his face concealed. He only became startled when he almost dropped the silver wrapper, bending over to pick it up as they walked.

"Worried about littering?" Bernadette joked.

"No, about leaving a trace," Caleb answered, which silenced her jest. "A lot of them can smell. Most of them. They'll still be able to smell us."

"Maybe not better than Poe."

Poe's head was in the air, chin tilted at an odd angle. She was mostly listening to anything, but Caleb made her remember to smell for anything as well. It was mostly fog, and on occasion, the metallic rot of leftover carrion.

They curved around a sidewalk from a square, a bird taking off from its perch on the fence and flying away. They could not tell if it was a regular bird or not but did not bother with it. Poe looked like a dead creature again. Just another thing out and about to see what it could find. She started to act like one again, too. She walked lightly up on the pads of her feet yet slouched in a stealthy hunch. They passed a tree with a large net trap suspended from its big branch, swaying in the wind, though nothing inside it. Instead, there was something sprawled out on the lawn. Its clawed foot stuck out, flexed into fighting from a battle lost. Caleb and Bernadette reacted to seeing it, recoiling a little as well as walking a little closer to see more. Poe smelled it before she saw it and knew that the thing was dead. The pile of blood and red feathers soaked the grass.

"Something got this one. But not before it was already got," Poe said. She braved a toe to touch the claw, only to see that the other leg was missing ... torn off in fleshy strips, leaving a short stub under the feathered belly.

"I wonder if Rex was here," she said.

"Do you think he fought it?"

"I can't tell ... I'm just glad this was the losing one."

A couple of flies buzzed around the eyes, open and melted. One landed on it, only to become covered in grayish guck.

"This was recent, but not too recent," Poe observed. "I think they all went home now, whatever ones were out trying to fight everything. I think they might have all turned in for the night. I think it might just be us now."

"Makes sense. It's got to be way after midnight. I forgot to check the exact time at the shop."

"I want to see the dawn," Poe stated.

At that comment, they observed the horizon of the sky, imagining the light orange haze to come up, light up the world, and slowly make the things that ran in the darkness disappear.

"I want to see what happens," she continued.

She saw that they agreed, knowing that they did.

They kept walking, eyes out for more creatures, whether they be living or in a heap on the ground. Poe walked with the most duty, speed-walking almost at a pace that forced the others to try to keep up with her. She hardly noticed losing them behind her when she felt like she was being pulled in so many directions. One to her left, a sound. Another, to her right, a scent. Things tugged at her ears and her nose and she felt they even did so at her skin. She could hear the scratches of nails running down planks of wood, something on four legs rushing through the weeds, and the ever-present metallic stench of blood. Poe stopped to allow her friends to catch up to her, Bernadette holding on to her hat and Caleb holding his sheet up so as to not trip.

"Hey, slow down. What did you find?"

"I'm not sure," Poe answered her. "It's everything. Everything at once."

They were about at an open field now, any rocky roads now changed to smooth grass. There was nothing there at all, not a creature of this world or the other, not even an innocent tree or stray of rocks. And yet Poe stopped. Her foot paused in mid-air, craning her neck. She stopped asking out loud if anyone could hear what she heard. It was a lost cause at that point, because she was convinced her ears could only pick up things that were too far away for the others. But this, this what she heard right then, was not something that was far. The words came in gusts of wind past her ears. Goosebumps broke out over her entire body. The voices sounded all around her, yet every time she turned, there was no face.

"What?" asked Bernadette.

"What is it?" echoed Caleb.

Poe stared at nothing, listening to the voices come in and out in spurts.

"I hear ... voices... coming from somewhere."

She braved a few steps, the chills sinking deeper into her pores. Something else did, too. Something else felt ... heavier, almost, but it was nothing tangible. She stretched her hands out, even though covered.

"You don't see any spirits?" asked Bernadette.

"No," Poe answered. "I can't see them."

"I can't see any either," remarked Caleb. He stayed with Bernadette. They both let her explore her senses, and she was glad they did. She could not really describe it to them. She licked her lips, mouth going dry, her bewitched tail swaying behind her. No one said it, but they were all thinking it. They were thinking it the same time she did, the same time she lifted another hand to catch that feeling again. It felt wobbly, like air blowing in different directions and crisscrossing somewhere in the middle. She found that middle, a tiny torpedo vacuum.

"It's here," she said. She pointed her finger to give them the visual. "Here. It's right here."

She lowered her hand while all three of them stared into the void, staring at nothing before them and at everything that they could not see.

"It's like there's an invisible wall here and I can hear the voices behind it."

"What are they saying?" asked Caleb.

Poe shook her head, moving her ears inside her mask but still keeping it on for disguise's sake. *Could they hear us?*

"I ... I can't really understand it," she said, softly.

They sounded somewhere, hanging in the air between the layers of wind and fog.

"It's in another language."

Caleb gasped.

"Those must be the—"

"The what?" Bernadette demanded.

"Demons," he said above a whisper. "You can hear the demons in the Nether realm. The high-ranking intelligent ones. They speak the Old Language."

"The Old Language!" Bernadette repeated. "I know it! I've been learning it and reading it for spells for years. Can you make out what they're saying?"

Poe pushed her ears, though they only lifted on her head. "There's ... I can't. It doesn't make sense."

"If you can repeat something, I could translate."

Poe lifted a finger for silence, allowing the voices to come and go and come and go.

"Tempasest macks?"

"Tempus est mox," repeated Bernadette. "The time comes soon!"

"The time," echoed Poe.

"That could mean for the veil to close," said Caleb. "When the night is over. They're waiting for the demons to come back ... and see what new souls they bring with them."

The disturbed hush allowed Poe to listen for more.

"Expected moose?"

"Exspectamus. We wait," said Bernadette. She and Caleb stared at the same nothing Poe did.

"So I guess this means we do too," Poe stated.

30

Every once in a while, Poe would look to the two of them to see if they were still with her. Bernadette's head drooped the most, though she fought to keep it up. Last time she observed Caleb's form in the sheet, he turned to her and said, "I'm still here," in a weak voice. That was hours ago. Now the two of them had officially succumbed to slumber, sprawled out in the beds of grass. There was nothing for them to do anyway, and she got the chance she needed: She needed to be alone. Perhaps if it were so, the answer would come to her. Though still in the darkest hour, it would soon wane in the upcoming dawn, and only then could she see the results. *Wait for what?* Did some unnatural phenomenon take place?

She looked at Caleb next to her, curled up into fetal form with his sheet around him just like he was back in his bed. On the other side of her was Bernadette, stretched out on her back with her arms over her head and her hat positioned over her eyes. Poe knew now that she would wake them up should anything happen, whether this veil became something visible or whether a new horde of underworld beings came onto the scene.

One of those would happen first. Perhaps both at once. Poe became accustomed to staring into nothing, at nothing, waiting for any kind of sign from any sense. The darkness settled, though nothing moved in it. The whispers now blended in with the wind offering no more voices, but still, she had her eyes glued to it, not once feeling the tug of sleep herself. In fact, if anything, the adrenaline spiked even while stationary. Or maybe it was something else. It became something else when Poe felt the tingles in her legs that suggested she had been sitting too long. Once she moved them, extending and bending, the tingles shot all up and down her legs as they woke up. She brought herself to a standing position as she noticed the black of the night had faded just so slightly to a dark shade of gray. Out in the thin distant horizon, though still hazy, was clear enough to find. Poe felt the tingles move to her stomach and jump around, making her focus jump around. The light hour was approaching, and the more it worked to clear away the night, the more she wanted to be in it. The more she wanted to be out in it. She had to explore it. Poe took one last look at her sleeping comrades, promising that she would not venture too far, that she would not leave them, and would be back. She would be back. She just needed to ... roam.

So Poe took off. The minute her legs worked again, they drove her with a speed she did not control. She sauntered through the tall grass of the field, ears perking, nose twitching, seeking out scents here and there of the living and the dead. All around her, the fog blended, gentle wisps urging her along, giving her the urge to follow. Her eyes jerked everywhere, wanting to find everything at once, the pull in her gut and at every pore in her skin. Something was there, everything was there. But what was it, and where was it?

She caught a scent ahead of her ... which turned into several scents. First was the fresh, wild smell of an animal followed by the fresh kill of blood. She could feel her ears pressed against her head in warning, though her instincts were telling her to seek it out. She rushed through the grass, turning to the edge of the wooded area they had left to meet a large shadow moving through it. The top of its head had two points, and the outline was shaggy, suggesting fur. It moved slowly, making brushing noises on the ground, to which Poe spied that it was dragging something behind it. Several things. She peered around a tree to see the carnage for herself: one, two, three, four different creatures slain, their claws limp in defeat. The figure moved through the thicket until it turned the corner. At the same time, Poe picked up another familiar scent.

He turned his face, tired and rugged, with a few scratches down by his eyes. His hair was in disarray, matching his beard and the fur jacket he wore. He turned abruptly after noticing Poe.

"Geez kid, you scared me!"

"Sorry ... wow."

"You better believe it!" Rex's words came in exhausted breaths. He stopped and eased the hold on his baggage. "Why are you still out here? You okay? Wait, the others, where are the others?"

"They're all right! They're just over there. They fell asleep. I'm just on watch."

"On watch?"

Poe nodded. "Yeah, we found something! We think we found an entrance! The veil to the Nether realm!"

Rex dropped his game and forgot his tire. "Where? How?"

"We could hear voices. We're waiting to see if anything happens, like if something opens right in front of us. We've been sitting there for hours."

"Why'd you leave?"

Poe hesitated. "I don't know. I felt like I wanted to check out the whole area first, you know?"

"Don't leave your friends," Rex said. "You doing okay out here?"

"Yeah. We still have solution. But, don't know how much longer we're going to need it."

Rex gave a nod in agreement.

"I don't think anything is going to happen," she continued. "We still don't know ... we just want to see. Bernadette wants to see."

"You're safer with a witch." Rex picked up the leather reins he had as a rope, stray drops of blood falling from them. "I gotta get all this back and store them before I can clean them all up and dissect everything. The society is going to have a field day with this haul and I think I can finally identify the claw I found two years ago that's in the basement!"

"I can't wait to help," Poe said, her nose tickling so much she fought not to sneeze.

"You're already a big one." When Rex turned his head to look around, she could see that he had another scratch by his face, blood already drying to scabs. "Go on, get back to them. I'm turning in for the night."

Rex walked on, dragging his hunt behind him with authority and finality. Poe could see one was something feathered, and a Nether flyer possibly, and another looked like a goblin or imp. Unable to help herself, she hyper-focused on the imp's ears, long and ending in points.

She shook herself out of it, suddenly terrified that her friends woke up and found her missing. She rushed back to the fields just as the blackness around her was starting to wane.

They were in their same spots as before, and same positions. Bernadette looked like someone napping under the stars, and Caleb looked like a stiff corpse under a sheet in the morgue. Neither moved in deep REM sleep. Poe stood before them with nothing better to do but to continue to wait it out.

When the blue started to permeate through the black, the orange fighting its way to the top, Poe stood in the very spot, the one that had to have significance, if anything did at all. She could see the night ending and the day dominating, and she pushed with every sense she had. She thought she picked up voices, but they turned to murmurs, and then turned to the rush of wind like something was moving very fast around her. And then Poe felt something rise from the ground and run through her entire body, from the legs all the way up to her head. It was so fast she could not place it, but it felt like a soft vibration. All around her, the fog disintegrated, blowing up like clouds of flour in milliseconds leaving the air completely blank and untouched.

Poe reached her hands out, grabbing and clawing at whatever she thought she could feel, but nothing was there. That same vacuum she felt before had vanished. She stood there, confused and defeated. In the distance was the first sound to indicate that the day had returned to normal: the early song of a bird. Poe lifted her mask, pulling it over her face enough so that it rested on the top of her head. She felt the air on her skin, let it seep through her pores, willing her skin to feel something that she did not feel before. But all she felt was her sweat evaporating, her struggle and confusion and tension just going away with it.

Poe bent down, one hand on other side and reaching the both of them.

"Bernadette, Caleb."

She shook them, calling them until they stirred and groaned, turning over.

"What?" Bernadette said, removing her hat and scrambling to sit up. "What is it? Did it happen?"

"It happened all right," Poe stated. "It's morning."

Caleb pulled his sheet up to his face, stiffing a yawn. "It's morning? What happened?"

"That's just it," Poe continued. "Nothing happened. I felt this weird tingle and then the fog disappeared and then a bird chirped. That's it. The end."

"What?" Caleb struggled to sit up, getting himself tangled in his sheet as he pulled it over his head. "What do you mean?"

"That can't be it!" Bernadette exclaimed, the morning grogginess disappearing. "Weren't you watching?"

"I watched all night, I never slept. And I'm telling you, that's all that happened."

Both Bernadette and Caleb wiped their eyes, looking around as though they themselves could see anything different, anything out of the ordinary. They stood up, eyes squinting in the newborn sun pushing its way out through the clouds. Bernadette walked one way, tilting her head forward like she was trying to peer into something. Caleb walked the other, hands holding his sheet up from his face. He finally took the whole sheet off, letting it flutter to the ground and he stood there with his arms out.

"Come on," Poe heard him mutter to himself.

"What are you doing?" Poe asked.

Caleb let his arms fall in defeat. He shook his head, brows at worrisome slants.

"It's gone?" he said.

Bernadette spun around.

"What do you mean it's gone?"

"It's morning now," Poe stated. "That's it."

"What do you mean that's it? We failed?"

"We didn't fail!" Poe said. "We couldn't have done anything. Nothing happened. Nothing happened that we thought was going to happen."

She jerked her head toward Caleb, to what he muttered that she could make out.

"Caleb, you don't mean that."

But the guilt was on his long face, eyes downcast.

"Caleb," Poe said again.

He shook his head. "I thought I was going to go last night."

Bernadette now was fully attentive.

"Go?"

"I really did. Many times something should have happened, but it didn't. It didn't, and I am still here."

Poe suddenly thought back to the day she first met Caleb, the moment he spied her at his bedroom window and beckoned for her to come in.

"I thought you were one of the beings finally coming to take me back."

"Caleb," she said. "You're alive."

Bernadette stepped forward.

"What? You wanted to die?"

She could always be counted on to be frank.

"Again?"

Caleb downcast his eyes again.

"Oh my god!"

"No you don't," Poe assured. "No, you don't."

"That's not how it works," Bernadette said again. "I mean, I don't know, it probably shouldn't, but were you really just going to let something kill you last night? Was that it? Right in front of us? Geez, nice to know."

"No," Caleb answered. "No, not like that."

"Seriously you wanted to die though, didn't you?"

"Not ... I mean, no," Caleb backpedaled.

Poe and Bernadette held themselves in the morning chill, hearing birds in the distance chippering peacefully, the only conversation out there that was pleasant.

"Not like that."

"Then what?" Bernadette demanded. Poe took a few steps to be in between them, not exactly wanting Bernadette to shut up. She faced Caleb with her own sense of urgency.

"What I really thought was that since I've been there before, I could go back. I could go back and ... at least fix it."

"Do it from the inside," Poe figured out.

"So you wanted to die again," Bernadette said again.

Caleb squeezed his eyes. He kicked around in the dirt.

"No, I told you. I thought maybe I could still...access it, or something. But..."

He shook his head.

"I wasn't supposed to come back."

He faced them, eyes pale and soft, delicate yet stubborn.

"Because that's not how it's supposed to work. I've been sick. I am, sick. My body decided it was time and I went. I went and I finally was going to be free, and not sick anymore. When my spirit was finally cleansed... then I was just pulled back. And that was it."

Poe tried not to see just how pale he looked in the dawn light, that up until that moment he temporarily had all the energy and drive of a regular, healthy boy, and now the end of their night activities brought the end to that.

"And now you're here," Poe said. "With us. You helped us. We probably couldn't have done a lot of it if it weren't for you. It *wasn't* your time. It still isn't."

Poe stepped in front of him so he could see her, face-to-face.

"Didn't our time last night teach you that?"

Poe now addressed the both of them, seeing Bernadette's alarm, yet worry in her eyes, alongside Caleb's guilt. She knew that one thing they for sure had in common was their stubbornness.

"We started something. We may not have finished it last night, but we're going to. This is the beginning. And—and you're both going to make a difference."

Caleb picked his sheet up, wrapping it around himself and therefore turning it back into what it was. Bedding.

"I need to go home."

Caleb's statement was enough of reality for all three of them, something they all had to agree on.

"My moms won't be awake for hours, but I don't want them to worry."

"My mom will be visiting my room in a few hours," Caleb continued. "For my morning medicine."

"We'll get you home," Poe finally said.

Bernadette stared at the field again. "We'll have to come back. I have to come back. I have to see what I can figure out. What I can find with magic."

"We will," promised Poe. "We will."

The three at last left the field, allowing themselves to slouch at ease, at rest. Nothing else was out in the world now. Just them.

31

Poe let herself in, quietly and slowly. A cursory glance to the rack showed Rex's fur jacket hung up, the eared hood hanging down at the back in slumber. His boots were thrown on the rug with bits of grass and dirt stuck to the bottoms, no doubt kicking them off after finally retiring from the night's work. Poe went up the stairs to her room and shut the door, peeling off her gloves and shoes and unzipping the body suit. She removed the mask last, in front of the mirror.

They were still there, sticking out from her hair. She touched them, feeling them as real and as part of her as anything else was. It wasn't like she saw her old ears too often, as they were always hidden by her hair, but did she always think that they were normal? Weren't they? Or did they always have the subtle hint of a point at the top that she overlooked?

Poe ignored the glisten of sweat around her brow and forehead, and how her eyes blinked at her to signal they wanted to go to sleep. She ran her fingers through her hair, pulling the too-short ends and willing them to cover what she wanted to cover. She turned and went to her drawers, fishing through things until she found a long knit hat, pulling it over her head and hoping that the next day she would not wake to find them longer and sticking out over her head. She changed out of her disguise, putting on long pajamas in the new-born November chill. She took the disguise clothing pieces and the mask and put them on the seat by her windowsill.

Poe climbed into bed and pulled the covers all around her, at once welcoming sleep as an old friend and wanting nothing but to let it comfort her. She pulled the hat down enough to cover her eyes, though barely in the brightness of the day she already wanted back the privacy away from the sun. She wrapped her blankets around by her chin, covering everything but her nose and giving herself as much of that darkness as she could. As though she missed it already.

Deep in sleep, Poe stretched her arms and scraped her pillows. She didn't hear the rip she made, the gentle tear through the pillow, and the bleeding of the stuffing out the thin slash. Her hand rested next to it, long nails growing to sharp points.

Book Club Questions

1. When we are first introduced to the main character Poe, anyone else who meets or encounters Poe for the first time reacts in either fear or interest. Why do you think this is? What was your first impression of Poe? What secrets do you think she holds?

2. Setting plays an important role in setting the mood for the story, especially in a fantasy setting where the main character is visiting for the first time, and it evokes wonder, mystery, and fear of the unknown. What other fictional town and/or setting can you compare to Mock Cob village, and why?

3. The town citizens are split as to the best course of action for the onslaught of new invaders. If you were a resident, which side would you be on and why?

4. The "father figure" is a common character trope in fiction, especially those characters unexpectedly thrown into the role of becoming a guardian for a child or young person. Poe just showed up at Rex's house, and she was not what he was expecting, but he accepted her. Describe how Rex changed in his home lifestyle and behavior after Poe came to live with him and became a part of his life.

5. The origin of Halloween traditions and themes is a strong theme in this book, though many retellings are based on real Samhain traditions. Name all of them and how they relate to the plot of the story and drive the behaviors of the characters.

6. The characters all have their own personal agendas during The Night of Passing, but the trio of Poe, Bernadette, and Caleb have joined together for a specific one that they have come to have in common in addition to their own separate, personal reasons. What are the goals for each character? How are they going to either help or hinder one another? Who do you think will find the most success and at what cost?

Author Bio

Jackie Sonnenberg brings characters to life on paper, and in person. With a background in journalism, she wrote for major area newspapers and published both fiction and non-fiction titles. With a background as an actor, it has also turned her into a costume maker, and she learned how to make her worlds merge. She is known for dressing as and appearing as her book characters for events and conventions in an interactive style of marketing, introducing people to her stories by first introducing them to the characters. She has won costume contests and creative awards in fiction and character design. Jackie is also an active member of the haunted house industry as both a writer, actor, costume creator, and in creative concepts for theme and atmosphere. She lives in Orlando, FL, where creativity and imagination surround her.

Discover more at
4HorsemenPublications.com

10% off using HORSEMEN10